"I read all 512 pages of Angelica Baker's debut novel greedily, in one dizzying weekend, unable to put it down. . . . The book gets beyond moneymaking hubris to a more basic kind of desire—the fretful, shapeless longing of those who are sidelined to be seen somehow as indispensable. Binge-watchers of *Big Little Lies* will enjoy the elegantly cutthroat politics of suburban life in wealthy Greenwich, Connecticut, while fans of Elena Ferrante will like the sharp portrayal of the delicate power balances in women's friendships. But any reader will appreciate the tightly woven drama of this book, which brings its five protagonists out of the margins of the crisis and into an explosive confrontation of their own."

—*The Atlantic*

"Baker skillfully grapples with questions of complicity . . . the novel is never less than gripping, and even if this is a world seemingly unfamiliar to you, it's impossible not to be swept up in the hard universal truths uncovered within its pages." —*Nylon* magazine

"Although the novel is set in the banking crisis of 2008, it feels as current as today's congressional testimony. . . . Ambitious. . . . The atmosphere in this novel is stretched taut as the characters wait for the other polished loafer to drop." —*Kansas City Star*

"A probing social novel about contemporary culture, family, wealth, and the line between ignorance and complicity: *Our Little Racket* is a captivating read that you must throw in your beach bag, posthaste."

—Refinery29, "Best Books of 2017"

"A classic page-turner. . . . As the story unfolds, the author takes us deep into Gold Coast life in 2008, just as the financial collapse was about to wreak havoc on the American economy. . . . Elegant writing and razor-sharp analysis of upper-class suburbia." —*Connecticut Post*

"A smart debut novel that examines power, greed, and the price of the American dream." —PopSugar, "Best Books for Summer 2017"

"Wry and perceptive." —National Book Review

"Working in the vein of Wharton, Cheever, and Yates, but with a voice and vision wholly her own, Angelica Baker has crafted a timely and powerful exploration of greed and hubris. It's impossible to look away from the family at the heart of this novel, who have acquired all the trappings of wealth—and then some—but are navigating troubled waters with a faulty compass. In clear and commanding prose, Baker exposes the myriad ways these people fail to care for each other and the questionable places they seek refuge as their world upends. Angelica Baker is wildly talented and this debut is her gorgeous opening note."

—Cynthia D'Aprix Sweeney, bestselling author of *The Nest*

"*Our Little Racket* is a golden web of a story hanging in the rubble of a house built by deceit and greed. A magnificent debut."

—Ramona Ausubel, author of *Sons and Daughters of Ease and Plenty* and *No One Is Here Except All of Us*

"Angelica Baker has written a terrific, whip-smart debut. *Our Little Racket* is a humane and serious window onto the troubling social world of the bankers who wrecked our economy. This is a great first novel."

—Stuart Nadler, author of *The Inseparables*

"A wonderfully rich debut from an incisive and elegant writer. Baker's women are worlds unto themselves, each with her own center of gravity, and it is a total pleasure to be held captive by them."

—Julia Pierpont, author of *Among the Ten Thousand Things*

"*Our Little Racket* is a gratifying peek over the hedgerows of Greenwich, laden with delicious anthropological detail. But like a modern-day Henry James, Angelica Baker uses the lives of the one percent to explore themes—of love and loyalty, family and friendship—that matter to all of us."   —Rumaan Alam, author of *Rich and Pretty*

"Blending high-stakes economic intrigue with high-class family drama, *Our Little Racket* is a sweeping and immersive novel. Baker fully inhabits each of her characters, voicing each with depth and breadth. . . . [An] engrossing and illuminating glimpse into Greenwich's upper crust."

—*Booklist*

"A personal, thought-provoking portrait emerges of the American Dream, complete with a web of visible and invisible cracks in the foundation."   —*Publishers Weekly*

OUR LITTLE RACKET

OUR
LITTLE
RACKET

ANGELICA BAKER

ecco

An Imprint of HarperCollins *Publishers*

"Little Racket" first published in *The New Yorker* © 2015 by Anne Carson. Used by permission of Anne Carson and Aragi Inc.

"The Plain Sense of Things" from *The Collected Poems of Wallace Stevens* by Wallace Stevens, copyright © 1954 by Wallace Stevens and copyright renewed 1982 by Holly Stevens. Used by permission of Alfred A. Knopf, an imprint of the Knopf Doubleday Publishing Group, a division of Penguin Random House LLC. All rights reserved.

HarperCollins books may be purchased for educational, business, or sales promotional use. For information, please email the Special Markets Department at SPsales@harpercollins.com.

A hardcover edition of this book was published in 2017 by Ecco, an imprint of HarperCollins Publishers.

FIRST ECCO PAPERBACK EDITION PUBLISHED 2018.

Designed by Suet Yee Chong

Library of Congress Cataloging-in-Publication Data has been applied for.

ISBN 978-0-06-264132-8

18 19 20 21 22 LSC 10 9 8 7 6 5 4 3 2 1

C.M.M.

The Dust Bowl was the darkest moment in the twentieth-century life of the southern plains. The name suggests a place—a region whose borders are as inexact and shifting as a sand dune. But it was also an event of national, even planetary, significance . . . the Dust Bowl took only 50 years to accomplish. It cannot be blamed on illiteracy or overpopulation or social disorder. It came about because the culture was operating in precisely the way it was supposed to.

—Donald Worster, *Dust Bowl: The Southern Plains in the 1930s*

There was a night, in the year before everything happened, when Madison's mother came to see her.

Isabel just appeared at the bedroom door one night, a few hours after dinner, and at first she said nothing. She hadn't done this since Madison was small. Madison could feel her standing in the doorway, watching.

"I wanted to see if you need anything before you turn in," her mother said when Madison finally looked up. And then Isabel smiled, her large blue eyes watchful above the crinkled mouth. There was something undefined about the smile, like an image reflected in rippling water.

It had been only a few months since Isabel's parents had died; first Grandpop and then Gran Berkeley, succumbing one after the other that winter. Madison knew her mother was still moving through the cluttered daily air of new grief.

"I was just going to do my hair," Madison said. "Before I go to sleep."

Normal touching, affection: For Isabel, that was contact without purpose. Grooming, on the other hand, had function. It was far from superficial; it was the only real bulwark against the world outside. Not only outside the house, beyond Greenwich, but even beyond this very bedroom, the whole world beyond their own two bodies.

"Sit," Isabel said. "Let me do it."

Her fingers began to work absently through Madison's hair, the way another sort of mother might sift flour before baking.

"People were talking at lunch today about how their parents met," Madison began.

"Which people?"

"I don't know. Me, Amanda, a few other people. Wyatt Welsh was there, but none of the boys seem to know their family's stories."

"Well," Isabel said, snorting. "Of course they don't."

"Would you tell it again?"

"Don't you prefer it when your father tells it? He tells a better story than I do. He always has."

"But he's at work," Madison said.

And her mother's fingers began to work more quickly.

EVERY DETAIL OF THE STORY was familiar, something Madison had rubbed smooth in her mind. The parts that were left vague, known only to her parents, were surely inconsequential; she imagined and reimagined the parts she already knew, so that the mysteries seemed less important.

Her mother had been working nights as the hostess at a club, right after she moved to New York. She was twenty-two.

"Your grandfather thought it was hilarious, me taking a second job," Isabel said. The bristles of the hairbrush grazed Madison's scalp. "He thought I was bluffing. He would show up to take me to lunch twice a month, fly the shuttle up from D.C. and take me to midtown, 21 or one of the steakhouses. He'd wait until the very end of the meal, as though I didn't know what was coming, and then he'd draw a check from his breast pocket and hold it out to me. And we never said anything, he just held it there for a few seconds and then laughed and put it away."

"And you didn't even have enough money every month to buy groceries."

"It's so funny to think this was only, what? Two years before I had you? And I was still such a child."

Madison could hear, though, the wistful pride in her mother's voice. Misery in the absence of danger, misery you'd signed yourself up for, carried with it an ersatz thrill, a shiver along your spine that couldn't be found anywhere else. It was like a soreness on your skin rather than in your bones. Madison had realized, by the time she hit middle school, that this feeling was something open to her that was open to almost no one else in the world. She'd kept this to herself.

"But one night, Daddy came in."

Isabel parted Madison's hair down the center of her scalp, as though preparing to split her daughter into two equal, tidy halves.

"And one night, your father came into the club, yes."

THOUGH SHE'D BEEN FOURTEEN when he died, Madison did not think of herself as someone who'd known her grandfather very well. Her memories of him could be sorted into several specific categories: his visits; Gran's cocktail parties at the town house in D.C.; his annual birthday dinner at the Yale Club, near Grand Central.

Madison's father liked her to mix his drinks, especially when other men from the bank were over at the house. By the time she was ten years old, she already knew every possible way Bob D'Amico might take his bourbon, or when he'd prefer scotch, which he only ever took one way. But Grandpop always sent his drinks back, usually for unforeseeable reasons. She learned quickly that she would not be able to anticipate anything other than his dissatisfaction, that he would reject the first drink she made. He never told her in advance whether he wanted an olive or an onion, for starters, and he always wanted what she didn't have. He'd tell her that anything worth enjoying should be sent back once or twice, because a good drink is wasted unless it's a perfect drink. He'd look askance at her father, taking steady slugs from the very first drink his daughter had proffered, and shake his head.

Sometimes, when they were in D.C., Grandpop would wait until Bob was talking to an important guest, someone he knew would have his son-in-law on edge—from the State Department, or something—and then creep up behind him, manic glee on his face, to tap Bob's beer with his own brown bottle.

The first time she saw this happen, Madison was seven or eight. It wasn't just that her grandfather had tapped the beer, that the geyser of foam had spilled all over Bob's sleeve. Grandpop had been mocking her father all night, usually waiting until a few guests had clustered in a corner before launching into some unflattering analysis of her father's role at the bank.

Twenty minutes or so after the spill, Madison wandered into the kitchen to see if she might poach something from a leftover tray, a toast point layered with buttery smoked salmon or maybe a cucumber sandwich, anything her mother's uninterrupted gaze had prevented her from touching earlier. But when she came into the room, she only saw her mother and father.

Isabel had him backed up against the sink, one hand tucked into the collar of his shirt, her hips canted up toward his. He pressed one hand to the small of her back, rumpling her silk blouse, and balled the other into a tight fist. Isabel leaned into him until his head fell into the space between her neck and her shoulder. Madison waited a few moments, trying to imagine her place were she to enter the room. Where she might tuck herself, whose arm would have to loosen to enfold her in their closed embrace. She couldn't see any place that made sense, though, and so she returned to the party, found Grandpop, crawled up onto his knee to listen to the thrum of his voice against his chest.

ISABEL TOLD THE WHOLE STORY that night, while she braided Madison's hair. She always did, once Madison convinced her to start; it was, after all, a favorite in their family. Every family wants to feel inevitable.

He came into the club one night, celebrating with his coworkers. He tried to get her mother to sit down with them, stay for a glass of champagne, and she told him off. Her exact words were never part of the story, but the point was that she spoke to him in a way that no other woman did. She called him a junior analyst, even though he was a good twelve years her senior. She put him in his place.

Then, to apologize, he held out a single, crisp, hundred-dollar bill. And Isabel threw it back in his face.

He found her, later, after she'd stormed off. He begged her to go out with him.

She was perfectly polite in her refusal, of course, she didn't bare her teeth. But he came back three times a week, for a month, having called management to find out the nights she worked. He told her that he could learn a lot from someone like her. He told her he needed reading recommendations. He kept coming back until she said yes to dinner.

MADISON LOVED THE DETAILS of this story for many reasons, but she especially loved that one tactic of her father's. Because he never read for pleasure. Anything that might shed light on the markets, sure. Earnings reports, diversity memos, whatever intel on the firm or its competitors that Jim McGinniss, his second in command and best friend coming up through the ranks, saw fit to funnel onto his desk. During the Russian crisis in '98, anything and everything about post-Wall Russia that he could get his hands on. But nothing irrelevant. Not for him the camouflaged meanings of fiction, the artificial tidiness of biography.

She thought often of her parents' story during that September after she turned fifteen, during the shell-shocked year that followed.

At first, when it all happened, people were expecting a scene. They wanted his howling at the perceived injustice brought out into the open—for on the day that it happened, quite publicly, he'd been vocal enough for them all to know that he considered himself one of the victims, too. They wanted the brash man they'd all tolerated for so long to turn, finally, on himself. They were afraid of, and so eagerly awaited, screaming and yelling, King Lear ranting beneath a white tent on a moonlit Greenwich lawn.

In this, her father never obliged.

NO ONE KNOWS what is lost at the moment it slips away. What you feel, then, is really fear. There is the inkling of what is to come, and the fear of that future pain leaves you paralyzed. Madison would come to understand, that year, that when Isabel had looked down at the crisp bill in the darkened club where she'd taken a job to spite her own father, she couldn't have seen the paths that closed themselves to her, right then, in that moment. She could have paused to examine the brutish, pleasingly handsome man before her and still known nothing more of the women she would not become, the lives she would not choose. She could only see the details, could not see the fragmented whole that it was all leading her toward. And for this past limitation, this necessary blindness, Madison felt for her mother only tenderness, only shared regret.

MADISON HAD LOOKED, a few times, trying to find pictures of the club online—her father had once mentioned red velvet couches that fit together to form swirling S shapes. But it was as if the place had evaporated once it closed, only a few years after her parents met there. She could find no trace of it, only casual mentions in magazine articles about the excesses of the eighties.

In the year after her father's implosion, she could think only of what she didn't know about that story. She could close her eyes and imagine her parents, could watch them find each other. But she could never hear the dialogue, not the crucial parts, and the story came to seem, for the first time, like only the pieces of a failed mosaic. It was incomplete; it belonged to the world she had known before that September, those fortified, moonlit lawns behind Greenwich houses. So full, verdant and cool, their stringed instruments, their tinkling glass. The lights in the trees.

But the pieces told her nothing, gave her no inside information. And she wanted it to be like that moment at Gran's cocktail party, in the kitchen, when she saw her mother's hand on her father's skin, saw his unused fist, knew something—she could not say what—about the invisible strings between them, the web she'd been living in all her life.

Wasn't she, after all, the only real insider? Didn't she live in a house, each day, with some versions of the two people in this story?

I

After the leaves have fallen, we return
To the plain sense of things. It is as if
We had come to an end of the imagination,
Inanimate in an inert savoir.

It is difficult even to choose the adjective
For this blank cold, this sadness without cause.
The great structure has become a minor house.
No turban walks across the lessened floors.

—Wallace Stevens, "The Plain Sense of Things"

If you haven't discovered your role, you're the villain
today. So you have to act like the villain today.

—Representative John Mica to Richard Fuld,
former CEO of Lehman Brothers, during congressional hearings

ONE

The summer before, they spent August at the house on Shelter Island.

"Bob," Isabel said one morning at breakfast, holding her teacup in front of her face. "Could you put that away, please?"

She stared pointedly at the BlackBerry sitting beside his coffee cup. They were all there, Madison and the twins, eating breakfast in the formal dining room. Madison had assumed that this year, the first summer without Gran, they might finally be liberated from her old rules and habits. But that hadn't happened. On some days, if they swam in the pool, they were allowed to eat lunch at the outside table, beneath the poplars Grandpop had taken such pride in showing to first-time visitors. But that was it, their only real casual indulgence.

Madison poured her own cup of coffee and immediately burned her tongue. She had been training herself this summer to drink it black, like her father. She didn't love the taste of coffee itself, but somehow she loved to drink it black. It felt like you were toughing it out, sucking it down anyway not for the pleasure but for the other benefits.

"What?" her father replied, still peering down the table at her mother.

"Vacation," Isabel said.

"I'm aware," he said, "that we are on vacation. I'm aware we're at your parents' house. I was wondering if you'd repeat the first thing you said."

Frank and Antoinette were continuing to ferry things into the room. There was already a samovar of coffee, a teapot for Isabel. They'd brought in a platter of bagels with lox, capers, onions and tomatoes and cucumbers. The strawberries in Gran's enormous old ceramic bowl were so red you looked at them and could think only of blood, that accusatory red you see when you've accidentally bitten the inner, fleshy part of your lip.

Madison could feel Luke beginning to vibrate beside her. She set down the fruit bowl and put one hand to the back of his neck.

"You heard me, I think," her mother said.

"But you know that I'm working. You know full well why I've got my phone here with me during breakfast. So I'm just fascinated, really, that you think I can just—" And her father snapped his fingers, an uncontrolled smile spreading over his face. He looked like a failing magician. "Make it go away."

Madison felt the sound of his fingers crackle down along her spine. She began rubbing her hand in smooth, continuous circles on Luke's back.

"I do think you can make it go away for the remainder of our children's breakfast," Isabel said. "I have that much faith in you, sweetheart." She tilted her head and smiled, that smile she had and used so sparingly. It made you feel she'd considered every detail of your person, your every gesture, and decided that you were truly and gracefully beyond reproach. She had offered the smile to calm him down, to bathe him in her own well-being. On his good days, it worked.

He squinted again. His eyebrows looked especially thick and unruly that morning, as if he'd repeatedly put his thumbs to his brow and rubbed with anxious distraction.

"You've got faith in me," he repeated.

Frank and Antoinette had suddenly vanished. They'd been Gran's only real staff out here for the last twenty years of her life, and this couldn't be the first unpleasantness they'd seen unfold over sliced bagels, Madison thought. They knew when to glide into the room slowly, so that by the time you realized you needed something, you'd grown accustomed to their soothing presence in the corner, but they knew just as well when to disappear.

She stared past her father's face, his jaw working away, to the big bay windows that looked out over the gray strip of sand on the beach below. The slightly longer grasses at the edge of the lawn were being bent wildly in different directions. What was she going to do if today was too windy? If she couldn't take the boys outside, and keep them there?

She wished that her mother had insisted Lily come along on this trip, that she hadn't given her the two weeks off to go home to her own parents in Brooklyn. Lily would have known, somehow. She would have seen this coming, before the meal had begun; she would already have figured out where to take the boys.

"Is that the case?" her father continued, his eyes fixed to her mother's face.

"I would like you to put the phone away until we've finished our breakfasts," Isabel said.

When he dropped his phone from a height and let it hit the dining room table, Gran's sturdy, beloved cherrywood table, the sound was so unexpected—even with all the signals he'd flashed— that the twins responded with almost primal caution. Luke jerked, ready to dive beneath the table, and it was only Madison's hand on his back that kept him in his chair. Even Matteo, always the more stolid of the twins, showed his hand, looking to his sister with a frantic jerk of his neck.

"You think I'm enjoying this?" Bob said. He leaned forward across the dining room table, his hands in his lap, his shoulders bearing down on his wife. "You think it'll still be vacation if things continue like this?"

Isabel looked away, out the windows, as if to ignore an embarrassing display of public drunkenness. When she looked back, she picked up her utensils and began cutting her cucumber and tomato slices into smaller and smaller triangles, arranging them in rows on her plate and spearing them in pairs with her fork.

Bob lowered himself back into his seat, smoothed his napkin across his lap. Madison knew that her mother had gifted him those moments, the time he needed to remember that she was the one person he did not scream at. The one person, besides Madison and the boys, who ever got to see him feel tender. Isabel got not just brisk loyalty, the way he spoke to his colleagues, but actual softness. Sometimes she passed by where he stood, and he'd follow her to another room just to kiss the back of her neck, the knob where her spine began.

This wasn't so unusual, Madison's father bellowing, using every object in the house to help him make some stressful noise. But not on vacation, and not when her mother had asked for so little.

"I can't put the phone away," he said. "I apologize, but now is not the time to fight me on this."

"Guys," Madison announced, "let's go put on our suits."

She bustled the boys into the kitchen. Antoinette was waiting by the sink, her arms crossed severely over her stomach.

"We're going swimming," Luke whispered.

"I would just leave them," Madison said to Antoinette, waving one hand back toward the closed door. "I wouldn't go back in until he's gone out."

HER FATHER HAD ALWAYS HATED EVERYTHING about that house. The way the carpet felt damp, sometimes, during thunderstorms. The exposure to the beach. The lack of any architectural protection from the wildness of the dunes below, so that if you forgot and left the doors open on the sunporch, the carpet would be sandy for days. It wasn't the sort of house he'd ever have selected, and certainly not one he'd have kept for decades. He'd tried for years to convince even his own mother to sell her building in northeast Brooklyn, to permit some developer to reimagine it as a sleek, silver column of luxury condominiums looking north toward McCarren Park and, beyond it, Manhattan.

But he'd never have refused this visit, at least not while Gran was alive. They had a standing agreement, Madison's parents. Bob's vacations could be as short as they needed to be. If he could take only four days all year away from the city, from the bank, then Isabel wouldn't say a word. But once he took a vacation, he took it. He didn't work the whole time, and he never cut a trip short. These were the terms of their agreement. Her father never forgot them, and her mother never had to reissue them.

Madison knew, though, that her father had assumed this year would be different. The house was now legally Isabel's. This gave him an opening, though he would never ask her outright to sell. Isabel's grandfather had won the land out here in a poker game in D.C. almost a century earlier. He'd basically built the house so he had an excuse to tell that story, as a shrine to the Berkeley men, and it was of course only natural that Isabel should love it for these very reasons. But Bob had his own ideas of the right sorts of beach vacations for a man in his position: private beaches in Mexico, the Turks and Caicos, the Bahamas. At the very, very least, a beach house of their own. Anywhere but East Hampton, really.

And so when her father dropped, nearly threw, his phone to the breakfast table that morning, Madison could have told herself that any one of these displeasures was the culprit. All month he'd been walking down the beach to take phone calls, standing at the water's edge with his khakis rolled up just below his knees. But that morning was such a departure from the normal vacation rules that it insisted upon its own novelty. Madison couldn't set it aside, though she tried all the rest of the gloomy, humid day at the beach. The only thing her mother had done, in the end, was remind her father of his own promises. And that had never infuriated him before.

The next morning, he was gone. He did not say good-bye to Madison, or, so far as she knew, to the twins.

Isabel kept them there for two more weeks. Antoinette's grandson, the part-time fisherman, took the twins out on his boat. Madison took a book to the beach each morning and dozed through the afternoons. She missed her own bedroom, where she fell asleep not to the sounds of water but to the rustlings of the false wilderness of Greenwich, the birdcalls her father claimed had so unnerved her when they first moved out from the city to live in the old house. Every so often her door would creak, an hour or four after she'd clicked off her bedside lamp, and her father's smells—the sweet bite of Maker's Mark, the choking staleness of nighttime sweat mixed with the morning's once-fresh cologne—would fill the room, and his coarse cheek would brush against hers. He'd be gone so quickly that by the time she was awake, she'd no longer remember what he'd said.

He had not done this in weeks, maybe months, maybe not all year. She couldn't remember.

It still felt strange being out on the island without Gran, walking along her stretch of beach without her there to fret aloud over the looming estate across the water, the one the fame-coarsened country singer had bought and immediately accessorized with his own helicopter pad. A few times Madison considered impersonating her grandmother, making the joke to Isabel. Shaking her head and putting the tip of her index finger to her lips, pressing on them, the way Gran had once done as she looked across the bay. But she wasn't sure this would be funny.

At night, they ate whatever Antoinette brought from town— scallops or lobster, a dessert tart from the French woman who had taken over the local bakery. Without her father there, meals were so quiet that Madison could hear herself chewing each bite of her food, could hear the obtrusive gulp as she tried to swallow. When they left, they flew home from the small airport on Long Island, which was unusual, and they took the plane her father had sent for them, which was unheard of. Her mother never flew the company jet unless he was with them, and then only if he insisted.

The car was waiting when they landed at Westchester County. The boys were carried from the plane to the backseat without waking, and when they pulled in at home, Lily was waiting at the front door, backlit by the lamps in the otherwise darkened foyer. And still no one had said a word to Madison that could serve as any sort of explanation.

She told herself this was just her parents: the electric weather of her father's moods and her mother's silences. And those were both harbingers of a sort she'd long ago learned to follow obsessively and to ignore blithely, in equal measure.

THREE WEEKS LATER, Madison came into the kitchen on a morning like any other and found not only the familiar sight of Lily preparing breakfast for the boys, but also the decidedly unfamiliar sight of her mother waiting for the toaster to pop.

Madison remained in the doorway while Lily moved with jerking motions between the sink, the stainless steel center island, and the boys at the breakfast nook. She poured milk over their deep bowls of cereal, smiled down at them as they began to eat. They moved the food from their bowls to their mouths with remarkable efficiency, like battery-powered toys. Madison had always envied them this, the incredible ease with which they approached mealtimes, that single-mindedness that allowed them to put aside every earthly concern that wasn't related to breakfast.

Lily bent at the waist to kiss each boy, brushing her lips to the very tops of their heads where, Madison knew, their hair was the softest. When Lily stood, she pulled a chair from the table for Madison, letting it scrape the floor. Madison's eye went immediately to her mother, to her tanned shoulders, her sleeveless linen top, but Isabel didn't flinch. Madison swallowed, and sat.

"Sit down," Lily said. "Eat."

Only then did Isabel turn to the table, her children. Her smooth blond ponytail grazed the place between her shoulder blades. The toast announced itself.

"Good morning," Madison said. She knew, now, what would happen. Her mother would spread peanut butter across five slices of toast. One slice for Madison, two each for the boys. She would then cut Madison's slice in half, and the two of them would share it. This was familiar—this was a weekend breakfast, what the D'Amico children ate on those rare days Lily was permitted to sleep in or catch the early train to New York, leaving Isabel at the helm. School days were left to Lily—goat cheese frittatas, fruit salad with out-of-season kiwi, red flannel hash with kale. Bagels for the boys, if they wanted them. Her father brought them home from H&H with great fanfare, though Madison knew for a fact they were delivered to the office with no effort at all on his part; even the order itself was placed by one of his secretaries.

Her mother always prompted her not to use that word, to say "executive assistants" instead.

"More milk, please," Matteo said, reaching out one plaintive hand. Lily rushed back to the table. She knew, just like Madison— who had often done this for him herself—that Matteo preferred to eat all but the final few pieces of cereal and then drown them in fresh milk, picking them out with his spoon. He was more placid than Luke, less easily frightened, but also by far the more finicky twin.

"Lily," Madison said. "What's going on?"

"Nothing. Eat something."

"I'm waiting for my toast." She permitted herself a tart spin on the very end of the sentence, but even this didn't get her any eye contact from her mother. Lily placed a halved grapefruit in front of her.

"Eat that, then."

Isabel brought over the plates of toast, then crossed to the boys and sat down beside them.

Madison looked at the food, looked at her mother, gave up on looking at Lily. Everything in the room felt unbearably slow; the edges of everything shimmered.

She picked up her spoon and her knife and began dutifully to divide the fruit into slits, slipping each fleshy triangle from its spoke in the wheel. Her brothers munched their toast without question.

"Your mother's going to drive you to school this morning," Lily said from the sink, where she was washing dishes. What dishes could she possibly be washing? No one had finished eating yet.

"You mean, to the bus."

"No—she's driving you straight to school."

"Why?"

"I'm sorry, do we need a special reason? Is this is a national disaster? Your mother wants to drive you to school, all right? Eat."

Madison turned once more to her mother, who had always taken great pride in the fact that her children rode the school bus. Isabel despised the mothers who insisted their children be driven to school, as if the buses provided by their elite private schools were no better than the filthy, crime-ridden Manhattan subway—which, Isabel loved to point out, was no longer even filthy or crime ridden. If there was ever a reason they skipped the bus, a late appointment or a faulty alarm clock, it was Lily who drove them straight to campus. Not their mother.

"Where's Dad," Madison said. Luke looked up at her, his bottom lip protruding and threatening to undo his entire face.

"We don't know," he said gravely. Lily popped the roof of her mouth with her tongue.

"Don't be silly, sweetheart," she said. "Daddy's at work. Where else would he be?"

Matteo turned to his mother for confirmation, and Isabel smiled and put one hand to his chin to snag a stray piece of cereal.

"You know that," she said.

"He's been in the city now basically since we got back from

Shelter," Madison said. "He's still there? Is he coming home anytime soon for, I don't know, a single night?"

She slid her half slice of toast across the table to her brothers, and Luke jumped on it. Even when I am an adult, she thought, the sounds and smells of toast will make me think of this. Crumbs brushed from fingertips, the inhaling of something warm and comforting that's been burned. I'll remember the five pieces of toast and my mother's mouth fixed in a thin line.

"When everyone's ready," Lily said, "let's meet out by the front door."

She couldn't be coming with them, could she? Lily and her mother could not possibly be driving them all to school together, as if they were fleeing some fast-approaching hurricane. Madison entertained a sudden, silly image, the car piled up with luggage on its roof, her mother hunched over the wheel, Lily navigating. The last Range Rover out of Connecticut. A dark, billowing storm in the sky, chasing them down.

Isabel began stacking plates and bowls in silence and carried them to the sink. Madison cleared her throat.

"I might stay late today," she said. "After school."

Isabel left the dishes in the sink and returned to the table with a damp paper towel, dabbing at Luke's chin, at the peanut butter crumbs clustered at the corners of his mouth. She took his shirt with both hands, pinching the seams at each of his shoulders, and with one tug pulled it so that it hung straighter on his wiry frame.

"There's a football game," Madison continued.

"That's fine," her mother said. "So long as you get a ride home."

And it was this more than anything else that left the world around Madison unchanged and yet ominous, as though everything in the kitchen had begun to list to one side. No questions, no suspicion from Isabel as to why her Super Bowl–ignorant tenth-grader might suddenly need to go to a football game. That plain fact, that it had been so simple to put one over on Madison's mother, that Isabel had not required even the basic acrobatics of a massaged truth.

Madison took her plate from Lily's hands and slid the hollowed grapefruit skeleton into the trash. She resisted the urge to prick at her mother, to insist that she was still hungry, and followed her brothers out into the front hall.

Isabel stood by the door, waiting for Luke and Matteo to shoulder their backpacks.

"Come on," Isabel said to her children. "Smile like we mean it." It was her constant refrain, anxiety sheathed in a joke, when the children accompanied her to parties or fund-raisers populated entirely by their father's underlings. No one asked why this should be a necessary enjoinder on a regular Friday morning.

THEY DROVE PAST THE GOLDEN CURLICUES of the Weillands' gate and the Kanes' private course and the Sapersteins' twisting drive, what could be seen of it before it was swallowed up by their cluster of white oaks. Madison could feel herself as she watched, some fluttering awareness somewhere that she should be paying close attention to something she hadn't seen yet. The houses, the glimpses sometimes visible from the main road. The small details—the machinery at the front gates and the landscapers' trucks parked at service entrances and the anomalous silver balloon lodged in a hedge at the edge of one property like a tiny ghost.

She had spent her entire childhood on this same expanse of land in Greenwich, and recently she'd thought she would leave this coast for college. But she knew how she would miss Connecticut. She would miss the shock of greenery when it returned in the late spring, and the way the falling plum-colored leaves from the dogwood trees clogged the pool during the first heavy rains. She would miss entering the house from the east door, leaving boots and parkas heavy with melting snow in the mud room and bursting through the swinging doors into the silver-and-blue kitchen, which in the afterschool hours was as huge and cold and silent as a mausoleum.

She would miss, perhaps most of all, the smell of Connecticut in the summertime. The smell of green, that unbearable moisture in the air, the smell of water somewhere not too far away and of just enough nature to bask in but far too little in which to feel lost. She would miss the smell of the grass and leaves being gathered into massive piles as the gardeners moved methodically across the back lawn, their bodies braced against the slope of the hillside, gathering all signs of summer for one last time before winter took over. She'd been to Los Angeles in summer, and she'd been in winter; it all felt like the same bleached sunlight, hotter and more likely to cause nosebleeds in summer, but otherwise the same. The summer in Connecticut was something lush and alive, something so powerful that to open your mouth outdoors in July was to breathe in the ripeness, the season that hovered just on the edge of rotting.

At the elementary school gates, the boys tumbled from the car without so much as a backward glance, and Isabel remembered only at the last moment to call out to them, to remind them that Lily would pick them up right in this very spot. When they parked at Greenwich Prep a few minutes later, a block away from the main entrance and the logjam of the senior lot, Madison lingered in the front seat. But when she looked at her mother, Isabel was leaning her head against her window, looking toward the bus line, as if the car were already empty. She looked not unpretty but deflated, all color withdrawn from her body.

After a few moments, she turned her head slowly and fixed Madison with the same gaze that usually appeared in response to something rude, an insult or maybe a personal question.

"You'll be late," she said, and Madison got out of the car. By the time she had reached the main entrance to campus, her mother had driven away.

TWO

The second she heard the SUV pull out of the garage, Lily returned to the kitchen. She sat down in the breakfast nook, just where Matteo had been, and put her head to the table.

Isabel had reclaimed this wood from some farmhouse in western Massachusetts, a town they'd passed through on their way home from the partners' retreat at someone's Berkshires estate. She'd apparently all but yanked the wood from its heap in a field, saving it from its bonfire destiny. But of course he'd insisted they restore it, clean it up, resurface the tabletop to get rid of pesky, uneven planks that might upturn a little boy's cereal bowl. And so by the time it was finished, just like the rest of the house, it had strayed a bit from Isabel's original plan.

This, at least, was the story Lily had heard from Isabel. Like the other stories about the construction of Bob's envisioned home, Lily was mistrustful of this one. She worked for Bob and she worked for Isabel, but she had yet to see any evidence that he could strong-arm his wife into doing much of anything. Which seemed to Lily like a fair trade, for a razor-sharp woman who expressed placid disinterest in the intricacies and machinations of her husband's career. It seemed only right that, in exchange, he accept the house as her domain.

Still, the brute-force approach might have been helpful this morning, if he'd been here. Madison had been in the kitchen for only ten minutes, but Lily felt like taking a bow, then a nap. And she wasn't usually wrung out like this before nine o'clock. There were a million balls in the air each day, yes, but Lily had kept this job for this long because she knew how to juggle. She wasn't usually asked to lie to these kids, though; she wasn't usually given enough information to make lying a viable course of action.

It bothered her, to be already thinking along these lines. No one had asked her to lie. All that had happened was that Lily had walked through the rose garden and into the main house an hour ago to find Isabel awake and fully dressed, her drained espresso cup sitting on the precious wooden table. And Isabel had presented her employee with a plan that wasn't so much a plan as a series of orders not to ask further questions.

As if that would work with the kids, as if they wouldn't balk at their mother suddenly driving them to school.

Jesus, they were only a month into the school year, Lily thought now. Too much was already flying out of her hands. The early return from their summer vacation, and now this.

She began loading the breakfast dishes into the enormous space-craft this house classified as a dishwasher. This was the smaller one, not even the industrial one they used for the events that were too small to be catered, and still it felt like an enormous churning maw that might swallow her at any moment. All this kitchen for a woman who didn't cook. But that wasn't Lily's business, obviously; judgment wasn't her job. Her job had taken care of Lily's parents, paid off her loans, built her grad school fund from mere scrimped money into something that actually deserved to be called "a fund." Something that could even pay for one of the big ones, law school or something. It was too easy to forget, sometimes, to roll your eyes and start to feel like the fact that you were the one cooking in a kitchen actually made it yours.

At what point did you have to stop saying you were "saving money for school"? If she never did it, never went back to school, never gave shape to her amorphous interest in child psychology, could she still say this job had served a purpose? In the past two years, she'd gradually withdrawn from anyone who might press her on this. Her old adviser from Columbia, who had gotten her this job in the first place because he trusted her to use it as a stepping-stone. ("These aren't the kind of people to whom you *don't* wish to be connected," he had once told her, taking delight in the wordplay, as if cleverness would make it sound less like social climbing.) Her friends from her major, many of whom had already gotten their master's degrees and were either mulling over or in the midst of Ph.D.s. And her father, who didn't share her mother's thrill at the sheer amounts of money she'd been able to earn.

Her father who always said that anything you did that you felt good about, you wouldn't feel any need to hide from anyone, no matter how noble the reasons for secrecy. Lily didn't believe he thought this actually, didn't believe any human adult could make it to his advanced age and still be spouting such inaccuracies, but still. He loved to say this when she was over for dinner, dodging his questions about when she'd quit her job and start "her next phase." When they were eating the groceries she'd bought, sending the leftovers home with the handyman she'd paid. (She never pointed this out, and also never reminded her father that if his landlord ever forced him out to make way for the invading gentrifiers, it would also be Lily's money he'd use to find another place.)

Of course, Jackson was different. Her boyfriend was always telling her that he didn't judge her for wanting to stay long enough to reap the benefits of all the work she'd put in. But you don't want to get *complacent,* he always said. You don't want to grow afraid of leaving; by then, it's too late. You don't want to fall for it. Start thinking you *need* them.

Lily punched at the faucet, ducking her hands beneath the scalding jets of water. Nobody, not any of them, wanted to hear that she liked this job. She liked being the woman Isabel D'Amico, who needed no one, relied upon for help. And these kids; she loved these kids. She wasn't in denial. She knew that eight years was at least five years too long for a girl with her options to remain a glorified nanny.

(Isabel had never really settled on a job title for her, instead always referring to her as "Lily, who keeps the train on the tracks," whenever her name was mentioned in discussions of logistics with other moms.)

But Lily loved the twins so much that she'd postponed the natural conclusion to her time with the D'Amico family, removed the word "temporary" from her inner monologue. She'd been here long enough that she allowed herself to take pride in them as if she were responsible for the fact that they weren't like other little boys. Which, quite frankly, they weren't. This was a truth she often had to remind herself to keep internal, when she was sitting with the other nannies on the corrugated metal bleachers at the elementary school. She'd watch the other children eating grass, scratching and pawing at one another and throwing elbows like barbarians. While her twins stood together in close conference like two little robber barons, heads cocked to one side, considering the soccer field in front of them as if puzzled by all the ways it diverged from whatever they'd rather be doing. They looked so thoughtful out there, so peaceful and old.

She did try to remember not to brag about them to the other nannies, though. You aren't supposed to take the credit for children you're paid to nurture; no one wants to see you form a true, unshakable bond with the angelic offspring of the man who signs your checks. The most jealous ones, actually, were usually the older nannies, the women born in Guatemala or Jamaica or the D.R. rather than on a safe, if unglamorous, block at the south end of Carroll Gardens. They couldn't stand the fact that Lily, so much younger than they were, so inexperienced when she'd been given the job and already so spoiled by an Ivy League degree, was so good at it. Took it so seriously.

She shut off the faucet and turned back to the table, leaning uncomfortably against the center island, the dishwasher buttons poking her lower back. Her phone erupted on the counter. She grabbed it, ignored it, and put it in the back pocket of her jeans.

Why couldn't it be research? That was the other thing all the men hassling her about this never wanted to hear, not even her old adviser. She wanted to work with children at some future stage. If she was considering a Ph.D. in East Asian History, would anyone argue against her spending five years, whatever, maybe even six or seven, in Japan? Would anyone criticize her for waiting to apply until she was fluent in the language, the people, all of it? No. The answer was no. But because her research meant caring for children, somehow she was stalling, putting her life on hold. Somehow it was unserious.

And what about the boys, their lives?

She'd been plucked out of the city by Isabel only a month after graduation. Her thesis adviser had insisted she call this woman he knew a little bit, this was a Wall Street CEO's *wife*, for God's sake, Lily's loans would be paid off within *a few years* and she'd be making more than she could make as a *paralegal*. Every trust-fund-baby Lit major at the school had heard the rumor about this job and was clamoring for it, but he would give *her* a personal introduction to the family. And so she'd given him a résumé that was polished to the point of fiction and waited for the call from Isabel's then-assistant, a creamy-cheeked redhead who had blinked compulsively and conducted Lily's entire interview, practically, in a frantic whisper, inspiring Lily to do the same for at least the first few months she'd lived out here.

She smiled now, remembering the constant seasickness of those early days, never quite knowing her role. But she'd picked it up; she'd followed Isabel's cues. She had a lifetime of experience as a mimic, after all, as the scholarship kid, as the girl surrounded by other girls who had grown up with more. It was that ear that helped her pick up the inflections of the other girls in her dorm freshman year, their specific emphases. How they had to live like *paupers* because they *literally* had like fifty dollars to their *name* right now, because they'd *blown* through more than a hundred *dollars* at an *open bar*, for fuck's sake. And they couldn't go to their dad, not again, to ask if he could do the deposit early this time, before the first of the month, please, Daddy. Just this once. I've learned my lesson. I swear.

By the end of that first year of college, though, Lily had realized that the best thing she could do with her ability to sound like them was to turn it on its head. It felt like she could only disguise her own marvel at these girls, their exotic, careless lives, by playing up the very things that they found exotic in her. They'd chosen Columbia, often, for the city. It had been a choice. To them, she was interesting by virtue of her lifelong residence there. They'd come from mansions in Holmby Hills or Rye or the North Shore, and they just assumed she knew all the byways and shortcuts to the city. So, she embellished. She invented middle school muggings, drug deals in Prospect Park, older men who took her to loft parties in Williamsburg before Williamsburg was even a thing. She never again tried to sound like them.

And she was proud of the fact that her early Greenwich whisper, that early fear, only ever really returned now when visitors came to the house. It had always come back with vigor when Isabel's father was around, the expansive Mr. Berkeley. He was the clear source of the twins' sun-drenched gene, that look of having spent one's early years crawling across some dappled croquet lawn in Rhode Island or Massachusetts or wherever it had been. Lily had only actually spoken with him a few times, though she'd often laundered his golf khakis and even more often prepared his breakfast. She'd never been able to keep from jumping, startled, when he cornered her in some upstairs hallway, his piercing eyes a milky blue, like a cloud-skimmed sky.

The boys looked more like Isabel's side of the family, definitely. But when you saw them all together, the twins and their parents, something clicked. All of their mother's light and beauty and yet none of the things that made her seem breakable, like some fragile glass bauble placed unwisely on a high shelf. The boys' faces spread out broadly from their strong noses, their flushed cheeks, then gathered with animalistic intensity whenever they were busy with some task. And in those moments you saw Bob's face floating over Luke's or Matteo's, like a menacing ghost.

Madison was different; Madison was her father's coarse energy poured over ice. She was her mother's goddess features, infused with her father's ceaseless certainty that he was right.

The phone buzzed, again, in her back pocket. Lily dried her hands, took it out, silenced it, and left it on the counter. It was Jackson, again, she knew.

He had always said she just needed something to shake things up for her, this job, so that other parts of the situation rose to the surface. And now he seemed to think that something had arrived. He was in Pennsylvania right now visiting his family, so it wasn't a question of luring her into the city to see him. She knew why he was calling. He wanted information. He assumed she had it.

She began loading the cereal bowls into the dishwasher. Bob spent plenty of nights in the city. He slept there all the time. This particular time had lasted longer, but that meant nothing. Isabel had chosen not to elaborate, and seeking the root causes of Isabel's moods was not in Lily's job description. Her job was to decipher those moods, to see how she could help the children to navigate around them, and then to withdraw.

Having done every dish she could possibly do, she looked around the kitchen for a moment. She could go upstairs to gather the detritus the boys always left in their morning wake, their sweat-choked pajamas on the floor and the fine spray of toothpaste across the lower half of the bathroom mirror. She could also sit down with the various sports and academic calendars and type up the kids' schedules from now until Christmas; Isabel would be thrilled if she had that all squared away this early. She was reluctant, though, to go upstairs. She opened the refrigerator and took stock of what she had. She decided to prep a marinade for flank steak; they could eat it tomorrow, for a late Saturday lunch. She took out the glass baking dish and began to chop the onion.

It was true Madison had that tough coarseness, her father's trademark, though she seemed powerless to apply it against her mother. But then Isabel was equally steel. When Isabel dictated the arrangements of the place settings for a dinner party, wasn't she just providing Bob with the polish he'd always wanted, the things he'd married her for? His nickname hadn't come from nowhere. He needed someone beside him who could transmogrify that noisiness, convince you it was dominance and not just a panicked tantrum.

And that, that definitely was something Isabel could do.

Lily hadn't seen marriage in this way before this job, as a mutually beneficial merging of goods and services. But then, that wasn't entirely fair. She saw the way Bob looked at his wife when she wore something backless, the near-ferocious blend on his face of aggression and pride and longing.

Again Lily felt the brief recoil of guilt. The part of her mind hired to play cop admonished the other part, the part that allowed for fear. Already, any minor doubt felt like a punishable offense. As if it would be caught on tape, recorded somewhere within the walls of this house, and played back to her later as proof of her momentary disloyalty.

Not that she'd actually understood much of what she'd read, the news all summer. Whenever Jackson mentioned it, either alone with her or on one of her nights in the city when she'd meet him and his J school friends at their favorite scummy bar beneath the BQE, she'd take that moment to visit the urine-coated, graffiti-mirrored bathroom. She was careful to keep her iPhone always locked around Madison, to conceal her periodic news checks throughout the afternoon.

So what did she really know? The other women, the nannies and the wives and—she could only assume—the mistresses, talked about these guys like they were firefighters and nuclear scientists and the president rolled into one. Meanwhile, she was not a moron and was in fact a champion eavesdropper, and yet she had not a clue what it was Bob D'Amico actually *did* for a living. Whatever activities filled

the corridors of his soaring glass building on Times Square were utterly foreign to her. So what did she know?

She knew daily routines. She knew the unpredictable weather
of summers in southern Connecticut, and she knew which layers of
clothing that weather might call for at any given time. She knew
favorite snacks and local shortcuts. She knew, in brief, his children.

And Bob, in turn, got to feel cozy and validated for hiring such a
well-educated nanny, and a young one to boot. She knew the other
yummy mummies—Jackson's nickname for the Greenwich contin-
gent, a phrase that had unfortunately lodged itself in her brain—would
never have stood for a recent graduate shuttling their children to and
from soccer practice, a young trophy-wife-in-training who might
remind them of what they'd seen in the mirror only a few years earlier. No, most nannies around here were middle-aged and terrified
of losing access to this world. Lily wasn't exactly competition for
Isabel, she was no nubile blonde. Still: Isabel had the confidence to
hire someone young, a girl with an education who spoke three languages (this was another blurred detail on her résumé, but whatever),
whose ass hadn't spread yet.

So, no, she hadn't studied the canon at Columbia so she could clean
up after the CEO of Weiss & Partners and his beautiful children. But
no one had ever explained to her how this was any less valid than the
amorphous digital-media analytics jobs her friends had signed up for
in open-plan offices near the Flatiron. She was taking care of small
people and helping them learn to negotiate the world around them.
What was more useful than that? If she wasn't here, their only available
guides would have been their parents, who were so deeply ensconced
that they couldn't possibly give their children any real, accurate information about the world. And so the next step, her next step—she'd get
to it when this job was done.

They treated her well. Lily couldn't speak for the others, the army
of gardeners and landscapers or Lena the silent Ukrainian woman
who arrived each day with her helpers at nine o'clock to scour the

house, one room at a time. The truth was that the D'Amicos could have a lot more people working in that house every day, and probably would if Lily herself hadn't negated the need for a personal assistant for Isabel. There was a girl in the city who exclusively handled the MoMA correspondence, sure, and that was the primary source of Isabel's business from day to day. But out here, with the kids? Lily had made herself irreplaceable, without even realizing how important it was for her to do so. Eight years was an epoch unto itself when it came to nannies in Greenwich; it was leverage.

She took the flank steak from the refrigerator, slit open its plastic cover. She took the strip of meat in her hands and laid it flat in its dish. She washed her hands with scalding water, covered the dish with foil, and slid it onto a shelf in the refrigerator.

Whatever was going on now, Lily had no real complaints, no smoldering resentments about her life with them. Anyone who didn't believe her, who didn't understand that this felt good, had clearly never felt it. She was embedded, now. And Isabel had to know this. There was no way, after this long. There was no way Isabel didn't understand.

THREE

I guess I'm just struggling. To understand. This sudden . . . enthusiasm."

Madison could see that Amanda was making a true effort not to roll her eyes. The end effect was twice as insulting as the most condescending smirk would have been.

"You hate football," Amanda continued.

Madison slammed her locker door with a degree of force she knew was unnecessary.

"That isn't fair," she said.

"Oh, no?"

"I know nothing about football. It isn't fair to say I hate it."

"Okay, well?" Amanda turned her palms to the ceiling. "Then why would we go? Plus, I've got swim practice."

"Friday drills are optional," Madison said. "And it's fun. Zoë Barker said that it's, you know. Fun. It's Friday."

She watched Amanda close her locker and lean into it, pressing her forehead to the chilled metal. Amanda had always been the one person for Madison, the one she felt close to in the way other people talked about feeling close—to sisters, to friends, to mothers or grandmothers. Madison had Lily, but that was different. Amanda was her one choice to seize the real intimacy that was presented in every book, by every movie, as a fundamental part of being a teenage girl.

Even when they were small, she'd begged Isabel to let her call

Amanda's house in the middle of the night because she was trapped in the paranoid fog of some dream in which Amanda had been angry with her. These late-night elementary school phone calls, along with their accompanying afternoon marathon chats, had been the primary reason Isabel caved and allowed Madison to install her own phone line.

But that had been a long time ago, and all this past summer it was clear that Amanda wanted Madison to know that things had changed between them. That they were sophomores now, and no longer beholden to the ties that had bound them together as children, whatever those ties had actually been.

Madison didn't understand why they would be growing apart. She couldn't see that either one of them had changed at all. But it was hard to miss, by the end of the summer, that her best friend had almost completely lost interest in her.

She watched now as Amanda performed her own exasperation, forehead pressed up against the metal. And she could see that there was a small, unacknowledged part of her friend that enjoyed this, that felt a little thrill at letting herself be this cruel. Madison could tell. It must feel the way it used to feel when they'd shoplift chocolates together from Greenwich Pharmacy, while their mothers stood chatting, oblivious. All these small slights, over the summer. Amanda didn't just want Madison to move on; she wanted to feel that electric charge, of being wanted by someone you no longer want.

"So the actual reason," Amanda said, "is that Zoë Barker told you to come watch the football game, so you're going."

"Amanda, they're not so terrible."

Sometime in August, as if they'd sniffed out what was happening with Amanda, all of a sudden Zoë Barker and her sidekick Allie Wasserman—girls who had previously shown little interest in Madison beyond a healthy fear of her parents—were inviting her places, asking her along. Madison had never had any real expectation that Amanda would go along with it, would allow them all to become friends.

"Can you just explain one thing to me, though? Can you explain why she is so obsessed with that umlaut over her name? I've seen her when it gets left off some name tag. You'd think they've printed 'Raging Slut' in its place, she goes totally nuts. Does she think anyone's actually going to be confused and pronounce her name Zoo? Or Zoah? Do you think it upsets her that it would rhyme with 'Ho'?"

"I really think if you'd spent any time with them—"

"Right, Mad, but the thing is—I have no interest. I mean, truly. Zero. You go ahead. Make new friends. And Chip's playing, right? But you know I have less than nothing to talk about with those girls."

"I don't know what that means."

"Madison, I don't have a lot they're interested in. Okay? Maybe in two years they'll decide that my father has something to do with admissions and they'll want to go to Yale and I'll get randomly invited to Zoo's next party. But until then, there's not exactly any magazine that named *my* father as the country's top CEO last year. You know?"

Madison could immediately see the regret on Amanda's face, her wrinkled nose and her gaping mouth. But as with most regret, it had flooded her synapses just a few seconds too late.

"You're telling me you think Zoë Barker reads *Institutional Investor*? I doubt it."

She tried to keep her voice dry, condescending, even. Amanda almost never violated this, their last unspoken rule. Their fathers.

"You know I don't care about that," she continued.

"Obviously, Mad. But you are one in a million. Most people around us aren't like you. And they definitely wouldn't be like you if they *were* you. You know what I mean?"

"Hardly ever," Madison said, sliding her lock shut and turning back to Amanda.

Amanda reached out with one finger and deftly lifted a strand of hair that had slipped down to hang loose in front of Madison's face, tucking it back behind her ear where it belonged.

"They can love you for different reasons than I do!" Amanda said. "You're, you know. There are lots of things to like about you."

It sounded like an insult, maybe even an accusation. They stood in silence, their classmates rushing past on either side.

"Look," Amanda said, "I'm not trying to be a bitch. If you want to go to the game, you should go."

"I don't," Madison said, and her voice had changed, flattened. She turned back to her own locker, her books, and ignored her friend's gaze. She thought of Amanda's father, of how they'd sat in on one of his Micro lectures at Yale a few years ago, in a soaring lecture hall with high windows that filled the room with late-afternoon light and rows upon rows of rickety wooden seats that would retract with loud, slapping sounds each time some lazy underclassman stood to duck out early. Amanda had flinched each time, as if the students were actually flipping off her father with each squeal and smack, and Madison had held her hand. Toward the end of the lecture, Jake Levins began calling out the slouching undergrads sitting in the first few rows, actually pointing at them with his index finger. It was something Madison loved about Amanda's father, something that reminded her of her own father, even if their methods were different. He could look at you with such vehemence that you understood him, wordlessly: he knew you didn't know what to say, but you were going to answer him regardless.

Amanda was still watching her.

"Mad," she began, "I know it's been a weird September so far, but you're taking it easy, right? Don't get stressed out yet, over nothing."

Madison rapped her locker once with her knuckles.

"You know I don't understand anything he does," she said. "It's not like he's going to talk to me about his job."

"That's not what I asked," Amanda said, but Madison had already turned away.

MADISON MOVED SLOWLY on the walk from her locker to the fields. She had always been aware, in a dim and unaddressed way, that Amanda might pay attention to things like that magazine award. But normally nothing like that would ever be said between the two of them. Amanda almost never talked about Madison's father. Amanda's parents, when Madison was over at their house—which, until these past few months, she had been several times each week—looked at each other and exchanged thin, toothless smiles whenever she said her father's name.

She saw Chip Abbott as soon as she got to the field. The other girls were huddled on the bleachers on the far side, so she kept her eye on him as she crossed the end zone. He stood with his hands on his hips, his shoulders hunched beneath his pads, his skinny legs squeezed into the shiny pants like straws in their paper wrappers.

She stumbled somewhat on a hidden divot in the field, the loose grass and bits of dirt flying up around her ankles, and she righted herself, brushed her skirt down over her thighs. She shook her head, just as she'd always done when an unpleasant thought crossed her mind in a public place, to dislodge anything like a frown from her face. Someone might be watching, noticing; she knew this, the awareness bred into her since babyhood by both parents. That your time, your face, your body—none of it was entirely your own, not when other people could see you.

There was a canvas, a slate, an Etch-A-Sketch, whatever. And she could control what was on it. What was visible inside her head. And what she wanted on there, the only thing she wanted on there today, was this: the fact that Chip Abbott had begun to say hello to her outside her third-period Trig class.

The first time had been one of the first days of the school year. *Hey*, he'd said to her, touching his fingertips to her left shoulder blade. He'd done it again the next day, at the same time, in the same crowded morning rush of the hallway. A boy down the hall had screamed, "Ball sack!" just as they made eye contact, and Chip raised his eyebrows and smiled at her, as if the rowdy eruption had been hers.

In the weeks since, that was essentially all that had happened. They had not had a real conversation. And yet it felt as though *so much* was going on. An entire catalog of glances and touches and jokes emerged, ready to be analyzed. A netherworld of nuance and suggestion rose up to greet her like an abandoned object suddenly emerging from the depths of a cobalt swimming pool; something she'd once lost, without knowing, and now had the unforeseen joy of retrieving. She had never felt, had only heard others bragging about, this constant excitement. This feeling that your body had been hollowed out and filled with something reactive that could be stirred, even by something so small as a smile in passing.

She kept her eyes low as she approached the bleachers, as she moved closer to him. Zoë and Allie saw her at the last moment, and waved.

"Are we winning?" she asked them. Allie was wearing leggings the same color as her own skin, so that from far away it looked, for a second, like she wasn't wearing pants. Madison's gaze darted back and forth from the girls to the field, Chip. This was what it felt like now, to be on a campus where she knew he was, somewhere. There was a part of her always drifting away from the conversation, floating into some untethered existence. Keeping her mind on one thing felt like keeping a room full of kindergarteners quiet and attentive.

"Winning?" Zoë said. "Of course, what'd you expect. It's just a preseason game, it's not serious. But Chip's killing it. He could beat this defense with his eyes closed. He's practically dancing around out there."

Madison had known Chip, or known who he was, since she was five years old. They'd attended the same elementary school, and now he was a junior at Greenwich Prep. In middle school, sometimes she'd see him on the main quad, throwing a football around with some of the older players on the team. The ball arcing high through the air, his arm extending in one long line from his shoulder.

Last year, as a sophomore, Chip had been the second-string quarterback, but everyone knew that was only a courtesy to Justin Peck, who had patiently waited until his senior year for his chance as QB. Now, it was Chip's turn, which seemed like a terrible idea to Madison. He was too lanky, too fragile. Chip was tall, and the ropy muscles in his arms jumped every time he raised his hand or shouldered his backpack, but even she knew that he was a shrimp compared to the varsity football players. These were the boys who spent their school days lounging around the same octagonal lunch table in the courtyard outside the cafeteria, their eyes permanently at half-mast, as though playing football for an affluent and predominantly white private school in Greenwich, Connecticut, was just about all they could be expected to handle in any given week.

But Chip: Chip smelled good, like soap mixed with fresh air and steam, like he was perpetually just stepping out from a hot shower. He clipped the strap of his backpack across his chest while he ran around campus, always fiddling with it, and sometimes he sang goofy songs at pep rallies and things. She had never known a single fact about football, a single rule, not even the scoring system. But she felt like she knew enough to worry about Chip, about the sound of his arm snapping beneath him when a bigger guy tackled him. About the way he would look with a black eye, with a fat lip. She'd already seen the way the football players walked on Monday mornings, that combination of swagger and a prancing sensitivity that favored their soreness, their multiple aches and pains. She sometimes thought that was how all men should walk: like they were all hiding something for your benefit, something that made them wince.

"Isn't Chip," Madison began with caution, "isn't he kind of skinny? Compared to the other guys?"

Zoë ran a hand through her hair, swirling it over her head in one glossy motion, tucking the ends behind one ear. "You're kidding, right? Madison! He's the quarterback. He's supposed to be small and fast, and then everyone else has to protect him. God, you really weren't lying when you said you don't know football."

"You guys know a lot about it?"

"Well," Allie said, dissecting a split end between her thumb and forefinger, "we don't have much of a choice, right? My dad has a game playing in the house at all times, from September to the Super Bowl. I'd have to literally plug my ears and blindfold myself to ignore it."

As the game meandered on, Madison did a quick mental scan of her tote's contents. English class this year wasn't much, but she couldn't wait for next year, to finally get to reread *The Great Gatsby*, something with actual humans feeling actual emotions and falling in love and with many opulent party scenes. She'd read the whole thing a few years ago, in middle school, but she remembered those party scenes most of all. The way the book caught how it felt in real life, when everything swirled past in the air above your head. The lights and the sound of breaking glass.

But sophomore English was, all signs indicated, going to be the same sort of hit parade English class had been every year so far, with *Beowulf*, *The Picture of Dorian Gray*, even, she had a feeling, with *The Scarlet Letter* next semester. A series of chances for a series of male writers to cram their ideas of what it meant to be a man down her throat. And if she wanted that, she'd just linger outside the door to her father's study the next time he shut himself up with some of his partners. Periodically paging her on the intercom to ask her to bring them drinks, his praise more lavish with each round. *Mad, you there? The natives are growing restless. Be a princess and bring us a tray of drinks. You know what we need, all the fixings. The boys'll be indebted to you, sweetheart.*

She shivered, then admonished herself for feeling guilty. She had thoughts like this all the time; didn't everyone do this, complain about their parents in the privacy of their own minds? Mocking her father this way usually felt gentle, harmless and inaudible, an appropriate counterweight to the rest of her life as a daddy's girl. And yet this particular moment of disrespect sat heavily at the base of her spine.

She pulled her cashmere hoodie more tightly around herself and peered over her shoulder at the other spectators. The fathers were all standing off to one side, clumped beside the bleachers; the mothers all sat on the higher levels, their backs straight, leaning forward with their hands cupped around their crossed knees. They all wore muted versions of the things their daughters wore—quilted jackets, velvet flats, gemstones sparkling at their ears whenever they brushed back a strand of hair. Several of them were staring down at her.

At halftime, the players gathered in a huddle not far from the bleachers, then scattered out across the field, some throwing a ball back and forth, others stretching on the sidelines. They all seemed determined to scowl.

"Chip is looking over here," Zoë said without inflection. Madison felt the moisture drain from her mouth. Moments later he was walking past the bleachers, cutting his eyes up at them.

"This the cheerleading squad?" he said, his voice rumbling from some place deep in his chest. When he spoke, it was like something warm had been poured down your back, from your neck to your tailbone.

"We just thought you could use the support," Zoë said, not looking at him.

"What about you," Chip said. "Madison. This your first football game?"

She nodded, voiceless.

"It's a rough one," he said.

She shrugged, and figured out something to say. "It's just the preseason."

"Yeah, we're hanging in."

"Really?" she said. "I heard you were running circles around their defense."

He grinned and looked back over his shoulder, wiping his mouth on his jersey, before turning his head back to her and looking her right in the eye. She felt something unfold in her chest, as delicate and expansive as a ship in a bottle. She sat up straighter.

"Well, you know," he said.

"Madison," a loud voice boomed, just beyond Chip, who looked back and then moved aside. Through the metal bars, she could see a man beaming up at her. "Madison D'Amico, how are you?"

A tuxedo, she thought. He'd been wearing a tuxedo—where? Had she met him at MoMA, maybe, one of her mother's events? His voice, like a stick dragged over gravel, made louder by the glass of vodka in his hand. Her father, catching her eye, raising his eyebrows and then letting a look slip toward the man as if he were emitting an unpleasant smell. Her hand over her mouth, hiding her own smile. The smell of her mother's makeup, which she'd been allowed to borrow, the waxy feel of the lipstick. The unpleasant static of her tights as they snagged on the tulle skirt of her dress. Years ago, at least—she'd been littler, then, an accessory for her parents' evening.

She could not, though, remember his name. Or who his children were, although his presence seemed to suggest that they must be somewhere at her school.

"Hi!" she said, her voice all manufactured brightness. "So nice to see you again. How are you?"

"Well, kid," he said, wrapping his fingers around the metal bars between them. She was sitting on a lower bleacher, so that his eyes were nearly level with hers. "I just came over to ask you the same question. How you doing? You holding up?"

Madison could feel the girls on the bench beside her, their presences settling, heavy with their efforts not to eavesdrop. The curiosity sinking to their feet like lead, holding them still. Beyond them, she knew, if she turned her head to look out over the rest of the bleachers, the mothers would be doing the same thing. Everyone would continue to speak, but their bodies would orient toward her. Somewhere, she thought with panic, *Wyatt Welsh's mom is here.* Suzanne Welsh, the most frantic gossip of all the mothers she'd known since childhood, was somewhere in the stands.

She smiled again, as if the man had just told her some wonderful news.

"Oh, I'm doing so well," she said. "They didn't *warn* us about all the *work* we'd have in tenth grade! But, I mean, otherwise I can't complain. What brings you to the game?"

His eyes roamed across her face, a smile tugging at the corners of his mouth. He looked like she'd just made a joke, and she saw with uneasy certainty that he felt in some way insulted, or dismissed. She hated when her father's friends looked at her this way, like her face was one of those brain-teaser paintings, and they were waiting for the hidden image of her true opinion to emerge. This man (What was his name? Which bank? Or maybe he was a client?) had ruddy, mottled skin, like he'd been standing in the wind and the sun for hours. His hair was gray in a way that was really almost white, unlike her father's, and there was a significant growth of stubble on his chin and cheeks. His fingers were clasped so tight around the bleacher bars that his thumbnails were the pale, nauseous yellow of lemon pith.

She saw, then, that the man standing off to one side was with him, that they were both looking at her intently. This other man was much, much younger, closer even to her own age. He had chunky-frame glasses and the sort of thick, dark hair that looks like it could be used to sweep a kitchen floor, and he'd given up any pretense of trying to control the hair other than keeping it more close-cut at the sides and around his ears than it was on top, where it flapped a bit in the breeze. His nose and mouth both protruded, in a way, came to a point beneath his glasses, which gave him an air of being constantly curious, of listening very closely. He was dressed too warmly for the weather, like a teenage boy who'd been dragged to an afternoon occasion of some kind with his parents. A forest green sweater over a shirt and a ruby red tie—had it honestly not occurred to him that he was wearing Christmas colors?—and khakis that had once been pressed but had been rumpled since, as if someone had tried to erase the crease along the front leg. This man stood rolling back and forth on the balls of his feet, his hands in his pockets, giving the unmistakable impression that he had them there to keep himself reined in, on his best behavior.

"Just saying hello, sweetheart. You tell Bob I sent him my best. Tell him I said hang in there. Stick to his guns. It's just a waiting game. That place has ridden out far worse than this."

"Of course," she said, refusing to look wildly around her to see who was watching. She could feel, of course, Zoë's focus next to her, emitting its own heat. And somewhere beyond her, Allie—more ambivalent and conflicted about whether it was rude to listen, but equally intrigued. "I'll do that. He'll be so happy to hear you said hello."

He works at Goldman Sachs, she thought, the final pieces of the memory returning. It was right, she was pretty sure, that she had initially met him at a museum event, with her parents. But the facts surfacing now came from a conversation she'd overheard another time. She was remembering gossip from Mina Dawes, Isabel's occasional best friend—he must know Mina's husband, Tom, that would make sense. She thought she remembered something about Le Rosey. This man had a daughter a few years older than her, but Mina had talked about them when her own daughter, Jaime, decided to leave for Andover. His kids had left America altogether, he'd "parked them"—Mina's phrase—at Le Rosey, in Switzerland. So why was he here now, on this campus?

"I wouldn't worry," the man said to her. His hands were still gripping the bleachers. She told herself that it was silly to think that they might reach through the bars, try to touch her hands, her wrists. "Your dad's a tough one. He's scrappy. But I don't need to tell you that, do I?"

"Sure," she said, still grinning like a maniac. The man pressed even closer, his cheeks now touching the metal.

"I don't need to tell his daughter, I'm sure, how skilled that man is. When it comes to getting off the hook," he said. "You know. Blameless. Untouchable. That's your dad."

She waited for a moment, looking back toward the football field, as if she had all the time in the world. Then she swallowed and turned back to look the man squarely in his weatherbeaten face.

"He'll be so thrilled," she said, "to hear that you came over to say hello. That you came all the way over here, and interrupted the game, just to make sure I'd seen you."

His face twisted into something ugly, but it snapped back so quickly that by the time she felt the first shiver of real fear course through her body, he was smiling again. He reached one meaty finger through the bleachers, and tapped it against her knee.

"Have a good weekend, sweetheart," he said. And then he'd turned away, to walk back across the field. The younger man seemed to want to say something, in that first second before they left, but the older one made a movement of his head, abrupt, and they'd said nothing. They walked side by side, still not seeming to talk, until she could no longer see them at the edges of her vision.

Madison turned back to Zoë and Allie, who were chattering at each other in a blissful, unabated stream. She willed herself not to look at any of the adults. Chip was jogging back toward the fifty-yard line, tugging his helmet on. She wondered how long he'd stood near her before returning to the field. Everything now was just as it had been, the man's appearance at her shoulder an uninvited, insignificant dream.

AFTER THE GAME, Madison stood in the senior parking lot, the trees darkening against the sky as it faded from stone gray to violet. She'd texted Lily earlier, hoping her mother would have conveniently forgotten that Madison had promised to find a ride home. She wasn't sure that Allie or Zoë were really her friends, that she could yet do something as casually presumptuous as asking one of their mothers to drive her home.

She didn't feel, just now, that she wanted to be in a car with a woman she'd never met before. Someone who didn't know her parents well. That seemed unwise.

Even before it happened, Madison felt that he was going to walk up behind her. She felt it with the confident knowledge that so often accompanied the inevitable, for her. It was like the moments of her childhood just before her father laughed at something she said and picked her up at the waist, held her high in the air. The moments just before she entered her bedroom to find her mother waiting for her, eager to point to some error or shortcoming. A stain undisclosed, a low grade she'd hidden away in a drawer, some public moment when she'd slouched. She always knew these things were coming; it was one of the things that made her feel like a spy in her own house. If you knew what was around the corner, eventually you began to feel like you could move through walls.

"Hey," Chip said, at her elbow. She turned to him—and she was so thrilled by this later, when she analyzed her own behavior—very slowly, with only a mild displayed interest in who was standing next to her.

"Hi," she said. "Nice game."

"You need a ride?"

"Do you drive?"

"No," he said, chuckling, and ducked his head, brushing one thumb to the cleft in his chin. This is a gesture I will memorize, she thought. I bet he does that all the time. When he's nervous, maybe.

"No," he said, "I meant, my mom could drive you."

"No no no," she said quickly, immediately mortified by the triple negative. "I'm just waiting for my mom. I got the timing wrong."

And of course, as she said this, there was Mina Dawes, someone who was decidedly not Madison's mother, careening into the lot in her inexplicable SUV. The woman had no children living in this state. She only ever had herself to drive around their relatively small portion of Connecticut.

"Oh," Madison said. "Family friend. I have to go."

"Hey," he said, and put his fingers to her arm, just above the elbow. "Thanks for coming to the game."

She wanted him to hold on longer, to let her be the one to shake him off, gently, as if he were an adoring pet. But by the time she'd had this thought, he'd given her a wave. He was already leaving.

FOUR

In the waning light of the predinner hour, Mina Dawes sat across the table from Isabel, desperate to keep their conversation aloft. During the silences her gaze wandered out over Isabel's pool, its surface entirely untroubled beneath the late-afternoon sun.

A pitcher of lemonade sat between them. Isabel's girl had brought it out within moments of Mina's arrival, placing it on an engraved tray that sat on the glass-topped table. Basil leaves floated just beneath the ice cubes, which was a classic Isabel touch. Every accent astonishingly simple: fluted calla lilies or random groupings of branches and vines thrown together in tall glass bottles, say, rather than the eruption and ostentation of actual centerpieces. Basil in the goddamn lemonade, Mina thought. She'd have to tell Tom tonight. He didn't like to be reminded of how much time she spent with Isabel, but he could usually be appeased with one of these finicky little details. That is, if he came home. He'd been on the couch in his office every night for the past week.

"It's always so lovely out here this time of day," Mina tried.

Isabel nodded behind her sunglasses. Mina sighed and looked off toward the guesthouse, the thick tree line at the back of the property.

When Bob and Isabel had settled in Greenwich for good, knocking down the old gray-roofed colonial and its accompanying stone wall, building up the property so that it loomed above the road below, everyone assumed their plan was a compound. Why else tear down that charming, quaint little slice of Connecticut history unless to replace it with something splashy? A palace for Bob? He'd just been named CEO; he was getting written up in all the city papers.

But everyone had underestimated, of course, just who exactly Bob D'Amico had married. Isabel Berkeley, the only Berkeley woman to decline a Yale acceptance since the school had first invited them in. Isabel Berkeley, whose idea of an appropriate vacation home was the white house with its green shutters on Shelter Island, shielded from the road only by a thick copse of trees. Where the upstairs guest shower leaked and the proprietors of all three bakeries on the main road in town had known her family's name the whole time she'd been alive. Mina had seen photos of some of this, and intuited the rest; she'd never been invited out to Shelter. Isabel's second home—well, third, if you counted the house in Sun Valley, but they were almost never there so Mina usually didn't even think of it—was not for entertaining. As far as Mina could tell, Bob was the only person without Berkeley blood who had set foot in the place, at least for the past few decades.

Mina remembered the party Isabel threw that first spring here at the new house, the guests wandering the grounds. The collective expelling of breath had been almost audible. She herself had explored a little, smiling at the cater waiters in that way she could never help, which surely inspired in them nothing but dripping contempt. She'd touched her fingertips to the different bespoke and reclaimed pieces of gorgeous furniture tucked into every nook, in every hallway, and she'd felt something almost like pride. Of all the women out here, Mina had known that this one was the real deal, and Isabel in turn had chosen Mina to draw closer.

Isabel wanted the other women to see this, too, to know that she saw them. How deeply they'd bought into all of it when they chose their husbands. Whereas her house was simple, elegant. It didn't cram anything down your throat.

You had to know the world would accept you nonetheless, before you could cast it off, was the difference. You couldn't possibly have the same attitude when your entire life came to you through your husband's success. But of course Mina never said any such thing to Isabel. She preferred to keep it to herself, and imagine that Isabel would know just what she meant.

Toward the end of that party, Isabel had kicked her heels to the floor by the stage and Bob had twirled her around the draining dance floor, her hair slowly coming loose from its chignon. Mina remembered the lavender-blue color of Isabel's dress, the hem puddling on the dance floor, the smudges of dirt visible at its very edges. That was the first time Mina had seen it, between them: that nothing about the way Isabel looked at him was performance. That his was the only opinion that would ever set Isabel's stomach on edge. Bob had all the qualities Isabel adored in her father, her own family, despite his naked hunger, his bulging eyes when he was angry. He was her best rebellion, a way to throw everyone off balance without having to jettison anything she didn't know how to live without.

No, in the end they built the house and a small guesthouse, redid the old tennis court and glammed up the pool, but most of the property was left somewhat wild by Greenwich standards. You had the impression that if you wandered to the edge of the lawn, you might take the step over the line, enter the woods, and find yourself lost.

And the house had been dwarfed, really, in recent years, by the newer ones. Twenty, thirty, even forty thousand square feet, some of them! Ice rinks, bowling alleys. *Tacky* was not really a word Mina was permitted to say out loud, not when she was talking to anyone in Greenwich, and so it was one she threw around often and with abandon in the privacy of her own head.

It was starting to seem like Bob might be the last holdout. Even the men who weren't like him, who were third-generation Wall Streeters, even those men were falling under the recent Greenwich spell. Ordering new construction that would sprawl out across the old land like an unruly teenage boy trashing a tasteful living room.

Mina turned back to the table, to Isabel's drawn face and large sunglasses, and poured herself another glass of lemonade.

"You know that new bakery had to close, already, did you see? The little jewel-box place on the Avenue, with the *macarons*? Lasted all of about six months," Mina tried again. Isabel nodded behind her sunglasses, and they both sipped.

Lily (yes, yes, she could pretend that she didn't, but she knew the girl's name perfectly well) had left them to their lemonade twenty minutes ago, during which time Mina had tried and failed to engage Isabel in any sort of small talk. She'd even confided in her about Jaime, whose roommate at Andover had been discovered concealing some troubling habits, doing things like slicing up her ankles with nail scissors. It was a horrifying turn of events, but one that had left Jaime with an enormous dorm room to herself for the remainder of her junior year.

Mina decided to return the conversation to their daughters.

"It's hard, no? Sixteen isn't so young, but it's hard to internalize that. That it's no longer in her best interest for me to drive up there and curl up with her on her bed and let her cry. You know, she was drawn to this girl, who turned out to be smashingly unstable, and now she has to suffer those consequences. Consequences are what we're supposed to teach them, right? So they don't just sink into all of this for the rest of their lives?"

She cast one hand through the air, including the house and the pool and the glimmering slope of the lawn in the gesture.

"Well, you know what I'm talking about. Madison's a sophomore, I'm sure you feel it, too."

Isabel responded with a smile, if it could even be classified as such. Her skin looked like a porcelain teacup that upon close inspection would yield up its faint web of cracks.

This impression was troubling all on its own. Mina had known Isabel for years, since the girls were small—although the girls had never been friends, not by their own choice. But Mina would say that she was as close to Isabel, certainly, as anyone else in town. Yet each time she came into this house she fought the fear that something was awry on her own person. Lipstick gathering and mixing with spit at the corners of her mouth, her blowout beginning to frizz with sweat just where her temple met her ear.

Because Isabel projected not perfection so much as uniformity. Her body, her hair, her tawny skin and the deceptive, unguarded clarity of her large blue eyes—it all met the eye like some sort of rivetless instrument. You couldn't see the joints, the creases, the tiny flaws that must be visible each morning before she was offered up to the outside world. *Believe me, Mina,* Tom always said. *Nothing going on beneath the waist. Beneath the neck! Bob can keep her.* And then he'd smack Mina's ass and grab her, exposing the soft part of her neck so that he could kiss her there. The sorts of unapologetic intimacies you were supposed to have the freedom to enjoy when you'd shipped your daughter off to boarding school.

Of course Tom would want to sleep with Isabel, in a world without consequence. This was not even a question. But really he was talking about her posture, about the way she held herself apart even when she was sitting in her own living room, as though the pool and the cars and probably the house in Sun Valley and definitely the jet—as though they all stank, ever so slightly, of something unsavory. What he meant was that he preferred his own wife, plucked from one of the lesser districts of Long Island and touched up and reprogrammed for Greenwich life and the occasional appearance in Manhattan. He preferred Mina, a woman reconstituted just like most of the other wives, to someone whose opinion might actually make his palms sweat.

She tried not to let these things bother her. Isabel was her best friend.

"Look," she said, "I fold, okay? I didn't come over to congratulate myself on the fact that my daughter's healthier than her neurotic roommate. I came to see if you need anything."

"We're fine, Mina. Truly."

"Isabel, I don't know much, but I do know that Tom has been working—so far as I can tell—quite literally around the clock for a week. So I assume Bob has been in hell."

Isabel laughed: a small, bitter sound. "That seems a safe assumption, yes."

"Have you spoken to him today?"

"No."

"Well, how did he sound yesterday?"

"You'd have to ask someone who spoke to him yesterday, Min."

"You two didn't talk?"

"Well, he's got his secretary—I don't know—*running interference*, so I haven't had the opportunity."

"I'm sure she doesn't mean it," Mina said, shivering at the scorn in Isabel's voice, as if she herself were the secretary in question. "I'm sure she's just frightened."

"That assumes she even knows where he is at any given moment," Isabel said. "For all I know he's in some bunker somewhere. She might not even actually be lying."

"You really think it's that bad?"

With a quick, unexpected motion, Isabel removed her sunglasses and tossed them down, letting them clatter on the table.

"What are we doing here, Mina? I assume you've been watching all the same cable news shows I've been watching. I'm sure you have every single piece of information I have, so why are you even asking me the questions? Hasn't everyone already decided?"

They sat in silence and Mina watched one single basil leaf, now fully drenched, begin its fluttering descent to the bottom of her glass.

"I didn't know that," she said. "I wasn't being insincere. I didn't know you hadn't heard from him."

"Well," Isabel said, fanning her hands out in an inclusive, welcoming gesture that encompassed the pool and the entire deck around them, even the woods at their backs. "Now you know."

"You know," Mina began, cautious, "that this is all mysterious to me. I understand that Weiss is in trouble. But if anyone can power through that, it's Bob, right? What does he say about it?"

"You're not listening to me. I don't know. He hasn't told me any-thing."

"I don't mean this week. I mean what has he been saying. The summer, and everything."

Isabel looked at her, her eyes settling on Mina's face as if she'd just noticed there was a second person at the table.

"Mina," she said, "my husband has not, in any significant way, told me anything about his bank for months and months. I swear to you."

The late-summer humidity hung in the air beyond the house, a palpable weight pressing down on the afternoon. Somewhere, be-yond the trees, Mina heard an industrial lawn mower. She imagined it moving across an indulgent expanse of green, leaving neat trails of exposed, cut grass in its wake. This was the sound of the afternoon, one of the sounds that, together, mapped her adult life as a wife, a mother, a woman inside her house in Connecticut. A woman waiting for her family to come home.

"Okay," she said. "But from what I've seen—I mean, they're still looking for a buyer, right? I mean it's much more likely that he'll sell the bank than that they'll just let it—I mean, bankruptcy would be a big decision to make. The government will step in, right?"

She was all too aware that she sounded like a teenager who hadn't done the reading. These were words Mina had gathered from cable news, in recent days, but not necessarily words whose significance she understood. Bob was considering selling the bank, Weiss & Partners, to the Koreans. This she knew. If the Koreans weren't interested, other U.S. banks were being convened to discuss the possibility of another buyer. This would include Goldman, Tom's bank. She knew this because Tom's boss's boss had been summoned to the Fed that week-end for a meeting with the other CEOs. She hadn't even known, until now, that the Fed was an actual location in Manhattan; she'd thought it was just another faceless government entity. She had, of course, kept that to herself when speaking with Tom.

But these were the broad strokes; she barely even had a hold on what it was Bob had done wrong, what missteps, exactly, had Tom and his friends shaking their heads in feigned sympathy six months ago. Back then they'd had to twist their mouths to conceal ill-disguised grins; now, when his failure was impending rather than hypothetical, they were all fearful themselves, ashen and under-slept.

"Mina," Isabel said. "I don't know what's going to happen to the rest of you, okay? My husband isn't here, is he? Do you see him here, enlisting me as his confidante? He's in the city. He's been there for weeks. He *flew home* from Shelter in August. I don't know what's going to happen to the rest of you. I can barely figure out what's going to happen to me."

They sat in silence once more. Tiny waves appeared on the surface of the swimming pool and the water lapped at the filter, making delicate sucking sounds. Mina had to believe that this finality, this resolve, from Isabel, was merely cloaked panic. That it was not really relevant, not to this situation. That they'd based their own lives, their children's futures, on something more substantial than sheer forward momentum, the unheeded enthusiasm with which those children had once built their sand castles at rented houses in the Hamptons, far too close to the returning waves.

"That isn't what I meant," Mina said. "You know that."

Isabel reached over to her, taking Mina's hand and spreading her own so that their fingers could interlace.

"Of course it's what you meant. I don't blame you. We're all allowed, right? My father used to say that no one would be afraid of an apocalypse as long as he knew there'd be enough canned food left to feed his own tribe."

Isabel laughed, and Mina smiled, too.

"That sounds about right. I mean, I wouldn't know. But based on the stories you've told me."

"I keep thinking about him, you know? He always acted like Bob's success was all imaginary. Like I was such a fool to take it at face value. While we were building this house, for those last few months when we were still in the city full-time, he used to call me up late at night and just . . . rant into my ear for an hour, sometimes. And I'd be alone with Madison, sitting in the apartment with the lights off, feeling the way I used to feel when I was a teenager and he'd come home and I'd lock myself up in my part of the house and he'd yell at me through my bedroom door."

Mina considered saying nothing; Isabel was speaking as if in a dream, and Mina did not want to recall her to where they were, how they usually spoke to each other.

"It's *not* imaginary, Isabel," she said finally. "I mean, whatever happens, it's not that."

And then Isabel looked up at her, her face wiped clean in the way that you'd sometimes see news anchors freeze in place when their audio feed failed to deliver the other half of the conversation.

"Oh," Isabel said, her voice so low it sounded more like an inhalation than speech.

Mina watched, over Isabel's shoulder, as Lily's head bobbed in and out of the lower corner of the kitchen window. She couldn't possibly be doing the dishes, could she? Surely no one had eaten since breakfast in this house. What did this girl spend her days doing, then? Mina knew there were others, even though Isabel's staff was relatively small, compared to the committees that ran some of their friends' homes. They had that expressionless Russian woman—was she Russian?—who always seemed to disapprove of whatever greeting Mina tried on her. And that woman had a small team of equally expressionless but younger and more buxom blondes from Eastern Europe who scurried around corners and disappeared from any room Mina entered. So what did Lily do all day?

Mina wondered this, often, about her own employees. The woman she had in charge of the house issued their marching orders, and as far as Mina could tell, every task was completed with efficiency and nearly invisible exertion. And still she sometimes felt like the inactive center of a clicking machine, divorced entirely from the muffled frenzy all around her. She hadn't known, when she was twenty-four, what it meant to run a household. Sometimes it occurred to her with clammy anxiety that she didn't know much more about it now, either. And if she hadn't learned by now, then surely—

"I miss my mother," Isabel said. "She would know. She'd know what to do."

"There's nothing you *can* do, not yet. Nothing's certain, right?"

"Not yet, no."

The irony here was that Isabel was by far the most literate of them all when it came to their husbands' work. Mina remembered a lunch at the club this past summer, their kids nearby, drinks sweating on the table. Tennis balls popping softly in the background like a summertime lullaby. A few other women sat with them. Suzanne Welsh was there, and Jim McGinniss's wife, Kiki, who would only have been there by Isabel's invitation, since she lived primarily on Long Island. Someone had complained about a husband slipping into bed at 4 A.M., for once not even smelling of scotch, and Isabel had nodded, tilting her head up to the sun, shifting her chair out from beneath the forest green table umbrella and stretching her browned legs in front of her. *The last time I saw them like this was when we were first married. You guys remember that, the whole yield burning nightmare? And they were all so terrified for those few months? I don't know how they do it, when things bottom out like that. They don't sleep for days at a time.*

There had been utter silence at their table. Suzanne Welsh had scrutinized her hands in her lap so closely that it looked like she was trying to see through them to her own veins. And Mina would admit it, too—that something in her stomach had solidified, some free-floating unease she'd always felt had gathered itself into some final, defined shape. Not jealousy, but fear. And fear of what? What did any of them care if Isabel understood what was going on, if she knew the language, the right phrases? She'd probably give anything, at this moment, to be ignorant. To *not* understand.

The day after that afternoon at the tennis courts, Mina had driven to the library. To Stamford, rather than their local library. She'd checked out ten books on finance—some just general nonfiction, social histories she guessed you'd call them, some memoirs by former Wall Streeters. She hadn't read any of them in the end. If Tom left her for another woman, it wasn't going to be because that girl understood his work. The nuances of whatever it was that he did to make her spending money. That much was clear to Mina. She might not be a brain trust, she might not be his equal, but she knew her husband.

Isabel let her hands fall to the table, her wedding ring scraping the glass.

"I just wonder," she said. "My husband has never failed in his life. I doubt he's heard the word *no* from anyone but me in decades. He's built up such a little cult of personality over there, from what I see on this end of things."

"Do you ever wonder," Mina murmured, "I mean—you should see Tom, when we run into the Weiss partners somewhere in the city, or something. Not Bob, of course. Bob's our friend. And, you know, him being so far Tom's superior."

Years of practice, here, meant that she could say that last phrase without wincing, without having to widen her eyes as she spoke.

"With Bob, it's irrelevant. But the other Weiss partners. We saw several of them at a wedding last year. And they won't even say *hello*, Isabel. Acknowledge each other's *presence*. Any single success they have at Weiss—I think Tom really does feel that this leaves less for us. I mean, not Tom. Goldman. All of them. It's like middle school with the firm's balance sheet. And sometimes I just wonder, if they looped us in more, if things like that might improve. If the summer might have been a bit less chaotic."

Tom didn't even like that she and Isabel were so friendly. How many times had he explained it to her, the firms' rivalry? Many times, she would reply. Many times, Tom. I know. I know.

"Maybe," Isabel said. "Maybe. Jesus, that was a long summer. I thought if we could just get to September. When Jim had to resign, when they had to fire the new CFO, that Erica woman. I really thought that might kill him. But then it was done, and I thought the worst was over."

"Poor Kiki." Mina knew how it must have killed, that *Post* cover with Jim stumbling out of the Weiss lobby, "MY GOODNESS, MCGINNISS" splashed across his face. His mouth gaping, his face like a lumpy cushion someone had slit open.

And if Mina hadn't had to sit through the preamble to one ladies-only dinner party where Kiki McGinniss had strong-armed them all into a tour of the walk-in closet she'd built for her shoes, if they hadn't seen (because Kiki had picked up individual shoes and made sure they'd all see) how many of the high heels had never once been worn, she might have been able to reach deep within herself and find the small place that felt sympathy for Kiki's humiliation. For what Jim surely felt was a betrayal from Bob, his oldest friend in the building.

That dinner out in Bridgehampton, when Kiki had shown them the shoe closet, surely wouldn't have included Mina if not for Isabel. She remembered that, as they'd left the closet tour, Isabel had taken her hand, held it just long enough so Mina knew they were supposed to hang back from the trail of women filing back out to the main part of the house. And Mina had lingered with Isabel, expecting some sharp comment about the shoes, the whole thing. But that had been it; Isabel had just wanted them to walk slowly, to keep themselves just a bit behind the group. Not to follow Kiki with everyone else.

It was in moments like those that Mina wondered how many other tiny sore spots Isabel noticed, how many things she saw about the other wives. Mina liked to think she herself wasn't entirely transparent, at this point, that she covered her constant fear that she'd forget all she'd learned when she got married. But Isabel always seemed to see her, seemed to know when Mina might need some unacknowledged warmth the most.

"Please," Isabel said, "please don't ask me to worry about poor Kiki."

They were quiet for a minute, maybe more.

"He's not very likable," Isabel murmured. Mina sat up straighter.

"Jim McGinniss?"

"No, no. My husband. He's not very likable, to most people but me. Plenty of people have been waiting for him to trip up and make an example of himself for years. Be a cautionary tale."

"Well, that seems a bit premature," Mina began, even though she knew Isabel wasn't talking to her.

"He's not," Isabel said. "He's not always likable. And if he can't fix this—I'm not a monster. I can see that it will involve much more likable people. Everywhere, I mean. Nobody's going to be worried about my husband's pain."

She trailed off on the final sentence, and Mina could think of nothing to say. Isabel sighed and spoke again.

"I really thought that if we survived the summer, that would be the worst of it," Isabel said, again. She leaned back in her chair and closed her eyes. Her eyelids were a pale blue, nearly translucent. "I've got to get the kids soon. I should pick them up, I don't want to send Lily. Madison's at a football game. Doing God knows what."

"Oh, sweetie," Mina said, "go upstairs. Take a bath. Or a nap. I'll pick them up."

Isabel nodded, but they sat there together for another half hour, and Mina couldn't bring herself to rupture the silence by standing up and walking inside, couldn't stand to leave Isabel alone out here by the pool.

WHEN MINA ROARED into the Greenwich Prep senior parking lot, the one closest to the gym, it was after seven o'clock and on its way to full dark. She saw Madison standing, her feet turned uncertainly inward, a tall boy's shape slinking away toward the other corner of the lot. Mina squinted through the lowering gloom but couldn't see who it was, and then Madison was opening the door and that was the more pressing thing.

"Hi, sweetheart," Mina said. Immediately, she felt, her tone was wrong. She couldn't very well speak to Bob's daughter as though rumor were forecast, as though the time had already come for pity and delicacy. He still might pull the rabbit out of the hat, after all. And if he did fix things, if it had all been just the nighttime anxiety that accompanied that particularly humid summer's fever dream, then there would be absolute hell to pay for anyone who'd shown even the slightest condescension toward his girls. For anyone who'd questioned the dominance of Bob "Silverback" D'Amico.

God, what kind of man let himself pick up that nickname? What kind of man *encouraged* it?

Madison was heaving her Vineyard Vines bag into the backseat, climbing into the front. Her kneecaps poked out like tennis balls crammed into tube socks. Her limbs had grown before she had, giving her that quality you saw only in teenagers or in young horses: the sense that they might trip over their own unfamiliar height at any given moment.

"Hi," Madison said. "Is there a reason you're picking me up?"

"Oh, well." Mina waved one hand in the air. "I stopped by to see your mom earlier and she was feeling a bit under the weather. I'm sure," she said, and here she allowed her eyes to slide from the road to Madison's profile, "I'm sure you've noticed."

The child next to her remained so still that she might have been sitting for a portrait.

"I haven't, actually. She seemed fine at breakfast this morning."

Mina cupped her hands around the steering wheel and hesitated, wondering whether she should speak. She kept silent through most of the drive, through excruciating minutes, but then couldn't wait

any longer. Why was it so treacherously easy to speak to teenage girls
in the car? So many indiscreet revelations she'd made to her own
Jaime had come about this way.

"Madison," Mina said. "I'm really asking, here. You can talk to
me. I'm sure you're aware of some of what's been happening, and I'm
sure you don't want to burden your mother with anything more than
she's already got on her plate. But I'm here, too."

Madison didn't turn, her profile so eerily similar to her mother's.

"That's so sweet of you, Mina. Really. I appreciate that so much.
But I'm doing fine. You know my parents—they've both got their
moods. If I let that upset me too much, I'd never get anything done."

Jesus. They had her trained well. Bob ought to call *her* into the
city to deal with reporters. Better than that spike-heeled blonde he'd
set up as the face of the firm for most of the year, right up until she
had to step down as CFO. Mina had pored over the photos of that
woman in her *Forbes* profile, her cleavage tipped toward the camera
like a fruit basket in one of those old, jewel-toned Dutch paintings.
Veritas. Were those veritas, or were veritas the paintings of skulls and
watches and things? *Sic transit Gloria mundi.* That was something,
right? Sometimes it felt like her entire education had slid from her
mind in one fell swoop long ago, like the tablecloth yanked from the
table in that old trick. So much for the four years of History of Art
seminars, the endless slides of paintings she still, back in college, had
thought she'd never get to see in person.

As for the blonde, though, Mina was probably being unfair.
Tom had said all year that she'd been promoted from nowhere and
then tasked with an impossible job. An impossible job for anyone,
but especially for an unqualified woman they'd only wanted to lend
some "diversity" to the C-suite. *What, there are no qualified women?*
Mina had asked. He'd been lying in bed while she sat reading a
book, his hand dancing up the skirt of her negligee, and he'd ignored the question.

"Well," she said, turning off the main road onto Isabel's private drive. A black sedan sat at the intersection, tucked down in the grass beside the tarmac. Come to think of it, they'd passed one just a few seconds ago, as well. Before the turnoff. "I just want you to know that you've got someone else nearby, if you ever need an afternoon away from the house. Or something."

"You must miss Jaime so much," Madison said, smiling. "I know Andover isn't that far away, but still. She's never home, right?"

"Well, yes," Mina said. "That's beside the point, though. I just want to make sure you know that your parents . . . it's just a crazy time for everyone. Us too! Tom has slept in his office for, God, I don't know. Maybe more than a week at this point."

"Wow," Madison said, eyebrows arching. She put one hand to the door handle, and it occurred to Mina that she was being indulged, that this girl couldn't wait to get out of the car. "That must be awful for you. You should keep coming by to see my mom. I mean, if you get lonely, or anything. Home alone. That must be rough, Mina. I'm so sorry."

There was no sarcasm in her voice, but it was entirely flat. There was no kindness in it, either. Then she was out of the car, shouldering her bag and loping up the driveway. And Mina sat there feeling twitchy, as though her skin wasn't fitting properly over her own bones, just as she had when Isabel snapped at her earlier. She flipped down the driver's-side mirror, ran her tongue over her teeth. Checked for lipstick, for streaks of makeup, for all the little flaws.

FIVE

It was an unexpectedly muggy weekend for September. Mostly, Madison lay on the floor of her bedroom conjugating French verbs, or stretched and baking on a canvas chair by the pool, her mother's old dog-eared copy of *Anna Karenina* propped open on her lap. It was the third time since July she'd tried to finish it. She dozed in the waning sun on Sunday afternoon, imagining Chip strolling up to the water's edge, dipping in a toe, coming to lean over her chair and down to her face, blocking out the sun. Of course, he didn't call. Neither did Amanda, or anyone. It was a quiet weekend. Madison never asked Lily where her mother was. Isabel was just elsewhere.

When Madison woke up on Monday morning from a night of unrecalled and thus unshakeable dreams, the house was quiet. Downstairs, she heard Lily cooing to the boys in the kitchen, heard the scrape of forks on porcelain.

Again that knowledge on her tongue, like the warm metallic tinge of blood, the taste of something you'd soon know. She was drawn quickly toward the table in the foyer. The paper had been left, unfolded, atop the electric blue plastic sleeve in which it had been delivered.

And there was the headline, the worst conclusion of every single malicious whisper she'd overheard that summer. Her father's bank had failed.

SIX

Amanda wasn't at all surprised to find her parents engrossed in their laptops on Monday morning, sitting hunched at the breakfast nook that doubled as their home office.

For the entire span of Amanda's memory thus far, her parents had lived in a perpetual state of anxiety that they might miss the next piece of breaking news. Whatever was "coming down the pike," to borrow a phrase from her father: the latest unemployment numbers or redeployment figures or the confirmation of some previous whispering of a congressional scandal. As if they weren't just tenured professors in rather humdrum fields of study, as if it were even possible for any one piece of the news to change their lives before the end of breakfast.

But this was probably the very thing about her father that allowed him to supplement teaching with his biweekly column at the *Times*, the gig that had made him famous, at least by professor standards. She sometimes thought it was that compulsive fear, that someone somewhere might know something he didn't, that drove him. If it was his theory in the first place, his economic forecast bugled out over the twenty-four-hour news networks whose omnipresence he always ranted against, then, at least on his small square of intellectual real estate, no one could possibly know anything before *he* knew it.

Her mother was another story. Nineteenth-century French lit did not exactly demand a brain hardwired to be constantly refreshing the page or cruising your Twitter feed. It didn't require, really, any awareness of the world outside your own window.

In any case, they remained engrossed on this particular morning even after Amanda came downstairs. This was new. On any given day, Amanda would have said that she'd kill to enter a room of the house and have no one notice her presence. The youngest of three, with two older brothers and excessively attentive parents, she was used to being poked and tickled and yanked and sneezed on from the moment she crossed the threshold. Every floorboard in their house groaned, protesting years of abuse beneath the tyrant energies of adolescent male feet and hands and elbows.

"Hi," she said. No one replied. She slid across the floor on her socked feet and twirled her hand through the air, performing a sloppy curtsy. The image of Isabel came into her head, unbidden— that carefully measured enthusiasm, the way Madison's mother always greeted a crowd. Charity auctions or teenage girls or Bob's colleagues; she treated everyone with the same warmth at a distance. Watching her move through a crowd felt like watching some electric-hued, exotic fish cut a swath through a school of minnows.

Amanda pasted a grotesque beauty-queen smile on her face and waved to her parents, assuming they'd get the joke. No one loved to analyze the D'Amicos like they did.

But all she got was a blurry look from her father, who raised his head at half speed, as if he'd sunk far underwater and then been warned not to resurface too quickly.

"Hi, monkey," he said. "Sit with us for a minute. Let's all talk before you take off for the day."

Sometimes, Amanda came home from school to find her father standing just at the edge of the swimming pool, motionless, his head tilted back as if a necessary theorem, or perhaps his next column, might be written in the treetops.

"I'll guess," she said, sliding into a chair across from them. "You're going to say . . . that we're moving! Finally. You've been listening to my misery all these years, and we're leaving Ye Olde Greenwich behind. Pedal to the metal, gone for good. You're giving me a chance to maybe one day spot another teenage brunette out there. I am so on board."

"Amanda," her mother began.

"Or, a black person," Amanda said. "It might be nice, you know, to occasionally sit in class with a black person."

"There are black people in Greenwich," her father began, and Amanda threw herself down across the table, miming the trauma of being struck down by his comment.

"Da-*ha*-ad. Let's not start telling straight-up lies."

"Amanda," her mother said again, sharper. "This isn't a joke. We need to talk to you."

Her father put one hand to his bald pate and cradled it for a few seconds. He took off his glasses and rubbed vigorously at his right eye.

"Amanda, we are all aware, I trust, that I'm no fan of Bob D'Amico. I've always believed the man to be just one step shy of a riverboat gambler. But there's been—he's going to come under quite a bit of scrutiny. And it won't just affect him, or Weiss. It's going to affect, you know, everyone."

Amanda stared at her bowl of dry cereal. Sometimes, when her parents took her into the city, she'd run down into a subway station and feel certain that she'd just missed a train. She'd hear nothing, none of the clanks and thuds of the departing trains, but the air would tingle with the sudden absence of motion, the new void, and you'd just know.

"I'm sorry, but I think you've buried the lede. What are we talking about?"

"I want to go over this before you leave for school," he said, shaking off her mother's hand on his wrist. "Lori, just give me a second. Let's get granular here."

Amanda busied herself with the toddler-simple task of pouring milk into her cereal. One of the intractable conditions of having a

Yale economist for a father was the constant demand for not merely awareness, but interest, not only conversational trivia, but actual understanding. She'd acquired a certain amount of skill that allowed her to manage this aspect of her father's parenting style; after all, she was an athlete living alone with two professors, so she either had to fob him off in an inoffensive way or else make a good-faith effort actually to understand what he did for a living. Why some people—who had presumably never seen him sit down on, and crush, the pair of glasses he'd spent an hour searching for—thought he was so brilliant.

But it was childish of her, she knew it was. Like she was too good to try to understand any of this? Madison had been her best friend for years.

The summer before this last one, she and Madison kept going to see the two Judd Apatow movies at the Twin Cinemas, sometimes paying to see the same movie three or four times in a month because they were seemingly the only girls in Greenwich with strict parents, and couldn't go to a party unless adults were present. That movie theater was closed, now.

All those hours she'd spent with Madison, and Amanda sometimes worried that her favorite thing about her friend was the way it felt to be around her parents. The way you felt both accepted and absolved, somehow. Amanda had been both grateful for and fascinated by the kind of rich people they were, that Isabel and Bob never acknowledged their ungodly amounts of money, never tried to remind anyone about it. Just kept buying house after apartment after house but otherwise didn't discuss it at all. So that Amanda was excused, when she spent time there, from acknowledging the colossal disparity between her life and Madison's. Their house had sometimes felt like the only place in Greenwich where she wasn't being asked, commanded, to display all the ways her life was different from Zoë Barker's, or Wyatt Welsh's, or even Chip Abbott's. They had a lot of flaws, Isabel and Bob, sure, but this was one thing they gave to her. And her own father had never, ever been able to accept that.

Now she did her best to drift somewhere beyond the outer borders of her father's voice, until the moment he said that his next column would be focused on Bob.

"No," she said. "No, you can't do that." She swallowed back the unpleasant bile taste of Madison walking down the hallway that past Friday, alone, her ponytail swinging through the air just behind her. The stale caramel smell of their lockers and textbooks mixed with disinfectant and air freshener.

"Amanda, I'm not asking."

"Why? So you can kick them while they're down?"

"Sweetheart," her mother interjected, but her father erupted immediately, coming down over Lori's voice and drowning her out altogether.

"Yes," he said. "Yes. Is that so hard to understand? They *deserve* to be kicked while they're down!"

"Why?" Amanda was sputtering. "Who will that help?"

"Us! The rest of us! It will help the rest of us to see them suffer."

"Guys," Lori was saying, "I don't see how this is a productive form for this conversation to take, and if we'd just—"

Amanda realized she'd been leaning back on her chair's rear legs, and now she let the chair fall forward with a clatter. Her knees smacked the edge of the breakfast table. She thought distractedly that the punch of the cold water would hit those spots first, those barely-bruises, when she slid into the pool later today, at practice. She left the kitchen.

LATER, DOWNSTAIRS, her father caught her by the arm just as she'd opened the front door.

"He'll land on his feet, Amanda," Jake said. "These guys always do. And then who'll speak up for the lives he's ruined? Who'll make him answer?"

"Okay," she said. "Enjoy your fucking witch hunt."

"No," he said. "I know you know better than that. People trusted him, Amanda. With their livelihoods. They gave him the freedom to make their decisions for them. They're the tragedy, not him."

She focused on the clouded copper umbrella stand by their front door, the one that held mildewing umbrellas and single gloves divorced from their erstwhile partners, and a golf club that had almost certainly been placed there in error during one of her father's fugue states.

"While you're doing this to him," she said, "I have to keep living here. I have to keep going to school with Madison. She's—"

Her sense of her own moral rectitude wavered, for a moment, but then her father didn't know, surely had not noticed, that she had been a terrible friend to Madison all summer. That she'd been moving on, sort of, until this started to happen.

"She's my best friend," she continued. "You're making a choice, and you didn't even ask me first."

"It isn't a choice," he said. "There is quite literally no explanation I can think of whereby he hasn't committed some sort of crime. They told their investors the firm was solid, sweetheart. They announced earnings in June that can't possibly have been real numbers. I know that's not—maybe I should be explaining this differently—"

She was looking, still, at the umbrellas. Small things, the sorts of things you cast off as soon as you came into a room, had always accumulated in the corners of this house. Those small things—that was what they had to show for their life, here. They left traces of themselves all over this house to prove how different they were from the antiseptic, tidy, public families all around them, even though these ephemera were still chosen quite carefully. Bric-a-brac from Ios, from Budapest, from Oslo. So her parents could tell stories about their semesters as guest lecturers, visiting scholars. So everyone would know they were in demand. All these seemingly offhand treasures left lying around, but anything actually embarrassing, actually unsightly, was packed away in a dusty shoe box under a bed somewhere.

These damp umbrellas didn't fit the narrative. They might be the only truly unglamorous things on display in this house.

"I don't think I'm wrong here, Amanda. Do you think I'd put you through this otherwise?"

But she knew, more every time he opened his mouth, that her father wasn't interested in her answers to his questions.

"You know how this works," she told him, and left the house.

AT SCHOOL, SHE WAS FAMOUS. It made her ill. Never in all her time at Greenwich Prep had she been approached, in one month even, by half as many people as were clamoring to get close to her today. The worst were the girls, girls she was certain had never known her name until now, had known her only by sight as someone who was always standing next to Bob D'Amico's daughter. These same girls were jealous now—of Amanda Levins!—because they believed that she was playing a series of exciting, demanding roles: confidante, nurse, enforcer, publicist. They assumed she had access, above all else. And wasn't that really, in the end, what everyone at Greenwich Prep wanted? To be the right kind of insider? That was why every one of these girls' parents had moved here, had followed one another from their starter apartments to their classic sixes uptown to, finally, "the country," their movements and decisions so thoroughly scripted by the migrations of the previous generations.

She probably shouldn't hate her classmates, then. For seizing the chance, on this juiciest day, to follow every code they'd been taught. None of them were actually so pathetic or misguided as to want to be Madison right now. Or at least they were smart enough not to cop to those longings in front of Amanda, an unfriendly observer. But they wanted desperately to brush themselves against the scandal. To know something the rest of the school didn't. To be *needed*.

That was maybe the first thing she understood that morning, each time an unfamiliar, manicured hand clutched at her elbow. Teenage girls were so desperate to be *needed*. None of them actually wanted boyfriends, or high drama, or true pain. They just wanted to feel essential, exposed in some crucial way to the vicissitudes of the world. And so they did things like give blow jobs in movie theaters, cry in public when something tragic happened to strangers across the country, throw themselves into her path in the hallway to ask her how Madison was *feeling* today. How she was *managing*. Did Amanda *know anything*. They just wanted the communal energy of crisis, the sense that they had to yank their best selves from somewhere deep within. They wanted, so very badly, to rise to the occasion.

And yet there was something more, too, she had realized by the afternoon. They didn't know what this meant. They didn't know what destructive forces had gathered in New York or how close they might come to Greenwich Avenue, to school, to the back steps of the public library on West Putnam where they all hung out waiting for their SAT tutors, to their very own houses. When they asked if Amanda knew anything, they weren't only asking about Madison. They were asking Amanda, of all people, whether their fathers were going to lose their jobs, too.

She tried to distribute information with as little fanfare as possible, tried not to enjoy her own clipped efficiency.

"She's doing well," she said repeatedly. "Really, really well."

And: "I think it's best if we just give them all the privacy we can."

And: "You know, I haven't even really read anything about it. It doesn't really interest me, to be honest. It's mostly gossip."

The truth was that she had not seen Madison yet that day. They had no classes together. This was the first year that neither one of them had flounced into the dean's office with Isabel or the more reluctant Lori in tow, to insist that both girls needed to have Mr. Schrode for Honors English, or Mr. Coombs for European History. Amanda tried to remember whether Madison had suggested their usual approach, whether she'd called in late August to compare class schedules. If she had, Amanda had probably ignored the call. Late August wasn't so long ago. Things must have already been teetering at Madison's house. Amanda put it out of her head.

It was just before eighth period when she caught Madison at their lockers. She saw her from the other end of the hallway and ran, fearful that if she waited a half second too long Madison might disappear again, rob her of the chance to say something, anything. To begin to atone. She lost track of her speed and came up behind Madison so suddenly that, when Madison turned, they both flinched. Amanda saw that Madison's first instinct had been to assume she was under attack.

"I've been looking for you all day," Amanda said. "You would not *believe* the things people have been saying to me. Not bad things. Just, like, people you've never even spoken to are coming up to me like you're their best friend, like they can't sleep they're so worried about you. It's gross."

Madison nodded and smiled, as though they were discussing other people far away, people whose pain could not be felt.

"I guess I just wanted to find you. I wanted to know if there's anything I can do."

"Oh, no," Madison said. "I'm late, but no worries—"

She waved one hand in the air like she was the queen on a parade float, and Amanda caught her by the wrist. "Stop it. Don't pretend."

Madison stared hard at Amanda's hand, at its grip on her wrist. She lifted her gaze to meet Amanda's.

"Oh," she said, her voice flat. "I'm sorry. I won't."

Amanda tried not to wince, tried to push forward. She let go of Madison's wrist.

"Did your dad come home from the city?"

"No."

"Is he going to?"

"I have no idea."

"Okay," Amanda said, "okay." She wanted to stall their way to comfort, run out the clock on her own guilt. Be, once more, the one in charge.

It's not my fault, she told herself for the fortieth time that day. It's not my fault that this all happened at this particular time. If I had known what was coming, I never would have pushed her away. I'm not a monster.

"How's Isabel?"

"Haven't seen her."

"She went in?"

"No, I just haven't seen her."

"Do you think she's there?"

"She was locked upstairs with Mina when I left."

"Has anyone else come by?"

"I don't know, Amanda. I've been at school."

"I just," Amanda faltered, "I thought maybe you just got here. I've been looking for you."

"We stayed home until, like, ten," Madison said. "I wanted to let the boys stay home but Lily won."

Madison was facing the lockers still when Amanda saw the boys moving toward them. Wyatt Welsh was at the front of the group. Other girls thought he was handsome, maybe, but he turned her stomach. He wore his hair spiked straight up from his head, and she was pretty sure that his blond highlights had been woven in skillfully by his mother's hairdresser, probably to the tune of hundreds of dollars. He always wore Lacoste polos in the most gorgeous, jewel tones, shirts she never saw on anyone else, but he was already developing a training-wheels potbelly and the shirts pulled, slightly, across his chest and stomach. He wore things like tight gym shorts and knee-high argyle socks on game days, when the football players were supposed to wear khakis and ties, because he knew he could. Because everyone would roll their eyes as he approached but start giggling if he pointed at them, smiled, said their names. Even the teachers. His mother, Suzanne, was one of the women Amanda and her own mother referred to as the gaggle: the women who spent most of their days somewhere in Isabel's vicinity, always taking in her jewelry, her daughter's clothing, what she'd served at the last dinner party to which only some of them had been invited.

Wyatt was walking slightly ahead of the rest of the group, his eyes moving across the hallway like a bird of prey searching for life, movement, beneath a choppy sea. And Amanda knew, even before his eye snagged them, that he wouldn't leave it alone.

"Let's go somewhere else," she told Madison. She tried to keep her voice neutral and small. "Let's go talk."

"Amanda, really. It's fine." Maybe the second-best thing was to keep Madison from turning around, just ensure that they wouldn't make eye contact. He might not feel bold enough unless he felt sure he'd be heard.

"I know it's fine! I just want to talk to you." She could feel her voice scaling up, too high.

And then Wyatt was smacking his chest, outsized and excited, casting his voice out across the hallway. He looked like an actual animal, Amanda thought, it wasn't just a phrase.

"I don't know," he was saying. "I'll tell you what my father said, though. Nice work if you can get it, right? Thirty mil a year to run a company into the fucking ground?"

It was amazing, she thought, how little they all knew themselves. She saw some of the other boys stutter out, their eyes flicking toward Madison, their faces frozen in the last second before they laughed, smacked a locker, shoved one another and stumbled over their own sneakers. They wouldn't dream of saying it first, she thought, but once he says it, they'll defend it until they die.

Madison stood, staring at the locker she'd already closed. She held a binder against her chest as though it were the only thing keeping her whole, keeping her from spilling out onto the ground.

"What do you want to bet his mother spent the day camped out in the produce section at Whole Foods," Madison said, softly, almost to herself.

"What?"

"I'm just saying. I'd bet you money she's been sitting there all day, pretending to smell the melons, flagging down any other women she recognizes. To tell them how terrible it is and how they *mustn't* gossip behind Isabel's back, not until they have all the facts. That Isabel and her children absolutely should not be blamed, for—"

She cut herself off, chuckled, readjusted the straps of her tote bag where it bit into her shoulder. But her voice was too distant, almost glacial. Something about it didn't really feel, in the end, like she was insulting Suzanne Welsh.

"Is Lily okay?" Amanda tried.

Madison shook her head, quickly, as if swallowing a pill without water.

"I don't know," she said. "Lily's, like, unmovable. She got mad at me for wallowing. This morning. She slapped me."

"Wait—like, on the face?"

"I deserved it," Madison began. But then they were no longer alone, Chip Abbott was standing there. He had his backpack clipped across his chest because he knew he was cool enough to act like a nerd. He might as well put electrical tape on a pair of thick glasses and walk around wearing them, just to prove that nothing could keep the women away.

His blond hair stuck out from his head in soft-looking tufts, and when Madison turned to him he cocked his head to one side, the corner of his mouth twisting.

Amanda fought the impulse to roll her eyes. She knew why Madison was so wrecked by this guy—you'd have to be chiseled from ice not to understand it, a little—but it just seemed so obvious. Like he was the hot guy in a teen movie and they were just female extras, hired to moon around in the crowd scenes and stare at him with their mouths lolling open. Amanda didn't see where the fun was if he already knew exactly how you'd feel about him from the moment he first said your name.

"Ladies," he said, his voice low and smooth. "How's our Monday afternoon treating us?"

"Oh, hi," Madison said.

The air had changed, and Amanda saw from her friend something she hadn't seen from her before, the ability to tug on the taut wire between her body and Chip's, an awareness of how this worked.

Chip was laughing, Madison had made some joke Amanda had missed.

"All right, Madison, take it easy. You walking upstairs?"

Madison nodded. She was doing it again—staring at the thing in front of her as though it held the key to the only language that could teach her anything. As though this boy could keep her alive.

Madison turned back, pressing her face to Amanda's ear.

"Don't worry," she said. "I'm totally fine. Who cares about Wyatt Welsh, forget it. I don't know anything else yet. But my dad will be home soon, and besides, it can't be worse than it's been today, right?"

Amanda watched them walk together down the hallway, toward the glass doors, their bodies becoming silhouettes against the late sunlight. She saw them stop and stand there, despite the swarms of people crowding the hallway, and she saw him pick at something on the sleeve of Madison's shirt, saw Madison tip the upper half of her body toward him as he did this.

A few days later, Amanda would take a shortcut to class, the one that cut along the leafy path just below the library, and she would see that someone had Wyatt Welsh pushed up against the side of the building. She would imagine the cottage-cheese surface of the wall scraping against the back of Wyatt's neck. Then Chip would shove Wyatt once more, his hands at Wyatt's collar, before walking away, and Wyatt would kick the ground a few times and then gather his things. He was a senior, a year older than Chip, even a bit bigger.

Now, Chip looked back, once, over his shoulder. Not at Amanda, but just to be looking away from Madison. Then he brushed his thumb against his chin, smiled, and turned back to her. They still were just standing there. Their feet were rooted on the ground, not coming any closer to each other, but their bodies swayed and curved, like the stems of a plant yearning toward sunlight.

Amanda knew, and tried to tell herself it had just now occurred to her, that she hadn't told Madison about the column, about next week's paper.

Madison and Chip started walking again, moving in tandem side by side, and their silhouettes merged. As Chip reached to open the door, Madison stepped in front of him, and then you couldn't see her at all anymore; he'd swallowed her up.

SEVEN

On that first morning, Madison didn't go into the kitchen. She didn't act like a sister, find her brothers to kiss the tops of their heads and preemptively explain that Isabel wasn't feeling well. She didn't act like a daughter, knock on her mother's door to ask how she could help. She didn't look for any of them. She did not want anyone to touch her, comfort her. She did not want to find out whether her mother would simply ignore the knock.

She went, finally, to her father's study. A television. A thick door to muffle the sounds from the foyer, from the kitchen and her brothers, their small voices.

She turned on the television, found the morning news, and what she noticed was that they were treating this as news of a crime. This wasn't a natural disaster; there was none of the patronizing sympathy, the eagerness to exploit, that you saw when the news covered a hurricane or a fire. They were scanning their spotlight over everything and looking for the culprit. All summer, each time she'd seen her father's name in the *Times*, each time she'd stood at the end of her parents' hallway and listened to her mother's low, urgent tones, to her father's quick, hissed replies—to the way his voice layered over hers until hers finally fell silent—Madison had not understood this. That there was a crime somewhere beneath everyone's anxiety, like the invisible letters on a piece of paper that reveal themselves only when you sketch over them with a pencil. That it was more than misfortune.

Now, a blond reporter was interviewing some guy on the sidewalk in front of the Weiss building near Times Square. The reporter looked like the woman who used to work at Weiss. She'd been forced to step down at the beginning of the summer, at the start of that period of time during which Madison saw her father rarely if at all. The same small features, the same frozen helmet bob of ice-blond hair. Amanda's father had written something about that woman, but she couldn't remember what. The woman had been there for all of a year, otherwise Madison surely would have met her at some point. It was odd, actually, that she hadn't. She would have to find Jake's article, later, online. She would have to read everything she could. She could not have anyone else at school know any more about this than she did. They only had half the story; they didn't know her father. She was the only one who could know everything.

She tried to remember the woman's name, but it kept receding further. Sometimes, when her mother ordered dry martinis on the rocks at dinner, her father would slide the glass over to Madison when the wine arrived. She would try to spear the olives with a toothpick, softened and useless from the vodka, and it would skid off the fat little globes, sending them tumbling down beneath the ice cubes. The longer she tried, the harder it became to skewer what she wanted.

The guy being interviewed on the sidewalk was talking now. He was a young trader, the reporter said. Fresh from the Ivy League. If he was really Ivy League and had a decent GPA, he wouldn't be on the trading floor, would he, Madison thought with a twinge of smug pleasure. He'd be an analyst. She imagined her father here with her now, on the couch behind her, stroking her hair absentmindedly when she pointed this out to him, proud that she knew the difference.

Madison turned up the volume.

"Uh, no, ma'am," the trader was saying. He was stocky, his head square, his face red as he spoke. She imagined a roll of fat on the back of his neck, just where his marine-short buzz cut met the collar of his shirt. "No, he's not down here. No one's seen him on the floor. I'm not surprised. You have no idea, really, how bad that'd be right

now. If I were that f—er"—and here the news bleeped out his color-
ful language and Madison started, not having realized they could
even do that on news shows—"I wouldn't want to show my face in
this building. Not today, not tomorrow, not for a long time. My buddy's got a bottle of Laphroaig he's been saving up for bonus season
next year, but we're busting it out right now. It's an Irish wake down
here, all right? No one wants to see Bob D'Amico's face down here.
Not on the floor. Not the guys he screwed over. They always used to
tell us one firm, right? That's our motto, 'one firm.' What a load of
horses—t."

Madison felt her cheeks warming, as though he could see her, had
spoken to her directly. One firm. That was how her father said good
night when the partners came over for dinner, as he sent them tumbling down the driveway to their waiting town cars, their wives unsteady on their stiletto heels after a night of drinking. *One firm*, their
voices raspy with alcohol, when he shut himself up in his study with his
friends and only Madison was allowed to come in, to bring them more
rocks glasses or, if he was in a good mood, make the drinks. That was
how they toasted, glasses clinking so hard that sometimes the other
guys, Jim McGinniss usually if he'd already had a few, cracked theirs
in excitement. Her father was famous for this: one firm. He always said
that loyalty was cheaper than staving off some idiot's revenge, that if
he took care of his guys for life they would be his forever. He told her
this sometimes after he'd had a few drinks, while she sat at his feet
watching a basketball game, her French homework spread before her
on the coffee table. She'd read an article once in *Vanity Fair* that was
all about this, about how much the firm meant to everyone there, about
how her father didn't like it when partners had showy affairs or got
divorced or eschewed their ties on casual Fridays. It wasn't horseshit. It
was her father's whole life.

The trader's shirt was too tight on him. It looked like it was choking his neck a little bit. She imagined putting her fingers to that
mottled red skin, both hands around his thick neck, and squeezing.

The reporter had said that few members of the trading floor had even come in to work. The men who were there had spent their morning packing their desks into cardboard boxes, which to Madison seemed a specious ploy for sympathy. These guys wouldn't be walking out of the building with cardboard boxes. They'd have their secretaries clear their desks of their few personal items. They'd do none of the dirty work themselves. This weepiness, this packing of the things, this would all stop as soon as the cameras did.

She could hear her father, even now: *Only the lazy or the ignorant get their news from those scum-sucking malcontents on TV news, all right? Got it?* Capiche?

Her father loved to throw Italian flourishes into their conversations, as though he spoke the language. He didn't. He wasn't first generation, he liked to remind her. You had to go back to his grandmother for any real Eye-Talians, but most of the men he worked with thought he spoke Italian. Sometimes, in articles about him, they reported that he was fluent. Sometimes he liked to introduce himself as Roberto rather than Robert or Bob. But Madison knew. *Capiche* was about as close to his roots as they got in this house. A few Italian words sprinkled here and there and the annual Christmas-Day car ride to Nonna Connie's house in Williamsburg, where Madison ate all the gnocchi she wanted because Isabel would never say anything in front of her mother-in-law. It wasn't the potential weight gain that bothered her mother, Madison knew, or that wasn't what bothered her the most. It was the wanton disregard for discipline, Madison's willingness to let everyone around her see how bottomless her appetites were, how raw her hunger. If you wanted something, her mother believed, you took steps to acquire it in the privacy of your own home, so that by the time you were out in the world again, you had everything you needed. You did not let other people see you as grasping, desperate.

But as soon as Nonna took the lid off the saucepan, Madison was always ravenous, even though the kitchen was the only part of that house that smelled good. She always held her breath in the hallways and the bathroom to avoid the smell of a house decaying around its longtime inhabitant, mixed with the nostril-invading musk of her grandmother's air freshener. The house was perfectly clean, of course—Bob D'Amico might not have been able to convince his mother to move into a luxury high-rise, but he wouldn't have let her live in actual squalor—and yet Madison didn't like to touch the surfaces, the lace doilies on the countertops, the butter left in a dish on the counter rather than sensibly in the refrigerator.

The trader was still being interviewed on the news.

They don't want him there at the office? Madison thought. Fine. We want him here. The too-loud rumbling of his voice off the marble floors in the foyer. All the noise, just from him being in the house. All the sounds that make us flinch. We *want* to flinch here, Daddy.

She closed her eyes. Just go downstairs, walk outside, and get in the cab. Just come home.

She had done this once before, and it had worked. Not right away, but it had worked. When the firm had evacuated on September 11. When her father walked up the West Side Highway and rented a suite of rooms at the Sheraton in midtown, sent one guy back downtown to slip between the barricades and retrieve the servers from the cordoned-off building that had once been their office. She'd read all of that years later, online. Back then she was still small, and she'd left her mother and Lily sitting in tears in the kitchen watching the small TV, a bottle of wine on the table between them, their fingers intertwined.

Madison had come in here to his study, curled up on his sofa, and whispered the same words to herself until she could sleep: *Just come home. Just come home.*

Now, something hit the thick double doors with a thud. Madison sprang up from the sofa, the remote control slipping from her fingertips and hitting the parquet floor with a dull shriek. Lily was yelling her name. She closed her eyes. When she opened them again, nothing had disappeared.

She unlocked and opened the doors, which forced her to make an elegant, swooping motion with both arms, as though welcoming Lily to some sort of morbid, empty party. *Vampire's Ball*—she'd heard her father and his friends say that, to describe the nights when they went out with the men who were about to be fired, who already knew they were goners. He thought she didn't listen, when his friends came over. But she listened to everything. Or she used to. Somewhere, at some point in the past year, she'd dropped the thread. All summer, waking up to her parents' voices cutting each other off, like poorly trained backup singers: she knew that this had unnerved her at the time, but all she could think now was that she hadn't been nearly unnerved enough. That she'd listened for months without hearing a single word.

And now she was being punished for it.

"Honestly, Madison," Lily said, her hands clenched into small, scrappy fists. "I've been yelling your name all over this house."

The fists were angry, but Lily's face was soft, malleable, as though she might be the one to cry. Madison returned to the sofa, to the television. The same blond reporter was now stressing that there were *unconfirmed* reports that Bob D'Amico had wanted to come down to the trading floor but had been dissuaded by senior management fearful that there might be an outbreak of actual physical violence. It wasn't yet clear, the woman continued, whether any Weiss executives would be subject to criminal investigation.

"Come on," Lily said. "Give me the remote. Don't do this. Don't watch." Madison pointed to the floor, to the bits of shattered plastic and the exposed batteries. Lily marched over to the television and turned it off at the source.

"Why do they say something and then remind you that it's *unconfirmed*?" Madison said. "Why say it at all, then?"

"Madison, come on. Come eat something. I know the boys would love to see you. They're nervous. They're little boys, not idiots. They know something's wrong."

"Well, isn't it your job to take care of them?"

Lily inhaled slowly, as though counting the length of her breaths, as though Madison was a frustrating challenge and she was going to meditate herself out of the room.

"Yes, but you're their sister, and I think having you in there would make them feel better."

Madison didn't say anything. Her father told her once that, in a negotiation, you just sat in silence until the other guy began to jabber. Until he'd reached the point where he'd offer anything, absolutely anything, just to hear your voice.

Lily started to talk.

"Look, Madison, I don't know. Is that what you want me to say? Because fine, I don't know. Soon, if your mother doesn't come downstairs, I'm going to have to say something. But they haven't seen the paper, and even if they did—your dad's work isn't really my business. My business is taking care of you three."

Madison could feel Lily trembling beside her, her coiled energy, like a hunted animal.

"Well, the boys should stay home. We all should. We shouldn't go to school."

"Absolutely not."

"I'm not afraid, Lily, I'm just trying to be realistic. You know what it's like here. Do you remember after Jim McGinniss, over the summer? You remember when we saw Kiki at Starbucks?"

A part of her, at the time, had thought that Jim's wife deserved it all—the gravid silence that seeped to the very edges of the store, the way she'd had to keep her sunglasses on the whole time, as if she didn't know every woman in line behind her. Kiki didn't even live around here; it had been a stupid, splashy gesture, to show up one afternoon at a Greenwich Starbucks. Madison had felt a chill, watching Kiki's shoulders draw closer and closer in on themselves. But Isabel had always said she was a foolish woman, and it had been foolish, parading herself around the same week Jim announced his resignation from the bank.

"Yes," Lily said, "I remember Kiki. I'm not sure that's a compari-son that really makes any—"

"You think everyone won't jump on this immediately, that my father fired his best friend in July, and everyone said *Jim* was the problem, my dad had the solution, and two months later some idiot trader is trashing them both, together, on the morning news? We just have to give it a few days. It'll blow over and people will lose interest and then the boys can go to school and Isabel can order her own soy lattes in peace and it'll just, it won't be just that my father—"

She felt a keen awareness of the shape of the words, of the effort it took to move her teeth and tongue and lips in just the right ways to say what she really meant. That my father, what? That my father failed. That his bank will not exist anymore. That my father lost his job. That my father lost everyone else's job.

"It's not just Mr. McGinniss," she said. "Right? The news—they're talking about this like someone's going to go to jail."

"That's absurd, you must know that's absurd," Lily said. "But no, I don't think it will blow over. Not yet."

Madison nodded.

"Listen to me," Lily said. "There's no point in worrying now. Your father will be home soon, and your mother will be up, and you'll all talk about it then. But for now, you need to go to school. Think about everything else. Anything else at all."

Madison turned to look at her, but Lily was staring straight ahead, out the window, beyond the pool to the trees. Her jaw was clenched so tight that it looked like her face had been carved from stone. She looked like a woman who should appear on a gold coin, on the bas-relief facade of one of those towering granite buildings in Manhattan, the ones that blocked out the sunlight.

"Where's Isabel?"

"I don't know, sweetie. I haven't seen her. Mina came over this morning. They've been upstairs ever since."

Madison laughed. She couldn't control it; the sound poured out of her in light trills, as though she were an adult, a few drinks too deep at a cocktail party.

"That's nice," she said. "The important thing is that she comfort Mina right now. Let's all remember that."

"Madison," Lily began. She was clearly hesitant and also, Madison could see with something like wonder, afraid. "I grew up, with my parents, in a certain—I never had a problem with the way I grew up. But then I got to college, and I was surrounded by all these other girls who had such, such different backgrounds. I wasn't embarrassed, because of my parents, but, you know. I mean, they became a different thing for me. Not, like, a liability, but—"

"Lil," Madison said, distaste on her tongue. "It's fine."

"No, I just want you to know. Obviously, I've never been through anything like whatever this is. Of course not. But I know that parents can be complicated. You know, your parents make decisions that affect you, but you don't get to have a say, really, and I know that's so hard. And in my family, really, we've had difficult things happen. And the important thing always in those situations is that you can all pull together, regardless."

"Okay, that's enough," Madison said. This was beneath Lily; this would be blush worthy when Lily thought about it tomorrow. That she'd chosen this pep talk to offer, at this moment.

"All I meant is that there are much worse problems in the world. And your dad loves you."

"Super," Madison said. "Thanks very much."

She could see Lily twitching, swallowing the admonishment, and she began to feel the new freedom, the bad behavior this might allow. No one, she realized, would deny her for a few days. She would become, for the adults in her life, evidence of all the potential damage still to come. Whatever she did, short of actual violence, would be considered "handling it so well." She felt this awareness spreading through her, loosening the knotted muscles at her neck, cracking at her knuckles.

"Your father will be home soon," Lily repeated, "and until then nothing is certain. Right?"

"He won't be home."

"Excuse me?"

"He's not coming home. Not for a while. Don't you remember September eleventh? He didn't come home for days."

"This is different."

"Sure. Now he has a reason to feel ashamed."

"Stop it, Madison."

"I'm sorry, what? Are you going to defend him?"

"Mad, I know you're upset, but pushing me to insult your father is not the way to go."

"Sure," Madison said, and she could feel the words gaining steam, sliding from their rails. She could feel herself approaching something she wouldn't be able to retract. "I guess I just have to wait it out. It won't be so hard, I would imagine, to get you to insult him down the road."

Even through her clenched jaw, Lily smiled in amusement.

"Yeah? What's down the road?"

"Well, you know. I'm sure he's going to start firing people. My father doesn't trust any of you anyway. He's not going to want a bunch of random employees in and out of the house, leaking things to the city papers, whatever. And if he wants to fire you without paying you severance . . ."

"Stop it, Madison."

"I think we both know he'll find a way. So I mean, it's not like you'll have *wasted* these past eight years, really, but I'm sure it'll feel sort of—"

The slap was so quick, so unexpected, that the sting on her cheek almost felt as if it had come from within, as if something inside Madison's mouth had pierced right through her cheek. She put one hand to the spot on her face. When she looked up, Lily sat thrown back against the opposite arm of the couch as though she'd been the one slapped, one hand covering her mouth. Madison saw the tears welling at the corners of Lily's eyes and felt a sudden and roiling disgust, the way she had for the trader on the news. If she wasn't crying, daughter of the downfall, then surely the rest of them could hold it together.

"Stop," she said, and Lily looked up at her in horror.

"Excuse me?"

"Just, stop. Please don't cry. This day is going to be hard enough."

Lily looked around the room, as though there might be someone else on the receiving end of Madison's reproach, and then laughed, once. She put both hands to her cheeks and swept the tears from her face.

"All right." Her voice was testy, long-suffering, and yet it was cool again, deferential. They'd both slid back into place. Madison moved closer to her on the sofa.

"Other girls would try to get you fired for that," she said.

Lily inhaled long and hard, so Madison could hear her breath skittering around inside her chest.

"Yeah," she said. "Be that as it may, listen to me, Madison. You don't know what happened, and you don't know what your father did or didn't do. But you are his family, and once you turn on him, that's it. You have to believe him even when no one else does. Are you listening to me? You have to tell the same stories, even when everyone questions them."

Madison curled her feet beneath her on the sofa cushion. The actual pain in Lily's voice, the foundation of anger beneath it, had bent Madison's rage back on itself. She knew, the way she'd sometimes see that her father's associates knew, even in the midst of having tied one on in a bad, bad way. She could feel the next wave of sick remorse that awaited her. She knew that the panic would recede, and that she'd feel terrible for having spoken this way to Lily. But it was too late, she thought. Lily's seen, now, that I have these thoughts somewhere in my brain.

She'd never thought of herself as someone who would be a brat in a crisis. She'd always imagined she'd be a rock, in a crisis, be like her mother. But apparently that wasn't the case.

"Everyone's going to take their cues from you. You walk through school like it's any other day, your father comes home tonight like he does every Monday. They won't be getting any blood when they bite, and they'll move on. Maybe the whole thing itself won't blow over, but they'll stay away from you. This isn't any more familiar to them than it is to us."

Madison wondered, with a pop of clarity like a camera's flash, whether Chip had seen the news.

"I'm fine," she said. "I'll go sit with the boys, but I don't want to eat."

Lily nodded, and they stood up.

"I guarantee you," Lily said. "Everyone at school is still going to be watching to see what you do first."

LATER, WHEN LILY LINED THEM UP by the front door for inspection, she grabbed Madison's wrist. For such a small woman, Lily was possessed of surprising strength, her fingers like wire around Madison's bony forearms. Madison let her body go limp; she's forgiving me, she thought, and waited for Lily's mouth pressed to her temple, her hands on her hair, for the wordless clemency of a kiss. They didn't hug each other as often as they had when Madison was younger, but Lily still always knew when it was the right moment for it.

But Lily held her there, for a moment, and did not embrace her. Finally she took two fingers and pinched a strand of Madison's hair.

"You had something," she said. "A crumb, or a leaf or something."

They both shook themselves away from each other, the same way they'd brush rain from wet clothes, and followed the boys out to the car.

EIGHT

Well, you know, he hasn't even come home yet." Mina wedged her BlackBerry between her shoulder and her ear. She finished potting the basil plant she'd bought that morning and carried it into her office off the kitchen, the room with the best light.

"He hasn't been home yet, and it's been three days. And I will tell you, because I can't tell anyone else—she's been a wreck, Dee. An absolute wreck."

Her sister Denise had met Isabel only once, when she'd spent the day in Greenwich and Isabel had stopped by to loan Mina an evening gown, but she'd been hearing about the woman for years.

"Well fine, tell me more. When you say wreck, we're talking . . . crying? Broken glass? Or just staying in bed all day? This is great! Keep going."

Mina sat down at the kitchen table. This was only her sister. Dee would tell her friends over white wine at her divorcée book club out on Long Island and none of them would have more than a vague idea who she was even talking about. It would never make its way back to Isabel, Mina told herself. It was only betrayal to say something to someone out here, in all the places she passed through each day. It was only betrayal if you got caught.

Besides, it was too irresistible, the way Denise would hear this. The most dramatic thing happening in the country this week, and Mina was in charge.

"This isn't gossip for me, Dee. This is her whole life. I mean, he may never work again. You know when he started at that firm? The seventies. Only place he's ever been, and now the name won't even exist. It's, I mean. It's a tragedy, really."

"Sure," Denise muttered, and Mina could hear her attention begin to wander, her voice pointed now toward the wet nail polish she'd be applying to her toenails, or the dried bits of tomato sauce she'd be scraping from the oven walls. Denise, the baby of the family, almost the wrong side of forty and back living with their mother, in the house on Long Island where they'd grown up. She'd come to Greenwich a few times, early on, when they'd first bought out here. But now she hadn't been out to visit for even an afternoon in more than a year, and neither sister ever said out loud that this was because Tom spent the entirety of her last visit darting around the house, wincing at their braying laughter, addressing Denise with the same absent censure he'd once used on Jaime.

"Oh, sure, we miss her," he'd said one night at dinner. They'd been eating pad Thai, which Mina had cooked from scratch, and peanut sauce had gathered at the corners of his mouth in a way that looked almost obscene. "But there's great things about having the kid gone. You wouldn't know this, Denise, but that's something that automatically arrives with the first kid. Constant noise." Denise had left the next morning, citing their mother, left home alone that week, as her excuse.

"It's really a tragedy," Mina repeated.

"Not for him, it won't be," Denise said, her voice sharpening. "Where's he from again? Italian, right? Not from out here though, is he?"

Mina snorted. "He is, if this is possible, even less Italian than we are, Dee. He's from that Italian part of Williamsburg, in Brooklyn. I don't even know if the neighborhood still exists, honestly. But the mother refuses to leave, she's renting to NYU kids, or something. Isabel's not big on the mother-in-law."

"Well of course," Denise said. "She's not new to this, and the newbies talk way, way too much about how much money he makes, right? I'm sure the mom loves to. God forbid. You know deep down Isabel probably hates the guy. No way that's a happy marriage, even before."

"The relationship guru of Long Island over here," Mina teased, even in a moment of levity careful not to use the word *marriage* with Denise. She shivered, too, hearing the hard *g* creep back into her speech, hearing the way her sentences sped up during a phone call with her sister.

Mina had first met Tom at Dorrian's, and it had taken him a week to call. He'd written her number on his hand and she'd been so certain he'd wash it off, think nothing more of it. It was the late eighties; you could lose information so easily back then, it was so much simpler for blithe fate to intervene. But still, she'd stepped it up while she waited for his call. Her campaign to smooth the Long Island from her voice. It had been a goal, that first year in the city; after she met Tom, it became an urgency. She'd watched old movies, gone to restaurants she couldn't afford and sat at the bars and listened to the women who were drinking vodka tonics and waiting for their dates. She'd always been a decent mimic—Denise had thought she should try to be an actress, as if that was all the job required—and it hadn't taken but a few weeks. By her fifth date with Tom, you wouldn't have been able to place, anymore, where exactly she'd grown up. She'd joined the ranks of young women in the city, the girls from Columbus or Pittsburgh or Overland Park or Moorestown. The girls whose personalities got them only so far, leaving them washed up on the shores of Manhattan. Where they could wipe themselves clean and unshackle themselves from their memories and histories, so the city could mark them as who they really were, without resistance.

She wouldn't have been able to imagine, back then, that half the women who married men like Tom had accents like hers, and that few of them ever bothered to try to sound like any other sort of girl. It was only when she'd ended up out here in Connecticut, when she settled in to live the life she'd spent years planning, that she realized how excessive it had been, that fear of discovery. Almost every woman out here, with the exception of Isabel, was settling in. Their husbands moved through days of shining, brand-new success; everything was constantly turning over, rewarding a lack of history, an unknown name. The old families, the people Mina had once imagined mocking her accent, were all the people who owned the decaying Greenwich properties Tom's friends started snapping up.

"Brooklyn," Dee was saying when Mina snapped back into the conversation. "Interesting. And what's this all about? He lost everyone's money?"

"Just one newspaper, Dee," Mina said, the satisfaction swelling in her throat. "You could read any newspaper. Not even the paper—just the front page."

Her sister waited in hostile silence, and Mina sighed.

"It's too complex to go into right now," she said. "They took too much risk, really. And everyone's getting hammered, right now, so if your neck's stuck out too far . . ." She snapped her tongue against the roof of her mouth. "Chopped off."

"I see," Denise murmured. Her sister knew Mina was grasping at straws. She knew that if Tom hadn't fully explained it, then Mina hadn't figured it out.

"Just his bank? They're all losing their jobs, I saw, but what about the others?"

"His bank was one of the big five," Mina said. "The others are—I don't know. I don't know, Dee. It's so sad, like I said. He's been there forever."

She wanted these losses to sound big, the way they'd felt when she was over at Isabel's these past few days. Coming down from the darkened bedroom with the same glasses she'd brought up the previous afternoon, the bubbled, day-old water.

She wanted her sister to feel what it was like, here. She didn't want it to keep sounding so small, so petty and meaningless.

"Well," Denise said. "I mean, imagine those secretaries. Imagine the girls there like us, Min. They're sure as shit not gonna pay out anyone's pension now, are they?"

Mina made a noncommittal noise, but she knew her sister would hear that this hadn't even occurred to her.

"Maybe you're right, probably they'll take care of their own," Denise said, smooth as ever. "I'm just saying. That's just how my mind works. I think about all the little ripples."

"I know you do," Mina said, leaving it there.

"What does Tom say?"

"Tom has been in the city for a week."

"You haven't talked to him? God, him, too, huh?"

"No," Mina shot back. "No, not at all. I just, I made the mistake of trying to talk to him about a fall visit, to drive up to see Jaime."

"No, it'll be fine," Denise said, dropping the idea of Tom as abruptly as she'd raised it. But Mina wasn't even irked; it was so remarkably soothing to hear her sister say that, just as she'd been saying since they were teenagers. Nothing else filled Denise with supreme confidence like other people's fear, coupled with an ignorant certainty that she knew they'd be all right.

Mina wandered into the den and curled up on the window seat that looked out over the front yard, the slope that led up from the gate at the bottom of the drive. She watched the gardener move across the flat lawn at the base of the hill. He'll be gathering the leaves soon, she thought. Everything about the outdoors was still summer, the dampness between her breasts as soon as she left the house, the weight of the air around her. But soon, that would be gone, and they'd forget, even, how it felt. She closed her eyes again and thought of being out with Denise, when they were teenagers. Taking the train into the city and sharing a fifth of rum they'd chase with cans of Diet Coke, and the way her sister always knew who at the bar to flirt with to get cocaine, and the way she'd grab Mina's arm when they were dancing and say, *Let's do some more, it won't kill us.*

"Say that again," Mina murmured.

"Say what again?" Her sister had kept talking, but Mina hadn't been listening.

"Nothing," Mina said. "Nothing. Anyway, I've got to head back over to Isabel's. I'm trying to check in every afternoon."

"You didn't answer me earlier," Denise reminded her. "It's been a few days. She's, what, sleeping all day? Screaming? Breaking the china, throwing his clothes out the bedroom window and into the pool? Inquiring minds, Min."

Mina waited, for a moment, but by then she figured she'd so completely transgressed the borders of loyalty to Isabel that confiding one last detail couldn't hurt.

"Sleeping pills," she said. "Sobbing, and then almost catatonic, and then sleeping pills ever since. But I should take her something else today, right? She can't just sleep forever. She's got to be able to stay awake without losing it."

"That poor woman." When she heard a faint sucking sound, Mina realized that her sister had lit a cigarette on the other end of the line. "That poor, poor woman. What a scumbag, leaving her out there all alone. He's probably holed up in their apartment with some twenty-three-year-old who takes turns between tonguing his balls and pouring vodka over his chest and telling him he did nothing wrong. Men are shit."

"All right," Mina said, her mind already darting ahead. She'd gotten a strange phone call from Suzanne Welsh, something about lunch later, but first she had to stop by to see Isabel. She tried again to decide whether she should take food or magazines or only Xanax.

"YOU KNOW, MINA. I hadn't even thought of doing this today, but since we're out! It'll just take one quick second, and then I'll run you right home."

Suzanne Welsh stood in the street beside her car, pivoting twice before reaching into the backseat and pulling out a large bag. She clicked her key fob four times before rejoining Mina on the sidewalk.

The bag seemed to indicate some errand to run at Saks Fifth Avenue, where they'd parked, but Mina remained baffled—as she had all afternoon—as to why on earth Suzanne had been so insistent they have lunch today.

Technically speaking, she and Suzanne were friendly. Wyatt was older than Jaime, though, so they'd never had much reason to deal with each other vis-à-vis their kids. Suzanne's husband had once worked with Bob D'Amico in some capacity, until Brad left to start his own fund, and so—despite Isabel's contempt for the woman's constant monitoring of every aesthetic, culinary, or social decision made by every single one of her peers—the Welshes were nominally included in many of Isabel's larger-scale events.

And it was true that, despite Suzanne's best efforts to conceal her discomfort, she came from a world much more like Mina's old life than Isabel's. Her father had made money, gobs of money. A department store he'd founded in Brooklyn, a beach house when Suzanne was a teenager, no doubt a small trust fund by the time she married Bill. But that had all only been cemented when Suzanne was a child, too recent to feel safe, and she was still ruled by a girlish terror Mina recognized all too well. That she was the only woman in town, maybe, who hadn't figured out yet how she was supposed to act while she spent her money.

Suzanne was above all petrified by Isabel, and this, too, Mina understood. Despite her exasperation every time she got one of Suzanne's famous rambling phone calls, ostensibly social but ultimately because she wanted to ask Mina whether she knew where Isabel bought Madison's shoes, or if she knew whether Madison's most recent Disney costume had been homemade. Despite the tiring charade of these phone calls, the presumptuous nerve of sucking up hours of Mina's day just because she existed in close proximity to Isabel—despite all that, Mina understood Suzanne, in a way.

But this, Mina would not call it a friendship. They rarely met for lunch alone. She'd had the thought that Wyatt might be applying early to Princeton, and that Suzanne might be angling for some sort of advice or even—could she be this brazen, though?—a recommendation from Tom. But this theory had been squelched over lunch, when Suzanne complained at length about the brusque treatment they'd received from the alumni development officer assigned to Bill on their recent weekend visit to Dartmouth. They were preparing for a big ask, something on the level of a new squash center, and apparently Suzanne had expected a thicker red carpet for the visit.

Besides, Mina thought now, Tom wasn't even that active an alum. If Suzanne wanted an ally, she would have known she had better options.

Isabel's name hadn't so much as haunted the fringes of any of Suzanne's inane stories. Which was just as well.

Mina followed her new gal pal into the store. Suzanne moved with purpose through the ground-floor displays—perfume counters, jewelry cases, fur-lined hats—all patrolled by middle-aged women in black suits who stood with their hands clasped in front of their bodies and had applied their foundation and their lipstick with too little care. Mina saw the way each woman leaned her torso forward as Suzanne passed; an afternoon torpor had settled over Saks, and until the very last possible second, they each hoped she might be the one commission to free them from it.

They arrived at a counter buried back in a deep, silence-cushioned corner of the second floor, the evening department. A woman whose cheekbones could have cut steak rose to greet Suzanne, removing the glasses that hung from a beaded string around her neck.

"Deborah," Suzanne said, "I know I'm a bit earlier than we'd said."

"Don't mention it," Deborah replied. Mina smiled at the thick Queens accent. If only we had a sign, she thought, something we could all flash one another in solidarity. Girls who don't belong here.

Suzanne slid a large, wrapped box from the shopping bag.

"As I said on the phone," she said, "I'm really just so sorry to be doing this. You can't imagine." Her voice was low but carefully modulated so it seemed a casual decision to be speaking this way.

"Please," Deborah said, "that's not necessary." She tugged at the box's gleaming ribbon.

"It hasn't been touched," Suzanne said, a flash of something, like a knife blade turned under a bright sun, in her voice. "I think it's obvious it hasn't been unwrapped."

"Of course," Deborah replied, and her voice coated the knife in soothing syrup. "I have to inspect the dress, but it's quite clear you haven't touched it. It's for your security as much as for ours."

Nonsensical though it was, this seemed to mollify Suzanne. She glanced down at her BlackBerry and typed something with her thumbs for a moment, then let out a sudden clucking sound with her teeth and tongue.

"I just hate to be doing this."

"It's no trouble at all, as I told you when we spoke this morning."

"Well, I mean, I feel terrible for your inconvenience, of course, but really I meant for me! Just look at it."

"It's a beautiful dress," the woman said. The water-smooth fabric emerged from the box in folds, a swollen purple. The three of them looked down at it for a moment. Deborah the saleswoman had yet to express any curiosity about Mina's presence.

"It just seems inappropriate," Suzanne said. "God knows what this event will be like, coming when it does, it's just such awkward timing. But it just seemed—I don't know, really. Wiser. Does that sound so silly to you? God, it must."

Her eyes moved briefly to Mina's, then away.

Deborah smiled in such a way that she committed herself to absolutely nothing, then craned her neck over her keyboard, one hand still on the dress.

"Why are you returning it?" Mina said, careful to keep her own voice level, not to raise it any higher than Suzanne's. "You seem crazy about it."

"Well, I did discuss it with Bill," Suzanne said, leaning in so that their three bowed heads formed a tiny triangle. "I know some others have tried to do this in secret, without telling their husbands. But I just couldn't do that. I know secrecy works for some marriages . . ."

Her eyes flickered in a way Suzanne probably imagined to be just barely perceptible, but which in fact could have been a frame from a cartoon.

"But I just felt I had to tell Bill."

"Tell him what?"

"Well, you know, we just discussed whether it was appropriate. A new dress for the Robin Hood event next month. He thought—you know, it would be good to seem like a team player. Wear something from last season."

"Suzanne, I'm here."

The deeper voice came up behind them, from the direction of the escalator, and Suzanne's head whipped around on her neck. Her face flinched, a rictus of greeting and pleased surprise.

"Oh," she said. She turned back to the saleswoman. "Of course you know—"

"Hi, Deborah," Alexandra Barker said. Mina marveled, not for the first time, at the lime green bow that drew Alexandra's hair back from her face.

"And I'm Mina," she said, trying to make eye contact with Deborah, who did not seem to hear her.

"So nice to see you," Deborah replied to Alexandra, evidently unfazed.

"I told her this was the way to go, and that she could just come to you directly," Alexandra continued.

"Of course," Deborah said. The glasses were back on and she was typing furiously at her computer.

"Mina," Alexandra said, "so nice to see you. I was so sorry to miss lunch."

Mina said a quick and dirty prayer of gratitude.

"Oh, that would have been nice," she purred.

"I suppose Suzanne has told you all about this."

"Well," Mina said. "I don't think so, no."

"Tell us, Deborah," Suzanne said, seemingly disoriented by the fact that Mina and Alexandra were now both here, though surely she had engineered the entire meeting. Or was it possible Alexandra had surprised her? But what would be the purpose of that? "We aren't the first ladies in here this week with buyer's remorse, are we?"

Deborah smiled without looking away from her screen. It became suddenly imperative, in Mina's mind, that this saleswoman know she was not really friends with Suzanne Welsh. How to communicate this?

"Well, she can't say, obviously," Alexandra said, wandering away from the counter and lifting the hem of a dress to hold it up to her face, inspect the stitching. "But believe me, Suzy, you're hardly the only one. I spoke to my sister this morning—they're still on Seventy-Sixth—and she was at Bergdorf the other day and said it was a complete mob scene. People couldn't get the stuff off their hands fast enough. She stopped by Loro Piana on her way home, too, and she had to sit there for twenty minutes before there was even a salesperson free to help her."

"Other women are doing this?" Mina had decided in that moment to remain silent, to try to catch Deborah's eye or, barring that, perhaps launch herself far away from this store. But her curiosity got the best of her, she couldn't help herself.

"And it's a shame we even have to," Alexandra replied. "Don't you think?"

"Oh, I don't know," Suzanne said, sounding seasick. "I do think it might be for the best."

"I'm not sure I understand," Mina said, hearing something flinty come into her voice against her own best judgment. "I'm worried I've missed something."

The woman was, to a startling degree, so much like the daughter, Zoë. Mina wondered if people saw her Jaime in her own face. Whenever she saw Alexandra Barker, Mina thought of the summer years ago when their daughters had been thrown together at a local day camp. She was sure, in retrospect, that Zoë Barker had made Jaime's life a living hell every single afternoon that summer; it was the first year Jaime had started to gain weight, had metamorphosed from a pleasantly round-cheeked kid into someone who was clearly to develop into a softer, sturdier young woman. And there was little patience around here for that, for a Long Island Italian set of boobs and hips. But Mina could remember showing up on the final day, sitting in the swampy late-afternoon heat at an outdoor basketball court, yammering on about how excited her daughter was that her basketball team had advanced to their "division finals." She'd felt, she remembered, an almost embarrassing degree of pride, watching her daughter dribble up and down the court slowly, her face bursting with unimpeded elation each time she made a basket. And foolishly she'd thought she might share this feeling with the other mothers. That they might be finding themselves consumed with that same sense of wonder, building up inside them so they felt it like a physical pressure threatening to push out from their cheeks, their hands, their entire bodies, erupting with love for the women their daughters would become. But Alexandra had interrupted to say, *Zoë was chosen to play in the All Star Game.* This had been treated, liberally, as a relevant contribution to the conversation. And then again, maybe bragging, sure, Mina had mentioned that Jaime's team might win the championship. And Alexandra had stared at her, had actually pushed her sunglasses up onto her head, drawing her strawlike hair back from her face, exposing her eyes, their incipient crow's-feet. *That,* she had said to Mina, *is not the All Star Game. She wasn't chosen for the All Star Game, was she?*

Alexandra finally let out a harsh chuckle.

"Well," she said, "I think the smart money says we should all be lying low for a few months, at the very least. We're ahead of the curve, really. Deborah here is going to have a mob on her hands next week, trying to do this very same thing. I just think it's so sad, you know, that we all have to apologize for our way of life. Just because one family has made some serious mistakes."

Mina wondered if she was ever going to get any smarter, any better at playing along in her own life. Of course it was about Isabel; of course she should have trusted her initial instincts. But they didn't want to gossip. They didn't so much want access to the information she had. At least not yet. No; they just wanted to know whether she even had it.

"God," Suzanne said, "I'd love to know who Isabel's hired to do this for *her*. I mean, I assume she can't be showing up at Bergdorf herself."

"*She* can't be showing up anywhere," Alexandra said, putting a smug little flip on the final syllables. "I assume she's holed up in that house for the foreseeable future."

Mina could feel the woman's eyes, but she'd turned back to the dress, letting the material pass between her fingers like water from a faucet.

"That's what bothers me the most!" Suzanne had regained her footing. "She just gets to hide away until it blows over! I mean, to be returning things *here*. You know, Deborah, I'm sure you must know this about me, I always shop downtown Greenwich whenever I can. You know how important it is to me that the store supports all our local causes. It just feels so unfair to be doing this here."

"It won't blow over," Alexandra said. Her voice was gaining ground, cutting through the air-conditioned hush.

Mina cleared her throat, trying to sound neither anxious nor angry.

"Suzanne," she said, "I hate to put you out, but I've really got to be getting back. I've got a gym session at the house at three."

"I just hope she knows that," Alexandra continued. "She can't just sit and wait for him to bully everyone into forgetting it. Though I know that's worked for her in the past."

"Alex," Suzanne began, her voice almost strong enough to constitute a warning, but Mina interrupted her.

"As I said, so nice to see you both," she said. "But I've really got to go."

Deborah was already in motion, spiriting the box away somewhere beneath the counter, taking Suzanne's trembling hand between hers and nodding like a metronome at everything she said. And then Alexandra was stalking ahead of them, and Mina was following with Suzanne, and they were all three of them totally exposed, was how she would later think of it, when Lily stepped out from behind a display of evening gowns.

Alexandra probably didn't recognize Isabel's nanny. But there was something so brazen in the girl's stance, in how close she planted herself to their path, that all three of them sputtered briefly, almost stopped where they stood. Mina felt the muscles in Suzanne's arm go tense, cling to the bone, and she knew Suzanne had recognized Lily.

Mina tried to make eye contact, but Lily wasn't looking at her. Her eyes were on Alexandra Barker. Even once they'd descended to the ground floor, emerged onto the street, Mina felt certain Lily was still watching them.

NINE

Lily fed the meter, so intent on casing her surroundings that she actually dropped a quarter in an attempt to fumble it into the slot. She left it where it had fallen and turned south on the Avenue.

In the best of times, she found this stretch of road draining. It sloped gently up from the train station, toward the library up on West Putnam and the winding residential districts of Greenwich beyond. It was dotted with sidewalk cafés and the kinds of clothing stores that didn't play pop music at earsplitting levels. Once or twice per block you'd spot a remaining storefront of Ye Olde Greenwich, as Lily thought of the longer-standing businesses like the old pharmacy.

It was a mommy playground, and by midafternoon all the frustrated energies of these underutilized women had them trolling this street in droves. They prowled the boutiques and the juice bars, quaking with everything they had but could not use. The Ivy League educations they'd been allowed to pursue, matriculating when they did, in the wake of feminism's second wave. The endless pluckings and bleachings and injectings that left them in a perpetual state of both tranquility (no wrinkles) and surprise (unnatural eyebrow arches) but also seemed to extract their sexuality from them as if by syringe. She'd never seen so many beautiful women who seemed to live life at such a distant remove from their own sexiness. An energy built up in their muscles all morning, as they ran on the "her" treadmill alongside the empty "his" model in their home gyms, built up as steadily as lactic acid. And by early afternoon, when it was still too soon to fetch their children from school—a task most of them outsourced, anyway—they ended up here. They steered from Maje to Saks to Lululemon to Starbucks, touching their fingertips to a cashmere sweater or unfolding a pair of boyfriend jeans, wondering if their daughters would mock them if they tried to wear these.

These women did not scare Lily. They actually amazed her at times—the wives of Greenwich were just so exactly what the rest of the world probably thought they were, at least in their outward habits. But for all their peels and shots, their lifts and tucks, they looked perpetually strained, to her, forever terrified that the one detail they'd forgotten to falsify would be the one to give it away. She never knew what "it" was for these women. It couldn't just be their age, or the subtle cords of animosity that stretched taut between them and their husbands as they lay in bed at night. And yet they had, quite literally, everything else. She'd never understood what they were so afraid of revealing to their colleagues, for that's what these women were to one another, really. These weren't friendships; these were mutual agreements to aid and abet one another's tireless campaigns for unspecified triumphs.

Lily turned from the meter and prepared to cross the street midblock, hoping the unnecessary crossing guard posted at the West Elm intersection wouldn't scream hoarsely at her insubordination, as he often did. She was headed to Brooks Brothers to pick up the boys' new suits. For the really big nights, evenings when Bob would be speaking on a dais, there were better options on offer. But for local Greenwich evenings, events with a kids' table that were more likely to send the twins home with grass stains or ripped elbows, it was always Brooks Brothers.

She was thinking about the boys when she saw Mina Dawes hop out of the silver SL parked across the street, smoothing her skirt as she walked toward the curb where Suzanne Welsh was feeding the meter.

As far as Lily had ever known, these two were friendly. There was no reason to believe that it was strange for Mina to be out with Suzanne Welsh, no reason at all to link their afternoon, with all its normal concerns, to what was going on with Bob. So it was one of those moments when Lily had to remind herself that the one thing she had on these women, maybe more important even than the fact that she was smarter than they were—which she firmly believed she was—was her ability to sniff out a fight, her identification with prey rather than predator.

She walked quickly downhill, then darted across the street as Mina craned her neck over the parking meter. By the time Suzanne returned to the car to withdraw an enormous shopping bag from its backseat, Lily was facing away from them, watching them in the darkened glass windows of the empty space that had once been a theater and was now, supposedly, going to be remodeled as an Apple store.

"It'll just take one quick second," Suzanne reassured Mina, who was twisting her left hand with her right, feeling her own wrists as if to seek out the pulse. "And then I can run you right home."

Suzanne's voice sounded almost frantic, even more anxious than usual, a bit hoarse. Was it possible she had one of the secret smoking habits? Lily had only ever seen a few of them smoke, and these always furtively, at the side gates to someone else's home. But they all must once have smoked all the time, to keep their appetites sufficiently strangled. When they were living in the city and waiting for these husbands, scanning the crowds each night at the Surf Club, which was always the place Lily imagined all the younger versions of these women. (She'd heard Mina mention the place once.) They must have all been whippet thin and had the most exquisite dark half-moons under their eyes all the time back then, when they were her age.

She followed them into the store, watched Alexandra Barker arrive to meet them, stood so close to them that it seemed ludicrous they hadn't noticed her presence. But then Alexandra Barker had always been one of those ninnies who put herself at risk precisely because she thought she was so tough, so terrifying. Lily had often imagined running into this woman in the city, on a crowded sidewalk or the subway—both places Alexandra would surely never be—and leaning into her hard with one hip, sending her careening off on unsteady feet like something cast off across the dirty, uneven ground.

She knew a little bit about that family, the basics. She remembered one time Bob had wandered into the kitchen to sit with his eating children, one of the times he'd been dressed and ready before Isabel. "He *had* to go out on his own," he'd said of Brad Barker. He'd been talking to Madison. "Everyone talks about that fund like he's so smart, he's such a genius. He had no sense of adventure! He could never take any risks with other people's money, he was too terrified of making the wrong move when he worked with a bunch of other guys. So he goes out on his own where no one's watching him. Who gets into this business and doesn't have the stomach for risk?"

At the time, Lily had credited this to Bob's bluster, his buried jealousy. Brad Barker was, after all, probably the richest man they knew.

But now, watching Alexandra, Lily was thinking how smart Bob was, in his way. How much Bob and Isabel knew about everyone they'd touched, without ever being seen scrambling for the information.

She almost stayed where she was, hidden. She almost let them go without revealing herself. Even as she was acting, having already made the decision, Lily knew that it would be more loyal, better, to remain hidden. But she just couldn't resist. She was not wired that way, and deep down, she didn't really think Isabel was, either. She told herself she was considering her options and stooped to examine a bias-cut black dress, floor length. It felt lethal beneath her fingers. She wanted to whip it at them, the opposite of a white flag, but she settled for just waiting until they turned, then stepping out into their path.

Mina caught herself before her face changed, but she couldn't control her limbs. Her arms retracted, clenched close to her body. Then she kept walking. All three women seemed to ignore the fact that they'd paused upon seeing Lily.

They'd slipped up. If nothing was wrong, then Mina would have waved, bustled over to embrace her. They'd be hoping, now, that she hadn't overheard their conversation. But she had.

She watched Mina's back as she disappeared down beneath the top of the escalator. The next time she shows up unannounced, Lily thought. The next time she tries to take a dish from me to carry in to the kids, or act like I don't know that she's been trying to push her pills on Isabel. That I know she just wants to be indispensable, to anyone. She'll remember this, the next time.

WHEN SHE GOT HOME that afternoon, she considered knocking at Isabel's door, cheering her with the image of Suzanne Welsh's face freezing, as if she'd just been told her husband had exposed himself on the dance floor at the annual Robin Hood Foundation gala.

But Lena had been waiting in the kitchen with a list of household questions, a lieutenant perturbed by the absence of her captain. Lily did her best to direct the woman, to remind her of which areas needed special attention, but she'd been shaky. Lena's eyes widened as she saw that Lily was improvising here. That she'd no more been told what to do this week than anyone else had.

"I clean everything," she said mournfully, before leaving the kitchen.

Lily turned, then, to dinner. She made the kids pasta Bolognese, something else she'd learned to cook during her first few months in Greenwich. Despite the mid-September air outside, she made it. Comfort food, something heavy and warm that would settle in your stomach. Something to push the dread somewhere else for a few hours.

"But if Mom's sick, why is she still at home?" Matteo said after she'd called them in to eat. "She should go see the doctor. Is she just mad?"

"No one's mad," Lily said. "Didn't I just tell you that?"

"I cleaned my whole room," Luke said. "If I go knock, I could show her. I put everything away in all its drawers."

"No one's mad at you for not cleaning your room," Lily said again. "No one's angry at all."

"You get mad at us all the time for not cleaning our rooms," Matteo said pointedly, tilting his head and widening his eyes so that he appeared to be giving the fish eye to his bowl of pasta.

"Okay," Lily said, "enough. Enough! How many times do I have to answer the same questions from you two?"

She pushed her chair back from the table, and both boys looked up in suspended amazement. Matteo held his fork in the air like an offering he'd hoped to surrender.

"We only asked one," he grumbled. Luke looked from his brother to his nanny with poorly concealed terror. Matteo considered his food with distaste, but in another moment he was humming. She knew he'd begin eating again soon, and that his brother would follow.

"I'm sorry I yelled," she said, but they'd both sealed their outrage and moved on without waiting for her to beg their forgiveness. The boys were like this; maybe all small children were. They didn't appear to hold anything against you, they moved through a world that was always the present tense, always shifting around them as if it were a rotating backdrop on a stage set. But once they'd been hurt by something, the hurt remained forever enshrined in the past tense. You could not heal it, once they'd put it away.

She thought again of Mina's face that afternoon. Lily could tell the woman was just dying for someone to confirm her place in Isabel's inner circle, to give her a clandestine wink so they could all draw a clearer line between "us" and "them." And it had been obvious all week that Mina was afraid of Lily. As she bustled in and out, uninvited, with her trays of prepared salads from Aux Delices, her pastry boxes. As if anyone in this house was eating junk food!

Luke let out a muffled gurgle, his mouth full, and Lily turned to look behind her. Madison was standing there, her body slouched against the door frame.

There was something sinister to Madison's new awareness of her body these past few months, as though she'd been told by an outside source that she was now at the age when boys would notice what her skin smelled like and whether she led with her hips when she walked. Watching her negotiate the things she hadn't had before—her coltish legs; the high, insistent globes of her newly rounded ass; the breasts that as far as Lily could tell had sprouted quite literally overnight—felt like watching a child finger a weapon.

It was always running, now, in the back of Lily's mind—even when she decided not to listen to it, the way she'd sometimes doze on the train in the city but still startle awake for her own stop. The same thought: that the boys were fragile, yes, but Madison was volatile, like something that needed to be kept in a test tube and stored in a safe. That if this had happened when Lily was fifteen, she would have swallowed anything that was handed to her, pressed herself against the first boy who offered, gotten as naked as she could as quickly as she could just to feel another kind of pain.

And yet when she'd slapped Madison's cheek, it had felt soft and barely able to hold itself together, like the fragile skin that forms on the surface of warmed milk.

"You hungry?" she said. Madison shrugged, and Lily waved a spoon back toward the table.

"Sit down, I'll bring it to you."

"I'm fine."

"Proper meals are important," Lily replied, hating herself even before she'd spoken. "Even when things are messed up. Especially then. Come on. Do me a favor."

These children had never been confused about her, living in their house, cooking their meals. It was something she was proud of, actually. That she managed to live between the two states of being that rendered the quasi-familial roles of so many others in her position so miserable and awkward. They never saw her as a relative or a friend; their father paid her salary, and as a result she was owed a certain respect. Lily saw the behavior of other children—bright-colored smoothies spilled intentionally on silken upholstery, food thrown at walls coated with paint as expensive as a weekend at a Manhattan hotel. All to punish the people their parents paid to teach them right from wrong. Not these kids. But it was now, asking this girl to "do me a favor," that Lily felt, radiating from Madison, an unfiltered hatred so strong it seemed to take its seat with them at the table. Madison sat down and looked up in a mockery of expectation. Her silence picked at Lily's skin.

"All right," Lily said. "Starve yourself. See if I care."

Madison turned to the boys.

"It's all right, Lou." She began to ruffle his hair, catching it between her fingers and pulling it straight up in the air, which he loved. "What's new in here?"

Lily leaned against the counter and watched the boys open themselves to their sister, uncurling legs that had been folded up beneath them, leaning forward as if to crawl across the table. They looked so small, their bones fit together like twigs and their bodies humming at quicker speeds beneath their near-translucent skin. But Lily knew this was her fear playing tricks on her.

SHE PUT THEM TO BED TOGETHER, in Matteo's bed, their foreheads touching. Madison was somewhere else in the house; she'd barricaded herself in her room for the night, most likely.

Lily went downstairs and clicked off the kitchen lights. She stood for a moment at the window, looking out toward the side gate beyond the garage, where she could just see the headlights of the black sedan that had been parked down the hill for the entire week. There was another one a few feet past the main gate, and another just before you made the turn onto the main road.

When she'd considered this for a few moments, she left the house and walked down through the yard, to her own house beyond the pool, the place Bob D'Amico had given her to live.

TEN

*W*ill the United States as we know it collapse this week? It may
sound like so much alarmist hand-wringing, but it's not an un-
reasonable question.

Does acknowledging that you sound like a fretful alarmist really
let you off the hook? Madison thought. Isn't that even worse than
being unaware, to know you're doing it and not care that you sound
crazy?

It had taken Jake Levins only one week, after the news broke,
to write a column about her father. Now she sat on the floor of her
closet, one hand twisting up behind her to hold the doorknob, the
Monday *Times* spread on the floor before her.

She couldn't think of many other situations in which it would be
necessary to have a lock on a closet door, but right now she could have
used the privacy. Who doesn't give a teenager a lock on her bathroom
door? Isabel and Bob D'Amico, that's who.

*Weiss and its ilk—which of course includes the late, not-so-great Bear
Stearns—are nondepository institutions. Their new way of doing things, in
theory, does a better job of minimizing risk. Or maybe it just does a better
job of ignoring risk. Because now, post-housing bust, you have to wonder if
they assumed that hidden risk would be the same thing as managed risk. Did
they think their investors wouldn't notice what was going on?*

Well, they didn't. We didn't.

How could people stand to read this? And people who, unlike her,
had no personal warmth for Jake, no memories to fight back as they

read his column. Madison could hear it read aloud in his own voice, the voice that had taught her curse words in Yiddish and Italian and German, that had asked her that very summer if she was enjoying *Anna Karenina* and let her unspool her entire tirade against it before telling her she was wrong. But what about the people reading this who didn't know him? How could they stomach the showmanship, the smug disdain?

Here's another quaint term for you: "bank run." You might think of this as a term for another century, when angry mobs of despairing deposi-tors pounded on the closed doors of a huge marble bank building. But this revolution won't be televised; it will happen with the click of a mouse, with an executive excusing himself to check his phone during an off-site at the Four Seasons or The Mark. It will be quieter, sure, but the effects will be the same.

Mentioning those hotels, that was amateur hour. It made him sound like he'd never actually met anyone who worked at a bank. These people had no idea how her father spent his day, they just wanted to feel like they knew.

She had never thought of Jake or Lori as "these people," but it wasn't really her fault that she thought this now, was it? Based on this column, it was clearly how Jake wanted to be seen.

And now we've arrived at my main concern this morning: Weiss & Partners. Weiss banked, in the end, on being too big to fail. But Treasury refused to put any more public funds on the line for Bob D'Amico.

It could be worse, Madison thought. It had taken Jake until the tenth paragraph to mention her father's name.

She'd read enough elsewhere, too, to know that Jake might have leaned a lot harder on the question of whether anything illegal had happened. On her father's public statements all year, and whether they could possibly have been truthful. On what really lay behind her father's decision to fire Erica, to fire Jim.

Some of the other bloggers, most of whom were probably half her father's age and had accomplished approximately one ninety-eighth what he had, seemed to be stuck on her father's childhood, which as far as she knew no one had ever cared about before. He'd never been that kind of famous. But now, apparently, it mattered.

How could a man from such a rough background, they wondered, be so out of touch with what life was like for the majority of Americans? Because he spent his days, whether on the Gold Coast or in Manhattan, surrounded by his underlings or their equivalents. Protected from reality by an army of sycophants. (This is a dark day for Greenwich, Madison thought, all these men and their wives learning via some journalism school graduate who couldn't get a job at the *Times* that they're technically just underlings of my father's.)

Her mother was often mentioned, too. Bob and his blond, pedigreed wife were the figureheads, the dolls atop the cake for a firm at which morality and loyalty were so cherished. *One firm*—the place where everyone was still married to his first wife. Or so they'd always claimed. But that loyalty extended only to the front door; D'Amico's loyalty, in the end, was always to his own guys.

Isn't that what the word *loyalty* actually meant, though? Who would talk about being loyal to strangers?

We've got a car rolling slowly toward a cliff. Some guy shows up and, shrugging his shoulders, gives it the final push over the edge. Do we blame that guy? Or do we blame the guys who drove the car to the cliff's edge in the first place?

She tried to read it without taking it in, her eyes glancing off each word like a stone skipping along the surface of a lake. But of course she could guess, without reading the next paragraph in detail, whom Jake would decide to blame.

Bob D'Amico and his erstwhile buddy, Jim McGinniss. Erica Leary, the CFO they hired and fired within the same year. The Big Three. But the only one who should have been in the driver's seat was Bob D'Amico. He's Wall Street's longest-running CEO; whether he likes it or not, his name is synonymous with the name Weiss & Partners. And as an article in the Times *put it, Weiss is now the Roach Motel—its investors checked in, but*

they can't check out. This will spread to the hedge funds, even if they're not
suffering yet. They're going to have some bank runs of their own, and they'll
have to raise cash with fire sales of their assets. And what of D'Amico himself,
the King of the Cockroaches? Did he scramble his way out of that car before
it went over that cliff? Or will he have to answer, in court, for his crimes?

Where did the term "fire sale" come from, she wondered. Was the
idea that there had been a fire, and you were capitalizing on it to sell
things to the people who had suffered? Who was the injured party,
during a fire sale?

But something about thinking that way, about her idle wondering, began to pour itself into the contours of what she'd read in Jake's
column in an unpleasant way. Thinking in those terms: blame, in-
dictment, exploitation, exposure. She swallowed hard and crossed
her legs. The newsprint had rubbed off on her elbows and fingertips.
Her laptop had disappeared without comment from her bedroom last
week, and Lily had said nothing since. The only other way to get online in the house—and Madison's tongue went dry at the thought
of someone seeing her reading any of this in the computer lab at
school—was the family computer in the den, which was far too exposed during the regular flow and shuffle of breakfast time. But she
needed to read in the morning; she needed to know what everyone at
school would have seen on their breakfast table. And so she'd woken
early, just as she had the day before, to swipe the newspaper from the
foyer before Lily had time to hide it.

What about the fact that Jake knew Bob D'Amico personally?
Shouldn't he have been compelled to say, I despise this man and always have, read on with a grain of salt at hand? Why were her father's
flaws the only ones worthy of examination?

She opened the newspaper and read the column again.

MONDAY SLUICED PAST HER, just as each day had in the previous
week. She woke up an hour before her alarm, snatched the news-

paper, sat with her brothers at breakfast. She avoided Lily's eye in the car. She went to class; she hid when she glimpsed Amanda at the other end of a clogged hallway. She came home, stole a few minutes at the computer whenever she could read what the Internet had to say about her father.

Other than brief glimpses upstairs, she had not seen her mother at all. It had still only been one week.

SHE WOKE UP IN HER BEDROOM, its familiar dark shapes all around her. It clearly wasn't Tuesday morning yet, but she didn't move to consult the clock on her bedside table, an ornate, gold-leafed behemoth her father had brought home on a red-eye from Milan. Isabel's first reaction had been that the clock was "a bit much," but Madison loved it, its bedside authority, its curlicues unfurling like the wings of a golden owl.

From across the room, she could see her phone's shrill red blink. Most likely that was another mealymouthed text apology from Wyatt Welsh, meant to cover the most recent time he'd insulted her father while she stood within earshot. Today, it had been in the cafeteria, while she paid for her paper carton of tomatoes and lettuce drizzled in vinegar. Someone from school must have mentioned it to a parent, who would have called Wyatt's house to chide his mother in a velvety whisper, because the two apology texts she'd received from him already were so clearly dictated to him that Suzanne might as well have sent them from her own phone. Which was worse, derision or the deflection of selfish fear? At least Wyatt made his thoughts known, with little remorse other than what was foisted on him by his mother. But Suzanne was so desperate for her condescension not to occur in the daylight, where others could see. She wanted permission to brag about the son she envisioned, wanted to wipe any evidence of a lesser, crueler person from the record. It was almost charming, in its way, so naive. You had to pity

Suzanne, really. The woman didn't even know where her own weak spots were.

Madison sat up, straining to hear whether someone was in the kitchen. Her bedroom was separated from the other parts of the second story by a hallway of its own, and noise floated up via odd channels, the house's unexpected currents. On the nights when the kitchen became headquarters for a real party, an actual event that required the French doors be thrown open so that guests could overflow out to the lawn, Madison might track the course of the evening without leaving her bed. She would hear mostly the afterthoughts, all the accoutrements of the evening. The chimes of empty champagne glasses assembled on a tray, the suck and whoosh of four industrial ovens swallowing and then ejecting croquettes or risotto cups or, finally, the miniature chocolate passion fruit soufflés that Bob insisted on serving no matter what the meal's theme. The smells, too, seeped up through the carpeting and filled her mouth with their oiliness, even though the food would surely smell amazing once it passed out into the party.

And the servers, she heard them, too, the grad students who covered their tattoo sleeves with tuxedo jackets, then sneaked out to the tiny enclosed courtyard off the kitchen for their pre-dessert-course cigarettes behind the hedge. Their wheezing laughter, their rasping whispers edgy but still timid. She couldn't hear their words, just their boredom, their lip-biting frustrations.

Madison heard it, smelled it, all of it. When something happened down in the kitchen, it felt like she could decipher its import. She told herself that it was for this reason that she slid from bed, her feet sinking into the mossy carpet, and opened her door.

But then she was not downstairs, she was darting up to her parents' wing of the house. She didn't think about it any further. She didn't care what was said, even, so long as someone—her mother—said it to her, said something out loud.

The fluffy sea-foam comforter on their bed was pulled so tight that small wrinkles stretched across its rounded surface, a voluptuous woman squeezed into a silk gown just a few sizes too small. Tiers of pillows in pearly shades bubbled up at the headboard, undisturbed. Madison knew that her mother hadn't let anyone into this room for several days; no one was cleaning up. She just wasn't sleeping in her bed.

There was a low hum, an energy, in the room that Madison took for the sound of her own blood in her veins. But of course it was only the bathtub, the steady rising fall of water cascading from the faucet. Her mother was drawing a bath.

It wasn't really snooping; she passed the bedside table on her way to the bathroom door. It was easy to imagine that the bottle, glowing burnt orange with its own secrets, had caught her eye from across the room. It was a bigger bottle, not the smaller one her mother's Ambien was usually kept in, and it was lying on its side, the cap next to it, as though her mother had torn it open in a hurry and then cast it away from her. It was Mina's name, on the bottle. The drug's name was an unfamiliar one, and Madison both read it and did not. She filed it away between the same folds of her brain that had swallowed every word Jake Levins had written about her family that week.

She looked again at the bed, at the myriad pillows piled up for no one, but this time she could see the slight impression where her mother had curled her body, night after night, without disturbing the sheets.

It was possible that the bottle was lying there because Isabel had decided *not* to take anything. It was absolutely possible, and if her mother had chosen not to take these pills, that meant that she was coming out of it, recovering. That she would be not only prepared to talk to Madison, but probably wanted to. She might even have made noise downstairs on purpose. She must be hoping for just this moment, for Madison's knuckles against the white paneled bathroom door, tucked discreetly into the bedroom wall.

The water didn't shut off after her first knock, but she could have sworn that she heard her mother's motions cease—whatever she'd been doing, whatever lotions or salt rubs she'd applied to her own body before lowering it into the hot water, stopped. Madison could hear her mother trying not to be heard. She knocked again. The water shut off.

"Who is it? Lily?"

"No, it's—it's me. I just wanted to make sure everything was okay. I heard a noise from the kitchen."

"Jesus, you scared me. Did I wake you?"

"I just wanted to make sure everything was okay," Madison repeated. She heard a gentle sound, the displaced water lapping against the edge of the tub. Her mother had climbed the steps that led up to the sunken Jacuzzi tub, and now she was in. Which could, technically, be an invitation. It definitely wasn't the usual deflection.

"I don't want to bother you."

"Well, Madison, I'm not going to beg you to come in."

Her mother almost never invited her into this room. They were both, it often felt, still treating it as the violated sanctum it had been when Madison was eight years old and Isabel had found her perched on the vanity, tubes of lipstick scattered at her feet, her hands pressed to the mirrored cabinet and her bare toes curled over the edge of the sink. Isabel had plucked her from the mirror like an errant ball of lint caught in the sleeve of her Barbour jacket.

Every surface in the room was reminiscent of a pearl: opal-toned marble, gauzy mint green curtains, pale pink towels, and numerous iridescent bottles and tubes and pots of velvety lotions.

To the right, a door led to her father's bathroom. In there it was different, everything dark wood, her father's effort to transport himself to the house in Sun Valley for his daily lather and shave. When she was smaller, he'd regularly let her curl up in the empty bathtub to watch him while he shaved, and even in summers she'd close her eyes and pretend it was snowing outside, that they'd been snowed in together. That he wasn't leaving. That there was no one else on earth who needed his time any more than she did, no one else to whom he'd made any real promises.

Isabel was lying with her head cradled against the far corner of the tub, the rest of her submerged completely beneath the bubbles. Her eyes were closed.

"Come sit with me for a bit," she said. "Everything's fine."

Madison leaned back against the wall.

"How has school been?" her mother said.

None of her teachers had said anything specific yet. In Trig she'd seen Mr. Warren try to catch her eye a few times, just after dismissal. He always looked so young when he tried to stand at the front of the room and give them all some command. His dirty blond curls looked perpetually shower damp, cropped short and beaten into submission. His cheeks were flushed and clammy, his short-sleeved button-down surely clinging to the part of his back just between his shoulder blades. He was in a band with a few of the other math teachers; she knew that about him. She also knew, just from the way he shifted his weight from foot to foot when he wrote the answers to their homework on the board, that he hadn't grown up any place like her part of Greenwich. And so she always wondered what he thought of them, his students. The blithe way they tumbled into each minute of the future, the way their hands curled instinctively around the screens of their iPhones, the sparkling BMWs in the senior parking lot. She had wondered these things even before, about Mr. Warren, even during that first week of school in September. She thought about things like this, even if everyone around her assumed that she didn't.

"None of my teachers have mentioned it," was all she said. Isabel nodded.

"You haven't been sleeping a lot, have you?" Madison said. "I've been seeing your coffee mugs downstairs, sometimes. When Lily doesn't get to them first."

"Should I have been hiding them from you?" Isabel's eyes remained closed but she let her hand flutter through the air above her.

"I didn't mean—"

"Well, you know, I wouldn't allow this if I didn't know Lily was capable. She's beyond capable. I mean the boys are more comfortable with her than they are with me, aren't they?"

"No," Madison said, because her mother's eyes were still closed, and what other reply could she possibly give?

"You never did that. But then of course you were older by the time we'd hired real full-time help. When you were small, I guess I was all you had."

The words were strange, altered; they sounded like they'd made their way all around Isabel's mouth by the time they hit the air. Still; her mother never talked about what it had been like, when Madison was a baby.

"I don't remember that," Madison said. She didn't think it was true that they hadn't yet had full-time help when she was a baby.

"You should have seen Gran's face whenever she was out here," Isabel continued, following some trail of thoughts only she could see. "There was no telling her, you know. She had no idea, what it meant to run this kind of house. It was a totally different life for her, hers was. And I should have been the one giving you your goddamn breakfast every morning? I don't know how she justified Frank and Antoinette, they weren't there on a volunteer basis. Do you even remember those first few years out here?"

Madison thought of the enormous, unmanicured yard, of the swimming pool so dark and murky, its surface clotted with leaves. She thought of the plaid blanket her mother used to spread beneath a tree for them both, the tea sandwiches in an actual picnic basket, and of falling asleep in the sun, opening her eyes to follow the swaying patterns the leaves of the tree cast down on her skin, the landscape marking her in the haziness of the afternoon. And of her father's car, the older Mercedes he used then for a station car, sputtering to a stop beyond the house and then her father himself, jogging down the slope of the lawn like an athlete to pick her up and press her sun-warmed hair to his cheek.

"What do you mean," she said, "like, our picnics?"

"Everything," Isabel said. "Our picnics. Just the two of us out here, and your father in the city. We never should have built this house, I should have never let him convince me. But your father wears every-one down. The Plaza, of all places. That has nothing to do with us, we don't need that. I don't know what he was thinking."

The words folded something in Madison's stomach, for she hadn't given the new apartment any thought at all in the week since the news, and of course she should have known that it was causing her mother distress. The year before, Madison's father had taken one of the new penthouse apartments in the Plaza. They hadn't sold the old place yet, but he said they'd have no trouble unloading it. He'd brought her into the city once, with her brothers, to see the place just after the deal closed, but Isabel had refused to come along. She'd said that chopping up the Plaza into condos was a travesty.

It was beautiful, the apartment, but Madison had felt nothing much for it. Despite its views, despite Central Park laid out beneath the soaring windows like their own personal carpet. Because she'd never expected to live there in any significant way, any more than she "lived" at the ranch in Idaho. Even her mother went only once a year with the other partners and their wives for the firm retreat. Some-times she brought Madison and the twins out for a week of skiing afterward, but the rest of the year it existed for them like the setting of a dream: somewhere they remembered, thought of sometimes, but mostly did not mention.

Isabel's head had begun to nod, making short, abbreviated move-ments through the air, as though she were tracing shapes with the point of her tiny, sharp nose. It was not a gesture Madison recognized.

"In any case," her mother said, "I'm aware. I haven't been around much these days."

"Well," Madison said, "haven't you been down there every night?"

Isabel sighed, as though she'd been holding the air deep in her lungs, and even the sound of the sigh had edges.

"Some things are easier to take care of while you guys are sleeping," Isabel said.

"Like the black cars outside?"

Isabel slid down in the tub, letting her chin graze the water.

"Mina gave me these pills," she said. "She said they would help, but they're not. I'm going to throw them away."

Madison knew that she would not get another chance, to ask about the pills, and she knew that was why her mother had brought them up in this moment. But see, she thought, it's fine, she's taken them once, she won't take them again. I won't give her the satisfaction of asking for more.

"There were more cars today," she pressed. "There were, like, two of them around back, behind the hedge. By Lily's house."

Isabel lifted one hand to her own chest, just at the dip of her clavicle. Madison couldn't see any other part of the arm; the hand just lay there against Isabel's neck as if a stranger lurked beneath the surface of the water.

"Someone tried to get into the apartment. In the city. So we wanted to—an abundance of caution. There's no reason not to."

"The apartment? While Dad was home?"

Isabel said nothing.

"Was he home? Is *he* being careful?"

"Madison, I'm not going to discuss it further. Plenty of people are worrying about it right now. Adding your name to the list doesn't help me at all."

Madison crossed the room, crawling onto the steps that led up to the bathtub and folding her elbows on the edge of the tub. She rested her chin there on her arms. She might have been doing this all her life, she thought, sitting above her mother as she floated in the bathtub, telling her stories. Isabel said nothing, though, just plucked a washcloth from the fragrant basket on the ledge.

"Have you talked to Daddy?"

There was only the slightest stutter to Isabel's movements, and she began to dunk the washcloth into the water. "He's very busy right now. It's been chaos in the city, or so I hear."

"Did he ask about us?"

"Madison, it's a very complex process. He can't do it from Greenwich."

"What is? What's complex?"

Isabel didn't answer. She put her palm to one of the frothy peaks of bubbles and sliced it in half with a slow motion, like a karate chop played at delayed speed.

"You mean when a company gets liquidated."

The word had the exact effect Madison had hoped for. She saw that her mother was wondering what she'd read, how much she understood.

"I just thought he might have asked about us. About me."

"Your father misses you, sweetheart, do you really need me to tell you that?"

Yes I do, she thought, *why don't you know that?*

"You know I leave the business to your father. Unless he needs me."

Isabel spread the wet washcloth across her chest and breastbone, leaned her head back, and closed her eyes again. Speaking to her mother this way, eyes closed, nose and chin in the air, felt to Madison like they weren't really speaking at all. The bathroom had become a pale bubble of untold strength, as though Madison could talk and talk without piercing its surface, without exposing them both to the world beyond.

"What have people been telling you?"

Who, Madison thought, who could she possibly think I've been talking to this week?

"He signed up for it," her mother continued, having barely left Madison any time to respond. "When he agreed to be the CEO. You can't get the worship without the blame. That's something your father's always struggled with. He wants all of one without any of the other. But where are you getting this? Jake Levins?"

"Did you read his column today?"

"Please. You think I care what that little man has to say?"

"I love Jake and Lori," Madison whispered, peering down at her toenails, at the chipped purple polish she'd applied a month ago, five years ago, it was impossible to tell the difference.

"I know you do. But in this particular area, Amanda's father is a man possessed, Madison. He thinks it's a good thing that he's the lone voice crying out in the wilderness."

"But that doesn't mean he's wrong," Madison said. "Just because he's thinking for himself."

Isabel let out a sound that was jarringly close to a snort.

"There was an article this morning about victims," Madison pushed. "It was about people who invested their money other places, and now—"

"Those people gambled," Isabel said, as if Madison's stupidity were exhausting. "They made a choice, Madison. They didn't do anything wrong, but neither did your father. And pretending that he did, so everyone can feel better, won't fix anything. He's no use to anyone if he's put—"

She stopped speaking suddenly, and Madison knew what they were avoiding, the forbidden words. Anything to do with prison, anything to do with criminal. The words Jake Levins so relished.

"I love Jake Levins, too," she began again, breathing deeply. "Sometimes. But look at someone like him, or even—take Tom Dawes. God love Mina, really, but Tom got everything he has because of his father. And what does he have? He's glorified middle management, and he always will be. He's no one of consequence, not really. So it would be too delicious for them to pass up, if he's run things into the ground."

"Jake?"

"No," Isabel said, her voice almost dreamy again, not at all per-turbed by her daughter's slowness in their conversation. Isabel was not usually understanding when you couldn't keep up with her. "Your father. If he's run it into the ground."

"Okay," Madison said. She tried not to picture them all on a plane, on the jet with the firm's insignia on its side. Her father storm-ing the cockpit in a drunken rage, seizing the pilot's controls, running the plane into the ground.

Isabel opened her eyes and fixed them on Madison, as though surprised to find her in the same place. Madison tried to hold her gaze but the eyes were so pale and blue, so unblinking. It was like looking up into the noon sky and trying not to squint.

"They hate how successful he's been," she said. "They always hated all of them, all the guys, because they weren't as polite as everyone else pretended to be. I mean, I felt it, too, when I first met him, you know that. They want him to apologize for that more than anything else. Can you understand that?"

Madison nodded. She did not look away from her mother's eyes. Isabel nodded, too, as if in response.

"The thing right now is to be strong. It's a system, Madison. He operates within a system. He didn't create it, but it's what he knows how to do. And he needs us to be strong while he fixes this. All right?"

Madison said nothing.

"I need to know that you understand what I mean."

"I think so. I do. But also, couldn't we go see him? For a weekend, couldn't we? What's stopping us?"

Her mother sailed her hand into the air, a dismissive gesture cur-tailed when it hit the water.

"I don't think that's a good idea."

"Why?"

"Madison, please. You think I might know what I'm talking about? A trail of shoe trees and crumpled ties along the floor, from his bathroom to his bed to the kitchen. All over the carpet. Clamshell cartons on the floor. Your father left to his own devices, it's not a pretty thing."

"He's only left to his own devices because we aren't there," Madison said.

The old apartment was on Park Avenue, fifteen blocks north of Grand Central. Everything inside was white or stainless steel, sharp corners and fabrics that felt cold to the touch no matter what the season. Isabel hated sleeping there. But it was an empty shell, really. To hate it so much—it was like hating a blank wall, a crisp white shirt.

Sometimes, when they were all there together and Madison woke up in the night, she'd wander into the living room to see if her father was up, watching television. If he was in a good mood, he'd bundle her into a cab, still in her pajamas, and take her to one of the twenty-four-hour diners on Second Avenue. He'd tell her they should wait a few hours, take the car to his old part of Williamsburg for two Italian subs at his mother's favorite grocery, but she never wanted to wait. She just wanted her father at the table across from her. The unnatural buttery glow of the lights in those old diners, everyone else there pale and faded, already resembling photographs of themselves. And the way those people eating alone at four o'clock would stop and stare at them when they walked in, she and her father, giggling, his hand wrapped around hers.

She was the only human alive, she knew, who had ever seen her father really giggle.

"We could be there," she told her mother. "We could be there with him."

"I'm done talking about this."

Madison looked at her feet once more, gripping the marble step she'd crouched on, and could not believe her mother's cruelty. It wasn't so much, she realized, that her mother didn't *care* that Madison might feel mistreated or resentful. It was that these possibilities had never even crossed Isabel's mind. It wasn't Madison's place to demand anything from Isabel, and her mother thought that this meant she never would.

"Well, then, I guess I'll go back to bed. If you're done talking about everything I ask about."

Her mother resettled herself among the deflating suds. Madison stood up and walked over to the door; when she turned back, Isabel was examining the backs of her own hands, rubbing at the wrinkles, the knuckles chafed and red from the warm water.

"I have one more thing."

"Of course."

"Are they going to take the house away?"

Her mother emitted a small, harsh laugh. "Well, who's they?"

"Please don't laugh at me."

And immediately the laughter died, like magic.

"Would that be the worst thing? You know this was never what I wanted. This cavernous house where if I put my sunglasses down, I'll never be able to find them again. I'm not sure it's how you three should be raised, either."

Madison tried not to stare at her mother, bare her own disbelief. *Yes,* she thought. *Yes, I think that would be pretty bad. I think that would be the worst thing.*

Isabel squeezed the washcloth, letting the excess water stream down into the tub. "I just wish he'd listened to me more. Of all the times to buy an apartment in the Plaza, I mean. Last year. Of all the times. And really, basically, your father is so disciplined. But they'll find everything, you know, his silliest things. The sheets, those sheets he has FedExed ahead of time to the hotels? They'll jump on that, I promise you. I promise you."

"Who?" Madison tried. "Who will jump on it?"

"Everyone. Listen," Isabel said, looking up at her again. She moved forward suddenly, the water sloshing at her shoulders. "We could have a fresh start, you know? In a way, as long as things don't take a turn for the worse, this is a blessing."

Madison tried to ignore the panic rising in her throat, flooding up from her feet. "What?"

"Sweetie, can you trust me? I need you to trust me that I am doing everything I possibly can to keep you all safe."

The word hovered in the room; the idea of safety, twinned as it must be with danger, was there now. Her mother had said it.

Madison waited for moments, watching the tiny beads of sweat form along her mother's hairline, clustered together like champagne grapes.

"I miss Buck," her mother said, unprompted, worrying her bottom lip between her thumb and index finger. Her mouth had slackened, giving her whole face an unfinished sheen.

"I know you do."

"He was very good in a crisis. Say what you will about my father, but he was good in a crisis. Your father, Madison, the man is excellent at preventing crises, but God forbid something actually goes wrong."

"That's not true," Madison said. "I remember the paper, after September eleventh. That's literally exactly what they said about him. He got them through a crisis."

"He got *them* through it," Isabel whispered, and again Madison felt the chilled knowledge all around her, that her mother was not talking to her at all.

"That was his job, Isabel."

Madison hardly ever tried to get away with using her mother's first name, but now it didn't even register on Isabel's face.

"You trust him, don't you?"

"I do," Madison said. "I trust him. Do you?"

Isabel shrugged. "I trust our tribe. Just like Buck used to say."

"All right," Madison said.

Her mother leaned back into the water, closed her eyes again. "But I'll tell you what really gets me. I'll tell you what kills me. That we're going to be the example. We're going to be the cancer eating away at everyone else. It doesn't matter that we're far from the worst. It should, but it won't."

The sentences came out slowly, as if her mother could see them behind her closed lids and was reading them to her daughter as they appeared, one by one.

"You have no idea, how petty. Everything my mother hated about the world you're in, once you're somebody's wife."

It wasn't clear to Madison anymore if her mother cared what she thought. Whether she truly wanted her only daughter to stay in the room with her, or just didn't feel a particularly strong aversion to having her there.

"But you aren't like that," she said to her mother. "You aren't someone's wife."

Then, without warning, her mother was in motion. The bathwater sloshed in shark-fin waves as her mother drew her legs into her body.

"Hand me a towel from the shelf, will you?"

Madison reached for one and when she turned back, Isabel was standing, the bubbles and suds sliding down her body like a second, ill-fitting skin she'd decided finally to shed.

Her mother's breasts were perfectly even, something Madison had learned to recognize as unique as she got older, as she and Amanda had started to compare their own with incessant anxiety. Most people had one bigger than the other, but not her mother. They looked perfect on her chest, hanging below her sharp collarbone, sloping down from her shoulders. Like the most elegant that breasts could possibly look. This is what people meant when they called her mother an ice queen. They just meant they were jealous.

Madison was embarrassed, to be looking at her mother's breasts like this, and she realized that she was waiting for her mother to re-call herself to her own physical body, remember she was naked. Her mother couldn't possibly want her to see this. But then Isabel put out one hand and stared at Madison, fingers waving in the air, waiting for her towel.

Two parallel cords of muscle led your eye down from her breasts to her hip bones, so angular, pointing you down toward the tiny, trim blond rectangle of pubic hair. There were soap suds wreathing her mother's hips and thighs but her actual pelvis—Madison could not think the word *vagina* about her mother's body, not even inside her own mind—was completely exposed, glistening with only droplets of water. When was the last time I even saw her naked? Madison thought, feeling herself grow more frantic. Did I even know to think about her pubic hair back then, to be jealous that hers is such a light color?

There were these women in Greenwich, Lily called them the Biddies. They had grown up here, always stayed, but now they lived in the guard cottages on land that had once been tiny corners of their family estates. The town had changed, for them. They'd approach you, sometimes, in the grocery store, near the plumped and glossy cuts of organic chicken breast. They'd lurk there, in the anticipatory frost of that aisle, and at first you'd assume they were just charmed to see a cute little girl. But then something would be off, and you'd realize they didn't know you, or where they were, had forgotten that they weren't still little girls themselves. You'd have to look away, because there was no way to watch them, driven in circles by their own frailty, the abandonment of the lives they could remember. There was no way to look without stealing something from them that you didn't even want.

She handed her mother the towel, averting her eyes, and then Isabel reached for Madison. She put one hand to either side of her temples, and kissed the top of her head. Madison wreathed her arms in her mother's and they stood there. Madison told herself not to cry, not to move, not to do anything that would make her mother notice the intimacy she'd given away for nothing at all.

It might happen again, she thought. Even if she throws away the pills, she might still do this with me again.

She understood, possibly for the first time, what it meant to be so comfortable with someone you could sit with them in silence. She had always felt this way with her father, but it had never seemed like silence with him. He was always in motion, always muttering to himself. Taking up space in the room. Now, with her mother, it felt like the room was expanding.

ELEVEN

Amanda didn't know what she'd expected, really, but this wasn't it. She sat on the steps of the Met, the last dregs of the city's summer influx of tourists straggling up toward her, their cheeks and necks pebbled red in the oppressive Friday-afternoon heat. She herself had unwisely worn leggings beneath her sundress.

"At least take a sweater," Lori had repeated as she drove Amanda to the train that morning. "You know how chilly they always keep those train cars. Always bring a cover-up."

Amanda knew her mother was really fretting over the fact that she had allowed her daughter to take the day off from school, to go into the city alone. All week, since the second column had been published on Monday, her mother had watched her like something that held the potential for sudden, shattering violence: a burnt package of instant popcorn, a champagne cork that had loosened in its berth and was just waiting to be liberated from its spindly metal cage.

Her father, on the other hand, barely looked at her at all. Apparently he was afraid that any stray bit of eye contact might indicate an apology or even, God forbid, remorse. And Madison had been the same, ever since that first morning. It really felt, to Amanda, that of everyone in their little circle she'd had by far the least involvement in whatever chain of events led to Bob D'Amico possibly losing his job. She really did not think all that highly of her own influence in matters of global finance, possibly even less highly than she thought of her own clout in the Greenwich, Connecticut, ecosystem.

And yet, apparently, she was the one everyone was desperate to avoid.

She stood up and brushed the folds of her dress, admitting to herself that she didn't have any interest in finishing the soft pretzel she'd bought on a whim from one of the carts at the entrance to the park. For a moment she'd convinced herself that it would be delicious, that it would be one of those many things native New Yorkers (she liked sometimes to lump herself in with this crowd) always treated with unfair disdain. What if all these touristy trimmings actually *were* the essence of the city, what if they were secretly wonderful and had been ignored for too long by those who thought they were in the know? What if this pretzel was delicious, and she missed it?

Of course, it wasn't. It was a throat-drying and yet also sodden lump of calories that couldn't be saved even with liberal globs of yellow mustard, and she threw it in a trash can, then joined the dampened flow of human traffic making its way down Fifth Avenue.

She cut east quickly, telling herself that it was time to catch a train home and call her mother for a ride, but when she came within sight of the subway station on Eighty-Sixth Street the thought of going down into the closeness and the heat was revolting, and she decided to walk to Grand Central.

All around her the Upper East Side flowed at its usual lazy weekday rhythms. She felt silly for having expected anything otherwise, but she'd been thinking so much lately of that other September, when her parents brought her into the city every few days. Jake told her later that people said it bordered on child abuse, taking an eight-year-old with them to TriBeCa to serve hamburgers and pizza to the first responders. Most of what she remembered was sitting on top of stacks of cardboard boxes filled with paper napkins and utensils, the other women volunteers patting her head as they bustled by. Her mother appearing every so often, crouching beneath Amanda and taking her chin in the cup of her left hand to make sure she wasn't afraid. It had smelled terrible, the smoke had clung to every tendril of her hair for days, but smells had never bothered Amanda and she'd liked being with so many adults, listening to them talk to one another when they forgot she was there. The way everyone liked one another for those few days. Susan Sarandon had been there, wearing an FDNY baseball cap and serving burgers, and that had been one of Amanda's first brushes with celebrity, with the way a man might change the entire register of his voice just because he was talking to someone whose breasts he'd seen on a movie screen twenty years ago.

After they volunteered, for those weeks—and her parents were often taking her out of school for this, spending days at a time in New York, camping out in the guest rooms of friends on the Upper West Side—they always took her to do something fun, a splurge. Tea at Alice's Tea Cup or an exhibit at the Museum of Natural History or scrambling over the craggy boulders of Riverside Park, despite Jake's known aversion to grass and sunshine and the ever-looming threat of Lyme.

All that fall you had felt not only the open quality of the city but also the way everyone knew how unusual this was. The way people took one another's hands to say hello when they passed in the doorway of Zabar's or Barnes & Noble; the way strangers stopped to tell her parents what a precious child she was. Everyone was anxious for any excuse to linger and chat, trade stories and hearsay. The constant evasive, obsessive gestures at the treetops on the south edge of the park, toward downtown, "down there."

There was nothing like this now, no such feeling of matched experience, and it was only in confronting this that Amanda realized how much she had expected this once more, this sense that everyone had dug, together, into their communal trench.

Near Sixty-Eighth Street a flush of older teenagers poured from the glass facade of one of the Hunter College buildings, their Converse sneakers dotted with marker drawings. The girls lifted their arms to expose wedges of soft skin between their tight tank tops and tight jeans. The boys clutched their headphones around their necks with casual pride, the way they'd carry sweaty gym towels after a rigorous workout.

Amanda let herself fall in with them, losing them when they descended into the subway but still imagining herself in some world where Bob D'Amico was a distant symbol rather than the man living in Madison's house. Where her own father had the good sense to criticize from afar rather than embed himself in the thick of it all like some clumsy, outspoken spy. Amanda wiped the sweat mustache from her lip and let herself think about these things, the things she wanted. Walking the streets in New York always did this, filled her with this unstemmed sense of all the things she wanted and might never have.

She passed the pizza parlors and old lady clothing stores in the East Sixties and Fifties, heading down toward the skyscrapers, that sense of business being conducted high above her. Steel and glass everywhere, the part of East Midtown that she secretly loved. She was letting her eyes roam over it all, this stretch of Lex with everything only a few stories tall, a little village, the Eat Here Now diner and Le Pain Quotidien and the boutiques. She was moving so quickly and thoughtlessly when she saw him that she almost tripped over the ankle-height iron fence that enclosed a tree planted at the sidewalk's edge.

She knew it was him without seeing his face: the barrel-shaped body, the way he had his hands in his pockets but leaned forward with his chest, a business-suit stance even though he was wearing sweats and a baseball cap. She could see the close-cropped pepper hair just at the nape of his neck, beneath the cap. And then he turned his body sideways, facing half uptown, toward Amanda, and she could see Bob D'Amico's face.

She did the quick calculations in her head. Their apartment was on Park, but where? Close to Grand Central, maybe. East Fifties. She should have known this would happen, why was she even walking to Grand Central in the first place? You wanted this, she thought, you wanted this agony, you walked right down this street like a little kid pushing at a loose tooth with his tongue until he feels the pop, the salt bloom of blood.

Mr. D'Amico hadn't seen her yet, so she didn't move. She stood still, and that's when someone just beyond him moved into focus, and she realized that there was a woman standing with her back to him, that he was talking to this woman. She was wearing a baby pink exercise top and skin-snug yoga pants, a Greenwich uniform if ever there was one, but Amanda didn't think she recognized the face. The outfit seemed so incongruous, every aspect of the woman's body language made it seem so unlikely that she was on her way to a yoga class, that the whole scene took on the outlandish cast of fantasy, of performance. These were their assumed identities, donned in a hurry so they could speak to each other on Lexington Avenue without anyone noticing. No one had; people continued to flow around them like they were two ordinary city obstacles left on the sidewalk. He was standing with his back to the street now, and she was facing away from Amanda, toward downtown.

And then he lifted his hand in the air and reached toward her right shoulder and let it hover there, not touching her, not wrapping his fingers around the bony curve of her shoulder, just letting his fingers hang in the air above her body. There was something protective and yet menacing to the gesture. Like he wanted to crush her with his fist but also wanted to keep her from harm, and so barely held himself at some equilibrium by refusing to spoil her, touch her at all.

Amanda watched them begin to walk down the street together, watched him take the woman's elbow and steer her onto the side street. She didn't watch them because she wanted to but because she couldn't move. She felt a tide of something undefined cramping her stomach, and she stood perfectly still for a moment more. As though her body were a water glass balanced on a delicate tray, and she did not want to splash its contents all over Lexington Avenue. Eventually, she kept walking and made it to Grand Central Station, to the scattered clamor of the main terminal.

All around her people gawked, stood unselfconsciously with their necks craned to stare at the ceiling, embraced one another and shouted. There was endless enjoyment and yet no fondness, not one display of warmth for anyone else. None of them cared what the others were doing. No hamburgers served to strangers, no one holding an unfamiliar hand.

The person Amanda wanted to call, really, was her father, but he was at Yale for office hours and besides, she couldn't call him. She had a piece of information now that he'd want, she had an insider tip. But she couldn't trust him, anymore, could she? She stood in Grand Central, listening to the ignorant buzz of the people all around her, and she did not want to board the train, did not want to go home.

TWELVE

Mina wasn't even hungry, not really. It was Tom who insisted they stop for dinner on the way up to Andover.

It was the first Friday in October, and he was furious that this was how they were spending the first night in weeks he could have spent at home. And then Mina hadn't said a word in the car, had denied him even the tiniest opening through which to shove the blunt force of his anger.

When she'd called that morning, to see what time she should arrange for a car, he barked at her. He was slammed. Jaime would understand, for God's sake, if they skipped her recital. If they dropped in on her the next afternoon, instead, and took her off campus for a celebratory brunch.

"I'll buy her a Bloody Mary if she wants," Tom said. "I'll buy the kid off. I swear to God, Min, it'll be worth it."

She tried not to dwell on the all-too-easily summoned picture of her daughter guzzling a thick, salty red drink, chomping the celery stalk between her front teeth, while the waiter looked on with distaste and Tom sat mute, his eyes tracking the parade of e-mails filling his BlackBerry screen.

Instead, she asked her husband if she could bring anything—his antacids, the papers. One of the crime novels he consumed at top speed on their vacations, novels he handled so aggressively that by the time he cast them off they looked pummeled, as if they'd been thrown from the window of a car speeding down the Merritt.

But then he'd surprised her, after his immediate and febrile initial protest, by insisting that they take the Jag out of the garage for the trip.

"Sweetheart," she began. "Tom. You must be exhausted. And we've got the room at the Andover Inn—you can go right to sleep. The recital isn't until ten o'clock tomorrow. So you'll really get a full night's rest. Wouldn't it make more sense to take a car?"

"We aren't taking the fucking car service. I already called the garage, they'll have the car ready for us by six."

Then and there, she swallowed what she knew would be four hours of Tom threading through Friday-afternoon traffic on I-95, tailgating any car that wasn't as nimble as the Jag, cursing under his breath. She swallowed a vision she'd had of a drive spent in companionable silence, Tom perhaps dozing on her shoulder, Mina sliding the rocks glass from his slackening fingers just before he might have let it tumble to his lap.

She swallowed all of it, her fragile hope for how this evening might unfold, and she swallowed it because she'd visited Jaime exactly twice last year. Once for the parents' weekend in the fall and once to pack her up for the summer. Tom hadn't come up with her for either visit. They were going to this recital, whatever abuses she might be forced to draw down on her own head.

He was punishing her, of course. That was why he hadn't been to Andover yet. When Jaime was first accepted, he'd insisted that they look at houses up there, in Massachusetts. So they wouldn't have to stay at any of the local hotels. The drive will be bad enough, he'd said. Might as well have it be a pleasant experience once we're up there.

She hadn't objected. It certainly didn't seem necessary, and it had only been a few years since they'd bought the house in Southampton. But she hadn't said a word. She'd even been, a little bit, excited. Decorating the beach place had been fun, if nerve-wracking—it had the potential to be their most public house, after all—but now she could do something cozy, a place where she'd always be alone with Tom.

She hadn't said anything to indicate to him that she thought there was anything wrong with his idea. But Tom was always sure she was policing him, always sure the girl from the *other* part of Long Island was going to peer out from behind his wife and suck her teeth at him, roll her eyes as he slid his credit card across the table. When he was upset, when he was on a bad run of weeks at work, it was always one of two things: either she was a killjoy who begrudged him any spending for himself, or else she'd married him for his money. That both probably couldn't be true did not seem to concern him.

In any case, after a few weeks, he'd stopped talking about buying a house in Massachusetts, and somehow this was Mina's doing.

"We really have to do this?" Tom said, just once, before they hung up. "It means so much to her that we go to some high school orchestra concert?"

Mina pressed her fist to her mouth, biting down on her knuckles.

"Yes," she said. "What with all that's been going on, I really do think it'll be nice for her to see our faces in the crowd. Reassuring, maybe. Do you disagree?"

He hung up without another word.

"You didn't even take her up at the end of the summer. You sent her in a car," Mina said to no one, her voice ringing clear against the marble floors in a way that it couldn't have when her husband was still on the line.

She should have known that Tom wouldn't allow himself to consider the possibility that his daughter was watching the news, interpreting the streams of jargon as indicators of her father's failure. Mina realized that this was how she'd been picturing Tom, in his office all these days. That same gaping mouth, the frozen quality to his face that took over whenever Jaime squinted at him briefly and then composed her own face into a smile, to thank him for the misguided gift or the foolish suggestion or whatever else her father had done to confirm that he did not know her at all.

Mina wondered whether Jaime *had* been watching the news. Did her daughter watch the news? She couldn't remember, but then Jaime had been fourteen when she left for boarding school, and hadn't spent more than a week at a time in Greenwich since. Did any fourteen-year-olds watch the news, really? Or were they all just getting that new thing on their phones, Twitter. Everyone striving to be as arch as possible, too witty to live.

She shook her head clean and went back upstairs to pack Tom's overnight bag.

THEY STOPPED AT RAJIV'S KITCHEN in Wellesley for an early dinner. Tom liked to drive up here several times each year, usually, but they hadn't been since the previous winter; the impending panic all summer had cut these small extravagances of time from their joint schedule, and dinners at Raj's restaurant had been one casualty among many.

Tom slid the car backward into a spot on the street and then parked with a jerk, cutting the engine so suddenly she was worried he'd do actual damage. He crossed the street just two steps ahead of her, so that she had to trot in a pair of already uncomfortable kitten heels just to reach the entrance beside him, rather than several paces behind him. She clutched vaguely at his arm as he shoved into the restaurant. She was well aware that Raj was probably on the floor, greeting patrons, that he might have seen them approaching through the restaurant's broad picture windows. That even before they crossed the threshold they would once again be in public. That might mean nothing to Tom, but then, that's why he needed her. She knew what it meant to rely on looking like someone other than who you were.

He shook his arm once, dislodging her hesitant fingers. *I don't care*, she said to herself. *I can take it all, just so long as he's over it by the time Jaime sees us.*

They were shown to their table by a tanned hostess with freak-ishly long, ropy limbs. Tom's eyes barely even skimmed her shoulders, her cleavage. No sooner had the gazelle deposited their menus than he bolted for the bathroom, knocking the table with his knee and nearly upsetting Mina's water. She cupped the cool glass and practiced breathing—four counts in, six counts out. It was just this dinner, really. Once they were at the inn, once he could sleep, things would look very different.

They would be late checking in, so she called ahead. "Why don't we just say we'll be there by midnight," she told an exasperated employee on the phone, some teenage girl chewing her gum loudly into the receiver. They were still a new family; nobody knew them yet at the Andover Inn.

When her husband slid back into his seat opposite hers, emitting the growl mixed with a sigh that was his usual sign-off each night when he finally climbed into bed beside her, Mina felt such relief, such longing that she was almost embarrassed, as she so often was by her private thoughts. She leaned across the table, mindful of their water glasses, and reached to cradle Tom's head with her hand, brushing her fingers through his close-cropped hair. She'd always loved that he kept it short, loved the way it sprung back at her touch like fresh-cut grass.

"How are you feeling?" she said. "I've got Advil if you need it?"

"No," he said, "I'm sorry I've been like this. I promise once I've got some dinner in me I'll be improved."

"Well, it's nice to see you, improvement or no," she said, stroking his hands with her thumbs.

"Min, I tried to explain last night, if you knew what hell on earth it's been in that office this month "

She shook her head, careful to keep a certain look on her face, something like tender dismissal.

"I wasn't," she said. "I was just being honest. It's so good to see you. We can go right to sleep, just the second we get to the inn. Once we've got a good meal in you. But I really do worry about you."

He nodded and drew his hand back. They opened their menus.

"Fuck me, Dawes, it isn't fair. What, do you have a painting of yourself crammed in a closet somewhere back at the manse, aging for you?"

Mina winced, still unaccustomed to the way Rajiv Dhalwala, the silver-tongued owner of the restaurant, seemed to cast aside his gracious front-of-house demeanor as soon as he spotted her husband. They'd rowed crew together at Princeton and trained side by side at Goldman until Raj had decided finance wasn't for him, and they still spoke to each other as though they were pumping up for a race, or goading each other into one more shot at some bar on Stone Street. Usually, Tom loved it—loved being called an asshole from across a genteel Wellesley dining room, loved the way forks paused for a moment before the general music of the restaurant resumed when people realized that the disruption had come from the owner himself. But tonight, she saw her own exhaustion mirrored as Tom's eyes widened and then adjusted. She smiled at him, and he nodded.

"Raj, my brother," Tom said, standing to shake his friend's hand. "I see you're still conning people into eating this crap."

"I've told your husband once, I've told him a thousand times," Raj said to Mina, kissing the back of her hand with a flourish. "If you call ahead, I'll always save you a window table! We can't have you out here among the riffraff!"

She never knew whether he was going to fawn over her or ignore her completely. Truth be told she preferred the latter; when he was like this, touching her wrists and clutching her upper arm and glowering at her like she was some just-ripened exotic fruit to be sliced and pared for one of his fusion dishes, it was all too easy for her to imagine what his role must have been back at Princeton. Always at Tom's side but shorter, stockier, sweatier. His face a collection of soft, rounded features, as though a stronger face had been smashed against the wall and remained that way. When he flirted with her, however harmless or false it was, she could only imagine him approaching the women at the crew parties, talking, getting them loose and lubricated, preparing them for the moment when her husband would swoop in for the kill.

"Maybe he prefers life among the riffraff," she said, smiling up at him and returning her hand to her own lap. Tom cleared his throat and sat down again. Raj remained at the table, looming over them, crossing and uncrossing his arms.

"Sure," he said. "Sure, sure he does. This is why you've all settled in Greenwich. Living in a little garden shed, was it? Have I got that right, Monsieur Dawes?"

"All right, Raj, ease up," Tom said. "I know deep down you're happy to see us."

"Not pretending otherwise," Raj said. "I've got a killer new dish actually, I've been hoping for someone I trust to stop by so I can test it out. Might be a bit out there for the good folk of Wellesley, Mass. They're happy with their tandoori chicken and nothing too spicy, thanks much."

"You don't even have a tandoor oven here, you fraud," Tom replied. "And you still talk about this place like it's the boonies. You are that worst kind of New York City snob. You can take the kid out of Queens, but . . ."

"Don't even finish that, it's tired before it's been said," Raj said, and began describing his new curry to Tom.

Mina watched her husband listen. So little about his face had changed since the night they'd met that the few concessions to age were all the more unsettling. He looked like a handsome young man who'd been exposed to some sort of apocalyptic weather conditions, the skin on his cheeks and nose and neck strafed by wind or hail. If he went more than a day without shaving, now, he looked grizzled rather than scruffy and adorable. There was a general heaviness around his eyes and mouth, as though the handsome original face had been simply weighed down, pebbles placed somewhere beneath the skin to drag it all toward his chin. When he smiled (or, as was the case tonight, grimaced) wrinkles fanned out from the corners of his eyes, like fragile clay that hadn't been kept long enough in the kiln.

And still, she knew, he was handsome. In an unusual way, more than just daily handsome. If he sat down next to you on the train, you'd blink and look again.

She felt a sudden urge to lean across the table, knocking over the water glasses if necessary, to kiss each of the wrinkles emanating from the corner of his left eye.

"So," Raj said, clapping his hands. "I'll pull out my special Tom Dawes bottle of scotch, of course, but what can I bring you, darling?"

She shivered again at the false obsequiousness, the hollow chivalry. "I'm sticking with water for the moment," she said.

"I'm not," Tom said.

"I don't blame you," Raj chortled, pausing for a moment and looking at them both before he continued. "Greenwich must be a bit of a fishbowl right now, no?"

Of course he was going to ask, because the man had not one truly tactful bone in his body. He knew that she was friends with Isabel. He'd come down to Greenwich for Tom's fiftieth; he'd probably kissed Isabel's hand, for God's sake.

"I've barely been there, to tell the truth," Tom began, and she could see him parrying with himself, trying to say as little as possible and keep a smile on his face. "You can imagine the scene downtown. It's not pretty."

"Well of course it isn't. Did you guys think it would be?"

Tom gripped his fork, lifting it from the table and then replacing it with such exaggerated care that it was more disturbing than if he'd thrown it right at Raj.

"Easy there," he said. "I wouldn't be saying 'you guys,' if I were you. Weiss is its own animal."

"But of course," Raj said, back to soothing. "And D'Amico made his own bed to lie in, I'm sure. How's he holding up? They've got kids, right?"

"Well, he has a lot to answer for," Tom said. "No way around it, right? History is not going to be kind to Bob D'Amico." Raj chuckled as though Tom had told an off-color joke.

"I think we can all give them some privacy," Mina said. "I think a little empathy might be in order. This could have happened to anyone. Or to many people, I mean."

Tom looked up from his silverware and fixed his eyes on hers. Raj stood above them for a few moments more, dead weight, before saying something about Tom's scotch and bustling off, removing his suit jacket as he crossed the room.

They sat in silence until a waiter returned with the glass of scotch. It was a generous pour, something Tom usually frowned upon, because he said only frat boys and unrepentant alcoholics poured more than a few fingers' worth. It had always seemed to her that only alcoholics had to craft for themselves such a complex rule system, but she kept this to herself. The fact was that the alcoholics she'd grown up with guzzled Crown Royal and so on down the scale, and in that way her husband resembled not at all what she thought of as an alcoholic.

He drank the scotch down in one gulp.

"Get up," he said then.

"Excuse me?"

"Get up. We're leaving."

"Sweetheart, we haven't even eaten."

"I. Am not. Fucking. Hungry. At the moment. Get in the car. We're driving to the inn."

Out on the sidewalk, the evening was unusually brisk for early October. Tom's fist was in the small of her back, propelling her across the street, toward the car. She stopped short when a car's headlights reeled up out of the darkness at the end of the block. Tom collided with her for a moment, an embrace without warmth.

"What the fuck was that," Tom said, though she noticed that he waited for the car to pass. You never knew, these days, who might be driving by with a camera phone. Her husband was nothing if not careful.

"I don't know what you're talking about," she tried.

"The hell you don't. It could have happened to anyone? Do me a favor, Min, try not to make your analytical debut when we're with the single biggest gossip in Princeton history. All good? Can we agree at least on that? You show an ounce of fucking judgment? Maybe some consideration for the man who's been working around the clock to keep you sitting in that house without anything to worry about?"

"Tom," she said, placing her hands out in front of her as though there was a table, or anything solid, to balance against. She kept them there, in the air between them. "I'm sorry. All right? I'm tired, too. I misspoke."

"Misspoke!" he yelped, and for a terrifying instant she thought he might erupt into laughter. "Well, I do know one thing. I bet you're damn happy not to be Isabel D'Amico. I bet your little-girl hero-worship bullshit, whatever it is that keeps you following her around like you're her kid sister, has taken some hits the past few weeks."

"Please stop. Please."

"You know how long it's going to take to clean up after him? Months, Mina. Maybe years. He put *us* in danger. I mean us, our family." He poked his own chest with his thick index finger, again and again. "Us. You, me, Jaime."

They both pretended not to flinch at their daughter's name.

"Jesus fucking Christ," Tom said, "I can't breathe." He started loosening his tie and then, absurdly, ripped it off over his head, started undoing the buttons of his dress shirt. He discarded the shirt like a damp towel on the hood of the Jag and stood there in his white undershirt, which he quickly untucked from the waist of his pants. He breathed through his nostrils for a moment, then continued.

"You know what nerve that takes? To put everyone in danger like this? It's not just us—I'm all for the people who hate him now, but they don't get it. *Everyone* will suffer. It's unconscionable, what he's done. It is. And now I've got my wife running her mouth off about how it could have happened to anyone? Jack all *happened* to him. He *did* it. And you think that could've been me?"

"All I meant," she said, "all I was saying, was that maybe he's just the first domino to fall. I mean isn't that what everyone's saying? Everyone was a little extended and now things will have to change? I mean maybe that's, you know . . ."

"Oh, thank you for pointing out the silver lining," Tom said, holding his thumbs and index fingers like guns and pointing them at each temple. "First domino to fall. That's a sharp turn of phrase there, sweetheart. You sound like quite the expert. Tell me more, by all means. Lay it out for me."

He had his hands on his hips and as he spoke sometimes he threw them into the air above his head in disgust. When he did this his undershirt rode up, showing his lower stomach, taut, and the tops of the pelvic muscles that cut across his lower torso at diagonals. It was her favorite part of his body.

She felt the stinging behind her nose, so similar to the way it felt when she was about to sneeze, and she swallowed several times, quickly. He hated it when she cried.

"I don't know why you're talking to me like this. I've done everything I can to be helpful and—"

"Damn it, Mina, do you think we're morons? Do you think I'm a complete fucking incompetent? I may not be the CEO of Weiss and Partners, and Lord knows I can imagine how hard it's been for you to keep your head high around your little friend, but I guess it just turned out pretty lucky for you that you didn't hold out for the CEO, right? I may not be the top dog, but things are pretty sweet for you, aren't they?"

She was crying now. She couldn't help it. He continued to rail at her—her ignorance, the pressures she put on him, the fact that he, Goldman, that they'd done *nothing* wrong. That Bob D'Amico had been the only idiot on the Street who thought he could keep taking the risks everyone else had forsaken months earlier, for fuck's sake,

Mina, *years* earlier. Bob thought he was so much fucking smarter than us, he kept repeating. Look where it got him. We were careful. You have no idea what you're talking about.

"Get in the car," he said, finally, when another car went by, its white headlights washing over them like judgment. She thought the car slowed a bit as it passed, but she couldn't say for sure.

"Get in the car," he repeated.

"No," she replied. He looked at her in disbelief. For the first time in so long, she did not question her own resentment. Her husband was being unfair. The fact that he wasn't a violent man, that she wasn't a battered wife, didn't excuse this. She was a grown woman, and she could call his bluff. It was a risk, to do so, but she could take it.

She put one hand to her chest and it fluttered there, as though it couldn't quite endorse her sudden boldness.

"Cut it out, Tom. Just, enough. I've apologized for, quite frankly, not really doing anything wrong in the first place. So just stop. If you're going to talk to me like this, I will get myself a second room when we get there. I swear to God I will. And you can sleep alone."

Tom's face set and he was still for so long that she really did believe, for a second, that he might hit her for the first time in their marriage. Wasn't this a crisis, wasn't everyone saying that their lives would never be the same? That this was the kind of meltdown that might come once in a generation? And that was them. They were this generation; she'd married into it. If their lives were never to be the same, what better way to usher in their impending doom than a short, sharp shock of violence to punish them both? What better way to say good-bye to the life they'd made than to realize that they barely knew themselves, in the end. That they could apply pressure to their own fragile bonds and learn that, rather than cracking them, it might turn them instead into completely different people?

"Get in the fucking car," he said. "I don't have to speak to you at all, Mina. Have it your way."

She knew it wasn't victory, not really. But she got in the car. The click of her seat belt across her chest, discomfort from an outside source, came as sweet relief.

LATER, SHE LAY IN BED waiting for him. When he emerged from his shower in a fresh white undershirt and a clean pair of silk boxers, the sleep outfit she'd packed for him, he did not look at her. She turned out the light, then waited before reaching over to him where he sat up against the headboard and lunging awkwardly to put her arm around him. He let his head fall to her shoulder.

He didn't open his eyes, didn't lift his head. He was stiff at first, his shoulders beneath her arms. He had corners, like a box, like a briefcase. But slowly, as she had so many times, she felt him ease into her body, lose his edges. His body was warm from the shower, though he'd dried his hair before coming to bed. He hated a wet pillow.

"I'm sorry I yelled," he said.

"I know." She ran her fingers along his skin, tracing the hairs on his forearms in little whorls.

"All I meant, when I said you must be glad not to be her. I just mean—I can't imagine him doing that to her. To those kids."

She made a soft sound in the back of her throat, a sound she knew Tom would interpret as gratitude, agreement. But she meant everything she'd said to him tonight. She believed, as strongly as anything else about this, that Bob had not done anything truly wrong. Because the man had his flaws, he was immature, he had an anger problem. But he wouldn't put Isabel in danger. He might make her look foolish, but not craven, not vile.

Mina believed that more than she believed anything about her own marriage; this was what she couldn't say.

"I just can't see it," Tom said. "Putting your wife through that. A real man doesn't do that. Can you imagine what that girl's been going through at the high school?"

"Oh, honey, they're just teenagers."

He didn't answer. When Jaime had insisted that they let her apply to boarding schools, she'd given them dozens of reasons. More challenging academics. Learning to live away from home. Meeting people from other parts of the country. They'd known, all three of them, what the problem was. Jaime was frizzy haired and stocky limbed and hated makeup, hated group sports, described herself without bitterness or recrimination as someone who needed only one or two friends. She'd wanted out of Greenwich Prep, out of the home Tom had built for her. He'd never used the words *betrayal*, or *rejection*, but Mina knew how he felt.

"I could never put my girls through that," Tom said again, his face buried in Mina's shoulder.

"We know that," she said, her lips brushing his ear. She had no certainty that Jaime *did* know that, but speaking up for herself was a privilege their daughter had relinquished when she left home at age fourteen, wasn't it?

"Would you really have left me alone in here?" came her husband's voice, small, sounding much farther away from her than he was. "Would you really have gotten another room?"

"I don't know."

Tom's shoulders shook, and she realized that he was about to cry. She circled him tighter in her arms and braced herself against his sobs, flooded with gratitude, with a silly, swelled gratitude, for the man she'd just realized he wasn't going to become.

"We're all right, Tom. We're okay. You said it yourself. It's not over yet, but we're okay."

"You were right," he whispered. His lips were so close to her ear that the sound of his voice tickled. He was smearing his tears across their cheeks, dampening the hair at her temple. "You were right. I'm sorry I screamed."

He kept breathing beneath her arm, his body expanding and then receding, reliably, like an ocean tide coming close and then moving away. He was here.

"I was thinking today," he said. "After you called. About the house. How we were thinking, maybe, we'd buy a house up here, even if we only meant to use it two or three times a year."

She put her lips to his forehead again, thankful that he'd said "we," thankful that they'd both been thinking of the same thing all afternoon.

"I'm sure all Bob can think of right now is how unfair, that this has happened to him and only to him. But it's happening to all of us. We won't be allowed to say any of the things we want out loud, not anymore."

"You can say them to me," Mina said.

"But I'm serious, Min. We have to be careful, for a while now. We're okay, but we have to act as if we've lost something. They're going to want us to decide that our life, our whole life, has been wrong."

"You can say them to me," she said again. His hand made its clumsy way across the comforter until it found hers, consumed it. His thick fingers dug into her palm, moving in such steady circles that she could tell he was unaware of the motion.

"I don't understand what will happen," he said. "If he belongs behind bars, I don't know where they draw the line. We've all done exactly what we're trained to do."

"Stop."

"It's dumb luck, Mina. It was a flood that came and he was on the ground floor, and I just happened to be a few floors above him. If it comes back again and goes any higher, that could be us."

"No," she said. She heard her voice coming from deep in her chest, low and calm. "No, it couldn't."

Later, when his breathing had slowed, when she'd brought him first a glass of water and then a nip bottle of vodka, they shut off the lamp and turned to each other like children, wrapped tightly beneath the comforter. They clutched at each other's shoulders, as if the bed were a swimming pool and they did not know how to swim, were afraid of drowning.

THIRTEEN

I don't care," Madison said. "I don't care what we get. If it's your treat, then that means you decide."

The late-afternoon sunlight came angling through the Starbucks windows, hitting the scummy floor. It was amazing, she thought, how very much *the same* every single Starbucks was, no matter where you were. The women who streamed in and out of here all day buying their six-descriptor drinks wouldn't be caught dead in any other place this haphazardly cleaned, this likely to be breeding a whole host of health violations. And yet here they were, lulled by the sameness and the acoustic guitar music. And, of course, the convenient location on its corner just across from the town hall, a corner every Greenwich mother passed by at least twice during her day.

Madison hated this Starbucks; she hated the way it always smelled, like burnt coffee beans and old egg sandwiches and baby wipes and air freshener. They shouldn't use air freshener in places that served food. It was distasteful to her; she didn't want to be here.

She kept her gaze squarely on Amanda. She even tried not to let her eyes catch on anyone else in the room.

"I don't know," Amanda said. "I feel like, it's too muggy still for hot chocolate, but it's October now and that's what I want."

"No one's stopping you."

Madison had avoided her best friend with dedication and precision for nearly three weeks now. But when school broke that Friday afternoon, Amanda cornered her at the lockers with such ferocious single-mindedness that Madison knew it would be easier to give in than to resist.

Amanda squinted at the menu as if they didn't order the same exact thing every time they stopped here after school. *My treat,* she kept repeating, as though Madison could no longer afford to buy her own coffee. She knew this wasn't what Amanda meant, but still. It was insulting that her best friend, after months of seeming like she'd wanted slowly to extract herself from Madison's clutches so that she'd be gone before Madison noticed, thought that a free cup of coffee would be an enticing lure. That Madison would so easily be tricked into baring her soul over Frappuccinos. When she knew that all Amanda really cared about was cementing her own role in this drama, establishing herself as the keeper of the information. Because at the moment, like it or not, Madison had information that Amanda didn't.

They drifted over to the counter to wait for their frothy iced drinks—no one, in the end, had been bold enough to order hot chocolate. When they were finally seated at a small, grimy table, Madison felt a pang for her friend's open, unguarded expression, for the wholly unnatural cheer with which Amanda seemed to feel it was best to treat the whole situation.

"I just feel like we haven't gotten much time to talk," Amanda said. "Not for, like, two weeks. And I do want to be here for you. And I actually went into the city last Friday, and—"

"That's really sweet of you," Madison interrupted, "but I don't really feel like I need someone to, you know, 'be there' for me right now. Things are fine."

"Really? How's Isabel?"

"She's fine. You know her."

"And how are the boys?"

"They're fine, Amanda. They're not worried. Things can be stressful for my father at work without it being this tragic drama everyone seems to want it to be."

"Good," Amanda said. "I actually have something I want to talk to you about. And I'm so glad everyone's doing well. I just don't want the other things going on to get in the way of us, you know—"

"What*ever* do you mean?"

"Mad," Amanda began. "Whatever else happens, I'm here. You know that, right?"

"Oh, of course. You're the only one I can trust, right? You and"—and here she couldn't deny it, even to herself, it was pleasant knowing what was about to come out of her mouth—"you and your parents, right? The Levins family."

Amanda was staring down at the table, folding her straw wrapper into smaller and smaller rectangles. "Okay, just, logically. When has my father ever consulted me about one of his columns?"

"Am I supposed to be grateful that you didn't specifically request that your father go after my family for no reason?"

"Madison—I mean, yes, my father has his flaws, you know that I'm well aware of them, but at least—"

"But at least *his* flaws only hurt you? Right?"

Amanda looked up, finally, and fixed her eyes on Madison's face. "Why are you doing this to me?"

"To you? *To you?*"

"Yeah, Madison, I am experiencing you being a cold bitch to me right now as something that's happening to me. Is that allowed?"

Madison laughed.

"Well," she said. "None of it's really surprising. Like father, like daughter."

Amanda gazed up at her, her lips parted. This was not, Madison realized, the conversation her friend had expected.

Madison felt sympathy for the hurt she was causing, but no real regret. One thing her father's world had taught her was this. If there was some future point at which people might need you, might need even just a moment of your attention, your gaze, then you could offend them with impunity. The wounds would heal, however superficially. There was a reason, beyond just gruff, performed affection, that his lieutenants called him Silverback, after all.

"It's not my fault," Amanda said.

"It's funny how much everyone's loving saying that," Madison returned. "There's only one person at fault, right?"

Amanda was actually sputtering now.

"What was I supposed to do?"

"Probably nothing. But is it so impossible for you to understand the fact that I, just. You are literally the last person I want to talk to about this. I'm sorry. But this is how I feel."

What Madison had learned, in the space of three short weeks, was that there were as many strains of sympathy as there were of the more celebrated emotions, love or hatred or longing. Everyone's sympathy hit her in a different spot, from a different direction, some strains closer to condescending pity and others smelling like selfish fear. When you became untouchable, you were radioactive. Your presence called up the memories of ways they'd wronged you in the past, or the ways you might have wronged them, the recalled injustices transmitted to them as if through your skin. She knew Amanda would be so much less showy now with her support if it hadn't been months, really, since they'd been close, comfortable with each other.

Amanda began vigorously to slide her green straw into and out of its slot in the plastic cup, producing a squeak that scratched the back of Madison's neck.

"You didn't seem all that worried about being there for me over the summer," Madison said. "Now that my problems are suddenly famous, you want to be best friends again? You want to know all my secrets?"

"I don't believe that's actually what you think of me. Not really."

"You can believe whatever you want, Amanda."

Then they both stopped talking for a while.

"You know you can call me at any time," Amanda said eventually. "My house is always open to you. Three o'clock in the morning or not."

"Amanda," Madison said, thinking of the way her mother would admonish her when she reached for a second éclair from the Payard box Mina Dawes had brought back from the city, the perfect Isabel blend of disinterest and authority, "I can't go over there right now. I need to be with my family, and your father doesn't approve of us. We're evil, right? We're oblivious?"

Amanda stood, shouldered her bag, and left her Frappuccino sitting on the table. She seemed to be weighing some invisible options before she finally spoke again.

"Why don't you just ask your father," she said, finally, with such steel in her voice that Madison couldn't help but be impressed. "If he's such a martyr, if it's so unfair that everyone's blaming him, why don't you just ask him to explain?"

Madison kept her gaze neutral, careful not to glare.

"Oh," Amanda said, "let me guess. He still hasn't come home. He still hasn't even thought to check in with his children."

"No, not everyone can be as *hands on* as your father, Amanda."

"Fine. So why don't you go find him? You're not kept on lockdown, Mad. Why don't you take the train in and ask him?"

"Amanda," Madison said, digging her fingernails into the skin of her upper thigh, ready to tear right through her jeans, "do you think that if I went to go talk to my father, it would be because of your advice? Do you think I need *your* advice?"

"Nope," Amanda said, "wrong. It's because you're afraid of what you'll find. So if I were you, I'd wait, Madison. I'd wait before I started calling everyone else a coward."

MADISON REMAINED AT THE TABLE after Amanda left; she wasn't sure how conspicuous she'd become to the other Starbucks patrons. Surely if she lifted her head, if she looked away from her fingernails and her drink, she'd see the telltale signs. The nervous eyes hastily averted, the mothers' hands firm on the backs of necks to make sure no one turned around, craned to get a better look. She'd been that child. It had been her neck, Isabel's hand.

And then he slid into the chair across from her.

"Hey," Chip said. He twirled a set of keys on his left index finger. She looked at his finger, watched the tendons in his hand jump each time the keys whirled through the air.

"Hi," she said.

"Just drove over from the senior parking lot," he said.

"Juniors are allowed to park there?"

"Yeah, well, I know a guy." He brushed his thumb to his chin and looked away, looked back at her and grinned. "But you're not asking the right questions, Madison." He jiggled the keys in the air in front of her, like a pet owner trying to coax a trick from a distracted puppy.

"Where, you should be asking, did these come from? Come outside."

He stood and left without looking back to see if she'd followed, leaving her to bundle her things together, endure an excruciating moment of uncertainty about whether or not to bring her unrequested Frappuccino. She left it. When she emerged onto the Avenue, he was waiting, shielding his face from the sun with one hand.

"Anytime, I don't mind waiting out here," he said. Then he clicked something on his key chain and a car behind him beeped its reply.

"You got your license," she said.

"Yes, ma'am."

"Well. Congratulations? Enjoy."

"Enjoy . . . what? Your jealousy?" He tipped his head to one side like he was trying to listen to something she couldn't hear and she felt that gesture settle in her chest, heavy at first but then settling down like a light dust over everything, like she wouldn't be able to have a single thought anymore that wouldn't carry with it a trace of that gesture.

"So here's the thing," he said. "I know you and Amanda are usually, like, attached at the hip after school, but I saw her drive off, and I wonder if I can snag you today."

"Schedule's wide open," she said. She liked that reply. It was encouraging but not desperate, which had begun to feel like an impossible note to strike.

"I just wanna drive," he said. "I just wanna cruise around, you know?"

"Yes. Yeah. Sounds good."

"It's the black Mercedes over there. Usually, you'd find it in spot 220. If you're ever looking for it."

He drove up into Cos Cob, the windows down. He seemed focused on driving, his hands at the ten and the two, his shoulders squared. She didn't know how much to talk. He put her in charge of the radio and she hunched awkwardly forward in her seat, her finger pressed to the dial, and couldn't decide on a station.

"Enough, enough," he said finally. "When you start driving you'll see how annoying that is, the music constantly changing." She froze in her seat, still holding her body awkwardly forward, afraid to move and resettle. But then he started humming along to "Fortunate Son" and she realized the word *annoying* had meant nothing at all.

"My dad loves these guys," he said, and she swallowed, caught herself before the knee-jerk response of, "Mine too."

It had rained that afternoon, perhaps the last of the late-summer sudden flashes of rain, and everything was unbearably green. The houses were all tucked up behind the trees, only their wrought-iron gates visible from the road, which curved and weaved its way up farther and farther from the train line down below.

Chip was a smooth driver, braking into the curves, accelerating out of them—he'd explained to her that this was one of the things you learned before you took the test—and she felt almost soothed, as though she could fall asleep in the seat beside him and he'd just keep driving her around. Her mother had once told her that she'd had a rough spell, as a baby, couldn't sleep through the night, and had only quieted down when Isabel walked her down Park Avenue to Grand Central, then back up almost to Seventy-Second Street, the wide avenue silent, nothing but them and the flowers planted in the middle of the street and the doormen winking at them from beneath forest green awnings.

Probably no one's going to teach me to drive this year, she thought. He always said he would, but now he won't have time.

She observed the idea as it visited her, passed her by. It had been almost three weeks, and he still hadn't come home.

"You haven't come to any more games," Chip said finally. Every part of her body felt lighter than it should be in an unpleasant way, like she hadn't eaten for days, but it also felt as though she'd been grinding her teeth for two weeks and had only just realized she'd stopped.

She cupped her hand around her seat belt and ran it back and forth. She wanted to hold Chip's hand, but he was driving, and besides that would be a bizarre thing to do down here in the real, non-dreaming world.

"I know," she said, "I've wanted to. I've been busy, after school."

He managed to look toward her without taking his eyes from the road, just inclining his head in her direction, really.

"Can't, or would rather not?"

She peered up at the leaves above her window, sunlight streaming through them and creating patterns like lace on her skin. Something about her bare legs in the seat, so close to him, felt too exposed. It was so much easier than it usually would have been for him to touch the skin on her upper thighs.

"I've been busy," she repeated.

"Look," he said, "Wyatt and those guys are assholes. I don't know if you know this, but people have spent way more time talking about what an asshole Wyatt is than about, you know, any other part of it."

"I don't care about those guys," she said, and it was only hearing this sentence out loud that made her realize it was true. Her father was her father. As soon as he came home, as soon as his presence reoriented the house. His thunderclap hands on her shoulders while she ate breakfast, surprising her, kneading the muscles between her neck and spine. That was her father. The men who worked for him called him Silverback, and to his face, so you knew it was admiring and not bitter or sniping. What did she care what Wyatt Welsh, of all the voice-cracking boys she knew, said about him? This was what they'd been for, all the little pieces of her father's advice. He'd given them to her like poker chips, trusting her to know when it was smart to cash them in.

"I don't care what Wyatt says, really."

"I know you don't," Chip said. "I know you're, you know. You don't seem like you give a shit, honestly. But just in case he's been bothering you."

Every few seconds Chip leaned forward to gaze up through the windshield, some unconscious part of him expecting things to come flying down at them through the trees, danger without warning.

She wanted to reply but she didn't know how petty she could be in front of Chip, how much of his sense of who she was relied on the fact that she was always terrified and mute in his presence.

"Actually, he's been texting me. To apologize. The texts are so weird, it's so obvious that Suzanne types them out for him. Like, so eager for me not to hold a grudge. It's actually sort of . . . I don't know. Funny? Pathetic? Something."

Chip smiled. "That sounds like Suzanne. She wouldn't, you know—she wouldn't want your mom hating her, or hating Wyatt. She's careful like that."

She felt something rising in her throat, something so stifling that she opened her mouth to speak but waited a few extra seconds, knowing that her voice would betray her with its thickness, its soft whisper. Not tears, not sadness or embarrassment, but anticipation. She knew the perfect thing to say, she only wished Wyatt Welsh could be here to hear it.

"I don't talk about Wyatt with my mother," she said. "That would never cross my mind."

They were stopped at a red light. Chip was driving back toward school, toward her house, civilization. No one but Chip knew where she was right now.

"We should drive into the city sometime," she said. She didn't look over to see if he nodded. She took her hand from her lap and put it over his hand on the gear shift. Chip's hand hovered there at intervals, as if the car were untrustworthy and might shift into a different gear without his permission.

She left her hand there, curling her fingers around his knuckles, and waited for him to turn to her. This had to be it, without question. He was going to kiss her. They were in a car, weren't they?

"Yeah," he said. "We should do that sometime."

They both smiled, but not at each other. She kept her hand on his until the light changed, until he had to drive again, and he didn't so much as glance over at her side of the car. She knew that if his hands were free he'd brush his chin with his thumb, and the victory felt just the same—better, even—than if he'd leaned across the car to kiss her.

FOURTEEN

Lily stood with Jackson at the counter, trying not to wince each time the man sweating next to her knocked his elbow into hers or slurped unceremoniously at his giant bowl of ramen. It seemed like it could only be a matter of minutes before he started just dunking his head down directly to the soup's rim.

"Isn't this kind of rich for October?" she asked Jackson, no less skeptical than she'd been when he demanded she meet him here. "Isn't ramen, like, a winter lunch?"

"I'm telling you, everyone can't shut up about this place," he replied, sliding his arm around her waist and resting his chin on her shoulder, reading the menu along with her.

One thing she knew about her boyfriend: he couldn't resist a buzz. If his writer friends were talking about a new place, he had to have eaten there. He'd sometimes bluff his way through happy hour small talk and pretend he *had* been there, though he always waited until she had a night off to come into the city before trying the places out for himself. She'd once thought this was because he wanted to wait for her company, but his habit of jumping up to head to the bathroom right around the time the check hit the table had eventually disabused her of this dreamy notion.

"Which one are we supposed to get?"

"Either. One is vegetarian, though, and if you ask me, ramen without pork is just soup. And honestly, fifteen bucks isn't half bad for a huge bowl of ramen."

"Sure," she said. It hadn't occurred to her that a trendy new ramen counter on Kenmare would be quite literally a counter. That she'd have nowhere to sit.

Their orders decided, he began trying to coax her to talk, punctuating his words with the kisses he knew she loved, along the side of her neck and her earlobe.

"I haven't seen you in way, way too long," he started, wisely. She shrugged.

"You're the one who wanted to eat a big heavy meal. I voted we go straight home."

"I still can't believe you've got to go back before dinner," he said, ignoring her innuendo. "It's Sunday! You haven't seen the guys in forever, we could have met up with them later."

"Gonna grab my baby, gonna hold her tight," Lily sang. "My boyfriend would rather eat noodles first."

"I thought you'd need something fun!" he said, laughing when she raised an eyebrow. "I mean something sort of fun before the important fun. I just thought it would be nice for you to get to take a breath, finally."

"It hasn't been that bad."

"Bullshit," he said, signaling to their waiter. They ordered. Within seconds, several tiny ramekins of various pickled, neon vegetables were placed in front of them. Here, Lily couldn't help but think, was a meal Bob D'Amico would hate. Cramped, DIY, no pampering, peasant food. Checks all the trend boxes in all the wrong ways.

"Bullshit," Jackson picked up where he'd left off. "I'm sure it's been a zoo. I just hope you're taking notes."

"Please," she said, "please don't start that."

"Lil, come on. I'm just saying. If you're going to do this for a decade of your working life, at least be smart about it. You remember that girl the year ahead of me at J school?"

"How could I forget," she said, and began mouthing the words to the story even as he launched into it once more.

"She was always threatening to transfer to Fiction, which was a joke because it wasn't even the same school. Like she just knew she could have applied to the Arts school and gotten in? Anyway, we all thought she would probably write a novel after we left. She was such a babe, every professor was always falling all over himself to help her out, take her around and introduce her."

"I would love, just once, to hear about this girl without hearing about how hot she was."

He nuzzled closer to her, partly in reassurance and partly because another couple had been jammed in beside them at the counter.

"Be that as it may, she didn't really seem to have the stomach to report anything, anyway. But then she sort of gives us all this big fuck you after graduation, when we're all basically interviewing for the same web jobs, some of which aren't even paid, and she takes this job working as the assistant to this Medusa publishing woman who's married to a big-time lawyer. Takes care of her kids."

"Yes," Lily said. "I remember."

"Well, she sold the memoir last month," Jackson interrupted. "Supposedly more than a million. So you never listen to me, but I'm always looking out for you, baby."

"I listen to you."

"Okay, but let's focus. What have you been thinking, in terms of once the worst part passes," he said. He'd unwrapped his chopsticks and started rubbing them together.

"What do you mean?" Their ramen arrived, and she looked down at the murk, the slab of pork floating somewhere just below the scallions, the noodles coiled around it. It looked like a cross section of human organs.

"I know you love the kids, so you've got to see them through this part," Jackson said. He started to attack his noodles. "But what about, like, say, January?"

It dawned on her. "In January?"

He pushed his bowl toward the edge of the counter and turned, wedging himself against their neighbors so he could look at her face.

"Please tell me you aren't going to stay at this job," he said.

"Why would I leave? Because of Bob?"

"Lily," he said. "Lily, come on. What do you think is going to happen when he comes home? It's going to be, you're going to be living under siege. The *Post* has been running pictures of him practically every day. Coming out of the lobby. The building's on Park, right? The apartment?"

She remembered one of the first headlines, the one Jackson had sent her the day after it happened: "DAMN IT, D'AMICO." She knew it had been a real crowd pleaser, not least with her boyfriend.

But that had seemed like it might be all. She'd been bracing the kids, that first morning—the morning she hated to think about—for some cataclysmic shift in their daily routines. Homeschooling, a more secluded house somewhere in another state, whatever it would take. But nothing had happened. She'd prepared herself for flashbulbs when she walked up to the house in the morning, reporters' stubby fingers reaching out toward Madison every time they walked through the streets of Greenwich. She'd imagined herself shepherding the children through their days like an underqualified bodyguard. But none of this had come to pass, and her initial bewilderment had given way to genuine awe when she considered how much Bob must be paying to make sure this didn't happen. The black sedans must be everywhere in their neighborhood, their drivers the human equivalents of an electric fence, heading the intrepid truth seekers off at the pass.

"I can't leave," she said. "It hasn't been as bad as I thought it would be, but there's a lot going on. They think someone tried to break into the place on Park. And she gets hate mail, you know. Isabel. She's in her office on the phone with their lawyers all day, because apparently he refuses to meet with anyone yet. And she's got to gather the hate mail every day, which means some of these people actually have access to their home address."

"So he's waiting and maneuvering. He's figuring out his best bet. You could learn something, Lil. You're the one always telling me you're watching him to learn more about how he got where he is, aren't you?"

"He's a pretty employable guy, Jacks. I'm guessing he'll be able to find another job."

"Well," he said, "no, maybe not. I mean, you should hear how the DealBook guys are talking about this. People are talking about actual prosecution, Lily. If you wait too long, you won't even be able to get another nanny job out there on the Gold Coast. Nobody's going to want to touch anyone near that name."

"Don't be a drama queen," she said.

Jackson raised his eyebrows in dismay, but he'd resumed slurping his noodles, and she took advantage of his full mouth.

"He did the best he could with the information they had at the time," she said. "Everyone loves risk takers when they're right. And everyone loves Monday-morning quarterbacking, especially when it's a rich guy they're second-guessing. But one man doesn't create a tsunami. People are just obsessed right now because it's a good story. It's just rumors. It's going to blow over."

"Jesus," he said through the food. "Listen to you."

"In some ways, I mean, he's suffering more than anyone else. His long-term financial interests, if you look at it that way, they're completely aligned with all the other shareholders. No one wanted that bank to succeed more than he did. If he's such a villain, why didn't he sell off his stock? He still owned millions of shares, millions, when they had to file. He's got to be in as much pain as anyone."

Her boyfriend stared at her. He had stopped chewing.

"Lily, come on."

"He must know it could get worse," she mumbled. "You think he's not in pain? Trust me, he loves those kids. He's in pain."

"How would you know?" Jackson croaked, having finally swallowed his food. He was still watching her, his face slack with amazement. "You haven't even seen him yet."

"You don't understand," Lily said. She dipped her spoon just below the surface of the soup, then spun it around and brought it back up for air. "He was a lifer there. It was the only place he ever worked. He was a lifer."

"Who gives a shit," Jackson barked. "You don't owe this man anything. You've already proved your loyalty, trust me. *You* don't have to be a lifer, Lil."

"I'm not there because of what he can do for me," she said, but even as she spoke she could hear how thin her voice sounded.

"Okay," he said, "we can stick to the party line. But I know you, and you aren't stupid. You know as well as I do what a reference from him will do for you, down the line."

They ate the remainder of the ramen in silence, constantly jostling their neighbors to hold on to their counter space. When the cashier left an oil-stained scrap of paper by their place mats, the receipt, Jackson slid his arm back into position around her waist. It was that wheedling sort of affection, the kind you both use to stave off the explosions you know are waiting for you in just a few hours, or even minutes.

"You've got this, right?" he asked her, and she took out her wallet.

THAT NIGHT SHE HAD HER HANDS in the sink, submerged nearly to the elbows in the soapy, scalding water. There was something satisfying about this feeling, satisfying in a way that weighted you to the ground. Knowing that your hands would be chapped and abrased when you drew them back, that you were aging them with every moment you let them float in the harsh water without the thick rubber gloves Isabel was always urging you to use.

She knew the gloves would help, knew it was silly to refuse them—they were hardly an extravagance by the standards of this house. But when Isabel had first waved them at her, Lily had been able to think only of her own mother. Of the fragile lines that arced from her nostrils to the corners of her mouth when worry cinched her features together. Her mother had always tried to get her to wear gloves like that while she did chores, and Lily had always refused. She couldn't refuse her own mother and not Isabel. There was no logic to this argument, but it was what Lily thought when she looked at them.

She lifted one hand from the sink and was examining her own knuckles, red and angry, when Isabel came into the kitchen. Or, to be precise, when Lily glanced up to see Isabel's reflection in the dark window, leaning against the kitchen door frame with performed ease, propping the swinging door open with one foot. Lily yelped and dropped the glass she was holding. A plastic one the boys used, thank God, but still. She hadn't seen Isabel for days and she didn't like it that, when they were finally in the same room again, her boss had caught her in the midst of incompetence.

"Jesus, sorry. How long have you been standing there?"

"Not long." Isabel crossed to the sink, letting the door swing shut behind her. She stood beside Lily and stared down into the suds, as though she'd been called over for a consult.

"Why are you scrubbing these by hand? I told you, just throw them in the dishwasher."

"You don't want to risk the crusted bits making it through," Lily said, her voice still wavering. Her whole body vibrated still from that moment, seeing Isabel standing just over her shoulder, staring.

"My mother taught me to do this, and it's a hard habit to break," she continued. Isabel nodded.

"Well, as is the case with all mother-enforced habits, I suppose." She sighed and looked down once more at the sink. "But did your mother pay for an extravagant, inconceivably expensive dishwasher? Because we did, and we've still got you in here every night scrubbing your fingers red. Anyone looking in our window might think you have one of those thoughtless, oblivious housewives for a boss, Lily."

They both quivered at the image, at the idea of anyone peering into the house, then pretended that they hadn't.

"That's something from *my* mother," Isabel said. "To spend the money but then fret over it every time I look at the evidence. That's her voice, lingering in the house."

Lily nodded and otherwise stayed very still. Isabel was existing in some unaltered space, and she did not want to remind her of reality, that they hadn't spoken for more than a few seconds here and there since the initial news. She didn't want Isabel to read on Lily's face everything Jackson had said today, about the things that mattered to this woman.

After lunch, after the ramen, she'd pushed aside her remaining, tugging annoyance with him and convinced him that they should go back to his apartment in Brooklyn before they went to meet his friends. She'd grabbed his keys from him as soon as they were inside the building and raced ahead of him on the stairs, removing items of clothing and letting them drop down behind her to hit him in the face as he scrabbled up behind her. She hadn't showered when she got back to Greenwich; she'd cut it too close to dinner. So she had that thing, this evening, where if she turned her head suddenly to one side, or darted her tongue to a corner of her mouth to catch a rivulet of sweat, she'd get a dizzying whiff of the smell of Jackson's skin. She had a soreness on her left breast that she knew was developing into small, purple bruises the sizes of fingerprints. She kept these sensations to herself, on nights like this, smiling at the zaps of pain whenever she made a sudden move to catch a tipped juice glass, or wipe a sauced chin.

"Everyone's eaten?"

"Yes, absolutely. They're in bed."

Isabel smiled, her face almost coy. She crossed to bring down a wineglass from an upper cabinet, then went into the pantry just off the kitchen where they kept the lesser bottles, the everyday overflow from the cellar. She returned with a bottle of red and opened it with two smooth tugs that drew the cork from its berth without resistance, as though it were being drawn up through water. These were the small things, Lily knew, the things you couldn't learn, no matter who you worked for, no matter how much you watched them. The way Isabel could open a bottle of wine and not be aware of her own movements, the way she could be graceful without observing herself—Lily knew she wouldn't have that, not ever. She'd made her peace with this. Cribbing from someone who did wasn't the worst thing in the world.

Isabel poured a glass of wine and then looked back over her shoulder, reaching up again to the cabinet. She raised her eyebrows.

"Sure," Lily said. "If it's all right with you."

"Well, I'm inviting, so I guess there are new rules," Isabel said, laughing softly. She reached up for a second glass. She was wearing tight black jeans and a black tank top that scooped low over her modest cleavage, the patterned scarf knotted at her neck the only bit of color on her body. She looked like a teenage cat burglar. The narrow hips, the muscles on each arm taut like stretched shoelaces. As Isabel aged it was all looking ever so slightly tenser, as though the muscles themselves were rising closer to the surface of the skin, but still this was a body any woman—a twenty-four-year-old, even—would want, would consider committing murder to have. Another reason, Lily knew, the other, older wives hated Isabel, even as they smiled and angled for invites to her fund-raisers. She was younger than they were and she exercised, sure, there was a full gym in the basement, Mina dragged her to a class every so often. But it wasn't her life. She wore the taut thighs, the flat stomach, the tennis player's angled hips, just as she wore everything else. As something she'd inherited, without giving it another thought. The only thing that kept Lily from wanting to pinch the whippet stem of her wineglass, pinch it until it shattered and cut her skin, was that there were so many other women in their town who wore their good fortune with no humility at all, and didn't it make more sense to focus your resentments where they really belonged?

Sometimes she fought the suspicion that it was worse to act as if you didn't notice all that you had, but that was only sometimes.

"Thank you," she said to Isabel.

"Oh, we should've done this first," Isabel said, clucking her tongue and gesturing at their wine. She tapped her glass against Lily's, producing a noise like a bell. Lily double-checked that the glass hadn't cracked.

"If we're cheers-ing to anything," Isabel began, "it's to you, Lily. I want you to know how much I appreciate your help these past few weeks. I haven't been—feeling well. As I'm sure you've noticed."

When will this woman learn, Lily thought, that I see her?

"You know I'd do anything for those kids," she said.

"They're barely kids anymore," Isabel mused, and Lily wasn't sure whether she was meant to reply. "The boys are already so big. And Madison, well. Madison's practically her own sovereign nation at this point."

"You know that," Lily began, fingering the stem of her wineglass. They both drifted over to the table, without agreeing, as if to acknowledge the fact that Madison as topic necessitated an actual conversation, not just hovering over the sink.

"You know that I'm keeping an eye on her. I just wanted to say."

"I appreciate that," Isabel said, gulping her wine.

"I know how smart she is, but sometimes, at that age, you know, that isn't necessarily a good thing."

"I'm wondering these days if it's a good thing at any age," Isabel said. She set down her glass and pressed the palms of her hands flat against the wood of the table, shifting her weight forward, then looked up at Lily.

"So," she said. "Look. I'm going into the city."

"Tonight? It's Sunday."

Isabel frowned at her wine. Lily could see that her bottom lip was chapped raw, that she'd been chewing at herself. It was jarring to see such an unsightly flaw on Isabel's face, to see that one part of her hadn't been buffed and moisturized somewhere behind a closed door before she presented herself to even so inconsequential a part of the outside world as her children's nanny. Lily bit her own lip, again tasting that flash of Jackson, the skin behind his ears, the soft skin just above his hip bones.

"I'll be here in the morning," Isabel said.

"I don't understand. You're going to drive in and drive back tonight?"

"I've called for a car. I'm going to get Bob. I think . . . don't you think? That it's time for him to start sleeping here?"

Lily kept silent. Isabel reached across the span of the table and put her fingers to the crook in Lily's elbow.

"Oh, Lily, come on. I know you feel you can't speak your mind right now, with all that's going on, but if I can't talk to you, then I can't talk to anyone."

This was frankly bullshit, Lily knew, but it didn't matter. It hit her right where it was meant to.

"Okay," Lily said. "The kids will be happy to see him. But I'm sure, if he's stayed this long, there's work—"

"Well, there's work *here*," Isabel said, something animal coming into her voice. She tightened her grip on Lily's arm. "There's work to be done here. They deserve an answer."

Lily wanted to ask if Isabel had meant to say, or had wanted to say, "We deserve," but she didn't think they'd wandered far enough from their normal lives yet.

"Why now?" she asked, and Isabel smiled. "I can imagine you must be concerned, but things are okay here. Won't he come back in his, you know, on his own schedule?"

"Madison came up to find me on Monday," Isabel said, pausing to let the image form in Lily's head. The kids knew they weren't allowed into the master bedroom uninvited. "As you can imagine, I was caught off guard. And she wouldn't leave, she had all these questions for me. She wanted answers. And now I've gotten a few troubling reports from the security guys. I'm sure you've seen the cars. Some kid was driving her around Cos Cob two days ago. And my daughter is, as we both know—how to say this—self-directed."

"And you're worried she'll go in by herself," Lily said. "To see him."

"Yes."

"And you aren't sure what she'll find."

They both put down their wineglasses and Lily knew that if Isabel stared at her, if there was an unadorned silence left to absorb Lily's rudeness, then this would be the turning point. That would mean things were moving slowly back into place, into the old rhythm.

But Isabel just smiled again, and nodded.

Lily's stomach contracted. She had always assumed, about Bob, but she had never seen a single sign. She'd been watching, more carefully than they could ever know. But she'd never seen him check the wrong phone at a strange time, or stutter when he had to explain a mysterious, midday errand. He was never one of the ones leering at the rare unattended single woman at one of the parties. Never, ever.

"I've called for a car. I won't be driving. I just need you to stay in the house. You can sleep in Lena's room downstairs, tonight. Just be somewhere you'll hear them if they need you."

Lena's room, a spare bedroom—not a guest bedroom but the spare, which was different—was wedged unceremoniously down a small corridor that led off from the den. It had never, to Lily's knowledge, been used by Lena. She couldn't think what sort of emergency would ever require that the head housekeeper, responsible only for the inanimate residents of the house, would have to spend the night.

Isabel's afraid, she thought. Not because Madison asked her some pushy questions the other night. She's never been afraid of Bob before. So, then, what?

"Of course," she told Isabel. "Of course I will."

BUT THREE HOURS LATER, as midnight approached, Lily was sitting on the top step of the main staircase. If necessary, she could be holding the boys in her arms in a matter of moments, calling for Madison to come out to meet them. But this was ridiculous logic. This was a contingency plan appropriate for a home invasion, something she felt certain was virtually impossible to pull off for this particular home.

Isabel had mentioned the black cars, she realized now. That had been a missed opportunity; her boss had been sitting across from her, fingering the stem of her wineglass, casually mentioning "security guys," and Lily hadn't asked the right questions. Hadn't even gathered any information. Security guys—did that mean they were watching *her*?

She felt her back stiffen, her chin punching the air in front of her face. Let them watch her. Let them see the millions of tiny things she did for these kids, every day, without thinking. Putting the fear of God into Mina and her crew the other day, that was the least of it.

The other possibility was that no one cared just yet about Bob's children, that they wanted a picture of the man himself brought low. Eyes bloodshot, cheeks carpeted with stubble, mouth slack with fear and exhaustion. Which meant that, starting tomorrow, her role as bodyguard might still come into effect.

Even as she considered this, though, she knew that Isabel wouldn't let this happen. They'd go hide out on Shelter Island, where the local law enforcement would act like Isabel's own private National Guard if she so much as asked them to do it, before she'd let that happen.

But at what point did hunkering down exclude anyone beyond the children and Isabel? Where was the line between, say, hiring security guards to protect your kids, and hiring a professional security firm to assess the work being done by your employees?

She thought of Madison, that first morning, of how quick she'd been to trace the blade across Lily's neck, remind her of her own impermanence.

Lily sighed, stretching her body from her toes, then curled herself closer to the banister. She wrapped her fingers around the cool wood, its curves shapely, almost feminine. She knew, of course, the real reason Isabel was so upset by his absence. Bob D'Amico didn't do any more to raise these children than the man who came to clean the pool filters, and Isabel didn't need his help. It was the apartment in the city. It was his presence there on the nights he was expected home, in Connecticut, his presence there now. It was his refusal to draw himself over the lives of his family, his disinterest in crawling into bed with Isabel, resting his head on her chest, listening to the sound of her breathing. That he'd chosen to be alone. After all this, all this time they'd been married and she'd been working for them, and one thing Lily would not have guessed about Isabel was that this surely illusory part of marriage was what mattered to her in her own.

When Lily heard the noises from downstairs they were not what she'd been expecting. She'd been waiting either for Isabel to return alone—this, in truth, had seemed most likely—or for the stately rustlings that usually announced their arrival home together, the sounds of keys hitting porcelain trays and wooden hangers knocking together in the concealed closet in the foyer. The tiny noises that seemed so loud and obtrusive when you realized that they signified two bodies, the owners of which weren't speaking to each other much.

There had been one night when she'd asked for some time to go into the city to see a cousin's graduation from Hunter, but had come back on the Metro-North and taken a cab to the house rather than stay over with her parents. She'd relieved the housekeeper, who had agreed to stay to put the children to bed, and had been reading in the kitchen when they came home. They must have assumed that Lena, an older Ukrainian woman who inhaled with guttural sounds and sighed in a falsetto whenever the twins did anything even a tiny bit rowdy, would be dozing already. Lily had heard the door slam harder than usual, heard a body thrown against it with unmistakable force. She was on her feet, moving toward the foyer, before she heard the rumblings of Bob's voice, Isabel's hissed replies, and realized that the words she was hearing were charged with erotic challenge and not malice or violence. She'd hovered there in the doorway for a second, more, longer than she would ever admit, before tiptoeing backward through the kitchen and sliding out through the mud room.

That might, in the end, be an ideal marriage, she'd thought then. Leave each other in peace, except for the days when you can't keep your hands off each other.

"Bob, *please*," she heard from downstairs. She crouched on the steps like a runner awaiting the starting pistol. There was a loud thud, some sizable mass hitting the floor, and she knew that whatever was happening would not be managed by Isabel alone.

But Jackson was wrong, she did listen to him, and she knew what he would say. Don't see anything. Wait until they've forgotten you're there, then listen.

The next sound, the clatter of something sliding from the table in the foyer, was loud enough that the boys might have heard it, and so Lily stood. She tried to jog down the stairs with brisk intent, the way she would on any other day, attending to any other task, and when she came into the foyer and saw them she kept her face neutral.

Isabel stood helpless above him, the front door still open behind her. Bob was splayed across the floor, twisted like he'd begun to flop himself over before thinking better of it. He had also knocked over the antique wooden table that stood beneath the mirror, its legs split like branches snapped for kindling. Lily had an absurd image, suddenly, of Bob D'Amico locking them in, barricading the house against outside intrusions. They could do this to all the furniture, tear it to pieces, feed the fireplace, wrap the children in blankets and teach them to survive without the world beyond their parents.

"Lily," Isabel was saying, "I need your help. Just help me get him standing. I can get him upstairs, just help me get him off the floor."

Isabel didn't seem surprised to see Lily, didn't seem caught off guard or overwhelmed with gratitude to see that her nanny had waited up. Lily swallowed the taste of something sour, but she didn't move. She didn't begin to help.

Bob rolled over onto his back, his knees pointing at the ceiling, and tried to lift himself up off the floor. It was threatening, almost, to see so much energy left dormant, like an exquisite gourmet summer meal left out to spoil in the sun, the cheeses growing sweaty skins, the salad greens wilting. His meaty upper arms, straining at the white dress shirt, looked more frightening now than they ever had in action. She was used to them flexing at intervals during even the most casual conversation, his hands in his pockets. She couldn't look at anything else, now; he was mewling there, on the ground, and all she could notice were his huge arms, the dark hairs on his knuckles. His thighs giant and tubular, clad uncomfortably in the silk legs of his trousers. The sickly, jaundiced-looking exposed strip of skin just above the top of his diamond-patterned socks. He'd always looked a bit off in the uniform, though, like he belonged in a wrestling singlet rather than formal attire. That wasn't because of what was going on right now. He'd always looked that way.

Why was he wearing a suit? Where had Isabel even found him?

"Jesus, Lily, help me!" Isabel barked.

"I'll never know," Bob was howling. "I'll never get it, not when they put me in the ground. They'll fucking bury me and I still won't understand why they let this happen to me."

This was private. Lily shouldn't be here, she did not want to go to them. She'd seen him drunk and jovial, drunk and vicious, they all had. But she'd never seen this and she couldn't be certain that some part of this wouldn't be preserved somewhere in some tiny, well-lit room in that black-out-curtained brain, that he wouldn't hate her the next time he saw her. She had never been afraid of Bob D'Amico before—nervous, anxious, but not afraid. But she watched him lift one leg and then let the foot drop to the ground, watched him keening like an injured animal, and she saw that he no longer had any reason to go along with anything, to tolerate any presence in his life that would remind him of any of these moments.

Why had Isabel brought him home like this? Her daughter was upstairs, the teenager with frown lines like a middle-aged woman, her shoulders perpetually stiffened lately, as if they were her only protection. The boys, the way they clutched each other in sleep every night. What about this man looked like something you'd want to bring into your home, the place where your children slept?

"Lily!" Isabel actually snapped her fingers. "Get over here. Please." She was back on her knees, trying to pull Bob up by his armpits. She gave up, letting him fall back to the floor, and clambered so that she was on top of him, straddling his body, holding down his pinwheeling arms.

Lily watched Isabel again try to lift her husband. What did you expect? she thought, and it was no longer just the moment, the act of bringing him home. Isabel had made a choice, sometime long before Madison, before the boys. She'd chosen him, and shouldn't this have been part of it, whatever she expected? Lily saw Isabel's humiliation, saw her futility, and she knew she should feel something closer to Isabel's pain. But all she could think was that Isabel had made some egregious error, long ago, and that now Lily and the children she cared for were going to be made to pay for it.

"Listen to me," Isabel said. He was still lying on his back with his eyes closed. She must have had a time of it, Lily thought, getting him into the car in the first place. He wrinkled his face in displeasure as Isabel's voice, so close, hit his ear.

"Listen," she said. "I don't care if you want to do this all night, but you are going to lower your goddamn voice until we get upstairs. Your children are asleep. I'm putting you into your bathtub and then I'll shut the door and you can scream at the walls all night if you feel like it, because I don't think they'll be able to hear you. I don't care. But not here. Get up."

He burped and it seemed to imbue him with a sudden clarity, for he sat up straight and took his wife's face in his hands. "Us, Iz," he said. "Happen to us. That's what I meant. It's not just me. I know that. I remember."

"All right," Isabel said. "All right, Bob. Let's go upstairs. Lily, are you going to help?"

"You shouldn't take him upstairs," Lily said. "I'll go check on the kids. They were sleeping, I don't know if they'll have slept through this."

She had already turned away and so didn't see Bob's face change, the clarity leave him again.

"I was always thinking of you, Iz. Always. Everything I've ever done has been for you," she heard him whimper, and maybe it was his sudden bellow, followed by a mottled gasp, that made her turn back just in time to see him falling.

He'd pulled himself up onto his knees, then flailed forward, slamming into the floor with his chin. She heard the crunch of his teeth, heard each of his limbs hit the ground separately. He lay there on the ground, splayed out like a crime scene outline, and Isabel stood just beyond where he could get at her.

He'd tried to touch his wife. He'd reached for her, Lily saw, and she'd stepped quickly away from him. She'd watched him fall.

Isabel looked up at her now, her face as blank as a bowl of milk.

"He fell," she said. She held Lily's gaze, for a moment, until Lily nodded. Then Isabel stepped forward, and they positioned themselves on either side of him.

"Honey," Isabel whispered, her voice artificially crisp. "You fell, Bob. Are you okay?"

"You fucking bitch," he muttered, and Lily gave his arm a little twist as they pulled him to his feet. Just a little bit, not enough to pull it from its socket. Isabel looked away, but Lily could see her twitching, maybe wanting to smile.

LATER, LILY CARRIED THE TABLE with its splintered legs into the garage. She'd look up the name of the repair place tomorrow, and drive it into town. Into the city, to one of Isabel's furniture specialists, if need be. She swept up the remaining debris—wood splinters and receipts from Bob's pockets and coins and glass, though who could say where that had come from—and emptied the bin into the kitchen trash. She thought of the receipts, then, and replaced the bag with a fresh one and buried the old trash bag at the bottom of one of the bins at the side of the house. She took everything that had once lived on the hall table—the sterling silver tray that held keys and phones and the photo frames, the glass for which miraculously had *not* broken—and placed them in new spots in the living room, in the den. She put the largest wedding photo in a far corner of the den, a room Isabel rarely used herself, on a high shelf, then told herself she was being silly and put it on a side table in the living room.

She walked back up to the top of the stairs and found her paperback, the book she'd been trying to read when they came home, and closed her eyes for a moment, breathed in, breathed out. When she opened her eyes, Madison stood at the edge of the hallway that led to the children's wing, just outside the boys' bedrooms.

She was wearing, unusually for her, a long white nightgown that matched one of Isabel's, the outfits they usually wore together on Christmas Eve. The lace detailing at the bodice looked like something growing vinelike up her neck, threatening to choke her.

Lily almost never told Madison what she ever thought of anything. She knew this was the biggest secret, at least between the two of them alone. That Madison thought they were close, thought of Lily as tough, candid, trustworthy, and loving, when in fact she never really told Madison any single entire truth.

Lily moved forward and extended one arm.

"It was an accident," she said, "but he's fine, we put him to bed."

Madison reeled back down the hallway, her body recoiling more precisely even than it had when Lily had slapped her, on that first morning. Her eyes shone white in the darkness, staring at Lily, anger turning them almost liquid.

"What are you talking about?" she said. "I'm fine, but you should see if the boys woke up."

She turned and ran back down the hallway, the folds of the nightgown in the darkness like white caps in a chopping sea. Lily made her way downstairs, clinging to the banister, and fell asleep on a couch.

In the morning, when she went to rouse the boys for school, she found Madison in bed between them. Both boys lay curled around their sister like newborn animals, untrusting and afraid of the coming light.

II

Scepticism is the chastity of the intellect, and it is shameful to surrender it too soon or to the first comer: there is nobility in preserving it coolly and proudly through long youth, until at last, in the ripeness of instinct and discretion, it can be safely exchanged for fidelity and happiness.

—George Santayana, *Scepticism and Animal Faith*

I can look right at you and say, this is a pain that will stay with me for the rest of my life. Regardless of what comes out of this committee, regardless of when the record book gets finally written. That's all.

—Richard Fuld, former CEO, Lehman Brothers

FIFTEEN

After her father returned to the house, the days grew shorter, but Madison's afternoons were endless. It was suddenly October, and the heavy, suspended quality to the air each afternoon reminded you that soon all the curtailed days would feel like slow slides into darkness, the morning sun just a feinting attempt at actual light. But the afternoons lasted forever.

No one, not even Lily, raised her voice. It was a time of freedoms circumscribed by some unuttered mandate, of moving through the house ready to remove anything that might, left in one's wake, reveal any information at all to the casual observer. They were all very aware of what it might feel like to be watched.

From Bob's study they only ever heard the sibilant consonants of his television, whispers that died somewhere along the hallway. Every so often the rhythm of these whispers would be punctured by something unusual—the smell of a fresh cigar or the lilting shatter, misleading in its vaguely festive air, of a glass against a wooden surface. And then they would freeze, but only for a moment, before everything resumed.

Madison knew, during this time, that a story was being built up around her. She knew it was far more than the boys at school, their hissing insults, their jokes coughed into cupped hands. She knew that her life was becoming a communal possession, shaped by the world lying in wait beyond the assaulted borders of her own daily routines.

This had always been true, she'd always needed an awareness of what her life looked like from the outside in. But now, every small detail was potentially treacherous. The empty bottles shimmering green and blue in the hallway outside her father's study, waiting with frankness for Lily to dispose of them each morning. The glossy black sedans that waited at the foot of the drive each day to follow their car to school, unobtrusive and unmentioned. The cigar ash left in tiny piles by the pool, just next to the diving board. Madison's home was now populated by people and things whose presences were not to be mentioned. There was no longer any such thing as blissful inattention; each day took on an unfamiliar and unsettling sheen of its own. Everything she chose not to acknowledge remained background, sparkling at the edges of her consciousness, no sooner identified than it disappeared.

She might have asked Lily, a year ago, what she thought about this. But Lily, since the morning they'd heard the first news, spoke to her with deference and caution and even, sometimes, joking irreverence for the overall mood. But never with candor, and never with warmth.

And so it seemed even more important that Madison's behavior not go unnoticed by her mother. During those first few weeks after he came home, she wasn't always sure of what she needed to survive, to keep up that illusion of forward motion, to match her mother's stride. She simply did it, tried to, in such a way—she liked to think later—that her mother *must* have noticed, that must have made Isabel proud.

SIXTEEN

Amanda couldn't believe she was going to this Halloween party. The previous afternoon, by the lockers, Zoë Barker had seemed actually to displace the air around them as she approached, sending it swirling past in coconut-scented eddies. Amanda could never tell if the fragrant cloud that seemed always to surround Zoë was her perfume, or something more innate, something that resided in her skin.

Amanda should have slammed the locker door and hurried down to the pool, because she knew exactly why Zoë was coming toward her. But she was, as ever, just a few seconds too slow to figure out her own life.

"Hi! Do you have plans tomorrow? For Halloween?"

"I'm not a big Halloween person," Amanda said. Which was true, but the truer truth was that she hadn't been asked, by anyone, to do anything. She liked the other girls on the swim team, but they mostly respected one another, urged one another on during meets, then said cheerful good-byes and went their separate ways. She'd had no new plan in place when she'd set Madison aside that summer.

"You don't seem like a costume person, either."

"Nope."

"Well, Wyatt is having a party," Zoë had said. "Wyatt Welsh."

"I know who Wyatt is."

Zoë smiled and let her eyes drift slowly beyond Amanda, to consider each successive group of people walking toward them. You had to admire her, that unruffled acceptance of her opponent's flint. Amanda could see the appeal, in its way. If you could only keep this girl on your side, she'd frighten so many other, lesser threats away from you.

"Actually, Madison's coming. I just thought, you know, she might be more comfortable with you there."

She'd left it there between them, Madison's name, like a poker chip on the green felt.

So now, like some total idiot, Amanda was in the front seat of her father's car. She was wearing a Peter Pan costume she'd imagined as clever and effortless, a clear rebuke to all the girls who used Halloween as an excuse to wear lingerie in public. Instead, she feared, she looked like an overgrown (and pudgy and possibly male) elf.

Her mother had agreed to give her a ride, but had then, at the last minute, tagged her father into the game. It was such a transparent move that Amanda had to admire her mother's guts, Lori not usually known for being either ballsy or manipulative. They were just such a *team*, her parents. It was its own form of showing off, really, their constant united front.

He said nothing for the first ten minutes, not until they were driving up into the quieter, winding roads. It got so dark up here, this time of night, this time of year. Usually she found it silly, that people in Greenwich still wanted to act like they lived in the country. But when you were coming around one of these darkened curves, beneath someone's gray stone wall, it's true you could forget this was basically a suburb of lower Manhattan.

"Which one is that party Suzanne always throws?" her father asked suddenly.

"The Bruce Museum benefit," she said. "It's always in April or something."

"That's right. Your mother was wondering."

"Tell her not to worry," Amanda said, snorting. "I'm just going to this one party, no need for us to make friends with the Wicked Witch of the Welsh."

"You know your mother," her father said, running his hands along the steering wheel. "She likes to have all the information."

"Even on people she doesn't actually care about?"

"Well," Jake said, and Amanda could sense him settling in, could sense what he'd been waiting to discuss. "I've tried to explain this to you before. You don't understand what it would have been like, growing up in her parents' house. They were both the sole survivors from their families. When they met they became all and everything the other one had."

"I know all of this," Amanda said, smoothing her green skirt across her thighs. They were almost to the house.

"No," he said, his voice flaring, "you don't." It was as sharp as his voice ever got, especially since they weren't even discussing Bob D'Amico or his cronies.

Which, though, they somehow always were.

"You're always terrified something will pass you by. It makes you desperate to know who has what, so you can keep yourself close to the person who's going to be able to help you. If it ever happened again. You cling to that idea."

"What idea?"

"Influence," he said. "Just, influence. You have to be able to get out right away if there's ever trouble, before it even starts. So you have to know the people who will know when trouble is coming."

She didn't say anything for a minute; the car stayed dark between them. He was wrong. He hadn't said any of this to her before.

"Then why would she marry you?"

She saw a flash of tooth, where his face was in shadow, and knew that her father was smiling.

"I'm not saying your mother always agrees with my tactics," he said. "But this is my job, Amanda. That's what I've been trying to get through to you. Your mother understands, it's my job."

"Good for her," Amanda said. "And good for you, I guess."

"Well, yes."

And then they'd come to the Welsh gate. They were silent as her father crawled up the sloping drive, through a second gate, then brought the car to a stop in front of the house. There was an actual fountain lit up in the courtyard, like some ruin they'd forgotten to tear down before they rebuilt their modern, if faux Mediterranean, mansion. The desire to make fun of it out loud, with her father, was so sharp it felt like an actual hunger pang. Amanda reached down to gather her purse from the floor.

"I'm not totally worthless, Dad," she said. "I know these aren't real problems. On the global scale. I know that. But you're bullying someone I actually know, and then you're making me stay here, where I see these people everywhere I go."

"It's my job, Amanda. I've told you that."

"It's not your job," she said. "Not all of it. It's not your job to enjoy it the way you've been enjoying it."

"It is," he said, "part of my charter. To speak truth to power."

"You know you sound exactly like him," she said. "When you two start complimenting yourselves, you sound like twins."

"This isn't yours to—" he was saying when she slammed the door. He'd taken her insult in stride; she'd hoped it would land with a bit more fanfare, maybe even unsettle him, to think that she might have been following news about Bob D'Amico from other sources. When she turned back to read his face, though, he was just peering up through his windshield at the big, glowing house.

WHEN WYATT WELSH ANSWERED the door and appeared to have no clue who she was, Amanda almost turned right around. She'd once sat at a table on the quad and actually told him and some of his idiot friends the story of how her parents met, on a subway platform.

But all that was waiting behind her was her father, driving home alone, and so she stepped over the threshold and into the house. Sure, whatever, Wyatt Welsh didn't remember who she was. This was fine.

There was another fountain inside, emerald tiles wavering beneath the streaming water. The entire entryway seemed designed to fool visitors into thinking that the windows and balconies would offer a sweeping vista of the Italian Riviera rather than a few acres of tidy Greenwich lawns.

Wyatt turned away from her after a cursory greeting and led her back into the house. She couldn't figure out what his costume was; he was just sort of dressed up. But then she heard voices, and they were walking down a short flight of stairs into a sunken living room.

The walls were painted the color of peach flesh, and two enormous forest green sofas faced each other at the center of the room. There was a tiled fireplace, with a fire going. The house was the kind of nice house that reminded you of its own taste, its own expense, but also of the way it had clearly been modeled on a magazine spread devoted to someone else's even nicer house. With every large art book stacked on a low table, with every ghostly seating arrangement of furniture that had clearly never been used.

Zoë sat on one sofa with her feet curled beneath her, a pair of chunky black heels abandoned beneath the low coffee table. Three guys stood above her, almost directly over her, so that she was forced to let her head loll back onto a couch cushion in order to look up at their faces. They were dressed in varying degrees of costume—one wore a hunting cap with earflaps, and another wore a Batman cape over his otherwise normal outfit, a black mask pushed back on his forehead. One of them was a senior on the football team; he wore only his Greenwich Prep uniform and carried his helmet in one hand, which Amanda thought was actually pretty clever. Everyone else trying so hard, but he had just come as himself.

Zoë caught sight of Amanda and stuck out her tongue.

"I love your costume," she called. "Get over here."

Amanda, for some reason, obeyed.

"Wait until you see Madison's costume," Zoë said. "We went shopping in the city last week. We had to, like, bully her into buying it, I didn't realize she was so against showing skin. Which you must know already. But she's dressed as an angel! I mean, tell me that's not perfect."

The big difference, Amanda thought, between looking like me and looking like Zoë Barker is that random parts of our bodies look so different. Maybe her stomach isn't any flatter than mine, but her collarbones look like really fragile straws, right beneath the surface of her skin. And I always have sweat on my upper lip, red bumps on the backs of my arms. And she has none of these things, and it doesn't look like she even tries not to have them. All her effort is always concealed, and all of mine is always right out in the open.

"I can't wait to see it," she said. "Sounds adorable."

"Allie's looking for vodka," Zoë announced. "All we have right now is rum and cranberry, it's repulsive."

She raised her voice artificially on those last words, so that Wyatt, who had been on his way out of the room, turned back.

"You were free to bring whatever. This isn't your house, Barker," he said, and left the room.

Zoë ignored him and patted the couch next to her, handing over a Solo cup. Amanda drank it down in one gulp, without having planned to do so, then held it out for more.

"So, I wanted to talk to you," Zoë said. "Before Madison gets here. I mean, things must be so terrible for her right now. Have you been over there? Is her dad, just, like, devastated?"

"He's been spending a lot of time in the city, I guess," Amanda began, careful. She didn't know if Bob was back in Greenwich yet.

"How would you know?"

"Because I saw him," Amanda said. She knew she would regret this. There were so many different ways she could come to regret this. But she could see how seductive it was, in its way, Zoë Barker's approach. She made you feel both interrogated and trusted, like a sidekick she was grilling to prove to herself what she already knew without question: that you were loyal.

"You saw him where? You went to their place in the city?"

"No," Amanda said. "Just, around. I ran into him when I was walking near Grand Central."

Zoë raised her eyebrows.

"He's just chilling by himself in the city? Do you think he's avoiding them?"

"No," Amanda said, and the story was so slippery, she was losing her grip, every corner she tried to grab was sliding away from her. "No, it was like—it was a meeting. He was with a woman who used to work for him. I'm sure it was something official, like a meeting about something."

Zoë smiled at her.

"A meeting on a random sidewalk," she said, and then Wyatt was back in the room, and Zoë's attention split away from Amanda's face, from her fumbling attempts to explain Madison's family.

BY THE TIME Madison walked in, Amanda had pounded—a term her brothers had taught her, a phrase she loved—three more drinks. She hadn't realized until she got here that Madison might not know to expect her, but something about Zoë's oily solicitousness had clued her in. And now she was drunk, and Madison was staring at her with undisguised contempt.

They both stood, waiting, before Madison smiled and walked over to meet Zoë's intimation of a hug: her arms wavering in the air above her head and then wrapping around Madison, pulling her off her feet with a jerk.

"So," Zoë began, "nobody brought the right mixers and Wyatt swears all the good stuff is locked up in his dad's office. I think he's just afraid to go in there without permission? He is the last person who should be in charge of this party, let me tell you. He will like *flip* if we leave this room and forget to re-fluff all the pillows, trust me."

"Why is he having this party, then?" Amanda tried. Maybe if she and Madison both spoke to Zoë, it would be like they were engaged in a conversation.

"Because I own him," Zoë said, shrugging her shoulders as though her opinions were founded on logic of such simplicity that it would be in poor taste to question them. "And this is the best party house of all time. That would be so wasteful."

"Where are his parents?" Madison asked. Amanda could see from her face, from the small twitches in its composed facade, that she'd promised someone there would be adults here tonight.

"Oh, right. I mean I would assume they're just in the city for some reason or other. You've just got to time these things right, but if we're smart, in the spring, we're there every Friday they spend here, and here for every Friday they spend there."

She glanced over at Amanda before continuing.

"It's near the museum," she said. "You know the area, both of you?"

Amanda took another sip of her drink and swallowed hard, feeling the liquid touch every inch of her throat.

Zoë, seemingly satisfied with Amanda's discomfort, listed toward Madison.

"Don't tell him I said this, but the apartment in the city isn't like this place. It's more, you know. It's not so over the top. The funny part is, I think Wyatt's dad is the one with good taste."

Amanda tried to catch Madison's eye, thinking that eventually, after enough of this conversation, it would become abundantly clear just how much they needed each other this evening, needed the release of shared eye contact.

She smiled at Madison and let her head tilt to one side, almost invisibly, her eyes going with it. Not quite an eye roll. A more secretive eye roll.

Madison fixed her with an expression so cold, so unmistakably enraged, that it had a probably unintended effect. Because seeing that fury, kept at such a shallow surface beneath her friend's outward face, made clear to Amanda how bad things must be at Madison's house. Madison looked almost grotesque, maimed by her own anger.

Just as quickly, that face was gone, smoothed. Madison turned back to Zoë, smiling and sliding their bodies closer together on the couch. And Amanda saw it: the clarity, in that moment, of Madison's choice between people who had the potential to hurt her. She must have realized, that month, that the one thing that couldn't be taken from her was that choice.

"I've never seen their place in the city," Madison said.

"Your parents have a place, too, right?" Zoë had made her first unforced error, Amanda thought. Bringing them up so quickly.

"Yes," Madison said, "they do."

A door opened that seemed to lead to a different hallway, and Allie clacked into the room, her legs wobbling on stiletto heels.

"Jackpot," Allie said. "I found a box of Crystal Light packets!"

"Uh," Zoë said, "not jackpot. With rum? At that point we might as well just do shots."

"Vodka from the freezer!" Allie waved an enormous bottle of Grey Goose in the air above her head, the muscles in her arm standing at attention.

"Are you telling me there's been vodka all this time and Wyatt's been holding out?" Zoë said, her voice pitched louder, as if to draw the attention back from the boys, who were in their corner removing coffee table books from a credenza and debating whether it was long enough to use for a game of Beirut.

"Yeah, girl," Allie said cheerfully. "And there's more in there, too, there's Ketel! Oh, Madison! Oh my God, Amanda! Hi. Didn't even see you there. Too excited about this new discovery."

No one seemed to notice that Amanda hadn't spoken.

"The Ketel is weird, though," Allie continued. "It's this bottle I've never seen before."

"It's sort of thick and squat? A weird shape?" Madison offered. "That's just what a magnum of Ketel looks like."

Allie clapped with glee, and Zoë cocked her head to one side.

"My grandfather has a pantry for his vodka alone," Madison explained.

"Oh, God," Zoë said. "You people are just as WASPy as they come, aren't you? Well, your mom's people, I guess."

Amanda watched Madison's jaw turn to stone, saw her placing Bob somewhere further back in her mind, keeping him far from Zoë's probing, childish fingers.

"Just teasing," Zoë said, seizing the bottle from Allie. She squinted at the label, like an adult casting an expert eye at a bottle of wine. Was it possible she didn't know that this kind of scrutiny made no sense for vodka? Amanda could see that Madison had recognized it, too, that she was feeling a generous superiority bloom in her chest, a slight calming of her trembling fingers.

"That's funny, that he lied about the vodka," Amanda offered.

Allie raised her eyebrows and said, in a stage whisper, "I'm not sure he actually knows to look for vodka in the freezer."

It was like this conversation had been designed as torture. Everything Amanda knew about drinking, about which liquors came in which bottles, came from the D'Amico household. Her own father was a single bottle of beer on a Sunday afternoon guy.

"I'm sorry," Madison said, "are you telling me Wyatt Welsh doesn't drink?"

"No," Zoë insisted, "it's not that. He just likes dark stuff. Whiskey and the other one, the one that's basically the same thing."

"Bourbon," Madison said. Amanda saw her momentarily fold in on herself and then straighten up, filing away whatever had bothered her, papers shuffled quickly past one another to keep themselves hidden.

"Nice costume," Amanda said, loud and direct so Madison couldn't pretend not to have heard. "I heard you guys bought it in the city."

"Yeah, we went to Scoop."

"Isabel's going to kill you."

"I doubt she'll notice."

On the couch, Allie had made some crack about Wyatt and suddenly Zoë was crawling all over her. A Solo cup went flying and landed with a shrill plastic yelp, spilling its fuchsia liquid across the Persian rug like a bloodstain. Unimpeded, Zoë buried her face in Allie's neck, nuzzling her or pretending to strangle her, it wasn't clear which, and their streaming blond hair blended together into one shining mass.

"If you do not stop talking right this second I will strangle you and then leave your body in a ditch!" Zoë said. "I will fucking destroy you. I will reveal all of your secrets. Madison and Amanda are here. They know you've been warned."

"Get off me!" Allie was shrieking. And in a second, Zoë had crawled back to her side of the couch, folding her long limbs into place, like a paper doll that had, for a brief flash, become animate, and then collapsed once more to its flattened world.

"Just warning you," she said, sipping her drink. It was Allie's cup, of course, that had gone flying.

"I'll go get something to wipe that up," Madison said, "but I don't know, the rug? Should we get that woman, the housekeeper? Her name was Maria or something?"

You remember her name, Amanda thought. Allie stood with Madison, as if to help. Zoë stared at them both.

"It's fine," she said. "Someone will get it later. Just don't say anything in front of Wyatt. Grab that big pillow, the one on the floor. Just, like, drop it on top of the part of the rug that's wet."

Allie followed instructions, dutifully. Madison sat down again and avoided Amanda's eye.

"Anyway," Zoë said, "when everyone else gets here, we'll move to the ballroom."

"They have a ballroom?"

"Oh," Callan called from the corner—that was his name,

Amanda remembered. The football player dressed as a football player. Callan. This was the first time any boy besides Wyatt had even acknowledged that the girls were sitting here. "The baaaaaaaaaaaaall-rooooooooooom?"

Zoë ignored him. Allie looked in his general direction, her face breaking into a smile, but said nothing.

"Oh, shut the fuck up, Cal. You are such an infant." Zoë fixed Allie with a disdainful pout. "Why you let that Neanderthal touch you is a mystery to me."

"Bite me hard," Allie replied.

Wyatt poked his head into the room again.

"Oh," he said, "Madison. Hey. Chipster's on his way, he just called."

"Oh, did he call?" Zoë cooed. "Did he want to see who was here?"

Wyatt's eyes darted to the corner, where Callan and company had now succeeded in clearing the credenza of its various decorative objects. A plum-colored vase, shaped like a calla lily, had been relegated to the floor.

"Fuck off, you guys, we can't play Beirut in here. Come on. The housekeepers are still around. Put that crap back. Yo, Barker. Who else did you invite? How many other girls are showing up at my door?"

"Don't worry," Zoë said, furiously mixing vodka into the Crystal Light in her cup, pausing at intervals to lick her index finger. "Plenty of ladies will be showing up."

"How. Many."

"Just a few."

"It had better be just a few. We have to set the security system before we go downstairs. Anyone who isn't here by then is uninvited. By me. The person who lives here."

He loped away, back down the corridor that led to the kitchen.

"It's so fine," Zoë continued, as if he hadn't left. "If the housekeepers bother us, we'll just go out there."

She shook a thumb over her shoulder, toward the picture window that ran the length of the far wall, and Amanda noticed for the first time that the room looked down over the grottolike pool, its waterfall a steep arrangement of stones lit the same unnatural green as the fountain.

"They won't tell Suzanne," Allie said. "I don't seriously believe Suzanne would care that we're drinking."

"She would if she saw the cars out front." Zoë held her hand up in the air and began to inspect her manicure, nail by nail. "You know how his dad gets, everything is a potential lawsuit to Bill Welsh. He thinks everyone loves to sue as much as he does."

"Who's driving home?" Madison asked.

"Zoë," Allie said, hunching her shoulders toward Madison with a conspiratorial air, "has been driving without insurance."

"They're going to *get* me insurance," Zoë said. "As soon as I pass my test."

"Which she can't even take for another six months!" Allie crowed. "They don't know she's been driving the car. Did you see the new car outside, Madison?"

Amanda had seen the car before she knocked at the front door. It was a black Mercedes, a tiny sports car, the kind of small, flippant car her father referred to as death-on-wheels.

"I don't know what they expected," Zoë said. "To buy the car early and then, what, let it sit there while I *don't* drive it? My dad *knows* I've driven it."

Amanda downed the remainder of her drink. It was sweet but hollow; there was nothing there but the promise that you'd be drunk soon.

"I have to pee," she said unceremoniously. She stood up and left the room.

IT TOOK HER A FEW MINUTES to find a bathroom, and on her way back she found herself lingering in hallways. Maybe they'd all decamp for "the ballroom" while she was gone. Maybe she would return to find only the ghostly quiet of recently abandoned furniture. Maybe then she could call her mother to come and rescue her.

But Lori might send Jake, Amanda remembered. There was no place for her, tonight, nowhere she could go without first making some bigger decision.

She wandered into the kitchen and opened the looming Sub-Zero, peering into its various compartments, fogged with condensation. You could learn a lot about people from what they chose to keep on hand, and apparently Suzanne Welsh was someone who bought in anonymous bulk for a household that contained only three people. This was a refrigerator meant to sustain a chaotic, bustling family. Towers of jumbo cartons of Greek yogurt, the tins of whey protein, a pile of frozen steaks in their taut plastic and Styrofoam packages. Rows upon rows of diet soda cans, still shackled to one another in their plastic rings. An entire drawer of complicated-name cheeses from Balducci's wrapped in their thick white paper. The hunks were of varying sizes and shapes, all of them still sealed and many of them past their expiration dates, purchased for impromptu dinner guests who had apparently failed to materialize.

Amanda closed all the drawers and, with her pinkie finger, wrote her initials in the mist on their chilly surfaces. Then she leaned forward and breathed, letting the heat overwhelm the evidence.

She shut the fridge and turned to the kitchen counters. In a side drawer, near the phone: the high school phone directory, a map of Rhode Island, a pack of Gauloises cigarettes that were surely the last lingering affectation left over from her junior year in Avignon, or some equally tragic backstory. She probably had them in her purse and parceled out artful glimpses of them when she rifled through it, looking for her tinted, La Roche-Posay SPF 50 concealer or a business card for whatever home décor business she'd once made a pseudo-effort to launch a few years ago. She probably kept them in a convenient pocket in the purse, hoping that Isabel D'Amico might see them once, casually. That they might bond.

Unfortunately for Suzanne Welsh, Isabel had spent her junior year in Tuscany, and she was rarely if ever looking for an extra window to open, for anything that might let one of these women further in. People always talked about Isabel like she was so icy, so remote, but she wasn't at all. She's always been warm to me, Amanda thought. She just doesn't devote her energy to putting people at ease when she has no respect for them. We should all be a little more like her, actually. It would cost us so much less if we could all agree to do it.

And whether Isabel cooked or not, at least her kitchen didn't feel like this place: a gaudy, well-lit rehearsal for a life.

For a moment, before she went back to the living room, Amanda thought of her father, of the proud way he'd practically puffed out his chest when he'd said that: "speaking truth to power." She knew, though, what he'd really been saying. It was, in the end, his answer for everything. How seductive this approach could be. Surrounding yourself with all the people you know you're better than. Then sinking into the contempt the way you'd sink into a bubble bath, just on the edge of too hot, after a grueling game of tennis.

It wasn't fair that in Bob D'Amico she saw it as evidence of his essential mettle, his intrinsic worth, where in her own father she just saw it as preening. She knew it wasn't fair.

WHEN SHE CAME BACK into the living room, Zoë was holding Madison's wrist high in the air, waving it around and calling back toward the boys' corner. A door slammed in some other part of the house.

"You guys," she said, "doesn't Madison have the world's tiniest wrists? Like a baby's! Look!"

Wyatt came back in, and then Chip was shambling into the room.

"Who's got tiny wrists?" He bent down to kiss both Zoë and Allie, each on the cheek, and nodded toward Amanda.

"I do," Madison said. "Haven't you noticed?"

"I guess I'm not usually paying attention to your wrists," he said, already looking over toward Callan and the other two. "That isn't where guys are looking. Just a pro tip for you ladies."

He crossed the room then, to high-five Callan. He was wearing a suit jacket two sizes too small for him, the sleeves stretched across his upper forearms, and beneath it a T-shirt with the Superman logo peeking out.

"Fuck you, Abbott," Wyatt said, and Chip pulled him into a headlock.

"No thank you, Wyatt, but I'm happy to just be friends."

"Wyatt, kiddo, can we perhaps get you something to chill you the fuck out?" Zoë called over her shoulder. "Does anyone have a joint for our gracious host?"

"Try does anyone have six Xanax," Callan snorted.

Amanda saw Madison's spine straighten, as though someone had jerked it on a string.

"Oh," Madison said in response to some gesture, some clue from Zoë. Amanda had missed it, whatever it was. "How long has that been going on?"

"Just sometimes," Allie clarified. "Like, really not often. Every few weeks. If she's bored. Right?"

"If I'm bored," Zoë said. "Yeah, we hook up. I mean that's Wyatt's best use, to be honest. I'm not going to tell him my hopes and dreams. Not a candidate for best friend."

"Or romance, I would imagine," Amanda contributed.

"I like those shoes," Zoë said, done with Wyatt as a topic. "What are those, Prada? I think I almost bought those. But not that color."

"Probably not," Madison said. "These aren't recent. They're my mother's."

"That's sweet," Allie said.

"What, is she cleaning out her closet?" Zoë said.

"No," Madison said.

They all sipped their drinks.

"Here's the thing," Zoë said, sliding lower on the couch so that her head tilted toward Allie's. "We could use a little something stronger, couldn't we? I'm already bored."

"Oh," Allie said, slouching down alongside her. "I've already taken care of it. Jared said he could get some. He said he'd get extra and we could buy it off him."

"For what? Fifty?"

"He said seventy-five, which I think is bullshit, but I'm just going to leave it alone."

"That seems like a lot."

Allie's hand danced in the air for a moment, then touched her hair, gently, as if to make sure it was still there. "I can get it this time," she said. "Whatever. He shouldn't even be making us pay."

"Madison," Zoë said, sitting up straight again. "You're going to love this. This is going to be dynamite."

The doorbell rang.

"Perfect. What do you want to bet that's Jared?"

"It had better be," Wyatt said, loping past them to head back out to the foyer.

"I think it's hilarious," Madison said, "that he's actually dressed as the guy from *Wall Street*. I think that's so—it's just so, so Wyatt."

She sounded, Amanda thought, exactly like Zoë.

"I thought it was supposed to be *American Psycho*, that movie from when we were kids," Allie said.

Zoë raised her eyebrows and grinned at Madison. "What's the difference? Right, Madison?"

WHEN THE OTHER GIRLS both left the room to follow Wyatt, Amanda knew that this might be the one time, all night, when she and Madison spoke only to each other. That certainty rushed to fill the empty, expectant places that had foreseen an evening that would end the way it was supposed to, with Madison needing Amanda.

"You're kidding, right?" she said. Somehow it came out hostile. "You're going to do that with them?"

"Amanda," Madison said, "I don't even know why you came."

"I came to see you," Amanda said, but all these thoughts were sliding from her brain, unruly, they were wrinkled and in the wrong order by the time she said them out loud. She sounded sad, when she said that, but all she wanted was for Madison to get it, to get how much more egregious any single person in this room was than anything Amanda had ever done.

Madison crossed her arms, pulling her knees in toward her chest.

"Do you want to talk about this now?" she said. "Then fine, let's go. I'm listening." And then, to Amanda's silence: "That's what I figured. So then why are you here?"

Madison stood up and went over to talk to Chip. Amanda felt an actual twisted pride, watching her do that. She walked all the way across the room, in front of those boys, and started talking to this guy she worshipped. She could do that now, when before—only a few months ago—she couldn't. Whatever was happening, had been happening, it was at least making her different, somehow. She was learning something.

Amanda waited for Zoë and Allie to come back with that senior, Jared Rodrick, and then slipped out the front door. Wyatt, thankfully, didn't seem to have set any alarm. She called her father on his home office line and waited by the fountain outside for what felt like hours, until she saw his car crest the hill.

SEVENTEEN

Mina was trying to remember, in chronological order, every single one of Jaime's Halloween costumes. She knew the first one had been a teapot, when Jaime was not even three months old. Mina had been frantic to find a costume that wouldn't broadcast to the entire party, a Manhattan event thrown by one of the older wives at the bank, how long it was taking her to lose the baby weight.

She'd been younger, then; she hadn't yet discovered her panoply of options, the mixing and matching of the other wives' weekly fitness regimens.

In the end she'd had a yellow dress made, cut low to expose her breast-feeding cleavage and with a high-waisted ball-gown skirt to cover her tummy. It seemed so perfect, for the bank, Beauty and the Beast, and a little teapot in tow. But of course it ended up being one of those things where kids had only been invited in spirit, and the "nursery" was the apartment's abandoned third story and a house-keeper who had clearly been asked last minute to work overtime, and Mina had been one of only two or three clueless women who'd shown up with a kid. And Tom seemed more embarrassed by her idea of a little joke, painting his nose black and putting a fake lion's mane over his suit, than she'd expected.

She trotted into the foyer now to fetch the giant plastic pumpkin filled with miniature Vosges boxes, their purple edges protruding from the pumpkin's maw like facets from a geode. It was so typical, that she'd been trying to remember her daughter's cutest looks and had instead wandered into a memory of recrimination and pain. She had to get a better handle on that. She knew why it was happening— any holiday was a spotlight shone on Jaime's absence, and Tom was stewing in the den tonight, annoyed that they had to deal with trick-or-treaters. It was all right to feel a bit off. But this constant wallowing—enough was enough.

"Oh my goodness," she cooed at the door, dropping a box of chocolates into the bejeweled handbag of a small girl who couldn't be much older than ten. She was wearing a face full of makeup and a dazzling outfit, one of the ones where flesh-colored nylon is sewed in place to make a young child look like she's baring skin, wearing something risqué. It had to be that she was dressed up as a pop star, or something, God knows it went right over Mina's head. The older your kids got, the less you were expected to keep up with whatever celebrity had them in raptures. And when your kid decamped for boarding school, you were almost completely off the hook.

She hovered in the kitchen for a few minutes after the latest batch of kids wandered back down the driveway—one reason Tom hated this process was that it required them to leave the front gate open, trusting that no one would trespass without candy-seeking kids in tow—before deciding that they might be reaching the dregs of the evening, that it might be late enough to call it a night.

Tom had been the sort of dad who cashes in on his daughter's Halloween haul. He had always tried to bargain with Jaime for her Snickers. I'll drive you to school, he'd say, and she'd squeal with laughter. I'll buy you some dinner. I'll take you into the city to see the whale on the ceiling at the museum. When we visit your Grandma Gennaro out on Long Island, I'll let you pile your food on my plate and if she asks, I'll say I took seconds, because it's not your fault you got the one Italian grandma who's a terrible cook. I'll do it for you! I'll do anything, anything. Just give me those Snickers bars.

They were all things he already did for her, things any daughter could expect from her father. They were the wages of love as they already existed, the parameters of Jaime's relationship with him as she'd been taught to understand it. That was the joke; he was offering her nothing at all. And their daughter had laughed and laughed, her giggles accelerating into near hyperventilation, her hands at her little protruding stomach, as if to hold her together so she didn't shatter from the hilarity.

That was another Halloween memory.

Mina topped off her glass of wine and poured a fresh scotch for Tom and carried both glasses into the den. He was in his chair, a CIA mystery propped open on his knees. He read paperbacks when they traveled, for the convenience, but at home he always preferred hardcovers from the library. He wasn't looking down at the book, or at the NBA season opener he had playing, muted, on the television. He was looking out the French windows, toward the swimming pool that would be visible if it weren't already dark.

"Honey?" she said.

He snapped to attention and considered her for a moment before closing the book and patting the wide wooden arm of his chair. She tiptoed across the room to curl up beside him. She caught his head in her arm and guided it toward her chest, and they both cradled their drinks in their free hands.

"Do you think she really won't come home for Thanksgiving?" Mina asked quietly.

"It's a long trip," he said.

"I'd go to pick her up," she said. "She knows that."

"It's good that she's made friends, Min. You'd hate thinking of her up there, alone in the room after that dingbat roommate left school. No one to talk to. You'd be so miserable if you thought that was the case. You were so worried about her, back in October. And it's nice that she'll have a family Thanksgiving."

"It's not her family."

"Sure," he said. "But it'll work."

Mina lifted her glass, but she realized that what she wanted wasn't really a drink, it was some Halloween candy. And not what they had in the hall; real candy bars. She wanted KitKats. She should have gotten Tom some Snickers bars, brought them in to him without warning. But then if he hadn't remembered, she'd have felt guilty for implying that he *should* remember.

"We could go away," he said now. "We could close up the house for the winter and go somewhere warm."

"No," she said. "She'll still come for Christmas, come on. And you need to be here."

"I'm sick of it," he said. "When I get out of the car in the morning, and see the building, I can't stand the sight of it. I don't want to walk in. I don't want to get into the elevator."

"Sweetheart," Mina said, lowering her face to his, brushing his temple with her lips. She felt him shudder, involuntary. "We don't have that luxury."

"He gets to just disappear," Tom murmured. "They should make him show up in my place every day, and explain to my team what's going on. That should be his penance. He should go from firm to firm."

She imagined them, her husband's hands tensed like claws and Bob's crisp white shirt wilted into his lower back with anxious sweat. Bob's head lowered in docile acceptance, letting her husband hurl everything at him, every piece of fear sharpened into fury, like shards of glass. She couldn't picture it; she couldn't imagine Bob, even now, so broken.

She knew Isabel was still waiting for it, because she was still waiting, too. For the last piece of information to fall into place, for the final card to land without the house falling. The proof, for every prying eye, that Bob had done his best, had really tried.

She said none of it out loud, of course, and they sat in silence. She could feel Tom shifting toward her, and she knew that in a few minutes they'd go upstairs, that her husband wanted to have sex with her. But in the meantime, they sat together and didn't drink their drinks, and looked out at the pool they couldn't see.

AFTER HE'D FALLEN ASLEEP, she decided to call her daughter. She could hear him even from their sitting room, his rasping punctured only every few minutes by a violent attempt to snore. She knew he had that apnea problem, he should probably be one of those men wearing a mask to sleep, but she couldn't even get him to go in for a consult to discuss it.

It would make more sense to go downstairs, where there was no chance he'd hear her, and where beyond that she had some tidying to do. The house still had to be closed down, everything turned off, darkened. But he'd been so sweet to her all night, so unlike the barking, quivering man he'd been all month, and now she didn't want to leave him, even his unaware sleeping body. She wanted to stay where she could see him, listen to his fragile breath, think about the nice evening they'd had together.

Jaime's cell phone, as it almost always did, went straight to voice mail.

"Honey," Mina whispered into the phone, craning her neck to peer out at the back lawn and at the distant lights from next door, where there appeared to be a party of some sort. There were orange lanterns strung through the trees back beyond Mina's tennis court. "Jaime, babe, it's me. I'm sure you're out or something, I just called to see what your costume was. I was thinking of that year you were Dorothy, do you remember? And Isabel had all the kids over to their house, and as soon as we got there, I realized you weren't just in a bad mood, you were running a fever."

It had been another brutal Halloween, with Isabel insisting that they didn't have to leave, Jaime could just lie down in one of the guest bedrooms, don't worry, Lily had every possible fever reducer and homeopathic remedy on hand. Just let her sleep there until you want to go home, Isabel had repeated, over and over. But Jaime had refused to be shunted quietly into some abandoned corner upstairs, and she had cried in big gulping sobs as Mina tried to explain that she couldn't bob for apples with everyone else, that she would contaminate the water.

"Anyway," she said into the phone, putting some sort of faith in the fact that her daughter would listen to this message, "you know how I love Halloween. I was just wondering what you dressed as tonight. You would have thought it might be quieter here, this year, but actually we had more kids come up to the house than usual. And the costumes—just as bad as ever. There was a little girl dressed as Britney Spears, or something. You would have been horrified, babe."

She rambled into the phone for a few more minutes before hanging up, feeling—as ever—that she'd been vaguely traitorous to her husband, her daughter, her sister, and her town, all at once, equally.

EIGHTEEN

The second Welsh gate had already shuddered behind her when the car's headlights slid across her body, and Madison recognized Jake Levins's Volkswagen. She could see his face, his body hunched like a turtle over the steering wheel, and that was how she knew that he surely had seen her standing there.

What possible reason could he have for being here?

"Jake!" she yelled, cupping her hands to her mouth. "Jake! Stop!"

The car pulled away from the house, disappeared smoothly down the drive.

"You're a dick," she called after the car, her voice useless. She kicked a cobblestone and narrowly avoided getting a stiletto heel caught in a groove. She told herself he'd heard her, and turned back to the house.

It leered up before you as you crested the hill, its upper stories dark above the ponderous sconces that festooned the ground-level facade. A fountain sat, unapologetic, in the middle of the courtyard, bottom-lit a garish green color, its water arcing in four directions. She marched past it, her shoes already rubbing raw circles into the soft parts of her feet; they didn't fit.

She'd stolen them from Isabel's closet while her mother was still locked in her office downstairs. She'd even put them on and worn them out of the house, the heels making curt little sounds on the floor as she passed her mother's door, but no one had said a word. No one had shown any interest in her whereabouts, even, except Lily.

"I'm not a chauffeur," she'd said when Madison begged to be dropped off at the bottom of the hill. "I'll drive you up there and wave to the adult you say will be supervising this whole thing."

Madison had almost replied that, technically speaking, chauffeur *was* one of Lily's jobs. But the last time she'd spoken to Lily that way, she'd gotten a quick slap to the cheek. And it felt like she should pick and choose those occasions. Save them for when she really needed them. These minor furies would choke her, not strangle her.

"You know the rules as well as I do. I could get your mother involved, but do we even need to do that? Don't we both know where she'd come down on this issue?"

"Be my guest, Lily. Seriously. Here—take my phone. Give her a call."

And they'd both stared at the cell phone extended between them.

Now, Madison was here, standing at Wyatt's front door because Chip had convinced her to come to this party. She rang the doorbell and prepared to smile.

"Good evening," said the small woman who answered. She wore a uniform, something that looked like hospital scrubs but slightly less antiseptic.

"I'm so sorry," she said. "I'm—my name is Madison D'Amico. I'm looking for Wyatt?"

She told herself she'd imagined it, that the woman's eyes hadn't flickered when she heard the name.

Wyatt, when he appeared, was wearing a blue dress shirt and red suspenders, hair parted and slicked back, dark with gel. It seemed impossible that he was actually dressed as a banker, but she didn't see what else he could be.

"Wall Street," he said. "I mean, the movie. From the eighties."

"Oh," she said. She pulled at the hem of her dress, which kept creeping up her thigh. This suddenly felt extravagantly careless, the decision to come willingly into Wyatt's home.

"It's fine, Mariana," he was saying. "Thanks for letting her in. You can go now. This is the last one. I swear."

The woman sighed deeply and put three fingers to the center of her forehead.

"She said you were not allowed to go out. She said this to me once when we were alone, and twice when you were there."

"Well," Wyatt said, "I'm not out. I am staying home."

Madison could tell that Wyatt was performing for her, slightly, that he was just a bit more brazen and cavalier than he would be if he were alone with Mariana. He was performing this disregard for his mother's employee, thinking it made him look suave, commanding. The sad thing, Madison knew, was that Wyatt wanted to seem so-phisticated, not spoiled—the product not just of his parents' money, but of its weight. And this was not the way to do it, not in front of some girl he barely knew.

Madison watched him as he listened to Mariana's scolding, as he adjusted to her darkening mood. Cocking his head to one side, squaring his shoulders to her. Holding her in the palm of his hand like a fistful of marbles, rolling them this way and that, completely in control in the way you can only ever control the people who have cared for you since before you had emotions, before you had impulses or desires. She saw, in that moment, that Mariana had been with this house for years, probably since Wyatt's birth, even.

"We'll be fine," he said, his voice soothing. "We don't need any-thing else, so you can go now."

"There's soda in the second fridge," Mariana said, sighing again. "In the pantry."

"Mariana, you're killing me," Wyatt said, throwing one arm around her in something that was halfway between a chokehold and a hug. "Anyone would think you didn't trust me at all!"

And then Mariana dissolved, rolling her eyes at Madison and pulling at Wyatt's ear so that he'd lean down obediently for her to kiss the top of his head.

"Fine," she said. "Have fun. Be careful."

"We will," Wyatt sang, already slouching toward a room off to the right. Only then did Madison notice that there were lights, voices, off that way. The party she was here to attend. Mariana disappeared into the darkened part of the house, and Wyatt gestured to Madison. He waited for her to pass through the doorway in front of him, as if he was holding a door open. As if this was chivalry.

ZOË IMMEDIATELY PULLED HER DOWN, wrapping her arms around her and making a great show out of kissing her on the cheek. Which saved Madison from having to register, in front of everyone, the fact that Amanda was in the room.

There were a few boys standing somewhat near the couches, their eyes wholly on Zoë as she snorted and then coarsely swiped at the lipstick she'd smeared across Madison's cheekbone. Madison knew she was a prop; Zoë had grabbed her not to show affection but to display something for these boys. Not because she was actually a bubbly girl in that moment, but so that they'd think she was.

Chip wasn't here yet. Why? Madison had come late, on purpose.

"Come on," he'd said to her at school earlier that week. "I'll be there. Everyone on their best behavior, and by everyone I mean Wyatt. I promise."

He had looked right at her, his jaw set, his gaze unwavering. He always looked at her for a few beats longer than felt normal, in daylight conversation. She did not know anyone else her age who did this.

"Don't worry," Zoë said now, shooting her a lascivious grin. "Chip will be here soon. Once everyone's here, then we'll go down to the ballroom."

Allie had some purloined vodka, and they were all mixing Crystal Light into it with their index fingers. Amanda was drinking as quickly as any of them, throwing constant looks in Madison's direction. Amanda, who had always been Madison's conscience, warning against dangers that had never had any relevance to their lives. You never set down your drink at a party, you never drink from something you didn't pour yourself. You never give anyone the chance to catch you when you're falling, carry you away to some violation you can't fend off. Look at her now, the smart one, the cynical one. Chugging from a Solo cup, her throat working, her eyes too alert and her cheeks too red.

"Downstairs?" Madison replied, turning to Zoë.

"Yeah." Zoë's eyes followed Wyatt around the room, Madison's question a secondary distraction to be dealt with. "It's right off the pool. Haven't you been here before?"

"I have," Madison said. "But only outside."

Zoë peered over the rim of her cup, her attention now squarely on Madison. "For the museum party."

Everyone's family had a chosen cause. Jim McGinniss, her father's closest associate, had lost his first wife to pancreatic cancer. And so even though she'd died several years after their divorce, he threw a party in the Hamptons every year. Madison's Grandpa D'Amico had died before her birth—his body shutting down within two years of his ALS diagnosis, robbing him of his will to live as soon as it robbed him of the ability to show up for his job as a doorman uptown. And so it was known among all her father's top men at the bank that they were expected not only to fill a table at the annual benefit but to give generously, in concert with that year's bonus, on top of that.

And Suzanne had the party for the Bruce Museum. It wasn't, as her mother had once said, much of an event as fund-raisers went, but then, this was Suzanne they were talking about.

Isabel had said that without thought, one April evening years ago. She'd been in the foyer plucking at Bob's collar while he held his BlackBerry at arm's distance, so he could continue to read e-mails while submitting to her various ministrations. Isabel swiped at his necktie with one final finger.

"What can I tell you, sweetheart," she said. "And I know you've always thought Wyatt was a bore."

"He's . . . fine," Madison said. "He's neither a bore nor an asset." At that point, it was still true. Her father howled, finally pocketing his BlackBerry and drawing her to his side with one arm, kissing the top of her head.

"Listen to that," he said. "Neither a bore nor an asset. Couldn't have put it better myself, kiddo. Could not have done a better job describing that family. Son and father."

"We're still late," Isabel said, fiddling with the faulty clasp on her bracelet, and then they were gone.

Then they were here, Madison thought now, looking around her.

"Of course," she said to Zoë. "They wouldn't miss the museum party."

SHE'D LOST TRACK of her drinks; she didn't know why they hadn't moved downstairs yet.

"My dad was so pissed I didn't move up into honors track for math this year," Zoë was saying. She kept sipping at her drink and curled her legs more tightly beneath her, like a cat preparing to jump.

"I'm sure you have nothing to worry about," Madison said. Zoë's father hosted several Harvard alumni events every year. It was, she knew, one of the things her father truly despised. Zoë's father had never had any real money of his own, had basically used his wife's money to keep afloat in the early days, but he had an old name. He'd gone to Harvard, and her own father hated this. The idea that Zoë might have a better shot somewhere than Madison, that an established history, however undistinguished, was better than no history at all. It was the same thing he'd hated about having to spend time with Grandpop and Gran.

"Madison, why aren't you drinking your drink?" Allie said. "The Crystal Light is terrible, I know. But if we used soda, that's like, thousands of calories. And obviously it's not like we're going to drink beer."

The boys were all still in their corner. It had taken only minutes for the party to separate efficiently and completely into two gendered groups, as if the presence of girls wasn't the only reason any of those guys had shown up in the first place. No one was allowed to look directly at the things they wanted, not until they were drunk.

"Right, Zoë?" Allie continued. "We *never* drink beer."

"Like drinking a loaf of bread," Zoë confirmed. She'd retrieved her phone from the coffee table and was scrolling through her text messages, but after only moments she dropped the phone and lurched forward, grabbing Madison's arm. It was the clumsiness of the motion, the way she almost fell across the table, that made Madison see that Zoë had been drinking, must have been, long before the rest of them had arrived.

She let her arm be jerked about in the air, let Zoë crow over its smallness. And then Madison's skin felt different, somehow, and Chip was standing there in the room with her.

Her eyes locked to him, his shoulders, the place on the back of his neck where the tendons met his close-cropped hair. She had to stop drinking, she'd already had two and the stickiness was making her nauseous.

He asked about her wrists, Zoë had said something about her wrists.

"Haven't you noticed?" she said to him.

She hadn't touched him since that day in his car, not at all. Everything about that afternoon had the sheen of imagined memory, leaving her so desperate for the slightest sign from him that she was certain her longing had begun to radiate from her body in some tangible, dangerous form. That he must be able to feel it, the charged air between their bodies, and must be ignoring it for some cruel purpose.

He made a joke, and walked over to greet the boys.

Just a pro tip for you ladies, Madison thought, repeating the words silently. She had never been more convinced of the dubious possibility that Chip's mind worked in exactly the same way that hers did. That he had known just what he was saying, just how she would hear it. Guys weren't looking at your wrists. Everything that has passed between us, Madison, is flirting, is real interaction. Our conversations belong in that same limitless catalog of things boys do to get the attentions of girls.

Except, of course he paid attention to her wrists, her hand on his wrist in the car. There were actual patterns forming, things that would one day be cemented as inside jokes. Things that had happened, would happen, each time they spoke. Those were the patterns that led you into actual intimacy, probably. It had to be casual patterns at the root of the web that seemed to drape itself around her parents, when they were getting along, that enclosed them in a quiet library of their own shared history.

Zoë was suddenly bored, was talking to Allie about Jared Rodrick, a senior. Was he coming? Amanda kept looking at Madison, but Madison wouldn't look back.

"Madison," Zoë said. "You're going to love this. This is going to be dynamite."

"I thought it was *American Psycho*," someone said. They were talking about Wyatt.

Zoë raised her eyebrows and grinned. "What's the difference? Right, Madison?"

TEN MINUTES AFTER she noticed Amanda was gone, they were crowded into a bathroom just off the kitchen. It had in fact been Jared Rodrick at the door. He was apparently dressed as one of the characters from *Miami Vice*, a show Madison had never seen. She'd be willing to bet he'd never seen it, either. It seemed chosen primarily as an excuse to rub copious amounts of gel through his hair and wear sunglasses indoors.

"D'Amico," Jared said, his voice rolling and dipping with approval, with a swallowed chuckle that she understood to be warm, not mocking. "Didn't know you were into this sort of thing."

She hadn't understood what Allie was going to buy until Jared took the two tiny Ziploc bags from his jacket pocket. She hadn't known you could find plastic bags so tiny. That's when she felt the burn, behind her eyes, when it was clear that Amanda had known exactly what was happening.

Jared looked around the bathroom, the ostentatious vanity beneath a mirror that ran the length of one wall.

"My question is," he said, "who is this shit here for?" He picked up a gold-plated hairbrush from a mirrored tray. "I mean no one uses this bathroom. This is a bathroom in a hallway next to a kitchen, right? Who's brushing her hair in here?"

Madison watched his face, his eyes narrowed with genuine curiosity. This was kind of amazing, she thought. This was kind of an amazing observation to come from a boy. That was a real, true thing he'd noticed, a little nugget of bizarre masquerade, one thing in a house that was surely full of such things. She herself was seeing these things, seeing the traces of Suzanne's insecurity everywhere in the house like fingerprints, but good for Jared, noticing them too. She felt the marvel of it rising in her chest, expanding like a balloon. *No wonder people love this*, she thought. No wonder so many people were always getting drunk. Everything around her seemed imbued with the potential to stun, as if every piece of furniture were animate, alive, and had just been keeping its own quiet counsel all this time.

She felt, for an impossible-to-capture moment, very close to her father. She felt the way the world must sigh and soften for him, after those first sharp sips of bourbon, the ice cubes knocking amiably against one another like spare change discovered in a pants pocket. No wonder he wanted her to be the one bringing him the glass.

"It's weird, dude," Jared was still saying. "Fucking gold hairbrush in this bathroom."

"Oh, come on," Zoë said. She picked the hairbrush up with two fingers, then dropped it to the tray with a hollow clatter. Madison let out a cry of delight.

"It's fake!" she said, realizing a moment too late that she shouldn't have sounded quite so gleeful.

"Well, obviously," Zoë said. "They're not going to leave anything nice down here. The housekeepers are probably the only people who even use this bathroom in the first place. Not everyone has, like, the entire security team for an entire company in charge of their house, Madison."

She felt the warmth ebbing across her cheeks. She thought for a few moments it was embarrassment she felt, before she became aware of her own heartbeat and recognized the sensation not as shame but rather as an anger so instinctive it felt as simple and unavoidable as a reflex.

Jared began clapping his hands together.

"Everyone please be the fuck quiet," he said. He cleared everything from the tray and began, with an expert tapping finger, to shake the cocaine loose from its plastic bag. It fell onto the mirror in small, delicate clumps. He took out a credit card, his every motion fluid and stylish, performed for their benefit.

Zoë drew a fifty-dollar bill from her skirt, where it had apparently been tucked against her hip, and rolled it tightly until it was thinner than a cigarette. Jared looked at Madison.

"That's what I figured," he said when she froze.

"Come on," Zoë said. "Just try it."

Madison thought of a word her father loved, *floozy*, and how he would hate to think of her doing this with these other girls, snorting something up her nose, rubbing at her face distractedly the way Zoë was right now, like she'd forgotten what she looked like in a mirror.

"I'm good."

Zoë turned to Jared and shrugged. "I guess it's understandable," she said in a stage whisper. "That she'd be so careful, right now."

Zoë bent over the tray, jerking suddenly from her waist, like a marionette on a string. Jared put his hand to the small of her back and kept it there, as if soothing a sick child. Allie giggled, for no apparent reason, and came over to pat Madison's hand with both of hers.

Madison took a round soap from a silver bowl and unwrapped it, waving it beneath her nose. It smelled clean, like lemons. The soap was freakishly smooth, like a tiny egg. She wanted to slip it into her pocket, but the white dress, quite obviously, had no pockets.

Then, through the pleasant gleam that seemed to overlay everything in the room, she thought of someone in her house, in the kitchen, in her mother's pearlescent bathroom. Tiny things going missing, things the absence of which they'd never notice, until everywhere in the house there were holes in the textures she remembered.

But she couldn't put the soap back; it was already unwrapped. She saw a burnished silver trash can beneath the counter and chucked it. It hit the bottom with a satisfying sound, and Jared looked over at her. She smiled.

Chip wasn't with them. He was somewhere out there, still, in the house. She liked the way it sounded when he said her name; he always sounded like he was smiling, somehow, when he said it.

For the second time that night, she thought of her Grandpa D'Amico. He had haunted her childhood, staring out sunken-eyed from the small number of photographs her nonna kept on display, arranged at the center of her chipped credenza like a shrine. Madison knew so little about him, in the end. Even though he was the one who had named her, long before she'd been born. The last building he'd worked at had been on East Seventy-Second, between Madison and Fifth, and he always told her father it was the perfect name for a street, even better for a girl. *Your mouth just wants to say it,* he would tell her father. *It sounds like a girl with no problems.*

She knew her mother had not wanted to name her Madison. Her

father had won, in the end. And then the twins had been given Italian names. Her mother hadn't gotten to choose any of them.

"Get over here," Zoë said, her voice growing more tender in its commands.

"Excuse me?"

"Come on, I'm sorry for what I said, Madison. I'm, like, blacked out. Come here for a second."

Zoë took Allie's lipstick and swiped it across Madison's lower lip with two expert strokes, the gesture so curt and graceful Madison knew she must have learned it from her own mother.

"There we go," Zoë said then, looking Madison in the eye. They turned together to the mirror and stood side by side, their hips touching, their lipstick the same. Madison tilted her head toward Zoë's. Zoë might not know it, but Madison was doing her a favor. She was allowing it, all the little comments, bending her head in gracious indifference.

"You seem on edge," Zoë said. "You know we're all just teasing, right? You can totally tell me what's going on. I'm here for you."

"We're going downstairs, right?"

"You have to have a sense of humor about yourself," Zoë said, which seemed irrelevant.

AFTER THAT, they were in the ballroom. There was a piano in one corner, somehow as out of place as if it had been wedged into a corner of the kitchen. One of the boys Madison didn't know sat down and plunked the keys with his fists.

There were mirrors everywhere and a wet bar sunk just a few steps below the level of the dance floor and the two chandeliers above them, and with the room dark except for the sconces in the corners, everything was flattering. The light bathed everyone's cheeks and caught the whites of their eyes. Callan picked Allie up, threw her over one shoulder, laid her out on the piano and tickled her. She sat up and threw her legs around his waist, holding him from behind. Neither of them pretended, anymore, not to notice the other.

Music began to blast from invisible speakers somewhere in the walls, that M.I.A. song. Zoë pulled at Madison's dress, yanking so hard that Madison's breasts nearly sprang forward from the vicelike grip of the white lace bodice. They started dancing together. Whenever the sound of gunshots rang out during the song's chorus, Zoë cocked both forefingers in the air above her head.

Chip was behind the bar, pouring Grey Goose into frosted shot glasses.

"No," Callan said, "wait a minute." He ran over to Jared, who was dancing by himself, sunglasses intact, a bottle in his right hand. Callan extracted the bottle and came back over to the bar. Chip watched, quiet.

"Madison," Callan said. "You'll love this, trust me. Let me show you."

She could see every part of Allie's body orienting toward Callan, wanting him to touch her again in the same unthinking, unguarded way he had just minutes earlier.

"Don't do that," Zoë said. "Don't make her do Aftershock. Jesus, what are we, in the eighth grade?"

"Why don't we let her decide for herself?" Callan said, pouring red liquid from the bottle into the two shot glasses. Wyatt materialized at his shoulder and smacked his hands together.

"Fuck yes," he said. "Madison, you done this before?" She shook her head. "Do you like cinnamon?"

"I fucking love cinnamon," she said. She was so surprised by her own words she almost clapped her hand to her mouth. Callan ceded the floor to Wyatt, who pulled a lighter from his pocket with a flourish and showed her how to light the shot on fire, how to slam your palm down over the lip of the shot glass and hold it there for a second.

"You need to wait for that suction," Wyatt said, winking at her.

"Don't we all, though," Callan said, and they slapped five. She ignored the nauseous flip in her stomach. It was refreshing, even, to be feeling nausea from so many different sources. It was like standing in front of a clamoring crowd of angry people, all shouting over one another. You were absolved of all responsibility; you no longer had to listen to any of them.

Wyatt lit the shot for her, and she covered the burning liquid with her hand, feeling the sticky suction ring forming. She was learning, too, that everything went down easier once you had a few drinks down there already. She was aware of how unpleasant the shot tasted, but it was remote. The pain was far away, she would fix it later.

Chip was still looking over at them, not even pretending to ignore her. Callan reached out and pinched her skin through her dress, just above her hip bone, and within seconds Chip was up from the sunken bar, shouldering Callan away from her.

"Give it a rest," he said, putting one hand to Madison's arm and moving her steadily backward, away from the boys, ignoring their laughter. He put his other hand to the small of her back and they were on the stairs, up and out of the room.

HER MOUTH WAS STILL TANGY from the shots, and Chip was moving ahead of her through an unfamiliar part of the house. She was only holding his hand by two fingers, four of their fingers all locked together.

You're not my mother, she had said to Lily in the car. Everything felt spiky, now. Every possible image applied an unwelcome pressure, as though with each errant thought she were pressing her own fingertips against fresh bruises all over her body. Lily in the car. Her father sprawled out on the floor. She walked with Chip down a darkened hallway.

She stopped near a pair of French doors that looked out over a side patio. There was an outdoor fireplace, mysteriously lit—so Zoë was right, there *were* still people around, wandering the house. Chip had moved away again, and she stood there, neither outside nor where she was, waiting for something to happen. So when he walked up next to her, put his hand to her shoulder and cupped it as though it were a fragile animal he was afraid to crush, it felt expected, inevitable even. She was barely even excited.

"Making a break for it?"

She smiled but said nothing, an instinct for which she later felt an absurd, awestruck gratitude.

"Everything okay?"

"I don't want to talk about it, if that's okay."

"I wasn't. I was talking about—you just seem tough. I see how you ignore, you know, Zoë's bullshit."

"She's the brave one," Madison said. "She would never have been this brave two months ago, trust me."

She could feel Chip's breath on her neck.

"Well," he said, "she's probably just trying to get a rise out of you. It's pretty exotic, you know, for someone like her. And I think Wyatt is actually afraid of you. Which is very impressive, I have to say."

"Sure," she said.

"I'm serious."

"Did he—I mean, is his costume a joke on purpose? Does Wyatt understand, you know, irony?"

She was worried she had used that wrong. They taught it in English every year, but no one ever learned it well enough not to keep making the mistake.

Chip laughed.

"All I know is, I wish I'd gotten here sooner to see his face when you saw that costume. It's kind of endearing, when you think about it. It would never have occurred to him that it might be awkward, not until you walked in. He's like this big idiot that can't help bumping into things."

"It's not awkward."

"No, I know. I didn't mean it like that."

His hands were on her waist, kneading the fabric of her dress. "Was everything okay with Amanda, earlier? She kind of Irish exited there."

"Could we not talk anymore?" Madison said. She'd said it from somewhere purely sincere, but he swallowed and she saw that he'd taken it for a dare, an invitation.

He cradled her chin, her jaw. His other hand was on her shoulder, drawing her toward him, so that even when he was reaching for her, it felt like she was leaning into him.

Once it was happening, once they were kissing, he took his hand from her shoulder and pressed it to her hip bone, his fingers warm through the fabric of her dress, and pushed back until her entire body was flush with the door behind them.

She thought for a moment of the phantom adults somewhere in the house, that familiar clinch of panic. That reluctance to be spotted if she didn't know she'd been spotted.

But then Chip took her bottom lip lightly between his teeth, pressed their bodies closer together, and reached for the thick silk curtains next to them. He drew a curtain around them, hiding everything but their entwined feet, and they stayed there for a few minutes, everything about him both hard and soft, pressing into her with delicious force. His hands never straying from her face and her hips so that she didn't have to make any real decisions.

"Where's Abbott?" Wyatt's voice came ricocheting down the hall, the open ballroom door allowing a wedge of warm light to pierce the darkness. "He said he was getting more beers from upstairs. If he is wandering around up there, I swear to God—"

"Dude, will you give me a fucking break?" Chip yelled over his shoulder, but he'd already stepped out, and he barely looked back at her as he pinched the skin above her elbow and then broke into a jog, disappeared.

She went back to the ballroom, to the soft lights and the reflections of everyone dancing in the mirrors all around them. To the T.I. song blaring as Allie mouthed along to the lyrics, which of course Madison had never realized were all about sex, of course they were. Zoë and Wyatt had disappeared from the party and Allie crawled on top of Callan on a brocade love seat in the corner.

Madison stood near the other boys, and tried to remember to smile whenever they all laughed.

Soon Zoë was back, black makeup gathering at the corners of her eyes and her face otherwise untouched. She asked if Madison wanted a ride home, she'd called one of her housekeepers. She'd come get the car tomorrow, whatever, she didn't want Allie harassing her about it. Allie didn't even look up at the mention of her name. She was still coiled on top of Callan, her legs thrown across his lap, when Madison left them there, the lights still casting colored patterns on all the walls and mirrors, the music blaring.

AN SUV THE COLOR OF FADED PENNIES was parked near the fountain. They stood uncertainly in the doorway of the house at first, Zoë swimming one hand into the air behind her, until Madison stepped forward and caught her. Zoë draped her body over Madison's like a scarf, her heels dragging on the cobblestones. A woman had already jumped down from the driver's seat, pausing only to clutch Zoë's chin in her hand and roughly shake her.

"She's fine. Just a mess. Get in," the woman said to Madison, her voice quieter than seemed to match her brusque, angry treatment of Zoë's unfolded body. "I'll drive you, too."

She had a thick Jamaican accent and her eyes in the rearview mirror tracked Madison's every movement. When Zoë had finally agreed to buckle her seat belt, they left.

Madison wondered if Wyatt could see them from his bedroom. If that's even where he'd taken Zoë, or if they'd stopped at some more accessible spot. It was so easy for them to shut themselves up in a room, like they owed you nothing at all. Her mother, Lily, even poor Mina Dawes—each one of them was running on the fumes of her own fear these past weeks, that Madison might ask a question with no acceptable answer. But men didn't feel that fear. They just took themselves out of the running, so that you felt foolish, grasping, if you wanted to ask them anything at all. Madison could never have wandered upstairs to knock on Wyatt's door, ask him to help her carry Zoë to the car. She knew this without question.

Zoë crumpled against her window and jammed her head at an angle, gazing up at the night outside as it streamed past. Madison's stomach sloshed, the edges of her vision both slurred and sharp. She tried to parcel out the memories of Chip, knowing that if she thought of all of them right now they'd begin to lose their luster, become imagined. They'd cross into the past, and she'd have to fight for her version of what had happened, defend these images to an invisible jury. This was real, the soft, fuzzy patch at the edge of his chin. Or the callus on his thumb; I felt it.

The car had pulled up at her parents' gate before she even realized that the woman driving hadn't asked her for directions. She wondered if this woman knew Lily, and then wondered if that was an offensive thing to wonder. She thanked her, and as she grabbed the door handle, Zoë, suddenly reanimated, grabbed at her wrist.

"Wait," she said, "you need this." She reached into her purse and slid out three sticks of gum. "Don't worry, it's sugarless, but you need it. They smell it on you."

Madison looked down at the gaping purse, at the pack of gum.

"These are your last three," she said. "You smell more than I do, you'll need them."

Zoë let her head loll back onto the seat, her job done, and closed her eyes.

"No," she said, "I don't. Just take them."

MADISON UNWRAPPED EACH PIECE of gum, one at a time, and then began to chew, letting the false sweetness spread across her tongue. As the car disappeared into the darkness she stood, alone, listening to the night around her. She could not see her house, of course; it was protected from view by the oak trees, set too far back on the property to be seen from the road. And yet she could feel it there, floating in the darkness up above her, waiting.

She turned to her left and looked at the black sedan parked about two hundred feet down the road, its right wheels sunk into the muddy grass beside the tarmac. She started to walk down the road toward the car. It was getting harder, as she got tired, to walk in her mother's shoes, and of course she was also drunk. No one was watching; there was no harm in admitting this here, on the dark road, to herself. No one was awake up above her. Whatever the house was waiting for, it wasn't her.

"I'm drunk," she said into the night.

The black sedan, though, was a different story. Someone was in there because he'd been told to sit there all night long. He was surely watching her now. He was waiting, she knew, to swoop in just before any potential danger made its presence felt. And wasn't this dangerous, right now? She was drunk, wandering down a poorly lit road, practically begging for some loaded suburban teenager to run her down. And wouldn't that be perfect, she thought, wouldn't everyone eat that up. In most of the things she'd read about her father online, she and the boys had been, at most, impersonal foot-notes included in the final paragraphs. In part, probably, because she was pretty dull, as teenage girls went. This was like the most exciting night she'd ever had, and she hadn't even done any of the available drugs.

But this, she thought, this could definitely be its own headline. Disgraced financier's daughter wanders dark suburb alone, unsuper-vised, jumps in front of reckless driver. Isn't that just what everyone expected of her, why Zoë watched her so closely, why Chip took pity on her? She was even better, at this point, than something truly volatile; she was something that, at any moment, might *become* volatile. Wasn't that why Lily hated her lately?

Even alone, even when she didn't say it out loud, the word, *disgraced*, settled in the back of her throat, threatened to keep her from breathing.

The point was that this man should already be out, walking toward her, hands up in a gesture equal parts defensive and soothing. He should be asking why she was out there, if she needed help. She was close enough, now, that he must be able to see her in the rearview. This man wasn't doing his job.

But no, because her father wouldn't have hired someone like that. Whatever had happened in the city, it hadn't been because her father didn't know how to keep her safe. She knew this even when she herself was angry, even when her mother had bitten her bottom lip while they talked about him that night, in the bathtub. They still knew this.

She stopped in the middle of the road. Another five or six steps would have brought her close enough to touch the trunk of the car. It sat there, untroubled, its lights dark, its engine off. How much nearer would they let her get before they admitted to themselves, to her, that she was trying to get their attention? It seemed strange to her, now that she was considering this, that this one car was enough to do the job. But then, didn't everyone think her father was still in the city? She thought again of the men in the car, of the information they had that she did not, of everything they might be able to tell her.

She stood there for so long she was convinced she could hear the men, because now she was sure there must be two of them. But of course their windows wouldn't be open. It was a chilly night for Halloween, unseasonably crisp. The car sat there still, unapologetic, giving up nothing. She closed her eyes, and waited.

EVENTUALLY SHE WALKED UP THE DRIVE, disabled the alarm system, and entered the house. She slipped off her mother's shoes in the mud room. She left them where they fell, like evidence to be tagged later by the crime scene investigator.

When she moved into the kitchen, her father was sitting at the breakfast table.

NINETEEN

It was the day before Thanksgiving, and it was the art collection. That was why Mina had been summoned, if you could classify the razor-polite conversation she'd had with Isabel earlier that afternoon as being summoned.

Her morning had begun with promise, when she'd gathered her household staff in the kitchen to explain that two other couples, no children, had been invited for Thanksgiving dinner, and that it was very important everything be finished, or at the very least doing something fragrant in the oven, by the time the guests arrived for cocktails. Everyone had understood right away what needed to be done, and all morning long the ground floor of the house hummed, like choreographed traffic zipping through midtown. But Mina herself sat in the breakfast nook, without much to do. She watched the traffic from a high floor, behind glass.

She'd taken the latest issue of *Vanity Fair* in there, hoping to hide from Cecia, her head housekeeper. Despite her genuine intentions, to read about the Colombian hostages, she'd been paging through a photo spread on England's future princess when Isabel's name showed up on her phone.

"Happy early Thanksgiving."

"You too," Mina had said. She'd moved into the den for the call; she didn't like the way Cecia had looked at her when the phone fizzed on the marble counter. They clearly didn't want Mina yammering in the kitchen while they all tried to get the house ready, which was laughable and offensive except that Mina took their unspoken point. She darted now back into the kitchen, cradling the phone between her ear and her neck, and avoided Cecia's eye as she withdrew a bottle of Pinot Grigio and a bowl of grapes from the refrigerator. She returned to the den.

"You're having people at yours, right?" Isabel said. Mina had the distinct impression they were treading water, but she wasn't sure why.

"Yes," Mina said, "and I've delegated so well that I'm not really sure what I'm supposed to be doing right now." She decided to embellish, for Isabel's benefit. "Everywhere I turn, it seems like I'm underfoot. I think Cecia wants me to go to a movie or something, and just stay out of the way until tomorrow afternoon."

"Well, that's how you know you've done your prep right," Isabel said, and though Mina had been trying to portray herself as a buffoon so that Isabel might feel more comfortable confiding in her, of course—as always—they had ended up with Isabel soothing Mina, rather than the alternative.

Eventually, the conversation came to a point: it was the paintings. A woman would be coming by, from Sotheby's. Beatrice North.

"I'll come over, Isabel. I'm happy to drop by. She sounds horrendous."

Of course, Isabel had chided her for that, but then Mina had known she would. Beatrice was just the *top* in her field, Mina, don't be catty. But she needed Mina to say it, to dislike Beatrice North, didn't she? Isabel couldn't. She didn't have that capital to squander, not right now.

This was how she kept you near her, Mina thought. This was why you endured the constant reminders that you were dull compared to her, that you didn't have her depth or her skin or her marriage. That you didn't sparkle, couldn't, when you stood beside her. This was how she kept you as her friend, regardless. She let you see the things she couldn't do, had never been allowed to do in either family, the one she'd inherited or the one she'd chosen, crafted. She let you see that she wanted to say something, but couldn't, and you got to say it for her, and she let you feel the value of it. She made you essential, in some small way, so that you knew you weren't as disposable as you felt. Mina knew there must have been other girls who did this for a younger Isabel, at Smith, in the city before she was married. But Mina was the one who did it for her now.

She'd waited for Isabel to say it, to ask. The house continued to buzz. Somewhere above her head, a door closed. The women in the kitchen spoke to one another with effortless urgency, their Spanish clicking and rolling past Mina's ears. She didn't speak the language.

"That might be helpful," Isabel had said finally.

She'd been out by the pool when Mina arrived, wrapped in a teal blue cashmere blanket, the boatneck of her loose-fitting black shirt severe against her pronounced collarbone. She looked even thinner than when Mina had seen her last, in October, but something had clicked back into place. What had been so uncamouflaged in those early weeks was once again monitored, what had been submerged, murky, was once again held at the surface. Watching Isabel by herself on the blustery November afternoon, drying leaves whirling at her ankles like skittish pets, Mina knew why they hadn't seen each other. She saw that their one icy phone call, right after the congressional hearings three weeks earlier, hadn't been a momentary lapse in their closeness. They were going to return, now, to their usual distance. *Oh, he's absolutely fine,* Isabel had said. *Most of the unpleasantness is well behind him, I think. He's looking like himself again.*

Still, she was the one Isabel had called today.

Beatrice North was, it had to be said, just as horrendous as Mina had predicted. Wherever Isabel was graceful in spite of her sharpness, her reserve, Beatrice North was simply hard-edged. Her dark hair was drawn back from her face in a ponytail so smooth and severe it was easy to forget it was her hair, her dress and matching jacket expensive and anonymous so you could imagine fifteen more identical outfits hanging in the walk-in that was surely the pride of her quiet studio in the East Seventies. She held a sleek leather portfolio close to her chest, as if it contained state secrets.

She was a trespasser, but Isabel had invited her in. She'd sanctioned it, as if that mattered. Or was it Bob's idea, Mina wondered. Was he the one insisting they circle the wagons?

What a funny metaphor; she wondered what could possibly have brought that phrase to mind. Why did people say that? As if even Los Angeles, the edge of everything, had any actual pioneers left. As if any vague chiming of misfortune's arrival could ever return them to the raw-boned, wind-bitten women who had preceded them, pushed a beleaguered path across all the old landscapes. *Circling the wagons.* How silly.

They walked from room to room, pausing before each work, and when they returned to the downstairs hallway, Beatrice craned her neck in the direction of Bob's door.

"That's my husband's study," Isabel said coolly. "There's nothing of interest there."

"We'll have to sit down and go through the listing together in more detail, of course," Beatrice replied, not losing so much as a blink. "I'd like to say we could have these in the lineup for a March date. If you're interested in moving that quickly."

"I am," Isabel said. "I think that would be best."

Mina let herself drift, almost as if she were just shifting her weight to her left leg, a bit closer to Isabel. At the same time Beatrice North seemed to shift to her right, and the unfortunate effect of both women moving slightly at the same time was to make it seem that the three of them were circling one another. It felt absurd, an accident of choreography, but still Mina felt the hair on her arms stiffen.

Beatrice North smiled, stretching her painted lips across her face in an expression that seemed to reveal some wound, involve some painful denuding.

"I should have everything I need," she said. "I really am so pleased you've gone with our house."

"Well, it was really a matter of the time frame," Isabel said. "That, and the guarantee."

"Of course. And you know, it's so rare that you see someone who works so closely with MoMA gravitate toward drawings rather than contemporary painting or sculpture. It's really quite unique, this collection. We can see a whole story, a history really, unfolding. There's a whole trajectory of cause and effect there. We can sell it that way. That's the narrative for the auction, I mean."

"Well, that's good," Isabel said. "I'm glad you have a narrative."

Mina looked at Isabel, at the slight puckering of her chin, and she saw that Isabel couldn't bring herself to make the woman leave.

"I understand that discretion is going to be—that this is a private matter, insofar as it can be kept that way," Beatrice continued. Blood-red fingernails curled around her portfolio, holding it against her hip.

"Well," Isabel said, "I'm sure you'll get a big splash when it's announced, whether you like it or not. But I don't expect that to fall within your purview. I don't expect it would matter, actually, even if we tried. Of course I've been selling things for years, but no one's ever shown any interest."

"That's the nature of the beast," said Beatrice North.

OUT BY THE POOL, later, it was clear to Mina that they had at most another ten minutes before the rain came. It seemed silly that they were outside at all, but after Madison barged in with Lily and Beatrice took a hint and let herself be sent on her way, Isabel had insisted they come out here. Mina hadn't been sure she shouldn't follow Beatrice out, but Isabel had touched her arm, so brief and light it felt almost secret, conspiratorial, and so she had stayed.

A chilled bottle of white wine, unseasonable though it was, sat in an ice bucket on the table between them. Lily brought it out without being asked, at least that Mina had seen. There was something new between Isabel and the nanny, some unrehearsed choreography now existing between the needs of one and the duties of the other.

"Are you sure you want white?" Mina said when Lily appeared with the bottle, and Isabel had waved a hand in the air, leaving it unclear who was being waved away. The wine remained.

Mina waited a few minutes before she asked anything.

"Weren't you afraid he'd wander out and come across that woman?" This was a gamble. She'd guessed where and how Bob was spending his days, but it was just that: a guess.

"I'm not afraid of him," Isabel said, her black sunglasses confronting Mina head-on.

"No, I know."

"He's out. He's been out all afternoon."

Of course, Mina thought. He might have come home, unexpectedly, but then she had me here with her.

"I don't know where he goes," Isabel said, and Mina saw that it was her role, here, to acknowledge this honesty by changing the subject.

"Do you really think you'll sell all of it?"

"If they want it," Isabel said.

"But not—not all of it, right?"

"Isn't it in poor taste?" Isabel said, a harsh, flat tone creeping into her voice. She picked up her wineglass and drained it. "Isn't that the point, now? I'm not allowed any of it?" She nibbled her bottom lip with great fervor for a few moments. "He asked me to hang on to Madison's painting, if we can."

"The Picasso," Mina said, thinking of the painting that hung at the end of Madison's bedroom hallway and then wishing she hadn't identified it quite so quickly. She knew the story well, that he'd bought it shortly after he made CEO, as a present for his daughter. But Isabel didn't so much as look away from the pool, the surface of which had held her gaze for their entire conversation.

"The Picasso," she said. "There's that Newman drawing, the study for one of the zips. The one he gave me when he proposed. He didn't ask after that one, however."

"That doesn't mean anything," Mina said, afraid that her own pity, for Isabel, would be written clear across her face either way.

"You know I started that first year or two," Isabel continued. "When we were first married. People were so dismissive of drawings. Obviously he wasn't CEO yet, but still. And they knew my father, too. They could never believe I was in the meeting to see about buying just drawings. You can't imagine how many times I heard that. *Just* the drawings?'"

Mina tried to hold herself very still, looking out at the pool with Isabel, watching the outlines of the trees beyond where they sat, coming into stark relief against the darkening sky.

"But it wasn't because that was what I could afford," Isabel said. "Or it wasn't just about that. I love those drawings. You can see the whole process. You can see how the man's mind worked. You can see him putting together the thing that will make him a success, everything he had to do to get there. Only the things he needed."

"They're beautiful."

Isabel shrugged.

"Some people don't think so," she said. "But those were mine." She wrapped herself more tightly in the blanket and let her head rest back against the chair. Mina imagined she'd closed her eyes.

"Madison loves that painting," Isabel said. "You should have seen her when we took her to Madrid. She stood in front of *Guernica* with him for a half hour, and he explained it all to her. They took so long I left and waited for them on a bench on the plaza outside."

Mina knew then that it hadn't been Bob's idea, the auction. It wasn't Bob who knew to stay a few steps ahead of whatever would be written about them. He was going to leave it all to her. Isabel had tried to hide away for a while, to refuse to leave the house and enter the world. She'd tried to force his hand, but it hadn't worked. He'd won, he always would in the end, and now Isabel had to be in charge. She had no other choice.

"You know what's next, Min."

But Isabel said no more than that, and Mina did not reply. She didn't know the answer; after all this time, she couldn't say which things Isabel would mourn the most. She must care about all of it. Isabel couldn't stand to live here, in this house of all houses, otherwise. But Mina didn't think they were talking about MoMA or the apartments or sending the kids away, getting them out of Greenwich. Or even Congress, again. It's something else, she thought. She's going to say one of the words we don't say. Prison, foreclosure. Divorce.

It's our husbands, she thought. The spirit or the letter of their laws. It's what our lives would look like, suddenly, without them.

There were so many things Isabel might be talking about, and the thought that Mina might reply as if she knew the answer, and be thinking of something that hadn't yet occurred to Isabel, was a paralyzing one. And so she said nothing, and Isabel didn't repeat her question. And even though they hadn't actually discussed any of those more graphic harbingers of misfortune, even though Isabel had confided nothing, it was in this moment that Mina felt closer to her friend than she had in years, since those first years before this house behind them had been built.

After another few minutes of silence, it began to rain.

TWENTY

It seemed to Lily at first that coming home to find that woman in the house, and Mina Dawes swanning around like the mistress of ceremonies, would be a surprise so scattering that they'd lose the afternoon for good. Madison had already been sassy to the point of insolence for the entire ride home from school, despite the early dismissal for Thanksgiving. By the time they reached the house, it seemed like all Lily could hope for just to get Madison upstairs and into her room where she'd have no target but herself.

And then they came home to find Isabel acting as if the past two months had been imagined. Throwing her weight around, acting as if she'd never disappeared, never hidden away upstairs. Giving a tour of the house to a stranger.

It wasn't good. Lily tried, at first, to convince Madison to sit down in the kitchen for a snack.

"We've got fresh strawberries," she said. "Fruit salad?"

"No thank you," Madison said. "Don't you find it a little, like, disgusting, the way we just demand every kind of fruit or vegetable at any time of year? Zoë was just telling me about this. In her bio class, they were talking about genetically modified crops. It's so pathetic, how we have to have whatever we want and don't ever even think about the consequences."

"I could even whip some heavy cream," Lily continued, undeterred. "You can eat them with cream and brown sugar. We may be able to get them, ugly Americans and sinners that we are, for the rest of the winter, but they'll be less juicy with every batch. I promise you that."

Madison looked up at her, her face open, unwrapped by pure anxiety.

"Don't make jokes like that," Madison said. "I feel like we shouldn't make jokes like that."

Lily's hands twisted with regret, then, at the words she'd chosen: sinful, ugly. She wanted to apologize, but she knew from these past few weeks with Madison that showing this teenage girl her soft underbelly would be a mistake. Even in capitulation, even during a moment of Madison's own childish fear.

She sat down beside her at the table.

"You don't have to watch what you say," she said. "Not in front of me, and certainly not when you're here at home. I understand you want to be careful when you're out there, I don't blame you. But you don't need to worry when you're here, okay?"

She could see Madison leaning in toward her, hungry for more. But since the morning of the slap, and again on the night of the Halloween party, Lily felt unsure of when and how Madison might choose to deploy her weapons. She turned away, and pretended not to see the way Madison put one finger to her sternum and held it there just for a second, as if to steady some heirloom left wobbling on its treacherous perch.

Lily washed the strawberries, making as much noise as she could, then told Madison she didn't have to stay to eat them.

SHE WAS MIDWAY through dinner prep when Jackson called. During her work hours, which he knew he was never supposed to do, and to talk about the holiday weekend, which she'd already made clear she wouldn't discuss further.

"I hear you," he said. "I've been trying to hear you. But you haven't been into the city in, like, a month."

"I don't think it's been that long," Lily said. "And I tried to explain this last night. I don't want to be gone for the entire weekend, and if I don't have the actual meal at my mother's, with my family, you know that will be six months of a soap opera. They're already furious that I don't visit more."

"We can go over there more often, too," Jackson said, and they both held still and let the offer pass into polite, uncluttered silence.

He knew full well that she'd never ask him to do that. He'd visited with her once. Her mother had asked him not a single question, had snapped at him when he offered to help in the galley kitchen, then demanded to know why he looked so "perplexed" when he stood and watched, helpless, as she removed casserole dishes from the oven in a flurry.

Lily had known, even as they sat down to lunch, that she would not ask him to visit the apartment again. She knew he thought he was proving his own seriousness, as a man, by dating a girl who'd worked her way through the Ivy League, and that he'd been ever so slightly disappointed by the stability and self-possession of her family. He'd grown up in a perfectly unglamorous family, managing but far from comfortable, and he was the first one to go away to college. And he thought these facts nullified any differences between him and Lily's family. But her mother saw those differences as fundamental; Lily couldn't explain this to him. His father was a drunk and his mother was sleepwalking through her own life, and as long as he never called Pennsylvania to ask for money, they saw his decisions as entirely his own. She couldn't explain to him, or chose not to, that her mother saw him as little more than the sum of his selfish, frivolous choices. Two Ivy League degrees so that he could be broke, writing mostly for the web, not even a "real journalist." Always dressed like a slob. Always sponging off her hardworking daughter, a girl who—her mother still seemed convinced—had brilliance and clout in her future.

"I need to be back here by Friday night," Lily said. "I'm sorry."

"I'm not trying to be a dick. But you are far, far too loyal to these people. It's getting delusional."

"There aren't degrees of loyalty," she said. "That isn't what that word means. You are loyal to someone or you aren't."

He said nothing.

"I just don't even think it's about loyalty right now," she continued. "We aren't even there yet. I'm just trying to get them through each successive school day."

"Okay," he said. "Well, I would like to see you soon, if only to discuss what's been happening. I am very concerned that you aren't taking this seriously."

"I take care of two eight-year-olds who haven't slept a full night in two months. I'm taking it seriously."

"You know what I mean," he said, and kept talking. She thought ahead to what still remained to be done for the weekend. Isabel had rented a limo, for tomorrow, to take the kids into the city for the weekend. They did not know this yet. Bob was, as far as Lily knew, still asleep on the couch in his study. He'd been in there, this time, for nearly forty-eight hours straight. He'd taken breaks this week only to field incoming calls from his colleagues, other men she could only assume were ignoring their own wives and families, drinking themselves into their own specific bouts of paralytic grief. In the immediate weeks after his return, Lily had been told to ignore the phone, leave it off the hook for hours at a time, but that was no longer a feasible strategy. If Bob wanted to answer it, he was going to answer it. And his infantry wanted to commiserate. They wanted their Silverback.

"I was talking to some of the DealBook guys," Jackson said. "That one guy just left, you know, to start his own site. You remember my friend Gabe? You met him that time at the Exley. He says it's going to get uglier. They're saying that when they really start going through the actual records, from Weiss, your guy is going to look incredibly—"

The phone didn't beep through right in that moment, though that would have been so much tidier. In reality, Lily had to go on listening to her boyfriend's halting cadences, the loud chewing of his Vietnamese sandwich in between grievances. It was several minutes before the other phone call gave her a graceful out.

"Someone's on the other line," she said, abandoning Jackson for a few moments, without warning.

"They filed for bankruptcy," he was saying when she clicked back over. "So there's going to *have* to be an actual investigation. He can't just clap his hands and make it go away. And neither can you, Lil."

She tried to picture Chip Abbott, who was on the other line. The Abbott family kept to themselves; she couldn't remember the mother's face, which meant she wasn't one of the group that was always arrayed around Alexandra Barker, moving with her from room to room like her own personal storm cloud. When had Madison started dating Chip?

"I have to go," she told Jackson. "There's a boy on the phone for Madison."

"You aren't doing this on purpose, are you?" Jackson said. "Like, you're not sticking around there thinking that you can use this to your advantage, down the road? Because I could get behind that, honestly. If there was at least a strategy. But you aren't doing that, are you?"

TWENTY-ONE

What Madison hadn't told her mother was that she'd already spoken to her father. Had encountered him several times since Halloween, in the kitchen, late at night. Just the two of them, always the unspoken agreement to pretend it was coincidental. He'd talk to her, ramble in long streams about people she'd never met. One night, he'd made them hot toddies and cooked soup. He told her one thing, then another, all these pieces of information stacking up somewhere inside her chest, like dollar bills.

The first time had been just a coincidence, though. She was relatively sure. She'd come inside, after Halloween, after Chip and Zoë and the silent cars down by the gate. Her father had been sitting in the kitchen. Not waiting for her, maybe, but there.

WHEN SHE CAME IN, he kept his elbows down and his chin propped on his hands, moving only his eyebrows. But when he cleared his throat she saw that he was holding the pose with shaky confidence, that he must have seen her on a security screen somewhere—or possibly, she thought with distress, gotten a call from one of the men in the cars down the hill—and known she was coming.

"Hi," she whispered.

"You're just getting home?"

"There was a Halloween party."

"And you're dressed as . . ."

She held up her angel wings, which had come off after only fifteen minutes at the party, a crumpled handful of white tulle and curved wire.

"Of course. What else would you be?"

"What are you doing up?"

"Oh, I couldn't sleep. I just came out here—I thought I might have a snack."

They both looked down at the bare table.

"Did you have dinner with the boys?"

"No, I wasn't hungry then."

"Is Mom upstairs?"

"Isabel?" He said this with genuine inquiry in his voice. "Yes, she's—she's asleep."

She looked at his face, the first time she'd been permitted to do so in weeks. The untamed eyebrows and the thick creases that led from his nose down to his mouth, like scores cut in wet clay. The large, jumping tendons that spanned the backs of his hands. He looked like the same man as always, but faded, rubbed with a dirty eraser.

"Would you like something to eat?"

"If you're hungry," she said, and he shuffled over to the refrigerator. She sat down, the alcohol hum between her ears amplifying every noise—the sucking sound the fridge made when he tugged at its door, the worn cloth of his old NYU sweatpants rustling against itself.

Her father hunched before the purring refrigerator, the Sub-Zero he loved so much. Often he would pat it as he passed through the kitchen. He took off his glasses and hooked them from each ear, letting them dangle beneath his chin. She was pretty sure this gesture had originally been an artificial one, designed to delight her when she was a toddler, when she'd loved to swipe at them, to put her fingertips to his chin. By now, though, it was a habit. He did it all the time, but she thought about how long it had been, this fall, since she'd seen him do it.

"I don't really know what we have," he said. "This is not my forte."

"I know," she said. "It doesn't matter. I'll just have some grapefruit or something. I'm sure we have fruit."

"That's a morning meal," her father said, twisting his neck to see into the corners of shelves as if new food might suddenly appear there. Madison smiled in spite of herself; her father, like Nonna Concetta, always had strict guidelines as to what foods could be eaten at what times of day.

"I'm not even really hungry," she said.

"Well, I am. Now that we're talking about it, I'm famished."

He looked around the room with expectant eagerness, then clapped his hands together.

"I bet I know what we have. Is there bread in that bread box?"

"Is that a serious question?"

He smiled, and she could see his embarrassment. "I don't know, Mad. I don't know when in the week Lily does the marketing."

"Does the marketing? Like, to stock the 'icebox' with Wonder Bread and cans of Tab? I don't know if anyone really 'does the marketing' in this day and age, Dad."

"Don't insult Tab," he said, smiling and waving the bread knife in her general direction as he considered the various quarter loaves clustered together in the bread box. "Tab made me the man I am today."

She was careful to breathe slowly, through her nostrils, so that it wouldn't sound anything like a sigh.

"We're on our way here. We'll just do a Nonna Connie special. Just some oil, some garlic, bread crumbs, red pepper. It's so easy, you could make it yourself."

"Thanks for that vote of confidence," Madison said. "So easy even a moron can master it!"

"It's hardly your fault, princess. We haven't taught you anything, have we? That's my fault. Your mother's a fantastic cook."

"She never cooks."

"I don't like her having to worry when we're entertaining."

"She could cook for us, though."

"Your mother has cooked for you many times."

"I can barely even remember five times she's cooked for me."

"Come on, Madison. That's not true."

"Don't tell me that," she said. She could hear her tone sharpen, shimmer. "Don't tell me what's happened. I was there."

Her father stood up stiffly. He'd been searching in a low corner drawer for his favorite skillet, the heavy cast iron.

"Then don't do that," he replied. "Don't pretend you don't remember our life."

He crossed back and heaved the pan onto the stove with a clatter. Madison flinched, but there were no sounds from upstairs. Her father drizzled the oil.

"We'd cook for you out on Shelter all the time. All those times your grandparents forced me to go eat stringy chicken paillard at that godforsaken club, you were at home eating something your mother and I had sautéed with love. So don't sit there telling me otherwise."

She waited for him to reassure her that he wasn't really angry, but he just put the pot of water on. Her father could be like that, though. His storms were just like real storms: they'd make themselves known in terrifying flashes, then move on to some other target and leave you cringing in a suddenly peaceful world.

It had always been him, she thought. He had always been the one to cook dinner out on Shelter. Sometimes her mother would come in for the end of his preparations, fastening an earring with one hand, reaching out to stir a pot with the other. Complimenting him on whatever he'd made. But the cooking dinner, together, had never been her mother's idea.

"Why are you awake?" she asked again. His knife struck the wood-block cutting board.

"I haven't been sleeping well." He began to grind salt from a shaker, holding it in the air above the boiling water and letting the grains fall.

"You know that's bad for the salt," she admonished, and he made a gun shape with his thumb and forefinger, cocking it in her direction and sucking his teeth for effect.

"Good girl."

"You've been sleeping in your study," she pushed. "Maybe you can't sleep because you've been on a sofa with the TV blasting all night."

"I wouldn't rule it out, Madison. I wouldn't rule that out at all."

He turned back to the pasta and she was left with her middling victory.

"Why don't you tell me about the party," he said.

"It was boring."

"I doubt that."

"Well, it took place in Suzanne Welsh's ballroom."

"Say no more. Why'd you go, then?" He looked over, one hand in the pocket of his sweats and the other holding the wooden spoon. "A boy, possibly?"

She said nothing.

"I wonder," her father said, "if I might be more inclined to keep some things to myself, say the vodka on your breath, if I had a window on what you were thinking."

"Blackmail?"

"Whatever it takes."

"He's no one special."

"No one is, compared to you." He smiled. "Everyone's got something to work with, and that will be yours. You'll always be holding more cards than the other guy."

"What was yours? Your thing to work with?"

He peered over the tops of his glasses. "I was cocky. And hungry. Risky combination. You generally want more of one than the other, if you're really ambitious you want to have that bottomless tolerance for eating shit, you know? You can't be too high on your horse. So sometimes it took me too long to figure out what was what. When you're living in Brooklyn with Nonna, you've got to keep pushing. There's a lot you've got to push right past."

"But you didn't push past Mom."

She felt it, then. That she was rising to his level, speaking to him the way he spoke to her. Even drunk, she knew it wasn't parity, but it was still something very, very difficult to do with her father.

"Well that," he said, "is my good fortune, kiddo. It's my good luck that she didn't always feel the way she felt about me that first night. She gave in."

The garlic and oil were heating up, and they sat for a while in companionable silence.

"Do you think Concetta will ever sell that building?"

"Who knows," he said. "We aren't still sitting on that thing for my own lack of trying." He prodded the garlic with a wooden spoon, setting it to sizzle. "Your grandmother likes any arrangement that gives her the maximum amount of power."

"Dad," Madison said. "Come on. Pot, kettle."

"I didn't say it was a bad thing. You know Nonna's story. Her father ran a hardware store and she thought your Pop was a class act just because he had proximity to important people. Two generations later, we've got you. So whatever your mother may say about Nonna's table manners, no one can say the woman isn't impressive."

"I wouldn't want her as my landlord, though."

"Having been in that exact situation until I was twenty-two, I can tell you that your instincts are correct. You've seen the apartment. She likes everything in its place."

"You like everything in its place," Madison said, gesturing vaguely out at the house, the pool, the woods.

"That's your mother," he said. "I know your mother acts like I forced this house down her throat, but I didn't. She picked every single fixture. You know I didn't have a say in anything but my own two rooms, and even for those ones, she's credited as consigliere."

Madison smiled.

"Maybe what we need," she said, "is a *wartime* consigliere." Her father laughed.

"Nice," he said. "Very nice. But no, you know that isn't what I care about. I only care that everyone knows where they are when they walk in. Which silk for the drapes—I could care less. Jesus, the drapes. I love your mother, but she thinks she's low maintenance because her indulgences are for her, not for other women. She wants to be high maintenance, trust me, she can be. I won't tell you what we spent on the goddamn hardware alone, for the drapes in the den. I'd have to cry."

"What do you mean, that everyone knows where they are?" Madison said.

"They walk into an event, here, in our home, they know who I am. That's what I mean."

"But then you do care how it looks."

"No," he said. "I don't. It's about other people and what they expect. I could care less."

"I don't care what people think of us," Madison said, not sure if this was what he was talking about, really. "I don't. Everyone keeps waiting for me to panic about it, or something. It doesn't bother me."

Her father paused, because now that she'd said something, they couldn't just keep watching the pasta.

"Are people talking to you about our situation?"

"No," she said. "I think they're afraid, still."

"So we've got that at least. For a bit longer."

He was folding everything together, tossing the pasta until it was coated with the crumbs and the oil.

"I know we haven't had much chance to talk, Mad. But I'm going to have to go to Washington again. It sounds as if that means they're accusing me of something, but they aren't. But it's still something that will happen, so I wanted to warn you."

"Who are you testifying against?"

He laughed, but didn't answer. "The whole thing is a farce, but it'll make everyone else feel better. Come on, sit down."

She ate the pasta so quickly she almost choked on the half-masticated mouthfuls, having briefly forgotten she was drunk. And then her father stood and crossed to an end cabinet, the one close to the mud room where they kept things like birthday candles and an expensive ice cream maker that had never been used and the old standing mixer that had been replaced but still haunted the kitchen. He reached onto a high shelf and brought down a bottle of Laphroaig. Madison's least favorite—the smoky smell of the peat always made her nauseous when she smelled it on him. He brought a glass over to the table and poured himself three fingers.

"What do you mean, make them feel better," she pressed. "Who?"

"I thought your mother would have explained some of this already," he said.

She shook her head.

"She told me to have faith in you. She told me you'd take care of it."

"She said that? That's good. I'm glad she included you in that."

He drank his glass down in two swallows, and Madison watched his hand reach out, without even looking in the direction of the bottle, to refill it.

"Your mother knows all about this," he said. "She takes the long view. Always has. This is what's important, Mad. You have to marry someone whose strengths are the opposites of your own."

"You don't take the long view?"

"I don't know," he said, but then he answered other, unspoken questions. "Some good might come from it. Maybe they can explain to me what happened. That'd be . . . that'd be rich, right?"

She lowered her voice to a whisper. "I don't understand," she said. "You don't know what happened?"

"Oh, I know exactly what fucking happened. Everybody lost heart," he said. "They couldn't just ride it out. Jim was my undoing, just like we always joked he would be."

There was silence for a moment, and then Madison asked, "Who said he would? What did Jim do?"

Her father stood again and crossed to the butcher block, dotted with bread crumbs and the ends of peeled garlic cloves. He stared at the remains of the meal he'd made, then began sweeping it all into the trash.

"Do you remember Alan Pratt? You were too small, right?"

"I mean," she said, "I've seen the pictures. You used to vacation with them, right? Mom still sees Karen, doesn't she?"

Karen was, she was pretty sure, Alan Pratt's widow. He'd died soon after quitting the firm, but she didn't really know anything else about him. She knew she'd heard old stories, about nights when her parents were just a couple, when they lived in the city. The four of them together: Alan and Karen and Bob and Isabel. Six-hour dinners, going dancing. The people her parents had been thinking they'd try to be, before they got married to each other.

"We haven't seen Karen in years."

He said this quickly, as if admonishing someone at the dinner table for a faux pas, a belch or an indiscreet confession.

"But Alan, he would have seen all this coming. He would have known. Alan was—I never should have let him go."

She hadn't known that her father had fired that man, Alan Pratt. She'd always heard the stories and thought they were friends.

"But it didn't matter," she said. "He died right after, right? Wasn't he sick?"

"Sick and tired," her father muttered. "That's what he used to say, when I'd go to visit him. He never wanted me there, really. It embarrassed him, he'd try to make jokes. Gallows humor and all that."

"But it's nice you visited him." She might as well have been speaking to the television, to a news report that would continue regardless of her response.

"But I couldn't have known, when we fired him. You spend your life figuring out what you're good at. You say, okay, I'm going to be the opposite of that guy. He's going to fail, and I'm not. I thought the best thing I could do was be the anti-Alan, be aggressive, trust my instincts. I might have made a mistake, there."

"Dad," she said, "I don't know what you're talking about."

He seemed to see her again, for a moment.

"No one does," he said. "Just watch, I'll be sitting there in front of Congress and they won't even understand their own lectures. You think they understand the repo market? They don't even know the term. You think they have a clue what was going on with the put options, those bets? The shorts? *That's* where they should be looking. Whatever I did, even Jim, whatever he did back in June, we were too late. It's irrelevant."

"Why," she said, but he wasn't listening.

"It just doesn't make sense. Of course you act, when nothing makes sense. You can't just wait there like a fucking sitting duck."

She had a feeling, then, that something cold and quick had come into the room and taken a seat at the table beside them. She wanted to reach across the table to touch her father's hand, to recall him to this night, to her face, but something had shifted and it had seemed possible he might react like a cornered animal, and strike.

"Daddy," she said carefully. "I don't understand what you're telling me. Have you said any of this, yet, to Mom?"

"Now isn't the time," he said. "I'm sorry, sweetheart, I just wanted to hear about you. About the party. Will you tell me about it? This can all wait."

It seemed so obvious to her that it couldn't, but she didn't know what she could say to him to force his hand.

"I saw people do cocaine tonight," she said. He put his palms to the table and pulled himself forward, closer to her.

"Jesus, really? Who? At Bill Welsh's house?"

She nodded. It seemed like this was the moment; if this night was an aberration, then this would break the spell. He'd become the same kind of father he'd been. There would be yelling, he'd be disgusted at her weakness in front of people like Zoë. She would be in trouble. If this was some temporary departure from their pattern, and not something wholly new, she would be in trouble.

"Did you do any? Tell me the truth."

"No," she said.

"Good girl. Believe me, Madison, it's not glamorous. You should've seen some of the guys, back before I met your mom. It's not a pretty story."

"Did you used to do it?"

"Oh, Mad, that was all so long ago. It's like different people. It's like actors playing us, when you try to remember it."

"So that's a yes."

Her father smiled, and rested his chin on his fist. He looked at her.

"What about now?" she said. "Did you do anything illegal?"

"No. You know me, princess. You asked me a direct question. Would I lie to that? To you? No, I have done nothing wrong. I swear. I wouldn't lie to you."

She stacked her pasta plate on top of his, even though he'd never served himself any food.

"Okay," she said. "I trust you."

She waited, and then decided to say it all.

"You won't lie to me, right? As long as I ask you, from now on. You won't lie. Because I told you about tonight. I could have gotten in trouble, right?"

Her father shook his head vigorously, but did not answer.

"I have some things to show you. You would be just the person to look it over with me, Madison. You know me better than anyone. And sometimes that's the best approach, in a funny way. You need a fresh eye sometimes."

"Oh," she said. She could not think of anything better to say to such a statement.

"But that's later," he said. "Do you want a drink?" Madison waited for the punch line, and when none followed, she nodded again.

"Madison," her father said. "I wouldn't put you in danger. You come first. You, Mom, and the twins."

"I know."

He clinked her glass with the lip of the bottle.

"Our secret, yes? Not a word to Mom."

THE MORNING OF THANKSGIVING, Isabel announced that they'd be taking a car into the city. She never mentioned that it was a limousine. When it arrived Madison said nothing, just stood in the driveway staring.

"I know," Isabel said, something vague enough to leave it up to the listener to decide what she knew. "I just couldn't resist, being able to sit and face you guys and chat for the drive in."

"Where's Dad?"

"He's not coming."

"Did you even ask him if he wants to?"

Her mother moved a step closer to her.

"Can we be on the same team? We just have to get through Thanksgiving dinner today, and then lunch with Nonna on Friday. I need your help, Madison."

It was the first time her mother had said that, anything like it, since the night of the bathtub. I can do this, Madison thought. If her mother acknowledged it, the strangeness of the whole holiday weekend, and enlisted her aid, then she could do it.

"I want you to tell me what's going on with the art."

"Not in the car."

She rolled her eyes at her mother, something she would never have been allowed to do even three months ago.

"No, obviously not. But later this weekend. I want you to tell me."

"Deal," Isabel said, and Madison got into the car.

By the time they were out of Greenwich, hurtling south on the Merritt, Isabel seemed to be relaxing. You could almost see it happening, one vertebra at a time. Her sunglasses perched atop her head and drew her hair back off her face, exposing the pink snail-shell coils of her ears. Her face appeared scrubbed of makeup in a way that meant she had spent an hour applying foundation, powder, under-eye creams, and forehead-tightening gels. She looked healthy, rested. She'd put this together carefully.

The boys asked for and received sodas from the minibar, a rare treat. Madison unpacked her stuffed purse. She had a date with Chip on Saturday, they were going to a movie. Her brothers had sodas, she had a few secrets. Everyone was happy.

When Chip had called her house, the previous afternoon, she'd found herself touching her own cheeks, the whole time, during the phone call. As if her skin were on loan from someone who had once worn it better, someone whom it had fit properly.

"So what's our schedule," she said to her mother, her eyes on the French conjugations she had to do. She'd always been able to read or work in the car, she and her father both. This was something she knew bothered her mother, for whom the words swam on the page as soon as the engine roared to life.

"No schedule," Isabel said, her voice airy. Matteo sucked down his soda, pausing after each tiny sip to deliver a loud, lip-smacking sound of satisfaction. Madison knew he actually hated the carbonation; they weren't used to it, growing up in a house where soda had always been an illicit, unknown quantity.

"Well, we must be going somewhere," Madison said.

"Yes, Madison, of course. We've got dinner tonight at Coco Pazzo, boys, remember? We used to go with Gran?"

"We're eating out?" Madison said sharply.

"Private room."

"Sounds good," Madison said, turning back to the French. She doodled in her margins and thought about the skin on Chip's face, just beneath his ears, where it had been the softest. She'd pressed the pads of her thumbs to that place.

"And then, really, it's whatever your little hearts desire," Isabel continued. "We've got the room at the Pierre until Sunday."

"I can't stay until Sunday," Madison said. Isabel was running her hand through Matteo's hair, measuring it between her index and middle fingers as if they were scissors. She looked up, but only for a moment.

"Why?"

"I have a date with Chip Abbott."

"Well," Isabel said, "all right, I guess. We can have a car take you back by yourself. Lily said she'd be back by Saturday."

"Really," Madison said. The boys looked up, hearing something in her voice, and Luke began to chew on his straw, his foot periodically knocking against his brother's. Her mother began rifling through her purse. She had said the Pierre; surely it had occurred to her that they'd be able to see the new apartment at the Plaza, probably, from the windows of their hotel room.

"Why are we staying at the Pierre?" Madison said, and it had its intended effect. Her mother's smile skipped a beat, like a flaw on an old videotape.

"Why not?" her mother said.

"Which one is the Pierre?" Matteo asked.

They all sat in silence, and now her mother was looking at her, looking her square in the face. Madison didn't know, really. Maybe it had been kindness, her mother's decision not to be strict about the date with Chip. Maybe she wasn't asking questions, or saying no, precisely because of that night in the bathtub. Maybe it was a reward; when Madison tried, she could see all of it this way, the nights in the kitchen with her father and the disinterest from her mother. As rewards.

Madison looked down at her French homework, because she knew the boys would get anxious if she and Isabel kept staring at each other.

"We haven't stayed there," she told her brother smoothly. "It's near the apartment, a little bit farther south."

"Why aren't we staying at the apartment?"

She knew that they probably didn't even remember the new place; they were used to being taken in and out of large, fancy rooms, places they were told they'd be coming back to, places to remember. Very often, they didn't actually need to remember them. Someone, usually Lily, would prep them on the particulars if they ever needed to return.

"We just don't feel like it," Madison said.

"Yes," Isabel said. "We don't feel like it. Thank you, Madison."

Outside the window, all the other cars were headed in the same direction, speeding toward the city's tall ziggurat skyline.

TWENTY-TWO

It was a bit embarrassing, Mina thought, to be shopping at Whole Foods on the morning after Thanksgiving. It seemed to indicate some sort of girlish unpreparedness, something charming in a twenty-three-year-old but not so much in a forty-six-year-old. That either she hadn't thought to buy groceries for the entire weekend when she made the big trip on Tuesday, or else hadn't cooked enough food for leftovers. Nothing to set out in aluminum containers at big buffet brunches in the kitchen, for the guests who slept late and straggled downstairs in shifts.

Of course she had no houseguests that weekend—two of Tom's younger associates had brought their wives for dinner, but they'd been speeding back to the city by nine o'clock the previous evening. But still, the leftovers in the kitchen was the image she always had in her mind, of what it would mean to host Thanksgiving out here "in the country." That was how one of the women last night, Pamela, kept referring to it. "The country." Like they were drinking milk fresh from the cow out back, or something.

Her phone danced as she walked into the store. She hadn't realized she was clutching it in her palm, and she was doubly startled to see Isabel's name on the screen. Having been called in for reinforcement on Wednesday, Mina had expected not to hear from Isabel for the remainder of the holiday weekend, at least.

"Well hello there," she said, keeping her voice sugary and light from the start. She didn't want to assume this was a distress call until she knew.

"Hi," Isabel said.

"How are you? How was your Thanksgiving? Tom's partner brought a new girlfriend, I swear to you Isabel, she looked twelve."

"Oh, Jesus," Isabel replied, getting into the spirit of things immediately. She sounded distracted, if game. "Did he want you to all let him tell you what he's thankful for?"

"She kept making these sweeping statements about—you know, what a shame it is that New York is so dominated by two industries, finance and fashion. How she finds it so tiresome that a new restaurant can put the word 'artisanal' in front of every vegetable or cocktail and claim to be doing something new. I mean, every single aspect of life in the city seems to have exhausted this girl, and I'm telling you she couldn't be more than three years out of school."

"Oh my," Isabel said.

"At first I thought she was trying to make me feel bad for not knowing the restaurants she kept mentioning, in Brooklyn, but I think maybe she was just nervous," Mina said.

"Well, of course. You remember what it was like, when you were that age. Spending time around them in groups, with the older wives, being the date on the arm."

Yes, Mina thought. Yes I do remember, but because I'm the one who did it. Not you. Isabel had never walked into a room and felt unwelcome, not once in her entire life. Not until this year, Mina reminded herself. You don't begrudge her that past simplicity. You bring her closer, because you understand how she feels *now*. Don't be so petty.

"How's the hotel?" she tried. "Where did you end up choosing?"

"The Pierre," Isabel said. "Madison's been great. She's so on top of things. You should have *her* come over to run your Thanksgiving."

"Did something happen?"

"Oh, no, not really. Well, I just felt bad. When we got to the hotel, yesterday, I snapped at her. I just didn't want her standing there when I checked in. I didn't want her to know, it's just, I used—I checked in under another name."

"Whose name?" Mina said, alarmed.

"No, no one's name. It was silly. April Wheeler. It's a character from my mother's favorite book. I just didn't want to use my maiden name or anything, any name some underemployed and overenergized young hack from the *Post* or the *Observer* could trace—I didn't want anything that really has to do with us," Isabel said, leaving the thought to its logical, unpleasant conclusion.

"No," Mina said. "No, that was smart."

"I didn't mean to keep it a secret, but at the last minute I just didn't want her to know it was happening? I don't know. I suppose I could have trusted her with it, but I just asked—I mean, I snapped at her, to go keep an eye on her brothers. And then by the time I got the room keys and turned around, they were talking to Suzanne Welsh."

"Oh," Mina said, still lurking just inside the store's entrance, her eyes scanning the checkout counters and the produce aisle for familiar faces. "Fantastic. Did she hear you use the name?"

"No," Isabel said. "It's funny you should ask that. My first thought was, thank God Madison distracted her."

"Wait, why are they at a hotel? Did they get rid of that place on Fifth?"

"So, I walked over, and Madison's just chatting with her, Suzanne keeps looking over at me. And she starts telling me, you know, Bill's sister is in town, the sister refuses to stay out in Greenwich, doesn't want to 'impose' by using the apartment, Bill has to put them up at the Pierre—"

"Well, sure," Mina said. "If your in-laws were Suzanne, you'd pick the hotel over their house, too."

Isabel paused for a moment and Mina was afraid they weren't allowed to insult these women today, that it was meant to be one of their more allusive, unmentioned conversations. Then Isabel laughed.

"Right," she said, "she kept saying, 'I can't imagine why they won't just stay with us, we have all these extra rooms!'"

"What else?"

"She kept asking why we were there. She kept referring to the kids as my 'gang.'"

"I actually really like that. They're your street toughs."

"Right," Isabel said. "Right, right, right." For a moment, it seemed as if that would be all.

"Is something wrong?" Mina said.

"She implied that we wouldn't be able to come to the museum party," Isabel said. "The spring benefit, and we're only in November now, and she was acting like our RSVPs were late coming back to her and so it must be that we couldn't make it this year."

"Classy."

"She used the phrase 'not up for it this year,'" Isabel said, her voice lowered.

"Just forget it," Mina said. "Just put it right out of your mind."

They both paused, as if to consider and then dismiss this thought without calling attention to its absurdity.

"I just kept thinking how we both used to be Weiss wives together," Isabel said. "When Bill Welsh left, I really thought that was it for me and Suzanne. I didn't think she could possibly aggravate me as much, when she was just another mom at school, as she had at Weiss. But I was naive."

"Well," Mina murmured.

"I used to try to be kinder. I'd try not to let her see what I thought of her. But then she'd start to talk about how smart he was, that Neanderthal son of hers, or she'd talk about some woman who wasn't there, whose husband hadn't been invited to the retreat that year, and how he was probably sleeping with his secretary. And I could just never be nice, not for more than ten minutes."

Mina nodded, but didn't speak.

"It always made me so furious, listening to her, just, savaging everyone else's marriages," Isabel said, softly.

"I know," Mina said. "I know just what you mean."

She waited in silence, waited for a cue from Isabel.

"I couldn't be nice," Isabel repeated.

Mina saw that it was her job to move them on from this part of the conversation.

"That isn't what's going on. Suzanne is far too afraid to hold on to any grudges, I promise you. I'm sure she was just worried that, if she didn't come say hello, you'd feel snubbed."

Isabel laughed.

"Is that where we've ended up?" she said. "I'm going to be worried about a snub from Suzanne Welsh?"

"Well," Mina said, helpless.

"She asked me if we've heard from Kiki McGinniss," Isabel said. "She asked if anyone knows how she and Jim are doing."

Mina waited for more, but it seemed Isabel might actually want the question.

"Have he and Bob been in touch?"

"I don't know," Isabel said. "I couldn't say this to her, obviously, but how would I know? Jim hasn't been on the phone any of the times when I've answered. It's always been guys one level below. They must have spoken, since the summer. They must have still been talking after Jim had to step down. But I don't know." Her voice had gone suddenly taut with ill-disguised panic.

"It's not her business," Mina said feebly. Commenting on the status of Bob's détente with his former best friend, the man who'd left the firm in disgrace last June, didn't seem like something she'd be able to do without a misstep.

"Exactly," Isabel said. "Oh, God, also. Madison says she's going on a date with Chip Abbott?"

Her voice trailed up at the end of the sentence, like a teenager.

Mina laughed and traded stories about Lacey Abbott—they agreed she seemed like a gem—and didn't ask any more questions. Suddenly, then, they had stopped talking about Suzanne Welsh. Maybe this was how it would be; Mina wouldn't be shut out entirely. Their friendship existing in brief bursts, like the fractured sunlight that spilled into Mina's library in the late afternoons, winking through the branches of her trees.

Just before they hung up, Mina remembered something.

"Wait," she said. "Suzanne Welsh, do you remember how she told you, that time—God, it must have been years ago—"

"Yes," Isabel said, picking it up seamlessly. "How he gives her a bonus, at Christmastime? Do you know I mentioned that, right afterward, to Madison? I told her that in the elevator on our way up to the room. I thought it would make her feel better. Suzanne, waiting on the edge of her seat all December, waiting to see how much money her husband was giving her at the end of the year. And Madison already knew! Apparently, at some point, Lily told her."

Mina felt a sharp, biting pinch at the nape of her neck.

"They talk about things like that?"

"I don't know," Isabel said.

This was the time, Mina thought, to mention that she had seen Lily at Saks. It wasn't even a secret. There was no information embedded there to hurt anyone; it was of absolutely no import that she'd declined to mention it at the time. But now they were actually discussing it, Suzanne, the idea that Isabel had to work to keep them on her side. Now it seemed relevant.

But then it was back, the chilled smoothness in the voice on the phone.

"I should go get dressed," Isabel said. "Lunch with Concetta."

"Oh, God, I completely forgot you'd agreed to do that. You really should have made him come along."

"Yes," Isabel said, and then the conversation was over, Mina knew it. See you soon, they told each other, and hung up.

MINA WAS IN THE PRODUCE SECTION when she saw Alexandra Barker, smelling a melon, holding it in front of her face and watching Mina from behind it.

Mina waved. Alexandra chucked the melon into her cart, waved back, and stalked around the corner into an aisle.

This was unpleasant. To be pumped for information by Alexandra Barker was bad enough; to feel that she was stalking you through the displays of misting vegetables, waiting for the moment when you might accidentally speak one of your private thoughts out loud, was much more distressing.

Mina was gathering the ingredients for Tom's favorite pasta sauce, debating whether to use sour cream or whole milk yogurt, when she felt eyes on her once again. This time it was a guy, much younger than her. Cute, maybe, in the way young women seemed to like these days. They prized the nerdier ones, now. In Mina's heyday, marrying a balding, slightly hook-nosed kid with glasses was considered settling, an admission of the fact that it was very difficult to find a handsome man who was also going to make the salary you'd been hoping for. Now, girls just out of school didn't seem to like them too pretty, didn't seem to write them off for being skinny. And certainly not for having glasses.

Of course, Mina had been grasping at whatever she could get, and had been as surprised as anyone when that turned out to be Tom.

This kid had glasses, and that coarse sort of curly hair that could look by turns adorable or distasteful, depending on the lighting and how recently he'd showered. His hairline was strong and consistent on his forehead, good for him. He had a hungry look to him, was the best way she could think to describe it. She'd noticed him a few times already in the grocery store, always somewhere in her general area, but now he seemed to be almost openly watching her. He was pretending to read the label on a carton of milk. Whatever he did for a living, she hoped it didn't involve subtle surveillance.

She turned back to the sour cream. When she pushed her cart

away, turning to leave the dairy aisle, he was suddenly right there looking at cottage cheese, and she'd rammed into his foot.

"Jesus," he said, "I'm sorry."

She laughed. "Why are you sorry? Are you all right?"

He bent over, his tight jeans looking like they might rip without warning, and massaged his ankle.

"Totally," he said. "And also totally not your fault. I was tuned out."

"Sure," Mina said, resisting the impulse to reply with "totally."

"I'm sorry," he said. "Do we—we've met, no?"

"I don't think so!" she replied, trying still to remain charmed, breezy, telling herself she had no reason to be concerned.

"I do," he said. "I think—your daughter is friends with Madison D'Amico, isn't she?"

"Mmm," Mina said. She looked beyond him, toward the front of the store and the registers. Was Alexandra Barker still here? The thing was for Alexandra not to overhear this, if it was anything. Alexandra might see it and just think Mina was bored, flirting with some younger man. Much preferable.

"That has to be it," he said.

"Really," she said, and she couldn't help it, the disgust was creeping into her voice. "Does it? You know Madison?"

"Well, no," he said. "I've met her. I'm actually a journalist. Formerly a reporter, now I'm actually starting a new venture. And I'd love to talk to you for just a second—"

Mina pushed past him, hopefully grazing his ankle again, and she made it through checkout without seeing Alexandra once. She raced through the parking lot, the cart rattling madly along the asphalt, and she had half her bags loaded into the car when he appeared again, like some sinister jack-in-the-box.

"I'm sorry," he said. "That was inappropriate, for me to approach you in the store. I just thought I recognized you. And if you'd let me explain what I do, I think you might find that we could work together. I understand you're close with the family. No doubt, it's been troubling for you to see the way they've been portrayed. In the media. I think there's more to the story. And you must know that there is."

"Enough," Mina said. "Please get away from my car."

"Bob D'Amico has not spoken publicly, really, since that week," he hammered on. "So the attention is, for all intents and purposes, on him. People are waiting for him to speak up. Once he does—or, alternatively, if they just get tired of waiting—the attention will turn to the rest of the family. To their close associates. People will want another perspective."

"If I see you near Madison D'Amico, anywhere in this town, I will call the fucking cops," Mina said. "And trust me, they'll take my word over yours, whatever I decide to tell them."

She put the last of the bags into her trunk and slammed the lid down, forcing the kid to leap back in order to save his fingertips. She sailed the cart away into an empty parking spot and hurried around to her door.

It was only later, driving away, that it occurred to her that even if he'd been bluffing to say that her daughter was a friend of Madison's, he still might well know that she did have a daughter.

Her panic spiked, but by the time she pulled into her garage she was calm, had gathered herself back. There was no possible reason to tell Tom, or even Isabel. She'd handled it, hadn't she? She'd been handling all of it, all along.

TWENTY-THREE

The day after Thanksgiving, which had consisted of a hushed dinner uptown and an early bedtime at the Pierre, Madison sat with her mother and her brothers at Grandpop's old favorite table at the roof restaurant in the Yale Club. It was the table farthest from the dining room's entrance, in the southeast corner of the room. In spring or in summer, the glass doors behind them would have been flung open to the rooftop patio, and they would have been able to step outside with their glasses to look down on the dingy grandeur of Grand Central. At the tiny taxis below, the people scurrying down Vanderbilt Avenue, reduced to just the tops of their miniscule heads.

Her grandma Concetta, her nonna, was late.

It was odd that her mother had chosen the club for this lunch, although only marginally odder than the fact that this lunch was even taking place without Madison's father there to moderate. Isabel must have assumed that Concetta would disapprove, no matter where they ate, and decided she might as well choose a place that brought with it warm memories of Grandpop, of the way every employee in the building had known which was Mr. Berkeley's table.

Still, this did not explain the fact that Isabel was having lunch with Concetta at all.

It was possible that this might be real estate related, that they might need to lean harder on Nonna, one final time, in an effort to get her to sell the building in Brooklyn. She'd now refused at least four times to let Madison's father broker a deal, find her a new place with a few more modern comforts. At one point Bob had even floated the possibility that Nonna could live year-round in their city apartment, but the mention of Manhattan had sent her into apoplexy. They'll carry me out feet first, she'd said, and repeated with gusto, until Isabel had asked her please to stop making death jokes in front of the twins, who were then five years old and found it upsetting to see the adults laughing about her theoretical demise.

They'd been waiting here for almost fifteen minutes.

"What are we thinking will be her opener?" Madison tried. "I'm guessing, how the rowdy black kids forced them to close down the pool and ruined her afternoon walks in McCarren Park."

"Be nice," her mother said.

"I am," Madison said. "I've been trying to store up things I think she'd enjoy, and I've got a good one. Allie's little sister told her that you aren't allowed to say 'flesh colored' anymore when you're talking about a peach crayon, because it's offensive. Heard that months ago but I've just been waiting to dangle it in front of Nonna and see if she takes the bait."

Her mother's mouth twitched, and she lifted her martini glass to her face.

"Madison," she said, "your grandmother loves you. She's from a different generation, the way she discusses things like that. Maybe you can just lob her some softballs, as a favor to me? Ask her about Genoa, about her parents before they came here. She wasn't there, but she still likes the stories."

"I love the stories," Madison conceded. "Not always the person."

"No one's trying to convince you that's backward, sweetheart, believe me. But just, as a favor to me?"

"Well," Madison said. "While we're waiting, why don't you pay me back for my last favor."

Her mother smiled down at the tablecloth.

"Your last favor isn't done yet," she said. "The weekend isn't over."

"Why are you selling the art?"

"Madison, I don't think you really need me to explain that."

"Are we in that much trouble, that we're going to start living off the money we make from selling art?"

"No," her mother said.

"Then what, it's a big symbolic gesture? Do we really think people are that stupid?"

She could feel her cheeks burning. She didn't understand how suddenly she'd grown so upset, without warning. But her mother's unflappable gaze, the absence of distress, worked like the opposite of a balm. It inflamed Madison's every nerve ending. How could her mother be this casual about the things they loved?

"I'm not saying they're stupid," Isabel said, "but yes, the symbols matter."

"But you love it," Madison said, "all of it."

Her mother sipped her martini. "You're worried about your painting, aren't you?"

Madison heard herself make a noise halfway between a scoff and a sob.

"I'm worried about all of it," she said.

"Well," Isabel said, "don't worry. Your father wants to keep your painting, Madison. It's the one thing he cared about keeping."

Madison chose this moment to unfold her napkin, to square the tips of her fork and knife, to smooth her small segment of table-cloth. She looked over at the twins, who were both sitting slumped in their seats, their hands folded in their khaki-clad laps, and she felt a barbed pang at the realization that she'd completely ignored them, that she should have pressed her mother later, when they couldn't hear. But it was too late. She turned back to her mother.

"He knows you're doing this? He's letting you?"

Isabel laughed. And then she fixed her eyes on something behind Madison and waved. Concetta had arrived.

She was bundling herself through the crowded dining room, the maître d' prancing and nervous in her wake. She reached the table and lugged herself around to the farthest seat, wheezing as if she was weighed down with shopping bags, when in fact she wore a demure blue skirt suit and had clearly been to her hairdresser.

Isabel made to stand and smacked the table with her knee, rattling the ice cubes in their water glasses.

"Sorry," she said. "Concetta, we were thinking you might sit there by Madison."

But Nonna had already heaved herself into a seat with a great sigh.

"I know," she began, "girls, I know, I know. I hadda wait like you wouldn't have believed on the G train."

She reached both hands out into the air above the table, miming a big hug for Madison.

"Lovely," she said, "you look gorgeous, kid. How are you?"

She still hadn't quite spoken to Isabel, who had drained her martini in one fluid knock.

Maybe, Madison thought, this was why Isabel had brought her along. It didn't bother her, she was happy to be used as a buffer. But she didn't see why Isabel couldn't have told her this right away, been transparent about it.

One thing her mother had learned, maybe from Gran Berkeley: how to turn everyone, everything, into a useful buffer.

"You know we would happily have arranged a ride, Concetta," Isabel said, immediately shattering the pane between them.

"Well, that's a slippery slope," Concetta shot back. "I let you all have your way, and soon we're at, you know, a limo to take me to the corner market every time I need groceries." She turned back to Madison and squinted at her. "Does your mother ever let you eat, little one?"

She tossed her purse, a bottomless leather monstrosity, onto the empty seat beside her, of course then calling attention to the unused chair at the table.

"Believe me," Madison told her grandmother with feigned gaiety. "I eat plenty."

"I doubt it, in your mother's house. You know they served beautiful rainbow arrangements of vegetables at that wedding instead of cake?"

She laughed loudly, a surprisingly ladylike trill that always seemed so unsettling emerging from Concetta, of all people.

"Well," Isabel's voice cut in coolly, "for all you know, Concetta, we did. You didn't attend."

Concetta's eyes flashed. Too early, Madison thought, for this tactical clumsiness. From everyone. The wedding, and Concetta's casual refusal to make the train trip to attend, was radioactive. It always had been.

They all looked at their menus for a few moments, and Isabel bantered with the waiter while Concetta frowned at the recitation of the specials.

Madison's phone buzzed in her purse and she surreptitiously clicked it to life beneath the napkin in her lap. It was another text from Chip: *U picked a movie yet?*

Have fun with your family, he had told her on the phone yesterday. *And if not, you can call me. I'm texting you as soon as we hang up.* He'd called on the house line, but now he had her cell number. When they'd hung up she had waited, watching the insistent rain outside batter the surface of the pool. Someone had forgotten to cover it. And then her cell phone had danced in her purse, on the floor.

Chip was still, so far, the only person who had ever mentioned her father to her indirectly without being nosy. Without prodding, and yet not explicitly asking her what she thought was happening or how she felt. He had managed to do this when no one else had, not Lily, not Amanda.

Isabel sent the waiter away for a few minutes, and Concetta set down her menu. She crossed her arms, resting her elbows on the white tablecloth.

"So we're here," she said, "for you to explain what's been going on. Where's my son?"

"Madison, would you take the boys to wash up before the appetizers get here?" Isabel said.

"No," Madison said. "They washed up when we got here."

Her mother didn't look at her, registering the refusal only with a blink. She turned back to Concetta.

"He did of course want to make it," Isabel said. "He met us last night, for dinner, but then he had to get right back to work."

Madison reached out to Luke and found his hands where they clutched each other in his lap. How could her mother know, for certain, that one of the twins wouldn't speak up at this, tell the truth?

"Please," Concetta said. "We all know he has no work."

"Not true," Isabel said, "but that's not a topic for today, Concetta. We wanted to take you to a nice lunch. Madison hadn't seen you in far too long." She made furtive eye contact with the waiter, who hurried over with the prosecco she'd ordered.

"No thank you," Concetta said, having been silent during the ordering process. "But, sir, I'd like a glass of red, if you please. And just—a few ice cubes. In a separate glass. You're all keeping your reds so warm these days, it's like you heat it."

Madison's phone spasmed against her leg. *seriously damico, very not cool to stand me up, if u aren't excited about our big date just say so, i can always return the red roses i got.*

This is a joke, she reminded herself. There is no way Chip will be bringing you flowers. *dont lie,* she typed back furiously, trying not to look down at the phone, *u bought those roses for wyatt and hell cry if you give them away.*

"I'm glad we have this chance to talk," Concetta said, clearly settling in for a speech. Madison's phone buzzed again. *touche,* from Chip. *how was turkey day?*

"Well, I have concerns," Concetta said. "I've been getting calls at the house. Even with the extra cars he set up for me, you know, they keep people from the door, but they're still on my block. All the time."

At this, finally, Isabel seemed spurred into reaction. She looked directly at Madison and, almost imperceptibly, shook her head.

"I'm sure if you let him know what's wrong, Nonna, he can take care of it," Madison blurted, not sure what her mother wanted.

Her grandmother looked at her, a face that would have been a smirk except that it didn't seem to be enjoying its own smugness.

"I know that's what they've taught you, darling, but you can't always take care of it that way," she said. "It can't all happen offstage, you know?"

"I didn't mean—" Madison tried, but her mother's voice layered itself over hers, so that as soon as Madison was silent her mother had already been speaking for a few seconds, as if they were tagging each other in and out of the conversation.

"Concetta," Isabel said, "this isn't appropriate. If you want to discuss this with Bob, you can call him at home. But it's not for this lunch."

"Call him at home! He never answers. Your phone rings on and on and on," Concetta said. "But then, Ms. Berkeley, you already know that."

Madison choked in surprise at the use of her mother's maiden name. But Isabel simply folded her hands in her lap and fixed her gaze on her mother-in-law, her entire body coiled like a question mark.

"You think I don't understand what's been happening?" Concetta said, her voice lowered in an alarming and uncharacteristic gesture toward Isabel's sense of propriety, the room they were sitting in. "I read, Isabel. I probably know more about his job than you do. I was there when he talked his way into that job, long before you even met him. And I'm not going to watch my son suffer, be made to suffer for other people's mistakes, just because you're not willing to get dirt on those little hands. You know where I'm from. I don't come from here."

"You were born in Brooklyn," Isabel said, almost muttering it, keeping her eyes on Concetta.

"You cannot wait this out," Concetta said, ignoring her. "You got no idea how many times I been visited, at my home, by some pissant reporter who says he used to write for the *New York Times*, like I'm supposed to find that impressive. He wears these big thick glasses, I guarantee you, just so he looks older than twelve. And he's always dressed like some kid headed to church on Christmas Eve. Hair like a bottle brush, badly in need of a haircut. Not impressive at all."

Madison stared, in shifts, into her lap, then at her grandmother, then at her mother, then into her lap again. She hadn't replied to Chip's texts. Her mother, for some reason, hadn't spoken yet.

"I don't know what he wants," Concetta barreled on. "He seems to think I'm going to put my heels up and fill him in on some embarrassing stories from my son's childhood. I close the door on him, goes without saying."

"No one is waiting anything out," Isabel said, finally. "You give me absolutely no credit, but by now, I guess I should know that. It's no surprise."

"Now," Concetta began, but Isabel had gained all the steam she needed.

"If you're so concerned," she said, "I'd encourage you to come out to the house with us. Come sit with your son. Try to get him to talk to you. Try to get him to describe his plans for the future. But you'd rather not, Concetta. You'd always rather call us from Brooklyn to remind us that we live a life you find repugnant. This doesn't, as we know, keep you from cashing his checks."

Luke had begun to make a soft, keening noise under his breath.

"Your favorite," Concetta said. "Your favorite little story, Isabel. That I sponge off you people. I never saw you striking out on your own. I never saw you turning down your own daddy's checks. You wouldn't know how that feels, would you? My son worked for every single thing he has, and he doesn't deserve to suffer because other people decide we need a villain."

Madison continued stroking her brother's little fist, holding it in her own. He'd brought his other hand up above the table, so that he could hold Matteo's, too. They both stared at their place settings. She knew she should stand up, get them away from the table. She knew she was failing to meet even the most basic requirements of being an older sister. But she could explain this, to them, when they were older. That she'd been afraid to leave; that she hadn't known whether or not they'd be able to trust their mother's account of what happened while they were gone.

"Your son's a very hard worker," Isabel said. "He'll work himself into the ground when things are going well. Not so good at picking up the pieces afterward, though. Not so good at meeting with the lawyers, or consulting the financial planners, or dealing with the press, or managing a need for additional security. Not the best."

"So do something," Concetta said. "He's mourning? Of course he's mourning. He needs his wife to do something."

There was something else, pulling ragged at the edges of Madison's mind, something that didn't have to do with her family, but she couldn't remember what it was. The description of that guy, the reporter trying to contact her grandmother. Something had knocked at a memory, like a book pulled slightly out of line on its shelf.

But Madison's phone was buzzing, had gone off twice since she'd last checked. She could just leave right now, walk out of this building and take the elevator straight down to the train and head home early, to get ready for the date tomorrow. He'd used that word. It was a date.

"You don't know how he operates," Concetta said.

"I don't know how he operates," Isabel echoed. Each word was given an equal weight, neither inquiry nor assertion in her voice.

"Now is not the time to worry about what your other little lady friends think of you," Concetta said. "You gotta live in the real world, now. You two have been living somewhere else for too long. If you wait, it'll be too late. This'll all blow over, but the question is where will you be when it does?"

"How refreshing," Isabel said, her voice so low it was barely audible. "Another expert opinion."

"What's that, dear?" Concetta barked.

"Everyone's an expert this year," Isabel said. "Everyone knows how to solve the problem. Apparently it's quite simple. How funny, then, that I can't see it."

"Well, sometimes we can't see our own dilemmas so clearly."

"What the fuck would you know about *any* of these dilemmas?"

At that, Concetta put down her wineglass. The ice cubes clinked. "Excuse me?"

Madison could not remember a time when Isabel had cursed at her grandmother. Had permitted anyone to see that Concetta made her this angry.

"You've never dealt with a world any bigger than your little block, Concetta. You've never taken care of anyone but yourself. Your son was responsible for thousands of employees. He has a big life, we have a big life, because that's what he wanted. And now you think— what would you know, about any of this?"

They all sat in silence. An obsequious waiter delivered their appetizers, flinching as he set the plates down as if Concetta might nip at his wrists.

"You know what, girls?" Concetta said. "This is really not to my taste, the cuisine here. I'm going to head home."

"Let me call you a car," Isabel said, her voice entirely without affect. Concetta ignored her.

"I'll walk you to the elevator," Madison said, wringing her hand away from Luke's and ignoring her mother's scrutiny.

Her grandmother stood, abandoning her napkin with a great flourish, and stared down at her daughter-in-law.

"I hope you're right," she said. "I hope you're damn confident about his priorities. Because the boy I know is not going down for this. And it might surprise you, what he'll do. You've never seen him really get to be scrappy, not in years and years. But then, of course,

I'm not saying things you don't know. Or I shouldn't be. You're his wife, aren't you."

Madison followed her grandmother as she stalked out of the dining room, catching up with her in the small foyer by the elevators. They stood, side by side, waiting.

Her grandmother turned to look at her, squinting as if through a thick fog.

"Don't let your mother make it his fault," she said. "He's one man and it's a big country out there. He wouldn't have gambled with you, or the boys, not on his life. And he's not going to hang his head now as if he did. She's always wanted him to be ashamed of what he has. At least when she thinks someone's watching. Don't let her fall in line with everyone else."

"I won't," Madison said. "I haven't."

Concetta took her by the shoulders and pressed their bodies together, some more militant version of a hug.

"You taking care of my son?" she said, and Madison nodded. The elevator dinged, and then Concetta was gone.

TWENTY-FOUR

Lily was racing through her afternoon, performing her errands at double their usual speeds. It was a bright white day, not too chilled for the middle of December. She was only a few minutes from the house, and there was still time to strategize.

The boys had a playdate planned for after school and Madison had told her that morning, without even a nod toward performing it as a request for permission, that she'd be going over to that Allison girl's house to kick off their winter break. So Lily had time to figure out what to do when her boyfriend arrived.

Jackson, on an express train that at that moment was probably slicing through Mamaroneck.

He hadn't sounded dangerous on the phone, exactly, because he hadn't seemed at all on edge or upset. But he was being unreliable, definitely. She didn't trust him not to do something crazy, actually just show up at the door. And while it was unlikely Isabel would suddenly start answering her own door again today, Lily still needed to get home before there was any chance of Jackson arriving.

Bob might be home, as well. Thanksgiving had come and gone without even a symbolic appearance; at that point she'd assumed he was still sleeping in his study, but now that they were staring down Christmas, she wasn't so sure. The small noises, the occasional untidiness, all the unconcealed clues that had been her guides back in October: somebody was watching them now, keeping them concealed.

Apparently there had been some sort of unpleasantness in the city, with Concetta. Isabel had mentioned it in only a slanting way— "Lily, if you see Bob this afternoon, let him know that we saw his mother on Friday and she's waiting for a return on her last call"—and Madison had just fled the room at the mention of her grandmother's name.

But that had been weeks ago now, and on this particular afternoon Lily's problem was her boyfriend.

Jackson had called the night before, drunk, from some grimy bar at the nexus of Greenpoint, Williamsburg, and Queens. He'd shouted the name a few times, but she had all she needed to know from his thick, rounded speech—Jameson and beers—and the music blaring in the background. You could hear the way his sneakers must be sticking to the spill-coated floors.

He'd been with his friend Gabe, the one he was always name-dropping even though she absolutely refused to be baited into showing interest. The one who'd just started his own website. She assumed Jackson wanted Gabe to bring him in on the new project, but she'd never asked for any more details.

But last night they'd both been there together, howling into the phone.

"I'm coming out there tomorrow," Jackson had said.

"Okay," she droned, lying on her bed paging through a copy of New York, one eye on the magazine to see if Bob was mentioned anywhere and the other on her picture window, where she kept the curtains open so she could see the house right up until she went to sleep.

"You're not taking seriously," Jackson had said. "ME seriously. She never takes me seriously!" She could hear him turning to someone else, a leering Gabe sitting next to him on the pockmarked wooden banquette, probably.

"Go home," she'd said. "Come on, Jackson, get a cab."

"You can't tell me I can't see my girlfriend," he'd bellowed.

"Sure."

"I'm coming up there TOMORROW."

"Okay."

She hadn't called him that morning, annoyed not just by his behavior but also by the fact that he had a point about one thing, at least. When he wasn't allowed to see her for weeks at a time, to press her against the back walls of bars and elevators and stairwells, to wake her up by kissing her hip bones, then she liked him a hell of a lot less. It was true that all the best parts of dating Jackson required that your bodies be very, very close together.

She had assumed, when they didn't speak all morning, that he'd forgotten their phone call. And then, an hour ago, he'd called her from Grand Central, about to hop on the 2:37.

"There's a bar car on this one," he had said. "Score."

He told her she couldn't stop him, he was going to sneak over to the house for the night, and when she exploded, he backtracked.

"Okay, well, I still think sneaking over to make out with the babysitter is very hot, but I can wait for you. Pick a bar! I'll meet you there later tonight, whenever. I've got a deadline, I could use a quiet afternoon out of the city to get some work done. It's like I'm meeting you at our country house, except the house doesn't belong to you and I'm not allowed over."

She parked the car and let herself in through the mud room. The house was silent, sealed. She tried to listen to see if Isabel was upstairs, but then told herself that it didn't matter. There was no way she'd bring him back here. She'd be firm. He didn't know that her authority was currently being performed behind a blackout curtain, that no one who mattered was listening to Lily anymore. She'd tell him he couldn't come here.

And then, as if on cue, she heard Isabel's car start up outside. She must have already been sitting out there, in the driveway, when Lily drove into the garage. She must have waited, not wanting to be watched as she drove away from the house.

The station was better, Lily decided. She'd meet Jackson directly at the station and put him on the first train back to the city, which meant she had only fifteen minutes to get back down there.

She left without taking the time to walk to the end of Bob's hallway, without listening to see.

HER STOMACH BEGAN TO CHURN when he stepped off the train. She tried to hold tight to her annoyance, her determination to cut things off at the source. He had his hands on her immediately, when they were still standing on the platform, his fingertips at the buttons on her pea coat and immediately under her sweater and up against her skin.

"Surprise," she said, wanting to shake her head at herself, her involuntary husky voice.

So now they were going for a walk, along Bruce Park Avenue of all places, because she worried that if they went anywhere secluded or warmer, she'd end up doing something like agreeing to give him a blow job on a park bench (this had been done before, though not in Greenwich) or, worse, agreeing to let him come back to the house with her, something she'd never done in the years they'd been together, never.

And then she saw the girls.

It was them, clear and obvious, no doubt in her mind. Zoë Barker was pulling into the station lot in an absurd convertible, and it was obviously Madison in the passenger seat. But the circumstances were so bizarre to Lily, in the context of the Madison she'd always known, that it was one of those times when you feel fate disintegrating your life into small pieces, sending the mundane routines of your days skittering away like marbles into hard-to-reach corners of a room. Because she, Lily, shouldn't even have been down there, obviously, shouldn't have been anywhere near Bruce Park Avenue except for the antics of her idiot boyfriend. Which could get her fired.

That thought, too, had crossed her mind. That Jackson was trying to make up her mind for her. If she was fired, he didn't have to keep trying to goad her into quitting. She didn't think he'd go that far—not he, who was so attentive to the right connections, to the casual meet and greet that could be nurtured into a future recommendation. She didn't think he'd be so cavalier about muddying her future job prospects, but still.

The girls, surely, should have been more cautious. They might have considered driving to catch the train at Port Chester or even Rye. What would they have done if they'd run into a friend of someone's mother, on the platform? The plan wasn't so daring, perhaps, but it still must have taken a brassy confidence that was new for Madison.

Lily didn't say anything. She never insulted Madison in front of Jackson. She didn't like giving anyone even a narrow opening through which to ridicule the kids, or giving away any information that was rightfully theirs to release. So many parts of their lives only made sense if you saw the whole picture, if you were there every day. If you saw how much easier it was sometimes to spend a little money just to make life less stressful. That, up close, it was so silly—pretentious, even, the worst kind of snobbishness—to refuse to spend money for a good cause, whether that cause was helping those less fortunate or simply making life a bit easier for your own children.

But Jackson's hand was in the back pocket of her jeans, and she'd made a soft sound of panic when she first saw Madison.

"What's up?"

"Nothing," she said. Even the way Madison carried her body was unfamiliar. Lily had never seen her move this way, as if she knew the world around her would take its step back to let her pass untouched. As if she knew that people would cede space to her, whether out of self-preservation or something deeper, some greater fear.

"Come on," Jackson was saying, "I'll leave tonight. I'll leave before dinner. Just an hour or two."

Lily watched the train pull into the station, watched them leave.

She couldn't see or hear them anymore, their glossy hair, their shrill calls back and forth to one another.

She thought again of something she'd been unable to erase from her mind for months now. *If it were me.* If the outside world had forced Lily to reckon with her own father, with the man in full, when she was fifteen years old. What would she consider possible, alone in the city, at a bar? Watching an adult man lick his bottom lip whenever she adjusted her bra strap or let her hair fall across her face?

She knew what she was meant to do, here. She knew, even now, what was important. Madison was a child, and her well-being was the job. Lily knew that she herself would, eventually, become unnecessary, this family's phantom limb, causing them pain in her own desperation to make her presence more than a memory. But not yet.

When she took out her phone and dialed Isabel's number, it rang sixteen times. There was no answer.

"Come on," Jackson said. "Who are you calling? If we drive back now, we'll have at least two whole hours. I took off work, Lil. I came here to see you."

Maybe it doesn't have to be mine to fix, Lily thought. What did they expect, ignoring her like this? And why shouldn't she get to scare them, just for an afternoon? For all I know, they've got a security tail on her. She'll be fine.

Jackson's hand was under her shirt again.

TWENTY-FIVE

Madison was on the train with Zoë and Allie, thinking about Chip.

About the nights in his car, how once she was back inside her own house it seemed like they'd been spread across her very skin. His face above her, the cinnamon smell of the gum she never actually saw him pop into his mouth but that he was always chewing by the time it started. All of it brought with it an almost subterranean pressure, as if she fell deep down into some cavernous space when she was inside the car, so deep that the sounds and rhythms of the world receded entirely. Time could actually fly; people had not been making this up. When you had your tongue in someone's mouth and wanted to touch every inch of his body, time could actually fly.

The first night, the movie after Thanksgiving, he hadn't kissed her until the very last second. The second time, she'd been prepared. When he asked about her curfew, she told him they had time to kill. When he pulled into the bank parking lot off the Avenue, she had the good sense to sit still and wait for him to decide what to do.

The third night, they'd pulled over on a residential street a few minutes away from her house—"not on my street," she'd warned, and because he was perfect he hadn't asked why—and that time the whole pageant of getting themselves to the actual moment had clearly weighed on them both. Because he hadn't even really reclined his seat, hadn't maneuvered the coffee cup in the console between them out of his way, before he had his hands in her hair. Before he was cradling her head at the nape of her neck, his tongue touching the roof of her mouth, once, twice, again.

Now, winter break was about to start. They'd been on four dates. Some dim, scrambled part of her brain knew that it must be a conscious decision on his part not to push for anything much beyond his tongue in her mouth and his hand up her shirt. But this felt charmed, she felt lucky. The sharp corners of any distressing thought felt muffled, unimportant.

Seeing him was the only thing she had any interest in doing for the next two weeks. Her mother did have a tree in the foyer, tall and fragrant, its spice filling every room on the ground floor and even the hallway at the top of the stairs. But Madison had known from the start that the tree wasn't for her. It had been standing there, a complete, twinkling package, when she came home from school one day in early December.

Decorating the tree as a family had been Gran's favorite Christmas tradition. She'd loved it more than her annual Christmas open house in Georgetown, more than she loved a solitary, quiet winter evening drinking mulled wine from a jelly glass out on Shelter.

And now it was apparently one more thing they were just going to discard in silence. It didn't matter to Madison, she wasn't upset over it herself. But it made her sad on behalf of the twins. They hadn't even asked any questions about the tree. They'd just walked into the room, looked at it in doleful silence, and then walked quietly upstairs together.

She let her head loll back against the torn leather of her train seat.

"I've been to this place before," Zoë said. They were headed to Grand Central, the first stage of a plan Zoë had dictated to them earlier this week.

"You have not!" Allie insisted. "You would have told me." She linked her arm through Madison's. Zoë still hadn't looked up from her phone.

"Are we going there because Wyatt will be there?"

"I have no idea where he is," Zoë said. "We're going to meet *new* boys, not follow around the same ones we've known since we were eight."

"Men," Madison said. She looked out the window and for the first time she realized they were coming out of this endless autumn, that the gray-streaked houses and parked cars were decidedly the elements of a winter scene. The sidewalks and pavements everywhere had that ice-bitten look so that you knew they'd be cold to the touch. It was only three thirty, but it would be dark soon.

"Excuse me?" Zoë looked up from her phone.

"If we meet anyone at this bar, it's going to be men. Not boys," Madison said.

Zoë snorted. "That's very optimistic."

Madison put her forehead to the window, feeling her skin shrink back momentarily at the chill, keeping it there, closing her eyes. She spoke very little for the rest of the train ride, but this did not seem to bother Zoë, and Allie was too busy letting herself imagine, out loud, every single thing that could possibly go wrong with their plan. Someone at Greenwich Prep would notice their absences during eighth period. Her mother's assistant would forget that Allie had called to say she'd be going home with Zoë. They'd run into a family friend at Grand Central who would realize it was far too early for them to have attended a full day of school. The fake IDs Zoë had gotten from her cousin's girlfriend at Choate would so little resemble their actual faces that they'd be arrested on the spot. It didn't seem to occur to Allie that cops in New York might have something better to do than come collect them from the street outside a bar that would surely rather just send them on their way.

Madison imagined a world in which she could turn to Allie and speak to her honestly. She had newfound access to things Allie couldn't possibly know. That it was always the plans like this one that actually succeeded, the white-knuckle moments that implausibly came off. It's the things you take for granted, she would have liked to tell Allie, the things you believe in without question or fear—the things you don't even know enough about to view as dangerous— that are sure to leave you vulnerable, exposed.

She had all this new knowledge, she was realizing these past few weeks, and no one who cared to hear it.

COMING UP OUT OF THE TRAIN always felt like being launched from a sluggish cannon. Making your way through the clammy tunnel that smelled of newsprint and exhaust, the air uncomfortably close to your skin even in the dead of winter, the archway that spit you out onto the endless, swarming floor of Grand Central.

There was a fluid rhythm to everyone's movement in that room. You felt like one small part of an enormous wave of humanity being swept up and out beneath the vast expanse of the restored ceiling, borne up to consider that span of burnished teal above you, its twinkling constellations. You fought the sensation that if you gazed up at it for a moment too long you'd be carried out into the city, not because you made the decision but simply because the anxieties and schedules of this many people propelled you forward with a strength greater than that of any engine.

Zoë moved with quick, decisive gestures toward the south exit. Out on the street they all stopped and looked at one another, as if the spirit of their caper had carried them as far as it could.

"Do you know how to get there?" Allie faltered. Zoë fixed her with a cool gaze.

"We'll just get a cab to Stone Street," she said. "I can look up the exact address on the way downtown. There's going to be crazy traffic right now."

They all continued staring at one another.

"Get a cab!" Zoë urged, and Allie tiptoed out into the street, her weight resting on the pads of her high-heeled feet, her knees buckling inelegantly. They'd all left their school shoes in Allie's locker.

"You'll love this place," Zoë said, her eyes once again on her phone's screen. "It's wall-to-wall bankers. It's all the way downtown, right near Wall Street, so they all go there for happy hours."

Madison looked up at the slate sky. It wasn't yet five o'clock and already the light was fading, leaving the windows of the tall buildings all around them burning in the gloom. It looked so beautiful, the city humming all around them, and all it was, really, was fluorescent office lighting viewed from a distance. Madison kept her neck back until she was absolutely certain her face wasn't red, or that if it was, it would be indistinguishable from the redness of her wind-chapped cheeks. It had been a mistake, coming into the city. She knew that now, but it was too late. It was inevitable that when the cab pulled up, she would climb into the backseat.

Zoë tried to sit in the front seat, next to the cabbie, and when he rebuffed her with a guttural exclamation, she took her place next to Madison in the back as if that was where she'd intended to be all along. Without saying anything, she patted Madison's knee twice.

The cab pulled into traffic and began its cruise down Park Avenue.

TWENTY-SIX

J ackson had never seen the house before, and from the moment they walked in, Lily remembered why that was. Why she'd structured her life this way, kept him always so far from this place.

"Jesus," he said when they came into the kitchen. "You always say it's tasteful. Are you kidding me?"

"Well, you should really see some of the other houses," she said, but her voice sounded unconvincing even to her.

"Lil," Jackson said, "I had no idea." He continued to wander around the room, touching various surfaces. "I would not put this on the tasteful end of the spectrum. You've got D'Amico in your eyes, babe."

What she actually had in her eyes were the beginnings of anxious tears, and her annoyance at their looming arrival was mounting. He hadn't even bullied her; she'd brought him here on her own recognizance. Why?

"You act like you've never met a rich person before," she said. "Half the guys in your year at J school were trust-fund babies. You had no problem holing up at their houses in the Berkshires all winter long. I don't remember that bothering you at all."

"Not like this," he murmured, not even wary of her tone. "You could play football in this kitchen."

He crossed the room and put his hands to her waist, lifting her up onto the butcher block island. He kissed her and let his mouth slide lazily down to her chin, her jawbone, and then the most vulnerable parts of her neck, her throat.

"We should fuck on this," he said.

"No," Lily said. "Come on. Get off me. I told you they've got those cars parked down there, I still think they might have seen you."

He pulled back and stared at her in mock outrage.

"As I'm pretty sure you remember," he said, "I hid. I buried my face in your lap, I believe it was."

"Whatever," she said. "Still worried."

"Come on," he said to her, notching his thumbs to her hip bones. "You've seen some crazy things in this football-field kitchen. What were the craziest ones? You never share the really good stories, I can tell."

She became conscious of her own breathing, of the air as it moved into her, filled her lungs.

"Nobody's going to give away anything juicy in the kitchen around the hired help."

He kissed her.

"Bullshit, Lily."

"This one couple came in once, having a hissing fight," she began. His fingers were kneading the skin just below the waistband of her jeans. "The husband was complaining that this was the last party for him, he was done, and she shrieked, 'You're the one who wanted to live in the People's Republic of Connecticut!'"

"Mediocre," Jackson said. "Not juicy, come on. I know worse stuff happens. The husbands come in and try to feel you up. People try to feel *her* up."

"I don't spy on them during their parties," she said. "I'm not downstairs."

He snorted into her hair.

"This one man came in here a few years ago, the summer," she said. "I was down here making some food for Luke, he couldn't sleep.

This guy came in and sat down at the breakfast table before I could stop him, and started to cry."

Jackson smiled. His hands flew up under her shirt.

"No," she said, "he was kind of sad. He was. They were trying to build this new house and all the little old ladies of Greenwich were outraged and went to the planning and zoning commission."

"Yes! The zoning commission of Greenwich. I love it."

Her stomach was churning, no longer with simple desire, but she ignored it. It felt like her voice was keeping his hands in motion.

"They went to the *Times* and then he didn't get to build his dream house anymore. He'd bought, like, eleven acres. And this was the following week, after the big article, and he was in here crying. He kept saying, 'It was tasteful!'"

"And then he made a pass at you, I assume," Jackson said.

The man had done no such thing. He'd had the look of a man who, on any other night, would have been a predator. But on that night he'd been battened down into submission by his own failures. He sat at the same table where the boys ate their morning cereal, his ruddy cheeks and veiny radish nose those of a man who's well on his way to liver damage. And he'd looked so rumpled, so small. Lily knew it wasn't that he'd been such a spectacular failure when he tried to take his rightful place alongside Bob and Isabel. It was just that being near them made it clear to him how far he would have remained, even in his monolithic eyesore, from someone they would ever respect, even take seriously. He had been promised, by some un-uttered decree, that there was some final plateau he could reach, that he'd then be able to stand beside Bob D'Amico.

But he couldn't feel large, not shaking Bob's hand in the receiving line. It was easy to roll your eyes at Bob from afar, easy to refer to Weiss guys as thugs, not the smartest, not the most dapper. Harder to do when presented with the man himself.

Lily had wanted to tell this man something, that night, something about what she'd learned about how not to feel small in this house. But comforting him wasn't her job, and besides it was annoying that he had broken down in front of her. Assumed she was nobody, underestimated her.

She'd found a security guy to wait with him outside while they brought his car around. She knew that this had been true, during her time in this house: that she had become more exacting, less willing to shield other people from their own exposed flaws. It was so easy, when you lived in it, to learn the behavior.

Isabel has never underestimated you, she thought now. She's basically given you free license over the lives of her children for the past three months. And today you watched Madison get on a train and didn't do anything because, what? You're sick of seeing her mother ignore her? If her mother didn't ignore her so much, you'd be out of a job.

"Come on," Jackson said, still kissing her neck. "Tell me. The guy tried to feel you up?"

"Sure. Yes. What else would you expect. These people are awful, right? Is that what you want to hear? They're clowns. All of them, equally."

"Not clowns," Jackson said. "But maybe criminals. You're going to see this, Lil. Sooner or later."

She pushed Jackson away from her and hopped down from the counter. She wanted to feel her feet on the floor. This was crazy, this whole idea. He needed to go.

"This is my fault," she said, "I don't blame you, but this is it. You got to come in and make fun of my job and roll your eyes at their house. I'm taking you back to the station, okay? You got what you came for."

But he was already wandering into the pantry, crying out with glee. The longer he stayed in here, the bolder he seemed to get. He wasn't whispering anymore. They had to leave. This was crazy; this was asking to be fired, begging for it.

And then, as if conjured by her fear, Bob walked into the kitchen.

He had on gray sweatpants and a blue hoodie, a sweatshirt she recognized from a past year's firm retreat. He was wearing his glasses, so he couldn't actually be going out for a jog, but otherwise he carried nothing, just his keys. He came into the room and then stopped.

"Lily," he said, "hello."

"Hi," she said. "Can I get you something?"

"I thought I heard someone here with you, and I wasn't sure—I didn't know we had company."

"We don't, I just—I ran into a friend, who's in town for the day, and I've got an hour still before the boys need to be picked up, so we're going to grab coffee in town. I just stopped by to—he needed something to eat."

"Fantastic," Bob said. "I'm heading out for a jog, myself."

Jackson emerged from the pantry with a bottle of red wine. No one said anything; Lily did not mention Bob's spectacles, and he did not look directly at the bottle in Jackson's hand.

"You have quite a collection," Jackson sputtered. Bob gave him a discreet nod, maybe simply an acknowledgment that he'd spoken. Lily saw it happen, saw Jackson's resolve weakening. She saw the way he stood up straighter when this man graced him with that gesture of approval.

"He's a big oenophile," Lily said, inexplicably even to herself. What, exactly, would she do if Bob turned to Jackson and started grilling him on wine? "He just wanted to take a look."

"Sure, sure," Bob said. "Are you a friend from the city?"

"Yes," Jackson said.

"An old family friend," she lied. Bob looked out the window, down the hill toward the front gate, and smiled.

"I wonder," he said, "if you might give Lily and myself just a moment alone? Just some business to talk over."

She could feel Jackson's eyes on her, his uncertainty, but she didn't look over at him.

"Of course," he said. He set the bottle down on the wooden table and walked back out to the foyer. Bob turned to her, crossing his arms over his thick chest in a way that made them look undersized, as if they strained to span the width of his body.

"I really am sorry," she began, but he cut her off.

"How is everything with you?" he said. "I don't want you to think I haven't appreciated that we've been asking a great deal more. From you. But how is your family? Are you getting in to see them?"

She nodded. "Yes, of course."

"And your father? I know it's been an unpleasant season. In Manhattan."

"He works for the MTA," she said. "And they're in Brooklyn, actually. Carroll Gardens."

"That's right. I did know that. Me too, you know. Different part of Brooklyn, I mean, but me too."

"I know."

He didn't say anything for a moment, just crossed to the sink. He flipped the garbage disposal for a moment, and the sudden keening of the gnashing blades startled her. Even though she had watched him walk to the sink, had watched his hand reach for the switch.

"Do you think that makes us tougher, in the end?" he said. "Do you think you're as disciplined as you are, I mean, because he's so unimpressed by the choices you've made? Your father, I mean. I've always gathered he wishes you were in law school, or something. Or at least still living close by."

She was too surprised to speak. She had never, in eight years, discussed her father with Bob D'Amico.

"I mean, he probably thinks this isn't a real job. I know something about that," he continued. "You've met my mother, I think. A few times."

Lily nodded.

"They sit there waiting. They find your choices frivolous, and so then if the slightest thing goes wrong—and things go wrong for everyone, lawyers and doctors, too, we know that. But as soon as we have any understandable misfortune, they clap their hands and back away and say, oh, of course. I told you it would. That's what your father would say, if something went wrong for you, yes?"

Lily shook her head, not in response, just a bewildered reflex. She had gathered, over the years, that Concetta didn't think he had a "real job," but it sounded like garden-variety fussing from a woman whose primary form of communication had always been complaint. She'd never thought, really, that his mother was waiting for him to fail.

Bob rattled his keys with finality, and Lily knew he was preparing to leave.

"I don't mean to pry, Lily," he said. "Not in the slightest. But I don't want you to think it escapes my attention. How tirelessly you—how much you give us. And you are, in many important ways, alone. That's why we've brought you so close to us. As you know, my wife is not one to befriend many people. But you are family, to us. You are as essential to this household as I am. I hope you know that, but more importantly, I want you to know that I know it."

Still she couldn't speak. She stood, in the middle of his kitchen, and nodded, mute. But then, this seemed the response he'd expected.

"I see how well you look after my children," he said, with finality. Then he cleared his throat and smiled more substantially. It was the glad-handing public smile she recognized, with none of the smoky distance he'd had on his face just moments earlier. She saw now that he had a manila folder in his other hand, held low and close to his body, against his thigh.

"It looks like it might rain," Lily told him. "You might want to save the jog for the morning."

"We'll see," Bob said. "I'll take my chances. It was nice meeting your friend. I'll leave you both to it. Help yourself to the wine, too."

He moved toward the mud room, pausing beside her to lower his hand to her shoulder.

"Pretend I was never here," he said. "We very nearly missed each other, didn't we?" And then he was gone.

Jackson reappeared as soon as the side door slammed. They moved together to the big window and watched him as he strolled down the drive, breaking into a light jog only as he disappeared behind the crest of the hill. But the security guys are down there, she thought. If he's meeting someone else, they'd have to pick him up farther away. Not in front of the house.

He'd just been trying to say something nice, something thoughtful. Maybe he was changing. He could, right? After something like this? He'd looked healthier, she thought, his skin once again had its nutty glow, no longer ashen and crusted, stale with stubble. But he must have a plan. He'd kept it from them, but he had a strategy. He hadn't really been leaving Isabel all alone, here.

She could choose to see it this way. She might not be wrong.

"Where is he going?" Jackson said. Lily felt that if she spoke, her voice would be only a croak. "He usually let you raid the wine rack?"

She knew they'd been given permission, and in exchange for something, but for what?

She took Jackson's hand, and they, too, left through the mud room. She knew now that she'd let her boyfriend stay. Later, they'd fuck.

TWENTY-SEVEN

As they jammed themselves into the darkened chamber between Stone Street behind them and the bar's inner door before them, Madison could already hear all the small noises you sometimes caught in brief shots as you passed the bars on upper Third, just north of the old apartment. That acrid smell she'd learned to identify as she got older, the smell of spilled beer mixed with old sweat. She smelled liquor at home, all the time, but stale beer didn't smell anything like day-old whiskey, whether on the floor or on someone's breath. Alcohol was all around her, and always had been, but bars were new.

Zoë surged ahead, her hips liquid through the muggy mass of bodies. There was a redness to the lighting, just as Madison had been led to expect from bars in every movie she'd ever seen. The bartenders were all tall women with sculpted arms, wearing modest black tank tops that still managed to look entirely lascivious on their bodies. The men—and the room was filled almost entirely with men—looked like they had been steadily wilting since 6 A.M. that morning. They all wore their hair parted, slicked back with product. Their combs had left razor-sharp paths along their scalps, so that their hair rebelled only at the napes of their necks. The slight flip to its ends let you know that they'd much prefer letting it flow free, preferably while sitting on the deck of someone's boat with a cooler of Bud heavy.

Bud heavy, she thought, the memory bobbing unexpectedly to the surface, had been Grandpop's favorite.

They all had bodies that had clearly been bulked and toned in service of some courtly sport, years earlier, but were beginning slowly to go slack. They all had a softness to their cheeks that was not baby fat but its older twin, the sort of fat that makes its debut about eight years after baby fat has departed for good. Many of them turned at the sudden influx of frozen air to watch the three girls enter the bar.

Madison felt the heat of their gazes on her cheeks, her hair, the exposed part of her collarbone. Miraculously, Zoë had already found an empty bar table at the back of the room.

"There's no bouncer?"

"I told you," Zoë said. "I've never been carded at a place like this. They don't care, we're girls."

"They'll probably card us at the bar," Allie said, smiling apologetically for the correction. "We're just still on the early side, for a bouncer."

"Well," Zoë said. "Yeah. But they don't have the time to care. Look at this place. Plus, I told you—the IDs belonged to my cousin and her friends. They aren't even fake."

Madison perched on a high bar stool, its seat upholstered in blood-colored leather.

"Should we go up to the bar?" she yelled in the general direction of Zoë's ear.

"We don't want to lose this table," Zoë said with a shrug. "If we wait, someone will bring drinks over."

And for once, she wasn't glossing over the truth.

The three guys who came over weren't all the same age; one of them seemed to have some sort of vague supervisory role in relation to the other two. He wore a wedding ring and was much quieter than his friends, periodically scanning his gaze over their heads, looking like he had hopes of levitating his way out of the conversation.

"You three look thirsty." One man had spoken first, when they slid over. This one was named Jack. He looked strong, his forearms bulbous like bowling pins. She liked the way his broad shoulders seemed to strain his dress shirt to its limit, but the rest of him seemed the wrong shape for a suit, his torso crammed uncomfortably into his pants.

"You also look a bit lost," said the other young one. His name was Craig. He was thinner, taller, like someone who'd only just graduated from being gangly. Unlike Jack, he still wore his suit jacket. Craig's hair was longer than Jack's, parted and tamed with some sort of product, but for the first few minutes he kept brushing it back from his face and sighing.

The married one, Hugh, was the one to take their orders. Madison didn't want a beer, but when they asked the girls to pick their poisons, Zoë immediately insisted that they'd all have whatever "you boys" were having. Did that even work? Madison wondered. Wouldn't we seem older if we all had our own drink orders?

As she drank, she told herself stories about them. Craig was the smoother talker, the better banker. Jack wasn't as smart, came from a more blue-collar background, was relying on becoming a good old boy as soon as possible if he wanted to advance. Her father would take him seriously; Jack was a guy who would get very good at golf, knowing it would help. She imagined that Craig liked Jack's bluster and Jack liked Craig's effortless comfort, the way he moved through their world like a knife cutting through cake.

The most noteworthy part of their time at the bar, she would tell herself later, was that she learned how wonderfully easy it was to tell lies if you strung them all together like buttery pearls on a necklace. Letting them fall in line, gain strength from their proximity to one another. You started with a big one and then followed it with several small ones to make the big one feel real, then as soon as it was truly established, added another big one. She could not believe how well it worked, the high you felt when you did it well, the way it filled you with the intoxicating desire to tell another, and another.

"Juniors," Zoë was saying. "We're at Yale," and here she indicated Madison and herself, "and Allison is at Trinity."

"See," Jack said, trying and failing to draw Hugh's focus back to the table. "I told you they were twenty-one."

Allie tittered over the rim of her pint glass.

"You girls all from Connecticut?"

"Oh, God no," Zoë said. "Los Angeles."

Madison couldn't look away; she had the bizarre sensation, ushered along by the beer, that Zoë was rewriting her own life for her, that when they were done here this would all be true. She would be from Los Angeles, not Greenwich. Her father would run a studio, not an investment bank. She would be whoever other people said she was, but instead of the people who usually performed that function, it would be Zoë and Allie who'd decide for her.

"So what are you doing down here six days before Christmas?" Craig teased. "If I were you I'd fly home as soon as December hit."

Zoë reached out to rest her fingers on the back of his hand. She told him about their mutual friend, an enormous Christmas bash at her place a few hours north, just over the Connecticut border. How they'd all gone a few years in a row, how when they were up there they had no cell service and it was so amazing, but on Sundays you had to drive over into New York if you wanted to buy alcohol.

"I still can't believe that's law over there," Jack said. "The first time I visited a buddy in Stamford, that blew my mind."

Jack was from Missouri.

"There's a law in Connecticut that more than five women living in a house together constitutes a brothel," Zoë continued. "So there are no actual sorority houses at Yale. Isn't that sad?"

Madison tried to remember if she'd known there was a law in Connecticut that prohibited buying alcohol on a Sunday. It seemed like something her father would have mentioned, many times.

"Yes," Craig replied. "That, guys, is tragic."

The room had gotten louder. Somehow, the underlying din was always male—deep voices rumbling past one another like tectonic plates shifting beneath their feet. The shrieks that punctuated those rumblings, the reaction sounds, were always women.

Hugh returned with three drinks, a second round only for the girls. Madison had asked for vodka this time.

"Ladies," he said. "This has been a pleasure. But we're actually late," and here he paused heavily to look at Jack, "for a client dinner. So you'll have to enjoy this round for us."

"Hugh!" Craig yelped, for the first time showing a rowdy streak that might match him more logically with Jack. "One more round!"

"Take a look, girls," Jack said, joining in. "This is what comes of marriage. He's got to catch the train to the 'burbs. He's got the wife waiting for him. There's a drip in the kitchen, the sink needs fixing. He can't be drinking away his Friday night with three California girls."

Hugh mumbled something about a glass of water, and began moving back toward the bar, his progress coming in waves—a wall of bodies would crush him, then something would give and he'd surge forward. Madison watched him move away from them. She took the straw out of her highball glass and gulped the drink.

"Let me tell you guys a little secret," Craig said. "He's twice as hammered as either one of us. He's probably been drunk since lunch."

When she left the table, the last thing Madison heard was Jack explaining something to Allie.

"Me, I'm there for two years, tops," he said. "Then maybe I move to a hedge fund, PE, somewhere else. Then business school if I have a good sense of what I want, but only down the road. The guys who go straight to school, honestly—those are the pathetic guys, the ones who become lifers at these places. You don't want to be a lifer, because unless you end up, you know, CEO, you're sort of stranded. And especially right now. Probably you don't know about this, but it's a weird time to be working at a bank."

Madison followed Hugh to the bar.

TWENTY-EIGHT

When Lily heard Isabel's car pull into the drive, it could have been ten minutes or three hours since they'd seen Bob in the kitchen; she had no idea.

A moment later, her phone chimed. Then again, then a third time. Beneath her, Jackson opened his eyes and cocked an eyebrow.

"What's wrong," he said, and it was hearing his voice, slower and clogged somewhere in his throat from the bottle of wine he'd already drunk down, that did it. That and looking around them, the curtains pulled, everything about this so clearly a terrible idea. Her own worst behavior wasn't going to jolt anyone else back into any normal degree of giving a fuck. It was just going to put her in the place of primary danger, which would only call attention to the months they'd already spent in that very spot.

She grabbed her phone; Isabel was calling, having given up on texting.

She got out of bed and slid back into her underwear, pulled on her jeans, ran into the bathroom to brush the wine sediment from her front teeth.

"The fuck?" Jackson was saying, but she was herself again, she knew what to tell him.

"I screwed up," she said. "I saw Madison when we were by the station, I saw her getting on a train. I tried to call Isabel but then—I should have done something more. I have to go talk to her."

"Okay," he said, "okay, but—"

"Just stay in here," Lily said. "Just don't do anything. Please. Do literally nothing at all. Don't make any noise. Don't go outside for a cigarette. Literally nothing. Promise me."

"Sure," he said.

Up at the house, Isabel was standing, perplexed, in front of an open cabinet, her arms stretched out to either side, hands clasping the cabinet handles.

"Did you move things around in here, Lily?"

"Hi," Lily said, and waited for the ignored question to snag her boss's attention.

"I've been trying to reach you," Isabel said. "It seemed odd no one was here. Where's Madison?"

"She went over to Allie's house," Lily said. She noticed, with something she tried to keep from becoming smugness, that Isabel couldn't place the name.

"But, actually, there's something—I tried to call you earlier."

"I haven't been watching my phone. It was off."

"Well, I'm a little bit worried."

Isabel's face shifted as Lily spoke, composing itself. Lily felt the same comforting click she'd felt back in her bedroom, climbing away from Jackson, remembering her job. She could make this sound normal, her part at least. She and Isabel could speak to each other, again, the way they had on the night Bob came home. Something had been disjointed between them ever since that night. It had really started then, not after Thanksgiving. She rewrote the history now, in her head, quickly. On the night Bob came home, she'd been too slow to respond. Her loyalty, her dependability, had stuttered. And now she was on the outside; Isabel had been keeping her at a distance. But it could stop now. Isabel could need her, again. There could have been a reason, a use, for her behavior this afternoon.

Lily told everything very clearly, in a very untruthful way.

"Are you sure it was that early?" Isabel said.

"Yes. Right when I called you."

"So they were getting on the 3:12," Isabel said, scrolling through train schedules on her phone.

"The other two were already on the train by the time I saw her," Lily lied. "I just barely got a glimpse of her before she stepped off the platform."

"So then how can you be sure?" Isabel said. Her voice was steamrolled, with little actual inquiry included in the question.

"Maybe it wasn't her," Lily said. "But my first thought was to call you."

Isabel stared down at her BlackBerry's screen.

"I only see one call," she said after a moment, and Lily seized on that lag time, took a shot.

"Well, your phone was off," she said, "you wouldn't have seen the missed calls. If you turned it off after my first call, I mean."

Isabel pressed something on her phone and lifted it to her ear, staring at Lily.

"Madison's phone is off now," she said. "But you didn't try her at the time?"

"No."

"And you called me . . . once."

They stood in silence, because again, Lily knew it hadn't been a question.

"We could call the school," she said then.

"No, I don't want to clue them in. Obviously they're too inept to realize she didn't attend her last class, otherwise we'd already have gotten a call."

Isabel moved to the sink, where she'd been cutting calla lilies before Lily came in. She washed her hands slowly, reflectively, then turned and leaned back on the heels of her hands, propping herself against the counter.

"What do you want me to do," Lily said. She was worried the wine had crept into her voice, into its volume and its cadences. But Isabel wasn't looking at her.

"The boys," Isabel said suddenly, pulling away from the counter with a small start. "I completely forgot."

"They're over at Kenny's again."

"Jesus, thank God. Is Bob down the hall?"

"No," Lily said. Isabel faced away from her, looking out the window, but her body stiffened. "He's not here."

"Did you see him?"

Lily waited, long enough, she hoped, before she offered her reply. "No, I didn't."

"This wouldn't normally matter," Isabel said.

"Of course."

"I just don't want to overreact."

"No, I understand."

"I've been waiting for this," Isabel said, her perfect Chiclet teeth chewing away at her bottom lip. "It's been too easy, with her. I've tried not to bother her, to see if that might keep her from striking back. If it seemed like I was giving her some slack, some space to process all of this on her own, without me all over her."

Bullshit, Lily thought. To attribute agency and wisdom to Isabel's indifference toward Madison that winter was one step further than Lily could sympathize. She'd sympathized with Isabel for years. The preteen trance she always fell into around this woman, how badly Lily wanted her employers to like her, had made it easier to shrug off the things Isabel didn't do for Madison. Lily had told herself for years that not every mother was warm, not every mother tickled and hugged. Her mother didn't, for one. And Isabel had been smart enough, hadn't she, to hire Lily. Lily was warm with the children, in her place, and Isabel was still a good mother, of a sort.

But that was different. That was temperament; this was neglect. Ignoring your daughter, ignoring her pain. This was how bad it had to get before Isabel did anything. Lily had to literally stop doing her job.

She tried to keep one part of her mind on Jackson, back in her bedroom. You can't be angry right now, she told herself. You've squandered that.

"Bob wanted to put a car on her," Isabel continued. "At all times. I thought that was outrageous. But if he finds out that she's in the city by herself, refusing to talk to us, he'll lose it, he'll kill me."

"He might know where she is."

Something like a smile flitted across Isabel's face, but she didn't bother to respond.

"He might have an idea," Lily said, "of what to do—if we ended up in this situation. He might have already thought about this."

Isabel ignored her a second time. She gathered the chopped flower stalks from the sink and threw them in the trash, each gesture made without urgency.

"I'll get the security guys on the phone now. I wasn't dealing with the new people directly at first, but I've spoken with them a few times now. I've got all the numbers."

"Okay," Lily said. Isabel ran a hand through her limp hair. She hadn't ever started to dress differently, really, since all this had started, but someone who saw her as often as Lily did could see the tiny false notes. There was a coffee stain on one sleeve of her crisp white shirt, and a faded spot of something peach colored—a makeup stain?—at the collar. Her hair was still thick and something to envy in its many shades of blond, but it had lost its luster somehow, as if Isabel had styled it the day before and then partied all night, brushing it back repeatedly from her face in a film of alcohol sweat.

"I can do it," Lily said. "I can call them."

"No," Isabel said, already turning to her phone, squaring her shoulders as if to hide its screen from Lily. "Here's what you can do for me. Call Mina. She'll be good here. Then let the guys in, when they arrive."

"Mina?" Lily began, but Isabel left the room, the door swinging behind her as if in grief at her swift departure.

TWENTY-NINE

Madison stood beside Hugh at the bar, ignored for several moments longer than she believed it had taken him to feel her there.

"Hi," she said. "I wanted some water, too."

The bartender came back over and set down a shot glass. Madison drifted back slightly, conscious of the lights above the bar on her face, but the bartender didn't seem to register her presence, her age. The bar was crammed; she'd had to all but crawl to make her way up to him.

He looked down at her.

"You want one?"

She nodded, keeping her eyes on his. He whirled a finger in the air, and the bartender brought over another before winking and gliding away. They clearly knew each other.

Madison took the shot. It was whiskey, bad whiskey. He looked at her again, his features spreading out across his face, less pinched.

"You like picklebacks?"

"Yes," she lied. Or maybe it wasn't even a lie, how would she know? He made another indecipherable gesture toward the bartender, who soon returned with four shot glasses, two of them filled with a murkier liquid. Madison liked the way the lights behind the bar illuminated the alcohol in the shot glasses, as if you were drinking something more special than what you could drink at home. That made sense, though. It was another reason to come to a place like this; to tell yourself that something you could find absolutely any-where was special, worth fighting your way toward.

"Jack's a big fan of these," Hugh said. "He got me into them and now, like an idiot, I'm always drinking them."

She watched and followed his lead, choking through her nose when she realized the name had been only literal; it was just a shot of pickle juice.

Hugh looked at her again. They'd performed some required ritual and now they were allowed to talk. She waited for his pupils to go soluble, for the corners of his mouth to slacken. She waited for the shift she knew so well.

"I didn't mean to be rude," he said. "You guys seem bright. You're lovely. It's just been a long day, and they should know better."

She nodded.

"You work on the Street?"

He smiled, letting his eyes move down her body to her hands, her elbow propped on the bar, then back up to her face again.

"My father works in finance," she said, feeling the words beneath her feet like a swaying tightrope. They were impossible not to say. It was like reciting a spell; if she mentioned it first, if she controlled their conversation, then it couldn't go anywhere too terrible. Then he wouldn't figure it out.

"Yes," he said. "I work on the Street."

"Bank? Hedge fund?"

"I work at a bank," he said. He didn't say which one.

"Trader, or banker?"

"Banker," he said. "I work in fixed income, do you know what that is?"

She nodded. She thought it had something to do with bonds—her father had muttered the name of his former head of fixed income several times during their last late-night talk. Her father's bank had been known primarily as a bond shop, at least before. She knew that part not from her father but from reading Jake's columns.

She pushed the thoughts of Amanda from her mind. She didn't want to think about Amanda's opinion of any part of the afternoon thus far.

"Anyway," he said. "I should apologize for being so rude back there. I just—it's been a strange few months. And then, being in here, you know, it can seem like nothing's changed. The younger people don't really know the difference, maybe."

He smiled down at her again and she saw his fingers reaching out to toy with one of the empty shot glasses, saw that he was longing to order another.

"We don't have to talk about any of that," she said. She kept her voice low, matching his, and he bent his head down toward her.

"I just wanted to explain," he said, now almost whispering in her ear. "Because it wouldn't normally bother me, those guys dragging me along to talk to girls like you. I wouldn't normally see that as a burden." He'd turned his whole body now, away from the bar, closing her off from the other men around them.

He kept talking, about the summer, the interns who had been hired before the tide had turned and washed them up at the office, potential prey instead of the predators they'd been trained to be. He talked about the weeks in September when no one had slept. When the head of his division had asked him, one night, if he thought they should bring in a doctor to make sure everyone was still physically capable of being there.

"You don't know," he said. "You're too young still to have known this feeling. But by the time you're my age, you're just living your life, putting it together piece by piece. You don't stop to think about it, you just do it. And nobody really—I mean, you can't be stopping all the time to think about how every small thing you do might affect someone else far away from you. You'd go crazy, thinking like that."

As he spoke, his voice dipping as if he were continuously suppressing a series of belches, she tried to keep nodding. It was like no one had asked him in months how he felt, if he was worried, why he'd been so quiet and withdrawn. Like he'd been waiting to meet an underage girl in his regular bar, just to have someone to tell it to. Every few seconds, often at the ends of his sentences, he'd toss his hair aside with a jerk of his head, to clear it from his eyes, and she saw that he wore it this way—brushed softly in a wave that crested back from his forehead—to cover the fact that he was losing his hair. The newly exposed skin ran back in furrows along the top of his head, like wheel ruts on a muddy road.

All she'd have to do would be to say one thing too much, one thing any girl her age—a college junior, she reminded herself—wouldn't normally know.

She had existed, thus far, somewhere safe. Whatever happened, however repugnant the pity she could see in other people's eyes, no one could touch her. They had all known her for almost as long as she had known herself, and they couldn't tell her anything she didn't already know, force her suddenly to credit their opinions. They wanted to reach out, to prod her with their fingertips, to see if she was still all there. She was sure they wanted her to cry, some of them, but they didn't dare try it. But here, she was no one. She was exposed, alone in the rifle sight, without any thick forest all around her to ward off the first shot.

"I must be boring you," Hugh said. He moved closer to her, put one arm to her waist. He let his head droop toward her, let his razor-burned chin graze her neck. He wasn't even trying to kiss her, really; he was just burying his face against her.

She thought of that trader on television, on the first morning. Of his mottled neck, of the way he'd spit her father's name. And then, just as she'd always been led to expect, just like the shot-guzzling junior associates for whom her father had so much contempt, she felt it—a wave of nausea, beginning at her ankles and spreading steadily up through her entire body, the delayed revolt of every sip of beer and vodka and whiskey she'd chugged down against that body's will.

"I'm sorry," she said, and when his arm didn't respond to her gentle pushes, she shoved him, harder, in the chest.

"What the hell?" he barked, his tender bewilderment vanishing. "What's wrong, sweetheart?"

She didn't say anything to him, just spun away from the bar, launched herself into the crush of bodies as if it were a rioting sea, and fumbled toward the street.

THIRTY

W e've checked with the doorman at the apartment—both apartments," the head of the security detail was telling Isabel. Mina liked him, his look. His name was Teddy. He had a military air to him, his head more square than ovate, cheekbones so broad and sharp they had corners. This was a man her sister Denise would go nuts for. Even if he brought bad news, it seemed safe to trust that he'd done his job.

Denise, Mina chided herself. That was what she'd intended to do tonight. She owed Denise a call. Jaime had decided not to come home for Christmas next week, and Denise was sleeping with some married guy. Gobbling up the Greenwich gossip together over the phone had been a reliable balm for them both, all month.

The married guy was in finance, but he was decidedly midcareer, and he was fearful for his job. Poor thing, Dee couldn't even find herself a man with a glamorous other life for her to envy. What she was choosing to obsess over, then, wasn't his wife but rather the many other women she was positive, *positive*, she told Mina, he was also sleeping with. She only knew about one of them, someone named Maggie. She'd seen them together once, at the bar behind the Oyster Bar, of all places. (This was a suspicious story in Mina's mind, because why would Denise have been there in the first place?) But now she was following the woman around the city, devoting whole afternoons to this. Maggie had given Trevor some expensive bar of soap from Morocco and when Denise found it in the apartment in the city he'd told her, unapologetic, who it was from. And so Denise bought him a thick ceramic soap dish—totally the wrong style, she'd reassured Mina, for his anonymous steel-and-white-marble pad— and used the soap compulsively, whenever she spent the night. Mina thought of her sister now, expecting her call. Hunched over his sink, grinding the bar of soap between her hands, and then slapping at her cheeks, rubbing the creamy bubbles in circles into her skin.

The security officer was still debriefing Isabel. Mina took a side-long glance at the kitchen door, where Lily had been lingering, suspiciously quiet and unhelpful, ever since Mina's arrival. They hadn't said hello. Mina had of course made to greet her, at first, but somehow Lily's entire body had held itself apart from Mina's arms. Not in disgust but almost with something like shyness. Which made no sense, but the truth was that for once it was nice to be able to stand at Isabel's side, to rub her back every so often, without feeling like you were stepping on the toes of an employee half your age. Lily also kept looking at her phone, which wasn't so unusual for some of these younger babysitters but for this one was, as far as Mina could remember, quite a bold display of insolence.

"I understand," Isabel said to the security guy. "But I really don't want to involve the police yet. We know she went into the city voluntarily, with her friends. I don't want to have our name attached to anything publicly until we think we have reason to do so."

"Has anyone contacted either of the other two young women?" he asked.

"I don't have their numbers," Isabel said.

"And could we contact their families?"

"I'm not," Isabel said. "I'm not willing to do that."

Mina thought about the girls. They'd all know, even if they hadn't phrased it thus to themselves, that they'd have no chance of keeping the trip a secret if anyone, however distant an acquaintance, saw them on their way in. Not with Madison in tow. Maybe it was just for fun; maybe she'd paid for their fake IDs, who the hell knew. Could they really be, at this point, unaware that the city might not be the safest place for Bob D'Amico's daughter right now?

She tried to remember what the world of men in lower Manhattan had looked like to her, back before it had become the place where her own life unfolded. Maybe this was how she would help; Isabel had never gone into the city as an outsider, and now her daughter was trying to do just that. Mina had some experience, here, that Isabel never would. But she couldn't think where Madison might go. She'd never been any good at reading the minds of teenage girls, as her own daughter had made perfectly clear.

"And we're sure that her father doesn't know anything further about what she might have planned to do in the city?"

"By all means," Isabel said. "If you can find him, please ask him."

"Well, then," the other security guy said, a skinnier man who looked troublingly like he'd love a nap. "There isn't much we can do but sit tight. But you need to consider, Ms. D'Amico, that one of these other families might have also noticed they're short one daughter. If somebody else calls the police, then this becomes a different situation."

"I know," Isabel said. "I know."

"There's also the question of someone possibly recognizing her. Someone with a grudge. But I'm not telling you anything you and your husband don't already know."

"Well, nothing I don't know," Isabel said, her syllables clipped.

"Isabel," Mina said. "I'll go wait at the station. I mean, what if she comes back? We won't even know until she makes her way up here. I'll just go watch the incoming trains. Why not?"

"I can go," Lily said.

Isabel didn't even look in that direction. She turned to Mina.

THIRTY-ONE

They rode the train back in silence, Zoë's a fuming silence, Allie's one of fear. Madison felt, given the panic that had driven her out onto Stone Street in the suddenly falling sleet without her winter coat, strangely peaceful.

Benevolent, actually, was the word. Zoë didn't have to make up an excuse, now, wouldn't have to adjust for the fact that any one of those men might have paid more attention to Madison than to her. She wouldn't be forced to square the mundane end to their actual evening with the evening she'd imagined: the three of them piling into a cab with guys who would buy them peach-colored drinks at whatever velvet-rope club they'd be shuttled into. Some man wedging his fingertips between her skin and her bra, allowing her to feel superior to Wyatt, who probably hadn't texted her in days.

The fact was that they'd all been spared these many small embarrassments by the sheer urgency of Madison's meltdown. Allie, who had brought Madison's coat out with her when they left the bar, seemed to understand this, too.

The train skated through Harlem-125th Street and then lower Westchester. Madison rested her forehead against the window, watching the raindrops tadpole their way along the glass.

Somewhere between New Rochelle and Larchmont, she decided to go for a walk. She'd never been on the train this late before, and she began to wonder who else rode the 8:39 local to Stamford on a

Friday night. Surely men with families would have gone home earlier, on a Friday, or else would be in the city drinking up the requisite
numbness to board a later homeward train. Overworked, entry-level
analysts like the ones at the bar? But surely they all still lived in the
city, hadn't yet been caught by the migratory drift into the more affluent precincts of Connecticut. Housekeepers, nannies, and other
domestic help with the weekend off? But they, too, would be on a
train in the opposite direction.

Madison stood and told Allie that she was going to look for the
bathroom. Zoë had curled herself into a tight ball, her high heels
abandoned on the unclean floor, her eyes closed to the music streaming through her earbuds.

Just like the slammed crowd back at the bar had created its own
pace, its own ecosystem, there was a pleasing rhythm to the train's
progress. Madison would come to the end of a train car, wrap her
fingers around the metal handle on the door, brace herself, pull it,
let the train's momentum carry her forward and onto the small jan-
gling platform between cars. Ignore the nighttime whooshing in her
ears, look neither left nor right. Grab another, identical metal handle,
this time heaving her body weight forward, letting it carry her past
the yawning, heavy door and into the new train car. Move in waves
through the car, her balance dictated by the motion of the train.
Reach the far end of that car, the next door. Repeat.

And then she was in the bar car.

A long, grimy bar with fake wood paneling stood at one end of
the car, with train seats lining the other end. Metal poles placed at
intervals had plastic discs on them, with holes cut out for cups. The
car was empty except for a few standing customers clustered at the
bar. A man who might as well have served as the actual Metro-North
mascot—thick neck, dark hairs pelting his forearms, spider veins
burst on his nose, guttural voice and authentic Bridgeport accent—
slouched behind the bar, entertaining two women who clutched
plastic cups. Two men stood closer to Madison, one reading a news-

paper and seemingly younger, the other with his back pressed to the wall, his chin drifting periodically toward his neck.

"What brings you here, sweetheart?" the bartender said, pulling himself with reluctance away from the two women.

"Hi," she said. "I'll have—you have bourbon?"

The old man at the end of the bar snorted, but the younger guy closest to her didn't look up from his paper. He had taken a small notebook from his pocket, one of those black leathery ones, and started jotting down notes.

"Let me make you a deal," the bartender said. "What do you say we make it ginger ale, and keep it between us?"

"Please?" she said weakly.

"Come on, Steve-o," one of the women chimed in. She beckoned him over and slid one of her cigarettes behind his left ear. "Let us buy her a drink."

The bartender grinned at Madison. "These girls have been trying to get me fired for going on decades," he said. "You wouldn't want them to finally get their way, right? You wouldn't do me like that."

Madison smiled and tried not to cry.

"No," she whispered.

"Ginger ale?" Steve-o asked her. She nodded, and when it came, she had to admit, it was delicious. She let the bubbles sting the roof of her mouth and it was much better than bourbon would have been.

She took her cup over to one of the seats at the other end of the car.

"Rough night?"

The voice came, unexpectedly, from the man who'd been reading a paper. He had walked away from the bar with his beer, and she saw that he was younger even than she'd thought, not far from her age. He had wild brown hair, thick and coarse like the bristles of a hairbrush, but it was still nice hair. You still wanted to run your hand through it, just to see if it was softer than it looked. He wasn't attractive, really, but there was something about him that made you want to keep looking. He seemed at ease, despite his wiry energy; he looked like he could feel he belonged anywhere.

"Rough night?" he repeated, a smile inherent in his voice. "It's still pretty early to have had a rough night."

"Just tired," she said.

"You live in Connecticut?"

"Greenwich."

Too late, she remembered her assumed identity for the evening, but like everything else from that night it seemed like it might be, at this point, rumpled and worn out. She figured it was all right to be herself again. There was something about this guy's face, though, like he was too eager to prove that they knew each other, that they were on the same team.

"Fun," he said. "I'm headed to New Haven."

"You're on the wrong train. You'll have to transfer at Stamford."

"Ahh," he said. "Where were you thirty minutes ago?"

She kept a blank smile on her face, confused.

"I figured that out already," he said apologetically. "I got on the local by accident."

"So you're not from around here?"

"I live in the city, but I don't spend a lot of time in Connecticut, usually."

"What's in New Haven?"

"Just visiting an old buddy who's up there for law school."

"Good for him." She knew that names like that one, Yale Law, were impressive to the point of rarity, that she shouldn't let it pass by unmentioned.

"He's the smart one," the man said, winking. He extended his hand. "I'm Gabe."

She felt it, again, the familiarity of his face. She tried to remember if Zoë had given out their real names that night at the bar.

"Eliza," she said finally, a bastardized version of her Italian middle name. His eyes seemed to flicker, but she told herself it was just a reaction to how long it had taken her to come up with her own name.

"And I take it you're underage," he said, flicking his eyes at the bartender. He slid his beer can down the seat until it rested near her hand.

"Our secret," he said. She took a sip and instantly regretted it. She still just did not like beer.

Just before she picked up the can, he'd smiled again but this time uncertainly, as if worried he'd made one gesture too many. And maybe it was that flaw in his seemingly polished veneer, in his sense of his own right to be there beside her, that surfaced it for her. Where she'd seen him before.

She stood up, knocking her paper cup from its slot. It had been months ago. The time between that and this collapsed in her mind and she felt it almost like physical violence, the arrival of something more than fear and less than knowledge.

"Look," he said, "I'm sorry. Don't worry."

"You were at my school," she said. "At the football game in September with that—that man." She felt the harsh edges of each word as it left her mouth. "What are you, following me? Because if you are, trust me, you don't want to be doing that once we hit Greenwich."

She was thinking of the sedans, of the measures she felt certain her father had taken. But then she felt it move through her chest like plucked guitar strings: no one knew where she was.

"I wasn't following you," Gabe said. His hands were up in the air between them, as if she were the one invading *his* space. He kept his voice low in that specific way that meant he was trying to urge her to do the same.

"Right," Madison said. "Feeding me a beer in the bar car, just a coincidence."

"Yes," Gabe said. "Of course I recognized you when I saw you. But that afternoon at Greenwich Prep, the football game, that was a coincidence, too. I was just there because I was shadowing Dick Corzar—he's at Goldman Sachs, he's a—"

"I know who Dick Corzar is," she hissed. She did not. She assumed it was the man who'd accosted her that day at the football game.

"Okay, well great. So I was writing something that involved him, and he went up to you without even explaining at first who you were. I didn't know. And then tonight, I recognized you, but you gave me a fake name, so I assumed you did that for a reason. I didn't want to upset you by bringing up that afternoon."

She said nothing.

"I assume that weekend was an unpleasant one for you," he pressed further.

She laughed a little, more just expelled air.

"I'm a writer," he said. "I used to write for the *Times*. DealBook. I'm sure you know what that is."

She stared at him, hard, until he began to fidget, to click his pen. She did not read DealBook, and in fact only knew what it was for sure because Jake sometimes used to make Amanda read it, but she wanted him to feel stupid for doubting her.

"I promise you," he said. "I got up and came to the bar car because I wanted a beer. I had no reason to believe that Madison D— Come on. How could I possibly have known you'd be on this train?"

"You don't want to be following me when we get off this train," she repeated. "My father has security everywhere."

"And I assume that's why there's been no press following you at home," Gabe said, his voice still low and soothing, his hands still hovering in the air as if he might have to block her from leaving. "He must be working very hard to keep everyone away from you."

She stared at him again.

"Well, the apartment in the city is, at this point I would imagine, unlivable," he said. "I mean, the press have been camped out there for months. I don't think most of them have figured out that your father's been back in Connecticut since October."

Her fingertips felt cold. This was her fault. She'd been childish, she'd pushed Lily away, she'd ignored so many things her mother had taught her. She was the one who'd brought it to this point, where this nerdy junior reporter—probably not even, probably he answered phones at the *Times* office—knew more than she did.

"If you think you're going to interview me," she began slowly, "about anything to do with my family, then you clearly have deeply misunderstood who we are."

He smiled, which made her want to smash the heel of her hand into his nose.

"Wow," he said, breathy—if ersatz—admiration in his voice. "Of course not. That's not what I meant, far from it. But let me just say this."

She started to sidestep her way past him, but he moved, with one step, to block her way.

"Please," he said, "just listen. I think your perspective is a valuable one. I think understanding your father as a human being—from the people who know him best—would go a long, long way toward re-habbing his image."

He seemed to realize that he'd slipped into his own jargon. He smiled and shook his head, almost sheepish.

"All I mean," he began again, "is that I think you have a lot to say. I think your father is being vilified unfairly, and I think you know that. And I think if people are reminded of who he really is—an outrageously successful family man who lives well within, even *beneath*, his means, when you compare him with his peers, who gives generously to all sorts of real and worthwhile causes, who is beloved in his own community—I think the tide might start to turn. I think people might do what they should have been doing from the start, which is view this whole thing with a wider lens. And I think that you could get your story out there, Madison. I think you could show people just how immature the reaction has been thus far."

Everywhere she went, no matter what name she gave, what drink she was offered, these men wanted to talk to her about her father. They wanted her to give some part of herself up to them, some vital thing she couldn't identify.

"I don't want to sound full of myself here," he said, allowing sugary self-congratulation into his voice. "But there is a part of me, yes, that thinks I'd be the perfect person to help tell that story."

"Please," she said. He seemed to realize, then, that he had his hand on her elbow, that he was pressing, however gently, back against her. He let her go as if she'd burned him.

"Just think about it," he said. He fumbled beneath the bar and came back brandishing a white card between his index and middle fingers.

She looked down at the name: Gabriel Scott Lazarus.

"This isn't a *Times* card," she said, trying not to be proud that he looked impressed. "It doesn't say the paper's name anywhere on it."

"No," he said slowly. "I left the *Times*. I'm launching my own site. The Tender Offer. It's going to be financial news, but human interest. Basically, anything you'd want to know more about after you read DealBook, but that you'll never see reported there. There's a lot happening, and only certain aspects of the situation are being reported. A lot has slipped between the cracks."

She nodded, and he smiled again.

"You're probably one of the very few teenage girls in the country who'd get that name," he observed.

She didn't respond.

"I'm not sucking up to you," he said. "I think we can help each other, but that's the operative phrase. Each other. I'm not interested in exploiting you or your family, the situation itself. I just think there are questions that aren't being asked. What's the real use of vilifying your father? That's not what the country needs, at this point."

When she said nothing, he sighed. "Just take this, all right? Keep my card somewhere and please think about using it if you ever want to talk to someone. I promise you that anything you'd want to discuss is of interest. I think you're valuable, Madison. I think you and your brothers are your father's most valuable assets right now. Soon, he'll realize that."

Somewhere around the word "assets," she finally pushed past him. When she got back to the last car of the train, Allie and Zoë were both asleep. She stood as they pulled into Greenwich, and did not deny herself the small pleasure of barking their names.

They hobbled onto the platform like cruise passengers sent to shore. Zoë threw her heels down on the ground, stepped into them, and stalked away. Allie began to follow her, then faltered and looked back at Madison.

"She's totally fine to drive," she said, her head nodding furiously in response to a question no one had asked.

"I'm okay," Madison said. "I'll call for a ride."

"Bye," Allie said, already turning away to run after Zoë.

The air was clear and unobtrusive, one of those nights when it was every bit as cold as snow but somehow didn't chill you to the bone.

Madison stood still for a moment, watched her breath unfurl into the air just in front of her face. It was a few moments more before she turned to leave the station and saw Mina, sitting on a bench, watching her.

THIRTY-TWO

Mina had forgotten that they kicked you out of the station lobby at eight o'clock, when they locked everything up for the night. It had been so long since she'd waited for a train. But by then, she'd made such a fuss about coming here, doing this, that she couldn't see how she could possibly return to that house without good news.

After another frozen hour, closer to two, Madison disembarked from the train.

She walked slowly along the platform, as if unsure of where she should go next. Her shoulders were small. She had applied lipstick with the excessive care and unsteady hand of a teenager, so that her lips were dark and imprecise, as if imagined onto her face. When she raised her head, she saw Mina.

Mina waited for Madison to cross the remaining space between them. She let the silence sit, for a painful moment, before speaking.

"Alexandra Barker could have called the cops," she said. Madison still refused to speak.

"Your father's name would have come into it, and you know that's the last thing he needs right now. Someone might have seen you in the city, Madison. Someone could see who you are and do something terrible."

"I know," Madison said, finally. "I didn't think."

"Well, no."

"I'm fine, Mina," Madison said, her voice weary. "It was stupid, I thought it would be fun."

"What do we do now?" Mina said, but she already knew.

She could bring Madison home without waking Isabel, who had gone to bed. She could prod the security guys to reveal to Madison one thing they'd learned, that Zoë Barker was cruising around Connecticut without a driver's license. As a warning, of sorts. For Madison's own good.

She could put Madison to bed. She could draw a bath, nice and bubbly and fragrant, something to sweat the alcohol out of Madison's body. She could fetch a glass of ice water and a small bottle of Advil from the kitchen, maybe a little saucer with cheddar cheese and a sprig of grapes and a filigree of crackers at the rim. Something to settle the stomach.

Mina could do all of this, she knew she could. She could paper over everything else in that house tonight—whatever Lily's offenses had been, Isabel's molten fury, Bob's howling absence.

Madison shrugged.

"Trust me," Mina said. "This isn't the smart way to punish your parents. Take it from me, I have a daughter who punishes me all the time. Find a way to do it without putting the whole team at risk. Not to mention yourself."

She desperately wanted Madison to respond, to tell her where she'd been that night, what was going on in that house. She needed Madison to meet her halfway, if she was really going to help. But Madison said nothing. She just stood up and walked toward the parking lot without waiting for Mina to follow.

THIRTY-THREE

Madison woke in the middle of the night, hours after Mina had tucked her into bed. For once, Mina's desperation to be included, central, hadn't bothered Madison. It had just been what was needed. But now her mouth felt dry, wrong, it was sticking to itself like Scotch tape.

She went downstairs for more water; she needed ice from the freezer.

As soon as she reached the base of the staircase, she heard the murmur coming from her father's study, saw the wedge of light coming from the open door. He's waiting for me, she thought. He left the door open on purpose.

A cigar smoldered in a cut-glass ashtray on the coffee table, which was otherwise covered with piles of paper of varying heights, each stack pinned in place by a book, plaque, cigar box, or some other improvised paperweight drawn from the room's furnishings. Her father sat on his couch, his weight forward and his elbows on his knees, taking notes on a legal pad. The television had been brought out from its cabinet again, and these were the voices she'd heard; a black-and-white movie was flashing on the screen. She couldn't identify the film itself, but she recognized the woman's thin slash of a mouth. Katharine Hepburn.

Her father looked up, ripping off his glasses as if he needed urgently to distance himself from whatever he was doing.

"I thought I heard you."

"What are you doing?" she asked. His eyes scanned the coffee table as if he, too, had only just now come in to discover the piles.

"Nothing much," he said. "Reviewing some documents. Just looking a few things over." He began hastily to wed the piles together, creating a precarious stack of papers.

"You don't need to move them," Madison said cautiously. "I'm not going to sit on the coffee table."

"Will you come sit here, then? With me?"

She sat, curling her legs beneath her and leaning back against the sofa's arm so that she faced her father. He reached to the table beside the couch, and when he turned back to her he had a drink in his hand. She cut a quick look at the bar, but nothing was out of place, it wasn't clear even what he'd been drinking. The bottles were all in their usual tidy rows, like cadets awaiting their orders.

"What've you been doing," her father began, keeping his eyes on the screen.

"Which movie is this?"

"You break my heart, kiddo. *Adam's Rib*. It's a classic." His voice was almost wistful. Madison twisted her rings on her fingers. Could they begin where they'd left off the first time, the night of Halloween? She hadn't seen him this open, unguarded, since that night. They'd talked since then, but not in the same way. He never seemed to be talking to her, really, never cared that he was using terminology she could grasp at only vaguely, with frantic hands.

"I saw a movie the other night," she volunteered.

"Oh, did you?"

"It wasn't very good."

"Oh?"

"*Slumdog Millionaire*," she said. Her father still seemed as attentive to the movie as he was to her. Had she been wrong to come in here? It had never in all her life been difficult to tell when her father wanted to be left alone. She couldn't accept, couldn't believe, that he might be so exhausted by the events of the past few months that he might have lost the will to castigate his children. To bark her out of an off-limits room.

"I thought it was silly," her father said. "Frivolous."

Madison hadn't paid that much attention, since she'd been at the movies with Chip, but she remembered enough to frown at this.

"Frivolous?"

"Poverty isn't a learning experience," her father said. "Being broke isn't noble. I worked my ass off and paid my own way through business school at night during my first few years at Weiss."

He hadn't, that she could remember, said the actual name before, not any of the times they'd talked at night like this. Not since September.

"You didn't really grow up in poverty, though," she said. "Grandpa and Nonna Connie did, but you didn't."

Her father smiled.

"Compared to you, kiddo, yes I did."

She felt annoyance rising in her throat, the troubling arrival of tears. She could not cry in front of her father, and certainly not if she couldn't explain to him why it was happening.

"Compared to me, everyone's growing up poor," she said. "Right?"

Her father looked at her, the spell of Hepburn and Tracy finally broken.

"I was just teasing," he said. "Pay me no mind."

And then another question, the one she should have asked first, surfaced.

"When did you go see a movie?"

Her father had looked away again, stealing glances at the piles of paper as if ruing the decision to toss them all together into one unruly group.

"I went on my own," he said. "I go to the movies, sometimes."

Madison felt a brief panic, first that her father might have seen her with Chip one of these nights, then that anyone else might have seen her father.

"Here?"

"God, no. You have to ask? I go into the city."

This did not seem an appreciably better state of affairs.

"When?"

"I don't know, I go into the city sometimes. When I need an afternoon off. Listen," he said, grabbing the remote from the floor beneath the table and extinguishing the movie with one swipe of his thumb. "I know I've probably been confusing you, a little bit. Our talks. I know it can be a lot of information all at once."

Madison felt her breath catch in her chest with the weight of an actual physical obstruction, as if it had snagged on something sharp she hadn't realized she had in there.

"No," she said. "Not too much information. Almost no information, actually."

"That's what I'm saying," he said. "I owe you an explanation."

"Dad—"

"Madison, please. All I'm saying is that I know it. And there is one coming, I promise. I've been going over and over some of this, figuring it all out. Everyone else seems to think they know what happened, but I'm finally getting to the bottom of it. It's all here," he said, waving his hand over the papers as if absolving them of their sins. "And it's important that other people know this, but I have to find the best way to communicate it to them. To everyone, really."

Her father was speaking in clipped sentences, his voice lowered to almost a whisper. She couldn't help but feel that he was enlisting her as a conspirator, but while he seemed to have a quite clear sense of his own conspiracy, she still couldn't tell what, if anything, he'd told her. He seemed wholly in control of his own faculties. But then it seemed like he'd been drinking tonight, too.

She considered, for the first time since her childhood, that she might not know the contours of her father's drunkenness as well as she'd always thought she did. And maybe it was this threat, the possibility that one of the threads that tied her and no one else to her father might have frayed, that edged her closer to him on the couch, prompting him to continue.

"What do you mean, the best way?"

Her father looked down again, lifting his cigar from its ashtray He looked at her before releasing the smoke, and she closed her eyes for a moment. This smell had always, always meant her father, meant that he was telling her things she needed to know.

"The truth," he said. "The truth is important. If you can just give everyone the whole truth about that final weekend, then show them where to look, everyone will know. We did everything—everything we could. No matter what, we couldn't have withstood the people who were out to get us. But we were—"

She watched his face. He wasn't looking at her anymore. He was looking into the middle distance, toward the pool, the woods, the world outside.

"An example," he said, looking back at her wildly. "A classic trick. You want to short a stock, you spread the rumor on a Friday. Late on a Friday. Nobody can actually do anything, but then it spreads all weekend, like a virus. No, like an epidemic. And then, Monday, if you were the people who heard that rumor, what would you do? Of *course* you'd eliminate your exposure. Who wouldn't? And then, the drop begins. The bottom falls out."

"It sounds like my life," she said.

Her father looked in her direction again. "What did you say?"

She'd spoken without thinking, but now he was focused on her.

"It just sounds like rumors," she said. "At school."

He only smiled. She had wanted him to laugh at the absurdity of what she'd said. It could not possibly be the case that her father's life was like hers, that he could worry about the nattering and ill wishes of people who behaved like Wyatt Welsh or Zoë Barker. She refused to believe it.

"We were different," he said. "That's why they're out to get us. We were as good as they were, but we were different. Do you remember Max Schaefer?"

She shook her head.

"Doesn't matter. He was good, but no one special. But the point is, he called me, the other afternoon. He just wanted to say—he told me that I was the only man in any business, anywhere, he'd ever seen leave a meeting, no matter with who, no matter which client, just because my wife was on the phone. He'd never seen it anywhere. Because it *wasn't* anywhere. There was no place else like us. Do you see what I'm saying?"

She could tell how desperate he was for her to agree with him. She nodded.

"And you have to ask," he said. "When you're calling for a head—I still owned ten million shares, Madison. I never so much as considered getting rid of it, any of it. I'll never be made whole. That's what it meant to me."

She swallowed hard before speaking. "Who—what do you mean, calling for a head?"

Her father was staring down at the carpet now. He waited a long time to reply, but eventually a snowflake of cigar ash on the knee of his chinos brought him back.

"Nothing, sweetheart. It's just words."

What did that mean? It was all just words, she thought. He said that as if he hadn't always known how precarious words were, as if his entire reputation didn't rest on his propensity for silence and reticence punctuated by vivid, memorable outbursts of rage. If it's all just words, she thought, then what the fuck did it mean every time he told me a story about himself?

"You're talking about jail, aren't you."

Her father did not reply at first. He stood, crossed to the bar, and returned with a bottle of scotch and another glass, one she now knew would be for her.

"No," he said. "Listen to me, Madison. No. Over my dead body. That's what I'm saying. Over my dead fucking body."

He looked up at her and held out the glass of scotch. She wanted to ask for an ice cube, but she couldn't look away from her father's face.

"Why don't you just go out there, then," she said. "Why don't you just go out there and explain what everyone else has misunderstood?"

"It's not the right time, Madison."

She laughed, unable to help herself. "What are you waiting for?"

"Princess, you know I wouldn't lie to you, but not yet. It wouldn't be wise now."

"Okay," she said.

"How are you," he said, looking down at his drink.

"I got into trouble tonight," she said. "Or at least I assume I did. Mom didn't stay up long enough to get me in trouble."

"She outsourced it," her father said. "Efficient lady."

Was it possible he'd been in the house when everyone was here? That didn't make any sense. Shouldn't he be curious, then, about what had happened?

She moved closer to her father on the couch, and let him talk for a few minutes longer. Eventually, she curled into her favorite place under his arm, letting her head fall to his shoulder, hearing his voice moving through his chest and throat. Sometime later, she felt him carefully prying her fingers from her abandoned glass, and the movie was on, again.

She closed her eyes again, maybe slept some more, and her head was leaning against the leather and not against her father. She opened her eyes and saw him carefully stacking accordion folders, one on top of another. He placed them in the bottom drawer of his desk, carefully, as if they were porcelain rather than paper, then locked the drawer. She watched as he stood, letting his eyes range over his bookshelves, and then moved forward to take a picture of the twins, tackling each other in the pool at Shelter, and taped the key to the back of the picture frame. He replaced the photo.

The sounds from the television circled her ears, as unknown to her as other languages, and she knew she was falling back to sleep. She wanted to make a joke, ask her father why he'd chosen a picture of the boys instead of one of the many pictures of her. There was a gloaming in the room, the gray of unconsciousness already fuzzing the picture, but she knew it was real, she wasn't asleep yet.

He returned to the sofa and took her by the hand and shoulder, sliding himself back beneath her.

The next morning, she woke up in her own bed. The golden clock said it was almost 10 A.M., but no one had come in to wake her.

III

Sunday evening, evening gray. All day the storm did not quite storm. Clouds closed in, sulked, spat. We put off swimming. Took in the chairs. Finally (about seven) a rumbling high up. A wind went round the trees tossing each once and releasing arbitrary rivulets of cool air downward, this wind which came apart, the parts swaying out, descending, bumping around the yard awhile not quite on the count then a single chord ran drenched across the roof, the porch and stopped. We all breathed. Maybe that's it, maybe it's over, the weatherman is often wrong these days, we can still go swimming (roll call? glimpse of sun?) when all at once the sluices opened, broke a knot and smashed the sky to bits, which fell and keep falling even now as dark comes on and fabled night is managing its manes and the birds, I can hear from their little racket, the birds are burning up and down like holy fools somewhere inside it—far in where they keep the victim, smeared, stinking, hence the pageantry, hence the pitchy cries, *don't keep saying you don't hear it too.*

—Anne Carson, "Little Racket"

I give you fourteen years of earnings. I have one bad quarter. This is how you respond?

—Richard Fuld, former CEO, Lehman Brothers

THIRTY-FOUR

Isabel sat at the mirror in her bathroom, slowly applying her evening face. Behind her, out the window, the sky was only just now beginning to seep into something darker. The clock had jumped forward the previous weekend, and now they were all waiting in that deadened space between seasons.

All of her children were elsewhere. The twins were at a birthday party in town, that Japanese hibachi place all the little boys loved, and Madison was apparently having dinner with Zoë Barker, of all people. Isabel had never taken her daughter for someone who'd fall under the sway of Alexandra Barker's spawn, but she couldn't very well say anything about it now. Madison had come to her, in those first weeks after it all began, but Isabel hadn't been ready yet. She hadn't had a plan in place; it had been too soon for her to start setting aside energy to comfort her children. She'd left the twins to Lily and she'd avoided Madison's questions. She'd still needed all of her own resources, back in the fall. And even at Christmas, she'd done the best she could. She'd had Bob walking around in an actual Santa's hat, she'd tried to make things cozy. It had not been, all things considered, such a terrible holiday.

When Madison came back, Isabel would be ready. She'd find something to say. But for now, her daughter was going elsewhere for comfort, and she had to respect that.

Isabel knew many women would have chosen a different tack, in September, would have clutched a daughter closer rather than leaving her, largely, to wade through it all on her own. Crawled into bed with her when you were both awake and heard each other wandering the house. Lavished her with compliments. Immediately gotten out of the bathtub, on that one night, and rubbed her back, brushed her hair, told her everything was absolutely fine.

It had been so obvious, really, how little she might have offered Madison, how meager the reassurance her daughter needed to feel safe. But Isabel had balked at those moments. She'd never been that kind of mother, and it seemed insincere to try to become one now.

SHE WAS DOING HERSELF UP tonight for dinner with Mina, who had called in a frenzy about something as yet unexplained. It was always tricky to locate the source of Mina's most immediate panic, since she lived her life in a state of constant apology. Apologies for any remaining traces of the girl she'd once been, apologies for the child her daughter didn't turn out to be, for what she hadn't been able to contribute to the world she found herself living in. Mina was hardly the only wife out here who'd come from Long Island, Redondo Beach, even the Jersey shore. But Mina was the only one who seemed to think treachery awaited her if she couldn't conceal every trace of that former self.

Still, Mina had been endlessly helpful this year. Many times since Christmas, she'd stepped in when Lily hesitated. Isabel could go to dinner with her, could reassure her that they were still friends. Remind her that even if Isabel chose to confide in no one, at the very least there was no one she'd be confiding in before Mina.

Isabel had known, as soon as her phone buzzed, that her hopes for a quiet evening had been futile. The house was empty, and it might have been nice. No one would have needed even a second of her time. Lily was still, whenever possible, hiding from her, just as she had been since that night in December when Madison had staged her faux escape to the city. In a way, it was a relief. Because Isabel had

not fired Lily that afternoon, had never even spoken of it again, the
nanny had been forced to put a stop to her constant, smug expres-
sions of unspoken disapproval. Lily had never been one for these,
not before. She'd never inserted all those little barbs into daily life in
the house, the sorts of tiny power struggles Isabel had always found
so petty, so sad, when other women described them. Housekeepers
who reorganized pantry shelves and other corners of the house in
which they had no real business, just to prove to you that they knew
the lay of the land better than you did. Nannies who issued orders to
your children that directly contradicted the things you had told them
earlier, or at least the implicit understandings you relied on in your
dealings with them.

But Lily had spent the fall implying, with her every raised eyebrow or disregard for Isabel's orders, that her boss was bobbling the
fragile, breakable thing she held in her hand. That she wasn't the
woman her family needed right now.

By all means, Isabel thought. She dipped a finger into a pot of
under-eye concealer, tilting her head away from the mirror so that
the light fell on the hollow just above her left cheekbone. Find me
that woman. Find the woman this family needs, and let her set up a
war room downstairs. She can sleep in one of the guest rooms. Our
treat.

But Isabel missed the old Lily, she did. It seemed laughable in
retrospect, like the cartoon version of some old rich lady, but Isabel
had always taken some measure of private pride in the fact that Lily
seemed to like her. More than she liked Bob, yes, but even without
that qualification. They'd liked each other; they'd gotten along.

This couldn't have been the desired endgame, being a nanny. But
Lily never breathed a word of complaint, never even put a disgrun-
tled edge at the end of a question. She'd been a force, with the kids.
She made the breakfasts. She planned the weekly playdates. She'd
known the family rhythms, this alleged outsider, just as well as she
must know to blink her eye whenever something painful lodged itself

there. She'd become one more element of the life Isabel had brought into being because it was what her husband told her they should want.

It was never me, Isabel thought. It *wasn't*. And look, this year had been proof. The house didn't need her. It would exist long after she was gone, this house she'd built. And wasn't that for the best? Who knew how much longer she'd even be permitted to live here.

She did *not* think: how much longer her husband would be allowed to live in a world that did not include orange jumpsuits, barbed wire, bitter phone calls through thick glass. She was not prepared to think this way, still. Not yet. No matter how many times she was chided by the lawyers. They weren't there just yet.

THE MEETING TODAY had been an intervention, of sorts. The entire legal team had been present, had combined forces to explain to her, respectfully, that they could not wait any longer for her husband to decide to join them.

She'd been meeting them alone, thus far. Many of these men had known her since she was a teenager. They were either Buck's former lieutenants, or men who had been trained by members of Buck's generation. She'd hesitated, at first, to start making these calls herself. It seemed prudent, for a while, to follow all the same codes Bob had always insisted on. This was a matter to be dealt with entirely within the family. This family, the one they had made together. The ghost of her father had no place in this matter.

She'd been utterly willing to extend Bob this courtesy until the night when she had to drag him back across this threshold, bring him bawling back from the apartment where he'd chosen to barricade himself. The apartment, the one place he knew would pierce her. The home of all the unspokens that resided at the very bottom of their marriage, like a teeming ocean floor. The things beneath their days together, the things they'd always agreed not to scrutinize.

At that point, she'd figured, just—screw it. If he didn't want to let her in right now, if he wasn't going to explain himself yet, that was his prerogative. But she'd called up some old friends of her father's.

And it had been unexpected, the sheer pleasure she drew from these meetings. From leaning on her father's reputation, on the relationships he'd left waiting for her. She understood why Bob hated these reminders. That he always felt like he was scrabbling uphill, and that he knew down to the soles of his feet that his wife didn't know that feeling, its bite.

But you didn't fritter away resources, not when you were teetering on an edge. That was her decision, and so this process, their recovery, or whatever it would become: this process had been hers.

The first meeting in October had been a turning point. It was the marker, in her memory, between the oppressive standstill of those first few weeks and the flurry of action that had consumed her these past few months. At first, she'd just been waiting to hear the results of his choices. But soon, she'd realized that she could fill the vacuum he'd left. By the time he woke up to it, the system would be in motion.

She trusted the lawyers, the accountants, the consultants. It was their job to remain several steps ahead of her, not because they were smarter than she was but because, for them, it was only a paper crisis. They could snap the briefcase, descend the elevator, go home to fix a drink. They'd be taking their cut, of course, but that cut dictated the borders of their own interest.

One of them had pulled her aside after one contentious hour in November to declare his admiration for how she hadn't once cried, hadn't bad-mouthed her husband at all. He'd probably just been angling, curious as to how far the rich guy's trophy wife had actually fallen, but it was flattering nonetheless. From the others, there were looks sometimes. The faces so blank and impassive that the judgment was fully visible. The metallic silences, from time to time, after a specific decision of Bob's was discussed.

And what could she say to them? She couldn't very well tell them, look, he's rude and he's arrogant but he knows what he's doing. He doesn't screw anything up so badly that someone like me, like us, can't fix it. He's embarrassed, he knows that in this year I've seen him right down through to his bones. He's ashamed, and he needs a few months to shore up his pride. Trust me, when I say that I trust him— not for everything, not for the small indiscretions, but for something of this magnitude. Trust me when I tell you that, eventually, he'll barge in here as his old self.

The lawyers were very careful, always, not to pity her. Even when she'd learned in an early meeting that the Greenwich house was now in her name, transferred last year for only a dollar, her signature faked on the papers. Even then, as she watched these men scan her face for clues, she'd felt no pity from them. Impatience, yes, distaste for how little she'd understood at the time. But no pity. They'd never asked a single question about what she'd known at this time a year ago.

She knew everyone must want to. Just look what they were doing to the Madoff sons, poor bastards. The older one had restored his farmhouse out here not so long ago, just a few years. A few years ago, Isabel thought, Greenwich would have looked very different to him.

She set down her eyeliner, a tacit acknowledgment that her hands were trembling.

It was so hard to know how her father would have handled all of this. That's what she wanted from these men, really. For them to speak in her father's voice. She knew he would disagree with her about Bob, about giving him time to recover, but surely he would approve of her ultimate strategy. The focus on her children, their futures. Those were the cards she had to play, as well as the ante she'd already left on the table.

Isabel shook her head, gathered herself. Mina would be here in another fifteen minutes, and she couldn't very well be crying when the car pulled up.

Through the window she could see the darkening treetops, mounded against one another like clouds, framed by the warm yellow rectangle of the window's light. Back in September, when it all first happened, she sat at this window smoking a cigarette and watched the sun rise, many times. She stayed up late, just like she had on those mornings years and years ago, the summer she met Bob. When she was working at the club and getting home just before sunrise.

She never saw him on the nights she worked. She kept those for herself, alone. She'd take the cab home, have it let her off on York just before her corner so that she could duck into her favorite bodega, the Koreans rather than the Turkish man across the avenue. She'd buy snacks, because the girls weren't allowed to eat during shifts at the club, but she didn't choose her food like an actual hungry person. It was always scattered and indulgent, exotic and nonsensical. Copious amounts of string cheese and two cartons of sliced pineapple, or something really mismatched, like a carton of chocolate milk to wash down a plastic tub of kimchi. Even now, on those rare trips into the city when she might duck into a bodega, needing bottled water for the boys, the smell would remind her. That swirling mix of tortilla chips and cleaning fluids and sizzling peppers and onions at the sandwich station, it always reminded her of herself, those nights when the younger Isabel would emerge back out into the dawning street. Off the clock, her bare legs chicken flesh, knowing she was headed home to curl up in her own crappy apartment to eat her own bizarre food. There would always be a scrawled message from her roommate on the pad by the phone, her disapproval evident from the fact that the notes never mentioned Bob by name: *call for you (from office) at eleven, told him you're at work like you are every Thurs, ANOTHER call again at one am.* Always, Bob would have called. He was always tracking her down, that summer.

But she'd been free, she thought now. Her father never ceased reminding her that he held the strings, but she got that hostess job for herself. Bob tried to tie her down right away, but she played around with him for fun.

The man who owned that bodega always laughed at her. She began to think of choosing her food as a performance for him, something he could rely on. He'd always know that at the end of the grave-yard shift, the white girl from around the corner would stop in to buy a morning meal that would make him laugh, her fingers looped through the straps of the high heels she'd swapped for flip-flops in the cab. Her eating habits were the only things he knew about her.

Well, Isabel thought. Now, if he's got a good memory for faces, if he still runs that store and stocks the *Post*, he knows another thing about me.

But it had *all* been only a performance, back then. Hadn't it? If she hadn't made her rent, at the end of that summer, nothing would have happened. She'd been in no real danger at all.

She'd had freedom *and* safety, and she'd been too idiotic and young to appreciate how rare it was that she had both. But Bob must have known. He'd brought her in with him, hadn't he?

SHE'D TAKEN THE NIGHT SHIFT at the club, a few months after moving to the city, because she wanted to know for sure that she could pay for her own life. It was hard to say why she'd thought this was any way to prove anything to anyone, but that had been the rea-soning. Her father found it hilarious.

She was working at a gallery uptown, and it barely paid enough to cover her rent, let alone utilities. And then her friend Binnie, from Smith, mentioned her new job as the coat check girl at a club near Isabel's apartment. She claimed she'd made three hundred dollars that first night, folded bills the men would pass to her on their way out. They're looking for a new hostess, Binnie said. You won't actu-ally have to carry a tray.

Isabel knew without question that she could easily spend her weekend nights flattering the type of man who pays to ensure that he's got a beautiful woman near him from the second he steps into the club. At the coat check, as he's walked to his table, when he orders the bottle. She'd been training for that job since childhood, hadn't she?

And she hadn't been wrong; it was easy. Other than having to stand on her feet all night, needing to soak them in salt baths after her first few shifts, it was a piece of cake.

She'd been most surprised by the waitresses, how tough they were and how glamorous. It wasn't what her mother had taught her to think of as beauty, the makeup hadn't exactly been applied so that it disappeared on your skin. You could get fired if you showed up without a manicure. But their targeted competence, those girls, the way they moved through the crowd on a Saturday at 2 A.M., holding the trays high above their heads, balanced on their fingertips. She loved to watch them. She knew she never could have waitressed there. She would have been fired after one shift. She could handle the straying hands, the sour breath in her face as some summer associate asked for her number and hiccupped in her ear. But hers was a different kind of steel. She would have looked tender and exposed out there on the floor, next to those girls.

Some of the men came in three or four times a week. The junior analysts from certain banks had the place designated as their last (or sometimes first) stop when clients were in town. They came in loud and cocky at midnight and left in the raw sunlight, six or eight hundred dollars lighter, smelling of scotch and sweat and, usually, vomit. She knew many of the waitresses were hoping to snag a fiancé here, had worked their way up to this place for that very reason, but that was another difference between them and her.

On the night Bob came in, he said nothing at first. His friends were much drunker. They all kept pulling at one another's sleeves and howling. But he was the one who asked her to sit down, to join them for a glass of champagne.

"What do you want to bet they'll allow it," he said, when she reminded him she was on the clock. He had a nice smile; even at the very beginning, when she still thought all she wanted was to escape his table, she could give him that. And even now, it was still true, Isabel thought, staring at herself in the mirror, at the lines in her face that had been such a distant possibility when she was still the girl in this story. From that very first night, right up to now, she'd liked the way her husband looked. The broad cheekbones and the angular jaw, its severity even when he smiled.

"They'll allow it," he repeated. It was always this that she remembered most, when she thought about meeting her husband. He had wanted to keep her at that table. He hadn't wanted her to leave.

"What do you want to bet that if we buy the most expensive bottle you've got, they let us kidnap the hostess."

He used that word. *Kidnap.* And she saw him realize, almost as soon as he did, that he'd touched something beneath her skin, something that would react as surely as a reflex.

The club continued its eruptions all around them. She looked him right in the eye.

"Oh, you're *so* right. You're the first man in history to come in here and spend a lot of money. Do you think—I mean, maybe they'll send me home with you, right? All in a day's work. All because some junior analyst gets paid an ungodly amount of money to pretend that his gambling addiction is an asset."

But then he pushed further. He held out the bill. She could see that he regretted it too late, that first impulse: to spur her on, to agitate. That was, maybe, the one thing that had changed most about him, once they were married. He'd stopped second-guessing himself; he didn't need to anymore.

But somehow, when he held out that crisp hundred, fresh from the ATM, he'd seen that *she* was second-guessing herself. He'd seen how terrified she was to be there, in that club, however well she understood the men streaming in and out. He'd seen that she was there because she was waiting for someone besides her father to tell her what to do with herself. He'd seen that she was skittish, in a perpetual state of both confidence and unease, like a purebred horse sent out into the unblinkered world. And he'd come after her.

The end to the story, as they always told it to the kids, was that she'd thrown the bill back in his face. In retrospect, that made for a good final flourish. But in reality, it hadn't felt like triumph. It had been totally unsatisfying. Throwing a thin piece of paper is difficult, and it had just fluttered in the air between them. It was no slap to the cheek, no drink in his face.

For her, the story wasn't ever about her telling him off, embarrassing him in front of his friends. For her, the important part was that he'd held out the bill and then seen that it was a mistake, seen the part of her that shivered and retreated. That he'd seen, in that moment, that their fears might combine to form some worthy weapon, the two of them together.

ISABEL TOOK HER PERFUME and applied it just as her mother had taught her, a spritz to each side of the neck, beneath the chin, and a final one to the crook of an elbow. It took an effort that was almost physical in shape and strain, as it had all year, to keep her thoughts from wandering out to the staircase, down the dark hallway to his study. To the room he'd chosen over this one, up here.

She'd considered looking for him when she came in this afternoon, knocking on his door. But whenever she tried, he wasn't in there. And the twins had seen her knocking on Bob's door, the last time. She'd turned and they'd been at the end of the hallway, holding hands, waiting to see.

She stood up and walked into the closet. It was just dinner in town, a restaurant they'd been to a thousand times, it hardly mattered what she wore. She knelt down, tucking her feet beneath her, and looked at all of the clothes. She reached up and let her fingers trail across the fabrics, the delicate swishing sounds bathing her ears. This was the corner where she kept skirts and suits—the materials thicker, sturdier, than, say, the evening gowns, with their supple fabrics touching one another like skin on skin.

It was funny, she thought: her parents had driven the same cars around Westport for decades at a time, the leak in Georgetown that warped the floorboard near the kitchen door had been left untouched until the day her mother died in that house. But her mother had taught Isabel never to skimp on her wardrobe. Her mother had always called her clothing "camouflage." It was one of those things Isabel hadn't registered as a quirk, not until she was in high school and heard other girls talking about their mothers.

She'd thought about that a few years later, after they moved to D.C. They sold the house in Westport while she was at Smith, not even mentioning it on the phone until it was in escrow. A few weeks after the move, her father took her along to New Haven for the weekend of his fortieth class reunion. Dinner at Mory's, the genteel seediness of the coffee stains on lace tablecloths and the wood-paneled rooms and the silver chalice full of champagne and Guinness that was passed around as they each took a gulp, while the rest of the party sang the song and banged their fists on the thick, unsteady wood table. When it was her turn, when her father's friends had already begun pawing her hand between courses, she thought of her mother, who hadn't been invited that weekend.

Some daughters would have run to the bathroom, shuddered at the powdery softness of the men's hands. This had not been an option for her, not a Berkeley daughter. She remained at the table, laughed when one of the men gave the silver cup a jaunty shove as she drank from it.

Her mother had always talked as if strength was a matter only of how you acted in front of other people, as if camouflage was all you needed. As if it was only self-doubt or hesitation that could leave you shaken.

But look at me, Isabel thought, her arms up above her, fingertips trailing the hems of her dresses. I never had a single doubt as to whether I belonged anywhere. That was supposed to be Bob; he was the one who had to bluff, when we first met.

She took one suit between her fingers, touched the nubbly wool to her cheek. I am an orphan, she thought. I have no sisters, I have no mother anymore. My father is gone. If this is the apocalypse, who cares how much canned food we've got. I have no tribe. Any freedom that comes from this, it's come too late. I have no other options now, and there's no fucking freedom in that.

She looked up at the suits above her, the business attire for the woman who did not have a job. She felt certain her work at MoMA required more intellectual energy than most women gave to their full-time jobs, but if she didn't need it, then it wasn't a job. There was a simple rubric, there.

She was expected to bring Bob with her to the next meeting with the lawyers, on Monday morning. Because it was a done deal: she was putting both houses on the market. The new apartment, too. She'd happily get rid of the old apartment, but that one was still in his name. He hadn't transferred it over to her name, whenever it was, exactly, that he'd done the others. He kept it, maybe for himself.

Maybe his little seclusion back in the fall, his month of anguished silence, was just a performance, too. Maybe it wasn't this house in her name that had been his lifeboat; maybe he'd wanted his own private lifeboat as well.

So this was what she had ahead of her right now: Mina, dinner, Monday's meeting, a plan for telling Bob. And then the party at Suzanne's next weekend. He'd already agreed to that, agreed to put on a tuxedo and leave the house to appear, with her, in public.

She knew what they wanted to hear, the lawyers and the accountants and the consultants. She knew what they wanted to know: Why didn't she just ask him? Why was she allowing him to leave her like this, alone and waiting?

She reached up to drag herself from her feet, and as she pulled at one of the hangers for support, she knew exactly what would happen. She knew that she'd caught a piece of dress by accident. Between her fingers. She knew it would rip with a satisfying sound, fabric rent from itself. But she was in motion already. She could only watch, as if from another body wholly unassociated with the errant hand. She watched her fist close around the dress, rip it cleanly as she brought herself up off the ground.

Good, she thought. Something, at least, in this room. Something would be damaged when she left.

Downstairs, the doorbell rang.

THIRTY-FIVE

When you were granted entrance to Brad and Alexandra Barker's home, after you'd been questioned and verified at the guard gate, you drove for a while before you could even see the house. Mina had been here only a handful of times—the Barkers were, surprisingly, not much for entertaining on a grand scale, and they'd only once or twice hosted the sorts of parties you'd expect from them.

This house always sent unkind thoughts scrabbling at the corners of Mina's mind. It wasn't jealousy, exactly. But ten years ago, when Alexandra bought this house just north of the Merritt and set about renovating it, she seemed determined to show them all how pathetically they'd failed at their own objectives. The house was a parody of their lives, and somehow this reflected poorly on them rather than her.

And of course you drove by it all on your way in, it had been designed this way. A low hedge bordered the driveway on both sides, low enough not to obstruct your view of anything. The tennis court, then the putting greens. Rising like a bubble in the distance, across a vast lawn, the glinting dome that enclosed the swimming pool. Which you could access through an underground passageway, by the way, so when it rained Alexandra could swim beneath the raindrop-spattered glass without even having to dart through the rain itself to get there.

What Mina hated about this house was that it was a house her own mother would absolutely love. And out of sheer joy, not even lurid curiosity.

Her mother had never seen one single point of pause with anything about the life Tom had established for them out here. It had taken Mina longer to acclimate; that whole first year in the house, pregnant with Jaime and waiting for her life to begin, there were so many times she'd held her breath so that she wouldn't cry. Like holding in a sneeze. By the time you notice yourself changing, Mina thought, you're already fully ensconced in your final position.

She coasted to a stop at the front entrance.

Alexandra's e-mail had referred to a vague "afternoon with the girls, just a handful of us." It had been a stressful few months, the e-mail also said. We thought it might be nice, just to have a relaxing afternoon in private.

It was that final qualification that had Mina on edge. This woman was far from one of her closest friends; they were cordial acquaintances at best. And it would be an unforced error, after that trip to Saks back in October, for Alexandra to corner Mina in hopes of getting some good gossip on Isabel. She'd tried that already, and she'd failed. She'd know better than to overextend.

"Mina, you're here! Fantastic." Alexandra answered the door herself, which was the first indication that Mina had perhaps been on the right track when she'd selected a bottle of Perrier Jouet to bring along, something nice rather than opulent. She had taken the code words—"relaxed," "low key," "in private"—as clues. Mina almost wanted to offer, as her RSVP card, that she'd snagged this particular bottle on sale at the Trader Joe's in Stamford.

"Always a treat to come over," she said instead, as if they did this all the time. She brandished the bottle of champagne before her, holding it high in the air between them.

Alexandra grabbed it and made a great show of examining the label, as if the flowers appliquéd all over the goddamn bottle weren't decent clues.

"Oh," she said. "Nice. Very nice." She winked with her entire face before spinning and beckoning Mina back into the house.

They walked through the main hall before reaching a back parlor that looked out across the grounds. Mina would have assumed it was Alexandra's office except there were no desks, no bookshelves, just artful groupings of stiff chairs and small cherrywood tables and ottomans. There must have been ten women in the room already.

"You know everyone," Alexandra said, not asking a question, and she handed the bottle absently to a young woman in a black shift and a severe ponytail who had at some point started following them.

"Could you take care of this, Celine?" The woman—girl, really—nodded and withdrew. Another young woman, this one with darker skin and wearing another black dress that was something decidedly closer to a uniform, stood at a wet bar in one corner of the room.

"Go get a drink!" Alexandra urged. "And just grab a spot anywhere. We're about ready to start."

Ready to start what? Ready to commence their afternoon of insincere small talk? Mina saw Suzanne Welsh sitting in one chair cluster with a champagne flute in her hand. There were no women from Weiss.

"You have anything other than champagne?" she asked the maid who'd been posted to the bar. She knew they weren't supposed to use that word to one another, but it always gave her perverse pleasure to refer to them as maids, at least inside her own head. It was honest, wasn't it? Tom didn't like it, though, either.

"Clear liquids only," the girl replied, her voice light and somehow sounding like a compliment. "I can offer you champagne, white wine, or perhaps a vodka."

Clear, of course. What on earth must this girl think of them, of this party, of this room? Mina felt her usual twinge of shame, her longing to tell the staff where she'd grown up, that she was really on their side. But you aren't, she told herself, you've never in your life met a maid who'd consider you now to have a single thing in common with her. She was always having to reteach herself this lesson.

"Can I get you anything?" the girl prompted.

Mina allowed herself to sail away, just for a moment, on the idea that she might start gulping down a straight vodka so early, with so much of this left to wade through.

"White wine," she said. "Thank you so much."

A little boy wandered in suddenly, another just behind him, a basketball in his hand. This was Alexandra's youngest, she realized—she'd forgotten they had a son. It wasn't clear what he wanted. Maybe just to be around the women; Mina remembered well the allure of adults of the opposite sex, the way their talk seemed constantly to flash signals somewhere above your head. The elusive promise that if only you could unlock what the fathers were talking about, then you might have a fighting chance with the boys your own age.

"Sweetheart," Alexandra said to him, drawing him to her body with one extended arm, not looking at him. She whispered into his ear. As she spoke, the skin just beyond the peaks of her eyebrows rippled, because this was a face whose anger was necessarily displaced and disjointed, playing over its features with the confusing rhythms of a submerged object seen from above water.

And then the child was gone, immediately, just as if she'd slapped him across his face. He and his friend simply vanished. Mina wondered—not for the first time and not for the last—how much it mattered to Tom, still, that they had never had a boy.

Suzanne Welsh was perched on the quilted lavender arm of her love seat. She smiled at Mina, then tapped one long French-manicured nail lightly against her glass.

"Ladies," she said, "I know we're all waiting for the main event, but I would just love to take a moment to thank Alexandra"—she paused indulgently for the chorus of assents—"for knowing that this would be something we'd all need so much right now!"

Everyone drank.

Moments later, Celine returned to the room in all her blond efficiency. Several other cocktail-dress-sheathed women followed in her wake, wheeling two stainless steel clothing racks. Everyone quieted; this was clearly the main attraction. Mina saw now that a space had been cleared at one end of the room, leaving only two fainting couches set at angles, as if facing the group of women for an interview.

Bags were unzipped with fanfare; silks and leathers and furs were draped across the couches. One woman seemed to be in charge of shoes, drawing out endless orange and purple boxes and removing a single python sandal, a single jewel-toned stiletto. She placed each shoe atop its own box and lined them up in rows.

"Oh, and I want to remind everyone that fifteen percent is going to the Equus Foundation!" Alexandra called from her place on the floor. She was curled up beside one of the tea tables, drinking what appeared to be a mimosa. Only fair, Mina thought, for the hostess to get a colored drink. "As if you needed any extra push!"

"She said it's a friend of her sister's who's spent several years putting together her own collection," Suzanne told Mina. "All the personal shoppers at Bergdorf's hate her. These past few months she's had a *boom* in her business. I mean, it's perfect. I've gone into Saks a few times, and last week Bill and I did some shopping in the city, but it feels uncomfortable. This is such a perfect solution. Leave it to Alexandra."

Everyone else began to gravitate to the women and their wares, asking questions, inquiring after specific pieces Alexandra had gushed about in advance, but Mina remained where she was.

"I can't decide," Alexandra said from her spot on the floor, and it was the first time Mina realized that she hadn't stood and followed the others. "Maybe this wasn't a good idea."

Mina nodded, keeping her expression noncommittal, wondering if it was possible she and Alexandra might actually agree on this.

"I just mean, I know it looks bad if we show up at these places in person," she said. "I understand no one wants to see me ducking into Hermès."

As if anyone would recognize you, Mina thought, holding it deliciously in her chest as she nodded, her brow sympathetic.

"But I just think if they get wind of this," Alexandra said, "it might be even worse. And I'm sure it's only a matter of time before someone writes up a snarky trend piece in the *Times.*"

Someone on the other side of the room squealed over a pair of Louboutins. Mina could see the red soles.

"It's just so silly, really, at bottom, isn't it?" Alexandra said. She lifted her palm to the ceiling, waving it in a circle, as if to include the entire room, the entire house, in what she would say next. "I know this is a lot. No one is more grateful for it than I am! I certainly don't come from this, I know how lucky we are. But Brad works his little butt off for everything we have. It's not like it's fallen into our laps."

Mina tried not to choke at Alexandra's description of her own background. As if aware of this danger, Suzanne floated back over with another woman, her eyes moving with unease between Alexandra and Mina.

"That's it," the other woman said. She held a pair of pleated silk pants the color of gold in her hands; she kept turning them as if to catch the light, then tilting her head in mock consideration. Mina tried to remember the husband's name. He was a senior vice president at Lazard, a mediocrity, someone who had been there for years without much to show for it. The guys from Lazard always looked so miserable. The place was stuck in the Stone Age, or more specifically in Paris circa 1976. Same difference.

"People talk about—well, about us, as if we just won it at the craps table in Vegas," Lazard Wife continued. "And I think we all know how far that is from the truth."

"Yes!" Alexandra's head bobbed. Her neck was strangely thick, Mina noticed, much thicker than you'd expect from the fine blond hair and the delicate fingers. "I just . . . we built this house as a place to spend time with our children, our friends, our grandchildren. We built it to have a place for future memories to happen. I don't see what's so worthy of attack, honestly."

Alexandra trailed off, and Suzanne, wearing a pair of sunglasses and clasping a jeweled cuff around her wrist like a vise, looked up in alarm. Oh, Mina thought. We've let too much time go by. We're supposed to speak up to agree.

"Of course not!" Suzanne said, complying. "And it just seems unfair and, frankly, I don't know. Shortsighted, I guess. The fact that one man is reckless, not good at his job . . . to act like everyone else, just by virtue of living in the same town, is just as bad as he is. I just don't get that at all."

Her eyes darted to Mina every few seconds, and then the final bit of understanding snapped into place. Mina felt it cleanly, like that last moment when you're baking and you slide the spatula beneath the cake and it comes away from the pan as its whole, uncrumbled self. She wasn't here because they wanted to know what was going on with Isabel. It wasn't just another installment of the dress at Saks, the concerned glances in Whole Foods. They no longer cared if she let them in, and they hadn't learned anything. No woman in the room had reconsidered shit about her own life.

They just wanted Mina to know this: if she didn't make up her mind the right way, they were going to make sure that she was the next one left out. The grace period had ended. They were coming out of their foxholes.

"Oh, I agree," Alexandra said, gratified. "I think Bob D'Amico is a fool. But my husband is not Bob D'Amico."

Mina felt a smothered admiration for the way Alexandra said this without even glancing in her direction, without softening her tone or wincing in apology.

"You know it won't stop with him," Lazard Wife said, holding her wineglass up in the air by its stem. "Steven says that John Briggs is hanging on by a thread. Not even a thread. He says it's a matter of time before, you know." She slashed her non-wine hand through the air just in front of her own throat.

"God, I can't imagine," Alexandra said, and Mina saw that this was why the woman had brought it up, to give Alexandra an unobtrusive chance to insist on this. Even though all they were fucking doing, any one of them in this room, was imagining it quite clearly. They'd all jockeyed, hoping to sit near Alexandra's place on the floor, so that when she leaned back she'd have to prop her elbow against their knees. Just so they could reassure her, yes, yes. You can't imagine. We can't imagine.

"I'm sure it will be fine," Alexandra said. "Everyone's been saying that about John's fund, and about Rhombus Equity, too, but it's all just rumors. I think we've seen the worst of it."

"Well, and the problem is that so often people don't know anything about it," Lazard Wife said. "But it won't stop them from adding their commentary. I mean, whatever happened at Weiss—and of course we still don't know exactly what that was—but it's hardly the same as the Madoff situation. And you know they just talk about it, like, Greenwich. In the same breath, as if any of these are the same things."

"I think I should take both pieces," Suzanne said to one of the young women; she had drifted back over to that side of the room. They were looking down at a piece of black velvet, at the diamond and ruby brooches strewn across its expanse. "They're just so different, in their ways. Whichever one I leave behind, that will be the one I have a sudden need for, right? Isn't that always the way."

"Buy them all!" Alexandra catcalled, before turning back to Mina. She'd edged along the floor to be closer to her.

"Just look at Kiki and Jim," Lazard Wife continued. "I mean, dear God, what do I have in common with those two! I always wondered what she thought about his little, well—his little foibles. That seaplane to commute from Bridgehampton, we know how it looks now, but how good did it look even then? But she would never really do her part, would she? They were so isolated, even though they were just in Manhattan. They certainly never entertained at the Hamptons house."

She seemed to have directed this last part at Mina, who took a sip from her unfortunate, non-vodka drink.

"I wouldn't really know even if she had," she said cautiously. "Goldman and Weiss were never much for cross-pollination."

"Oh God," Suzanne chimed in. "Of course. I forgot that when you're still at one of the banks you have to put up with all their little feuds. God, I bet you're wishing right about now that Tom had thrown in with a fund a little bit sooner."

Mina smiled. Suzanne turned back to Alexandra.

"And speaking of, has anyone seen either of the Madoff boys? You know both houses out here were attached to one of the first lawsuits. By the Fairfield County pension fund, if you can even imagine how that must feel. I know it's not the same thing, but when you hear stories like that, you can't help but wonder. Isabel must be terrified."

Again, Alexandra let the moment go by, gracefully, like a ballerina bending at the waist to dip alongside the arc of her extended leg, to brush the floor with her fingertips.

"I think we can all agree that Isabel must be suffering," she said, her tone vaguely admonitory.

"Oh, yes," Suzanne trilled, sipping from her freshly topped-off champagne flute. She sat next to Mina and put one hand to her arm, as if eager to remind her that she, herself, had said nothing against Isabel. "She's such a smart woman. If only he'd listened to her."

"And it's only going to get worse," Alexandra continued. "I mean, I don't want to go into detail, but once they start really digging into what actually happened in that building . . ."

The other women leaned in.

"This, too, shall pass," Alexandra said, dramatically abandoning her earlier sentence. "But I have to tell you, I'd be shocked if he doesn't have to leave town. That is, if he's even got that option. But

I shouldn't even speculate, that's bad luck. Well, Mina. You must know what I'm saying. I don't doubt Goldman has access to all the same information Brad does."

"Oh," Mina said, cautioning herself even as she began to feel her pulse in her temples, her jaw. "I agree. I'm sure they've all got the same information. I'm sure all the men who hated Bob for so many years because he was so much better than they were at making money—I'm sure they're all lining up to call him a criminal. I don't doubt that at all."

Alexandra said nothing, revealed nothing. She simply stared at Mina, and smiled.

"Well," she said with an air of finality, unfolding her limbs and standing finally to walk over to the dresses, the jackets, the shoes. "In any case, I do feel bad for her. Really, I do. But she might have to get used to the fact that this isn't over anytime soon."

As small talk slowly caught up to them again, Mina knew that she would have to buy a pair of pumps she'd never wear because of their association with this day, this room. She couldn't be the only woman to leave without buying something. What choice did she have? She wasn't ready, yet, to storm out of Alexandra Barker's house, and she'd already said far too much. She was not ready to lash herself to Isabel's sinking ship, not without some sort of guarantee, from Isabel. Some honesty to tie them to each other.

SHE CALLED AHEAD as she drove. Lily came to the door and didn't bother to conceal her contempt, her resentment at Mina's assumption that it would be permissible to show up with so little warning. Isabel hovered, a white shadow at the top of the darkened staircase.

"You sounded pretty panicked on the phone," she said. Lily withdrew.

"I was at Alexandra Barker's house. She hired some women to

bring clothes to the house. So they could all keep shopping, but in private. So no one will see them buy anything expensive in public."

Isabel laughed once, and the sound was terrible. Mina could hear it coming up from deep within her, could hear it scrape and tear its way out of her body.

"Very resourceful," Isabel said.

"No, it's not funny. You should have heard them. They were talking about Bob, Isabel, totally out in the open. About whether anyone from Weiss will do jail time. They kept mentioning Bernie Madoff and how it wasn't *really* the same thing."

She tried not to spit the words, knowing that she needed to frighten Isabel only a bit, not too much.

"Why are you telling me this?"

"Because we're going out, right now. What I said on the phone. We're going to go have dinner somewhere where a lot of people will see you. You're going to sit at a table with me and smile and laugh and stop at people's tables to say hello on our way out of the restaurant."

"Mina," Isabel said, "you must have me confused with Suzanne Welsh. I don't care what those women say about me. I don't—"

"No, I don't think that's true," Mina said. "I think you care very much. And we're not in the staging area anymore, Isabel. They're going to move on either way, whether we give them their cue or not."

Isabel tilted her head, as if Mina's voice were reaching her from a distance.

"We?" she said. Mina ignored it, the pain of Isabel's tone. This was no time for hurt feelings, for polite deferral to Isabel's imperiousness.

"You have to go to Suzanne's party next week, for the museum. I know you don't want to, but you still have to."

"Mina, please. We've already planned on it."

"Good, then. Good. You know as well as I do—you know better than I do, Isabel. The boys have another *ten years*, Jesus, ten, before they'll go away to school. And Madison still has to live here. It's been more than three months since Christmas."

Isabel recoiled at the mention of Christmas; you could almost see the skin at her temples begin to vibrate.

"And we said, at the time, we said that her little rebellion could have been so much worse. Didn't we?" Mina continued. "If someone had seen her, spoken to her? It's sheer luck that it didn't happen then and that it hasn't happened since, Isabel. You have to start playing along, even if he still won't. You have to go out, and you have to protect them."

Isabel didn't say anything for so long that Mina thought this might be it, that she might finally have spent everything she had in the bank here.

"We're getting wine with dinner," Isabel said finally, and Mina felt herself deflate with success.

"Yes," she said. "And it's my treat. I'll call Tom to drive us home if we have to. Or we'll get a car. Have it meet us around the corner from the restaurant."

IT WAS LATE, the end of their main course, before Isabel said anything that pierced the veneer of mild conversation about their daughters. They made another brief mention of Suzanne's benefit the following week, but this was only natural, since the museum was near the restaurant. They laughed a lot, and Isabel sat relaxed in her chair. The dining room at L'Escale was full of women they both knew, but no one spoke to them except the maître d'. He brought over a complimentary bottle to express his great chagrin at having so offended them in the past that they'd withheld their presence from him all winter, then seemed belatedly to realize his error in calling attention to that fact, and quickly retreated. Isabel didn't flinch.

"It's not even the house itself that bothers me," Isabel said, unprompted, after their plates had been cleared. She did not lean in, or give any bodily clues that she had lowered her voice to a loud whisper.

"I mean, I have no respect for the house, but I don't care enough to spend time judging someone else's criteria for happiness. It's the reluctance to commit to it once you have it. It's just what you said about today—insisting that it's not done to build herself up. When you build a dome around your swimming pool, how can you possibly say you aren't showing off?"

"Sure," Mina said.

"But I don't know," Isabel said. "I know in her mind I'm below her on the ladder, Brad's hedge fund trumps Bob being a lifer at an investment bank. I know she's the ringleader of the women who think that way. I always knew. So I never avoided any small opportunity to twist the blade, you know? I always asked after his first wife, whenever I saw him, if she was standing there. I'd always make sure to reintroduce her to Bob every time they met, like I was worried he'd forget which wife it was. You know, *you remember Brad's wife Alexandra, little Carter's stepmother.* It seemed like a small way to keep myself entertained. It didn't seem so terrible, at the time."

Mina was feeling much calmer now, a whole dinner away from those women. She saw now that she'd done the right thing. She'd told Isabel what she needed to hear, and Alexandra's little party had just been the final flourish she needed to drive the point home. But things weren't quite as dire as they'd seemed. They never were.

Well, she supposed, sometimes they were. She thought of poor Bob, of how slow he'd been to act. She felt real sympathy for him, for the first time in months. Of course he'd assumed the whole thing wouldn't actually collapse; when in their adult lives had that ever happened? He was only playing the odds. He'd done the best he could, in some ways.

"Isabel," Mina said, "I don't think this will last. People are just afraid right now. It wasn't just you and Bob. You should have heard the way they were talking about poor John Briggs. As if his fund folding will give them any sort of insurance that their own lives won't change. People will move on, once they feel safe. They won't care what's happening to you."

She saw, for one brief moment, that this was not quite what Isabel wanted, either: to pass into irrelevance. She actually cared, still. But then Isabel composed herself, returned her face to still reflection, like the glassy surface of an unoccupied lake.

"Maybe," she said. "I once worked with a girl, though—this was in Manhattan, around the time I met Bob—and she dated this reporter who'd been with a paper in San Francisco in the early eighties. He was a little bit older than us. And he made his name, really, with this series of pieces he was writing early on, at the very beginning of the whole thing, in 1981, I think."

"The beginning of what?" Mina said, but then she knew. "Oh. AIDS?"

"Right, exactly. He was there for the whole beginning, and it was so mismanaged I guess those first few years, it took them so long to do anything about it, and everyone who was a spectator, all the journalists who cared to cover it, they could see how bad it would get."

"Denise had a friend," Mina said. "From high school. He moved out there after we graduated, and then he was dead, and I remember, just. You repeat the story endlessly, to everyone you meet. A twenty-four-year-old just died of this rare form of cancer. You keep saying it out loud as if you'll learn something new, get smarter about it."

"Yes," Isabel said softly. "That's exactly what you do." She picked up her wineglass and held it for a moment without drinking.

"I'm sorry," Mina said. "I interrupted you."

"No, it was just—this man, he had this story about all the infighting. He said there was an editor of a small local paper who'd spoken out against the gay community, I forget the whole story, insulted some of the local gay leaders, and thirty-six of them signed a letter to the publisher calling for him to be fired. The editor, I mean. And he printed up that list, the people who'd signed the letter, and kept it above his desk. And every time another one of them got sick and died, he'd take a red pen and draw a line through that name. This was even years and years later."

Mina said nothing at first.

"What made you think of that," she tried then, careful not to betray her surprise, certainly not any dismay.

"I'm not saying my problems are—"

"Of course not," Mina said. Don't say more, she thought. Please don't compare this to that.

She felt the same cramping fear she'd felt that night in December, waiting to find Madison. That Isabel wasn't reacting as Mina had hoped she might; that all the things she'd always assumed existed so far beneath the surface, in her friend, might not be there.

She didn't want to watch Isabel retreat further from reality, continue to lick her own wounds. There was a part of her, she knew, that wanted to watch her friend strike back, make him suffer for his mistakes. If you couldn't do this now, when your husband had humiliated you like this, then when? When would it ever happen?

"I'm just saying, that's what we are, at bottom," Isabel continued. "People, I mean 'we' as in humans. That's how we think. And I guarantee you, our names are on that list now."

Mina wanted to ask her to clarify "our." She wanted to ask whether that was so wrong, for someone's name—Bob's, at the very least—to be on such a list. Someone's name, after all, needed to be there, when history returned to this time, found that list. But she knew that these questions were too much, even for this moment, porous as it was.

THIRTY-SIX

When Chip came to the door he looked, improbably, as if Madison had just woken him from a deep and isolating nap. He was wearing the shirt she'd come to think of as his trademark ever since the weather had turned from crisp to cold: a blue-and-green-plaid button-down, its sleeves cuffed neatly just below his elbows. She tried to control her gaze, to keep it from wandering to those elbows, to the soft parts of his inner arms where his veins pulsed beneath his skin. She also tried not to be insulted that he wore the shirt with a pair of Harvard sweatpants, their hems frayed, the fabric pilling.

His skin still held a trace of its ski tan from when he'd flown to Aspen in January, that weathered brown skin across his nose and cheeks; was that possible, even, more than two months later? He was leaving for Florida on Sunday, she knew.

"You made it. Cool," he said. She shifted her weight from one foot to the other, feeling the cold beginning to eat through her mother's boots. "Oh, right, yeah. Come on in. No one's home."

"Perfect," she said, but he'd already turned away from her. She'd known already that the house would be empty; of course this was why she was here, on the first full day of their spring break. She hadn't heard from him in so long that she'd already begun to think of him in the past tense until he'd started texting her this week. There'd been the attention over winter break, the late-night phone calls, a text he sent her at seventeen minutes past midnight on New Year's

Eve. February, and the necessity of Valentine's Day, the way it sucked her attention away from anything else for weeks—early February was when he'd gone completely quiet.

And then, of course, more than a month later—a month during which she'd been so careful not to say his name in front of Zoë or Allie—his name popped up one night on the screen of her Black-Berry.

"D'Amico," he said. "Where you been?"

As if nothing had happened. As if his life swirled past so quickly that he couldn't be expected to observe the reactions of the people who'd been caught up in its wake. Valentine's Day was never mentioned, like something they'd have had to choose to acknowledge together, as a team, if it were to exist. And now here she was, at his house, agreeing not to mention it.

She followed him inside.

The foyer opened directly onto an enormous, open living room, every surface jammed with photographs. Madison longed for a pocket of time to explore them, to look at the younger Chip decked out in the studied casual uniform of coordinated denim that had been so popular for family photographs in the midnineties.

"Do you want something to eat?" Chip tossed back over his shoulder. He led her down a hallway that ended in a kitchen with paneled hardwood floors, yellow curtains, a dripping faucet.

"Or, we can probably sneak two beers from my dad's fridge in the garage."

"Oh," she said. "Yeah."

"Because we've got a few hours at least before they come home."

"Whatever you want." She wanted to snatch the words back immediately, because hearing them out loud made her see how true they were.

"I was thinking we could watch a movie," he said. "Have a beer. My dad has all the Oscar screeners."

"That's so cool," she said. Could this possibly be the same boy who had followed her into a dark hallway on Halloween? Were they the same two people who had bantered back and forth, successfully, she was pretty sure, so many times?

She waited in the kitchen until he came back with the two beers and opened them on his kitchen counter. They ended up eventually in a second, more casual den, a room that had clearly been colonized, over the years, by the Abbott men. There were half-eaten bags of Doritos left at intervals throughout the room. Three different game systems and their accompanying power cords lay vanquished on the bottom level of a large, multitiered piece of furniture that held, among other things, a flat-screen television. Another wall was taken up by another built-in bookshelf, one entire section of which held DVDs.

"My dad's a big movie guy," Chip offered, as he walked over and began rifling through loose cases in search of something. "My mom says in another few years no one's going to watch DVDs, and we won't even be able to give these away."

"You never know," Madison said. "The things they're always telling you will disappear next are never the ones that actually do."

Chip didn't look up.

"We've got this one," he said, shaking one DVD in her general direction. "It's supposed to be pretty depressing."

"Way to sell it, Abbott," she said, lifting her beer bottle to her lips. "Who could resist that pitch?"

And finally, he looked up and smiled at her. His eyes moved over her body as if he'd just noticed that she was in the room.

"This one it is," he said. He crossed to the television and she curled up at one end of the couch. There was a nubbly chenille blanket balled there and she took it, spread it out over her knees, and burrowed deeper into the side of the sofa. She should have let him sit first, she realized then. He might have chosen the middle. He might have wanted to force their bodies closer together.

The movie began, dominated throughout by a steady ebb and flow of mournful piano music. As far as she could tell, the movie's main thesis seemed to be that marriage would slowly kill you. That it would sap your physical capacity for any joy, metaphysical or otherwise. There was one fairly tame, if awkwardly violent, sex scene. She began to wonder why neither one of them had realized this might be an uncomfortable thing for them to watch together, side by side, in silence. Her beer bottle was sweating into her palm.

When they'd seen movies together at the theater, Chip had whispered almost continuously, tickling her during quiet scenes, putting his finger to his lips and admonishing her loudly when other moviegoers urged them to be quiet. But that had been a while ago, now. Months.

About thirty minutes in, he stood up and left the room, returning with two more beers after a suspiciously long absence. He sat down on the couch, right next to her, and opened the bottles on the scuffed edge of the wooden coffee table. He passed one bottle to her without taking his eyes off the screen. Then he leaned back and stretched his right arm out across the back of the sofa.

"I didn't know you could open beer like that," she said.

He took a swig from his beer and carefully set the bottle down on the floor before turning back to her.

"I can do it with my teeth, too," he said. "But it's really bad for them. Your teeth."

She reached out with one hand to trace his bottom lip, letting her fingertip hover near his two front teeth, and waited.

He turned off the movie, tossing the remote onto an armchair.

"Come here," he said, lying back and pulling her toward him so that her chin rested on his chest. He took her beer from her hand and placed it on the floor, beside his. Then he put both hands to her waist, just above her hips, and hoisted her up, so that their noses were touching. It took a moment of fumbling, but she dug her knees into the couch and pinned him beneath her. He reached up, letting his hands sift through her hair, fitting her jaw snugly into his palm, and pulled her down to him.

It took, she was pretty sure, a long time for him to do anything more than that. But once he had decided to, suddenly, it was all happening quickly. She felt his fingers scuttling at her hip bones and then her shirt was off, his fingertips were nicking at the clasp of her bra, he'd picked her up again by the waist and flipped her onto her back and he had her jeans down and off, over her ankles. And then she was aware that she could feel his erection through his sweats, that it was pushing between her legs in rhythmic thrusts. Eventually, a few minutes after that had already started to seem silly to her, he stopped and twisted his body so that he was lying next to her, turned onto his side, which pushed her into a perilous position on the very edge of the couch. He put both hands on her shoulders and pressed down on them; she'd liked it better when his hands were in her hair or on her face, but this was fine. But then the pressure continued, strong enough so that she actually had to square her shoulder muscles to keep from buckling under the weight of his hands, and she realized what was happening. Just to test it, she stopped resisting. And he was pushing her down, quite clearly, toward his groin.

"Oh," she said, "I don't, I don't think—"

He stopped kissing her and torqued his neck at an awkward angle so that they could see each other's faces.

"Oh, I just thought," he said. "Or, I've got a condom, too."

She froze, faithfully certain that if she refused to move any part of her face or body, then time, too, might not move forward, might give her a chance to find the combination of words to dissolve this situation.

"I'm just not," she tried, willing him to meet her somewhere in the now-clouded middle. He was still moving every few seconds, pushing against her and then retreating. But he didn't say anything. He let his neck droop, a little, so that his face fell into her hair, spilled out across the cushion. Sweat had gathered at the back of her neck. And then he turned his head toward her and kissed her hair, kissed her on the temple, beneath all her hair. She closed her eyes.

"I can't," she said.

"I would do stuff to you," he said. "I would do stuff, too."

"Oh," she said, struggling to conceal her breathless panic. "I can't."

His voice had been soft, thick with the preceding fifteen minutes of silence and clotted with the fact of their kissing, the inhaling through his nose and the quickened breath and the tamped-down excitement. But now it turned, somehow. He sighed, and not in the way he'd sighed into her hair only moments earlier.

"Okay," he said. "Well, do you want to totally stop?"

Yes, she thought, *yes, isn't that obvious*, but then she realized she did not want to stop, she just wanted to hold still, to remain where they were. Or to put her bra back on and maybe at least take off his shirt so that she wasn't basically naked while he was fully clothed. And then stay where they were. She wanted to just kiss him for another hour or two or however many hours they still had. Couldn't they agree, decide on this together? Just make out? Kissing him was like being caught in free fall in amber; nothing changed, no surface ever interrupted your delicious flight. It was the absolute freedom of no other choice.

Chip bent to kiss her again, and for a moment it seemed like exactly what she wanted to happen would happen. He took her hand in his, and pulled it down toward his pants, which was fine. And a moment later, she felt warm skin that she knew, without having to look, wasn't the skin of his stomach, and she understood what was happening. That this was a bargain she'd made; that this was, technically, as close to winning as she would get this afternoon.

After another few seconds, he stopped kissing her. He reached up above them to the accent table that ran behind the length of the couch, and produced a bottle of lotion—from where? He took her hand without asking and squeezed some lotion into her palm. It smelled overwhelmingly of gardenias, which seemed absurd, but you didn't need boys' and boys' worth of experience to know that you weren't allowed to laugh, not at this particular moment.

He rolled away from her and turned his head into the back of the couch, his hand cupping her shoulder, squeezing it periodically.

Before it was over he said, hoarse, "There are Kleenex over on the bookshelf, can you go get some?"

And then she had to stand up, naked, because as it had gone on he had pawed a few times at her underwear and she'd understood she was to use her free hand to wiggle out of her thong, which she'd abandoned to the floor. So she had to walk naked across the room, and pluck a few Kleenex—how many would she even need for this?— from their box on the bookshelf, and then turn and walk back to the sofa where he lay splayed, his shirt still on and his sweats only pulled down a tug beneath his hip bones, almost none of his skin exposed. He was looking not at her but down, his mouth set in concentration, his jaw working, and as she lowered herself to the couch again he put his hand out and touched her hip, not far from her belly button, and said, "Wait, would you stay there? Sit up like that. Yeah."

And so she sat at his side, as if he were a patient and she were his nurse, until it was finished, then gave him the Kleenex. She didn't know if he'd wanted her to do something with it but it made more sense to let him take care of it, he understood the situation better, surely, than she did. Then she lay down next to him again because that way they didn't have to look at each other's faces. She figured if she were him, she'd be embarrassed, that the other person had just seen his face, in that moment. He didn't seem embarrassed.

She thought about whether she was allowed to turn to her side, to press her body against him, or kiss the part of his neck just where it became his shoulder. Eventually he put his hand to her bare thigh and squeezed, once, then pushed up, past her, pulling at his sweats.

"We should probably get up," he said, gathering the beer bottles from the floor. He frowned at hers, which was practically full. "They might be home soon."

"I thought you said they'd be gone for a while."

"Yeah, but I don't know what a while means," he said, and it was this sentence more than anything else that made her want to cry. "They might get back soon. Do you need a ride?"

She hadn't made any plan. She had lied to Lily, said she was meeting Zoë for dinner on the Avenue. Getting here to be with him: that had seemed like it would be such an achievement that no further planning was needed. She had just assumed that elation would dissolve the pesky roadblocks of logistics, obligations.

"Yeah," she said. "I need a ride." She snatched her clothes from the floor and pushed past him, unwilling to look at his face.

She got dressed in the bathroom, then ran the water and pressed a perfumed washcloth to her squeezed-shut eyes. She wanted to look untouched by the time she left this room.

The front door opened and closed. She heard Chip's voice, loud and performed, and she heard what could only be his mother's voice, too.

She had no choice but to leave the bathroom.

"Oh," his mother said when Madison came into the living room. "I see. I didn't realize we had company."

Madison ran one hand through her hair and stepped forward.

"Hi," she said, "I'm Madison D'Amico."

The woman's lips parted and she took a reflexive step back, as if to consider Madison more fully, but she caught herself quickly and extended a hand in return.

"Of course," she said, "Madison. I can't believe we've never met—well, we must have, but years ago. Your mom and I used to play tennis together sometimes. When I could keep up with her."

"She played in college," Madison said. "You're not the only one. I'm impressed you could play with her at all."

"I'm Lacey," Chip's mother reminded her. They shook hands. His mother had Chip's face, almost, but everything that was sharply defined in him—his jaw, his smile, his brow line—was somehow more casual on her, gummier, more lopsided. When she smiled it seemed to touch the very edges of her face, and tiny fans of wrinkles appeared at the corners of her eyes. Her wavy blond hair was cut short, to her chin, in an indifferent, untouched sort of bob.

"Well, I'm just getting home with groceries," Lacey said. "We weren't planning anything special, because we all still have to pack for Florida, but Chip's dad will be back from the city in another hour or two. Do you want to stay for dinner?" She looked at Chip, without turning her head away from Madison. He was standing several steps away from them, disavowing the conversation. "It would be fun—we could get to know each other."

Madison scanned, quickly, what she knew about Chip's father. He was, she was pretty sure, a lawyer. And not in-house counsel anywhere; she was almost certain he had no ties to anywhere that mattered. But it was irrelevant, anyway. Chip cleared his throat.

"She's got to get home," he said. "I was just going to drive her."

"Oh," Lacey said. "It's looking like rain, honey. Why don't you stay here? Madison, I'll run you home. Are you guys still up in that same place? Off Baldwin Farms?"

"Yes," Madison said, and she couldn't keep her fear from her voice, even though she tried. "Of course we are."

"I just haven't been up there in years," Lacey said, her voice dipping to acknowledge and dispense with Madison's curt reply. "Your mom hosted the Silent Auction a few times, when you guys were still in elementary school."

Madison breathed again. She nodded her head furiously, eager to agree.

"Sure, I remember that."

"All right, well," Lacey said. "Chip, I'll be back in twenty."

He nodded, and then turned to Madison and stiffened his hand, touching it to his temple. He was saluting her good-bye. Their bodies had not touched since they'd been lying on the couch.

"Have a good spring," Madison said to him, looking away so quickly that she couldn't see whether or not he flinched, if he even understood. Or if he just wanted her gone, out of the house.

LACEY LOWERED HERSELF slowly into the Mercedes, checking her mirrors and her purse methodically, as if they were embarking on a cross-country road trip. Madison glanced over her shoulder and saw a pair of cleats tucked tidily beneath the driver's-side seat. She felt her blood in a rush, pooling behind her eyes, and she faced forward.

"So, what are your plans for the break? I assume you aren't traveling."

Here was the opening salvo, and Madison met it midarc, almost enjoyed catching it right away. She tossed her head, lifted her chin. She was developing a routine, an actual series of steps in response to rude, veiled questions about her parents. But as she opened her mouth and looked over at Lacey, her eyebrows raised as she watched the road, the vestiges of a smile on her face, she realized this woman might just be asking the question itself.

"No," she said. "We had thought about going out to Shelter Island for a week, but my mom just wanted to stay here."

"Oh, I didn't know you guys had spent time on Shelter. One of the partners at Nick's firm—Chip's dad—has an old family place out there. It's quite gorgeous."

Madison nodded. "It was my grandparents' house. I thought it would be fun to go, even if the weather stays like this. It's fun to kind of hole up there."

"I'm sure your mom will be happy to have you all around the house for a little while," Lacey said. "So, are you in Chip's class? You're a year below him, aren't you?"

"I'm a sophomore," Madison said, "yeah."

"Well, let me tell you, enjoy it while you can. I know girls are different from boys, but this year has been a constant struggle getting Chip to stay on top of all the different SAT dates, the ACT dates, his AP tests coming up soon. Everyone warns you about junior year—and we went through it already with his brothers! But I think it's even worse, for you guys. It gets worse every year."

Madison nodded.

"Madison," Lacey began, "I know we don't know each other, and if I'm offending you in any way I hope you'll stop me. But I just wanted to let you know how much I've always liked your parents. My husband and I are, a little bit—"

She paused and fiddled with a few buttons on the dashboard, cursing softly under her breath when the windshield defogger didn't at first turn on.

"Anyway, Chip's dad and I are a little bit removed from a lot of the other families at your school, you know? We just have a little bit of a different life. And I don't mind that; we moved here because I didn't want to raise the boys in the city, not because I wanted to pretend my husband worked at a hedge fund. And we moved here a long time ago, Chip is our youngest. And it's changed a lot. But my point is just that your mother has always been so sweet to me, and she has no real reason to be sweet. The only reason is that she's just a classy person."

"Oh," Madison said, "I'll tell her."

They were stopped at a light, and Lacey reached over to touch Madison's knee, just for a second.

"No," she said, "you don't have to. I'm just telling you, for you. I think it's important to remember that who your mother is doesn't change just because of what other people might say."

"Thank you."

"That said," Lacey continued, "I don't know if you and Chip spending time together is such a good idea right now."

Madison wrapped her hand around her door handle, though they were still minutes away from her house, from the chance to launch herself from this car.

"Really," she said.

"I'm sure you understand. This is an important year for him, and for you, too—in a different way! It's just really best that you spend some time with your parents over this break. I'm sure they'd like to have you around. And of course if you need anything at all, you and

Chip are friends. We'd be happy to help. I told you how much I've always liked your mom. But she must have her hands full, dealing with all these women. Such gossips. I'm sure I don't have to tell you."

"I can hop out here," Madison said. They were at her gate; she didn't want Lacey to notice the black sedan parked across the street. "Thanks for the ride."

Lacey, perhaps seized by a spasm of compunction, reached out to clutch Madison's arm. "Oh, honey, I hope I haven't said too much. It just struck me that you could probably handle it, were I to be blunt. But I don't mean any of this to seem like a judgment on you, Madison! Of course not, that would be absurd. But things must be quite—difficult, right now, waiting to see what's going to happen. And I think it's best if you don't involve Chip."

"Oh," Madison said, "I always involve boys from school in my most intimate family problems. Why wouldn't I?"

Lacey smiled, her face vacant, clearly not sure what to make of this, yet.

"Thanks so much for not being just another gossip," Madison said, and she got out of the car. "Thank you so much, Mrs. Abbott," and she slammed the door.

THIRTY-SEVEN

That Sunday the boys had a tee-ball game at the fields, their fourth game of the season. Lily had taken them to each game so far without any input from Isabel, who was usually still upstairs at that time of morning. Lily had never suggested to anyone that she found this odd.

This was only one part of her recent campaign—begun sometime after that night Jackson had been at the house—to try not to see things. Not to notice when and if Isabel neglected the kids or ignored their reasonable questions, whether spoken or implied. Not to think about how she herself would have done things differently, since Bob's initial return but especially since Christmas, since the turning of the seasons. This meant she didn't clock it when Madison lied about where she'd be, didn't point anyone else toward these lies. On that day in December, it felt, Lily had made some calculation. She'd allowed herself to step outside the house, all the way out. To watch these people through different eyes, the eyes of someone else, not the grateful girl applying for her first job out of school. And she'd been surprised at herself, at the bitterness that rose up in her like mercury on a thermometer. She was afraid of what she'd do if she indulged it too often, if she lifted the foot she still had on their side of the line and brought it to rest elsewhere.

But this morning, by the time Lily herded the boys into the kitchen for breakfast, Isabel was already there.

"I thought I'd come see the game today! Morning, sluggers."

She'd dressed carefully, Lily could see: dark jeans, a cashmere pullover that matched her eyes to an uncanny degree, a Barbour jacket. Her brown leather Ferragamo boots, with the thick heel. She'd dressed for the fields, for muddy grasses and climbing up to sit on chilled metal bleachers. She really was going to the game.

The boys stopped short just inside the kitchen door when they saw her. They wore their baseball uniforms, their jerseys thick and boxy on their wiry frames. Their backpacks hung from their hands, dragging on the floor.

"You're wearing Gran's jacket," Matteo said, walking to his mother, fingering the large golden ring hanging from the tip of its zipper.

"That's right," Isabel said, carrying the fruit bowls over to the table and pointing the boys toward the banquette. "Gran always wore this jacket. She got a new one about once per decade, but this was her last one, and she gave it to me."

"And you'll give it to us," Matteo intoned, tucking his feet up under him and digging into the food.

Lily remained in the doorway. Was she supposed to leave them here, alone with their mother?

"Well, this one's too big for you, bub." Isabel sat down with them.

"Why are you awake?" Matteo demanded, artless as ever. Lily felt some pride at this, the way these boys were so aware of everything going on, and showed such little inclination for concealing their confusion, even their distaste. She felt an ownership of their honesty.

"Do you still want me to drive them?" she said finally. Isabel didn't respond.

"All right!" Luke cheered, suddenly, the events of the morning just now catching up to him. "Is Dad coming, too?"

"That's a good question," Isabel said, then turned to Lily. "I was thinking we could all drive in together. Madison, too."

"I'm going to go ask him," Luke said, officious and determined. He climbed down from the breakfast bench and disappeared.

"Is Madison awake?" Lily said after a silence, but then Luke was already back.

"Dad said he'll meet us at the door," he said. "When we leave."

"Luke," Lily said, "go ask him if he'll drive you boys right now. Then I can wait, and help your mom get Madison ready."

Isabel quite pointedly watched Matteo eat, fondled his earlobes and fluffed his hair, and did not look in Lily's direction until Bob's voice rumbled in from the foyer and Matteo bolted from his chair.

"Play ball!" they heard Bob growl, and the boys erupted into peals of manic laughter, and then the door slammed. Neither twin had really eaten breakfast. Isabel left the kitchen without saying anything, and Lily followed.

Upstairs, Madison seemed to have been marshaling her resistance even before she was awake or apprised of what was going on.

"I just don't understand what I'm going to get for doing this," Madison said. They hadn't had to build their way up to this; her voice had pitched itself at its shrill peak almost as soon as Isabel went into the room. Lily lingered in the hallway just beyond the door, watching them.

"Excuse me?"

"You said you want us all to do something together, fine, but that doesn't sound like something that does me any good. It sounds like I'm doing you a favor. So what am I going to get in return?"

"When did you start talking like this?" Isabel said, almost laughing in disbelief. "This is the third or fourth time you've done that now, these words like 'favors' and 'what do I get.' This isn't a negotiation, Madison."

But apparently, when met with her daughter's silence, Isabel had to concede that it was.

"What do you get?" she spat. "How about this extravagant roof over your head and your food to eat, and designer jeans, and your grandmother's jewelry. How does that sound?"

Madison rolled her eyes and almost actually stamped her foot, and Lily saw that Isabel couldn't look away. She was literally riveted by her daughter. What did she think would happen? Lily thought. She hasn't been cultivating her, she hasn't been doing anything to keep her calm. This is what other people mean when they talk about the nightmare of raising a teenager. They'd all practically had to implode to draw it out of Madison, but here it was. She was finally playing along.

"Madison," Isabel began, the words emerging from between her clenched teeth, "I am asking you to do something very small for me. You are already awake; it's quite clear to us both that you aren't going back to sleep. All you need to do is ride in the car with me and sit in the bleachers at this game for an hour. You can bring homework, if that's what you're worried about. And actually—no, I'm not asking. I won't ask again. Be downstairs in ten minutes."

No, Lily thought. Just touch her. Just put your arms around her and wait for her to buckle. She'll tell you what's happening, she just needs you to give her any small sign of encouragement.

She wanted to reach out to them, to move their limbs like dolls she could control. Or, really, she wanted to step forward and hug Madison herself. It's what she would have done, when they had an argument, even just months ago. It had usually been her role.

"Madison," Lily said, finally, softly. "Just get dressed. You know you don't have a choice here. You're just delaying the inevitable."

Madison stood in silence, her body still angled at her mother like a cannon about to go off, her head turned to glare at Lily.

"You're *both* unbelievable," she said finally, her emphasis somehow making it clear how deeply and in what different ways they had both offended her.

"I have a lot going on in *my* life," she said. "But no one seems to care about that. If you all want me to just show up and act like your performing monkey, then all of a sudden you care where I am or what I'm doing. No one has cared for months, not until now, but fine. As long as I don't tell anyone anything they don't already know about us."

She got dressed, of course, and later the three of them sat in the car near the fields. Lily hovered in the backseat, watching mother and daughter volley back and forth. She couldn't see what the urgency was, why Isabel cared so much that they be here, that her daughter walk out onto those bleachers.

Isabel hadn't reacted, back in the bedroom, when Madison spoke. She'd shown no alarm, asked no questions at all: anything *who* doesn't already know, what, why would you phrase it just that way.

"I've done everything you've asked me to do," Madison said to her mother. "You have no idea what it's like."

She was pressed toward the passenger door as if her mother's brief silence had been a bulky object that might displace her from her seat. She gripped her door handle with her right hand; her knuckles were white. She wanted Isabel to know that she was hurt. She wanted to prove, with her every tensed muscle, that she could not bear to spend even one excess second in close proximity to her torturers. Anger could be discounted, made to seem petty or small, misconstrued as a tantrum or ascribed to Madison's status as a teenager. But Madison wanted it to be clear that she was not merely angry. She wants us to know, Lily thought. Or she wants her mother to know. She might not even care, at this point, that I'm here.

Lily watched Madison so carefully, the teenage face trying so hard to remain composed, and when Madison's lip quivered then Lily, too, felt a stinging behind her eyes. I'm here, Mad, she thought, chewing her inner cheek with the effort to get Madison to look back at her. I'm here.

"There's no chance you'll do this for me, just because I've asked?" Isabel said finally.

Madison sat in silence, her back still pressed to the window.

"Okay," Isabel said. "I don't owe you this explanation, but I understand that you're frustrated by the fact that I haven't talked to you much about what's been going on with your father."

"I'll go find the boys," Lily murmured, knowing full well that

Isabel would, without looking away from Madison, hold up one finger to keep Lily in her seat. They were all in this car, under the same spell, and Isabel no more wanted it broken than Lily wanted to be the one to break it.

"It wasn't his fault," Madison said suddenly.

"Of course it wasn't entirely his fault—"

"No, I'm not saying this in some pathetic, no one person was responsible, whatever, way. I'm saying that there were other forces at work. People who had it out for him. There are things people don't know yet."

These were so clearly not phrases of Madison's own imagining that Lily felt a chill in her chest, felt something contract and squeeze for a second too long before relaxing. Isabel must hear this, too. Was she going to file it away? Was she going to deal with it?

"I just need you to come sit out there with me," Isabel repeated.

Madison turned again to her mother, her cheeks still streaked with tears, her face red and swollen. "This is such a fucking joke."

"Madison," Isabel said, "what's going on? Is something else going on?"

And then she was out of the car, tumbling from it at high velocity, like a hostage with just enough coiled energy left to orchestrate her own escape. She slammed the door behind her, of course, pellets of mud and grass arcing through the air around her ankles as she stormed toward the bleachers.

Lily held herself still, wondering if she had been truly forgotten, but then Isabel spoke.

"She wouldn't have left the house if you hadn't intervened," she said quietly, staring ahead.

"I doubt that's true," Lily said. "Besides, we could always have called Mina for help."

Isabel didn't take the bait.

"You could have just explained it to her," Lily said. "Whatever has you so hell-bent on trotting her out to watch the game. You could have been honest with her. She's not a baby."

Still Isabel said nothing, and Lily turned toward the field. Her eye sought out Matteo and Luke, standing—as always—somewhat apart from the others, their little robber-baron stances. Sometimes, waiting for them at the school gates, she caught sight of them walking toward her before her brain recognized them as her own charges, these little boys and no other. That oscillation between disinterested observation and ferocious recognition, the recognition of your own kin.

But they weren't. They weren't her kin, not at all.

"Look at her," Isabel said. Madison was climbing the bleachers now, shouldering the Vineyard Vines bag she'd brought along. It was stuffed so full that it sagged theatrically on her shoulder. "I forget that she's half D'Amico. Look at her, she looks like some Neapolitan washerwoman who's never had a day's rest in her whole life. That's pure Nonna martyrdom."

When Madison reached the bleachers a few rows up, where the mothers were clustered, she kept climbing. They watched her as she climbed to the very top row and then edged her way along one bleacher to the far corner, where one man sat alone, folded over himself, a Brooklyn Dodgers cap jammed low on his head.

"He's lost weight, hasn't he," Isabel said.

"Well, he was never overweight."

"No, that's what I mean. He's just missing, you know. His bulk."

And she was right. He was missing muscle, health, the occupied space of a man who had once successfully asserted himself in the world of his choosing.

Isabel watched her daughter, and Lily watched them both. Madison came to stand beside Bob, and after a few seconds he looked up. She sat down beside him.

"Are you going to ask her, later, what she meant by that?" Lily said.

"Which part?" Isabel said.

"I think you know which part," Lily said. "She's talking about it like she knows secrets that other people don't. That doesn't worry you?"

Isabel squinted at the field, still not turning back to face Lily. "Lily, you've seen him yourself. He's haunting the halls. He hasn't spoken to anyone in months; you think he's debriefing his teenage daughter on his company's bankruptcy?"

"Are you going to ask her what she meant?"

Isabel sprang forward, clicking out of her seat belt and slamming the driver's-side door without saying a word. Lily locked the car and followed.

"The boys look good," someone said as they took their seats. Everyone said hello, and Lily saw that no one would mention Isabel's husband, sitting alone up in his corner. As they sat down, Isabel put her hand to Lily's, touched the knuckles.

"Thank you for being here," she said quietly, during a home run that elicited noisy outbursts from the other mothers.

Lily put two fingers to her mouth and whistled, quite aware that several of the women sitting in front of her winced noticeably, before she replied.

"You pay me more money than my own father makes, pay for my health insurance, and fly me around the world with you twice a year. To be here."

"You know that's not true," Isabel said.

"No," Lily said. "It actually is." They were murmuring, not looking away from the field.

"I'm sorry if you disapprove," Isabel said, "of how I handled her this morning. But she is not the only variable in my life right now, Lily. I have other things on my mind."

"Right," Lily said, "of course," and she knew right away that she'd let too much of her opinion drip into the words.

Isabel stood up. The thick heels of her boots chirped against the corrugated metal bleachers as she moved, shaking the entire row. She sat down with a cluster of women a few bleachers closer to the field. Lily could see her ease herself in with small talk, could see that she had manufactured some reason for relocating. But she could also see that Isabel's movements had that jittery, fragile quality of someone who was trying hard to conceal her anger, who was smiling to soothe an eruption. And it was satisfying, to see that.

Once or twice, she looked back over her shoulder. Bob sat in total silence, hunched and gray, his chin resting on one fist. He hadn't shaved in a few days. Madison sat silently beside him, her history textbook propped on her knees, chewing the end of the highlighter she held in one hand. They looked, Lily thought, like partners. Conspirators, even.

That was how she would remember the morning, much later. Bob and Madison in silent communion up behind her, Isabel chatting up strangers down below. And Lily, left alone on the cold metal between them.

THIRTY-EIGHT

When Amanda turned from the cash register, her Pinkberry in hand, Madison was standing at the end of the line. It had been so long since they'd interacted beyond brief encounters in the hallway at school, eyebrows raised in vague distaste. The way you'd lock eyes with another pedestrian if you passed a patch of vomit on the sidewalk, or something. Amanda had accepted this back in October; she had been relieved of her job, whatever that job had been.

But now, she saw Madison before Madison saw her. Alone, without the boys or Lily or even her mother, Madison projected an uneasy alloy of steeliness and grace. You could see the grated vulnerability of her knowledge that if you forced her to meet your eye, then she'd have to respond with avidity and warmth. She looked like she was trying to keep herself locked away without claiming any physical space for herself.

When she finally saw Amanda, they stepped out of line together. Amanda kept her back resolutely to the other women there, but she saw Madison's eyes flicker.

"Hey," she said.

Madison smiled, and this in itself was so surprising that Amanda felt emboldened, safe.

Her father had gone quiet for a while, but the past few weeks had been every bit as bad as October. Jake had written about Madison's father, either indirectly or by name, for his past five columns.

"I was just killing some time while Lori runs errands, I didn't want to sit at home alone. Do you want to walk around?"

"Sure," Madison said. "Isabel is with the twins, at Le Pain. I told them I wanted yogurt instead, but I probably don't have to go back right away. Isabel got stuck talking to a bunch of other women there."

"Yogurt?"

"No, let's just leave. I'm not even hungry."

"You don't really get hungry for frozen yogurt," Amanda said, swirling her spoon into the creamy peak she'd dotted with yogurt chips and graham cracker crumbs.

"Well," Madison said, "that's dessert. So don't delude yourself."

"You know me," Amanda said, and they walked out onto the Avenue.

"The boys had a tee-ball game," Madison said. "We all had to go."

"Oh."

"Yeah, he came, too."

"I wasn't going to ask," Amanda said.

"No, I know, but you were thinking about it, right? We all went."

"That seems good."

"Maybe. I didn't see him actually speak to my mother."

"Well, how often have you gone out in public, so far?"

"Yeah, I know."

"They're probably just nervous, you know? I mean, I don't know if he gets nervous."

"He does," Madison said, and she was nearly whispering. "People always act like this. Or I mean, used to. Like just because my dad is scary and yells and everyone who works for him is always terrified—I mean, that's not his real personality. That's a performance. It's not like he's scary with us, like we're all tiptoeing around him. He has normal emotions when he's at home."

"I know he does," Amanda said.

They were walking past the park, then the bank, still walking up the hill. They'd moved in the exact opposite direction from where Isabel was waiting for Madison's return, and this knowledge made

Amanda anxious. Even now, she thought, I don't want Isabel to dislike me. It's kind of pathetic. After this whole year, I don't want to be any kind of wedge between the two of them.

"Are you going to the party next week?" Madison said, and Amanda shuffled names and dates frantically in her mind. When it dawned on her, she almost laughed.

"The museum benefit? Suzanne? I think I got plenty of that house at Halloween," she said. "I don't think we've gone since I was little."

"Right," Madison said. "I wasn't sure. We ran into Suzanne a while ago, in the city, and she made it sound like it would be bigger this year, like she'd invited way more people, so I thought maybe."

Amanda let this pass, let her yogurt mass at the roof of her mouth before she swallowed it. She knew Madison hadn't meant anything by it.

"You don't have to go," she told Madison. "If you don't want to go, don't go. What are they going to do to you?"

They crossed the street and began moving back down the hill. Amanda knew that soon, they'd be at Le Pain, and she hadn't yet done anything she couldn't have done months ago. She hadn't learned anything in all this time they hadn't spoken.

"I need to ask you something," Madison said. "You'd be a good person to ask."

"Doubtful, but go ahead."

"What if you knew they were doing the wrong thing? Jake and Lori. Like, you knew they were just too upset about something to think clearly, but they weren't asking for your opinion even when they probably should. What if you were actually a big asset and they didn't get it."

"You're describing my daily routine, but okay."

"I mean, no one's going to listen, right? Nobody's going to listen to us. But what if someone would, and you could explain it better, because those are your parents. Like, nobody watches our parents as much as we do. Right?"

"I guess," Amanda said. "Tell me what you mean. Give me an example."

"There's no example," Madison said, shaking her head, looking beyond Amanda down the Avenue. "But would you trust your own judgment? More than theirs?"

Amanda bit her lip, and looked down at the empty yogurt cup. The yogurt had liquefied, gathered itself in the seams of the paper cup. When this conversation had started, she had thought maybe they would commiserate, that they'd complain about their parents in generic, normal teenage ways. That maybe if it seemed like forgiveness was really coming, she could even tell Madison about the Riverdale boy she'd met at the swim team weekend retreat in the city last week, or something. And Madison, in turn, could fill her in on what, if anything, had ever happened with Chip. That was the conversation she'd thought they might have. Just, for once this year, a conversation that wasn't about their fathers.

Madison put her hand to Amanda's arm, and they looked at each other.

"I would trust your judgment, I guess," Amanda said. "I always would, Mad. You're the smartest D'Amico by a long shot."

Madison didn't smile, but somewhere back behind the face she was showing to Amanda there was a small turn, the recognition of banter, of closeness. Of insulting their own tribes as a show of loyalty toward each other. Amanda squeezed Madison's hand.

"But if you had stuff people wanted to know about," Madison said, again. "You'd want people to know, right?"

"I've never had access to anything important," Amanda said. "Come on."

"It just seems like there are better ways to handle most of it. I'm sick of waiting to see if something's going to happen. I'm sick of waiting for it to get worse."

"Understandable," Amanda said. "Just tell me what you're worried about. Maybe I can help."

THIRTY-NINE

Madison noted with pleasure that Gabriel Scott Lazarus looked almost nervous when he spotted her near the back of the darkened bar. He stood just inside the street door for a moment, shaking the rain from his pea coat. It was too big for him. When his eyes met hers, he put one hand into the air, as if it wasn't clear that she was already looking right at him. He walked back along the length of the bar.

She didn't know anything about this place, Corner Bistro, but she'd heard Lily mention it once as having the best burger in the city. She figured straining to choose somewhere chic, somewhere Zoë would approve of, ran the risk of tipping him off to how little she felt she controlled the situation. This place, quite clearly, wasn't a move made to impress him with her street smarts or her prowess.

"I love this place," he said. "You've been before?" She reminded herself that she shouldn't fire back some tart dismissal of the way his voice was smooth with condescension, of how carefully he was trying to show her that he knew she seemed older than she was, wise beyond her years. She just smiled, as if she came to this bar all the time. Like he should have known it without asking.

His glasses were fogged, and he took them off and slipped them into an inner pocket of the pea coat before slinging it over the back of his chair. When he sat down, the chair rocked him forward. For the remainder of their conversation, he would totter back and forth like this, on the uneven legs of the chair.

"Are those fake?" she said. His face scrambled for a moment before she saw him realize she'd meant the glasses.

"Not at all. If you were standing on the other side of the room, holding up cue cards, I'd definitely need them. But the situation we're in, I think just my own eyes will do."

He smiled at her again. This is someone who doesn't really have a problem flirting with a fifteen-year-old, she reminded herself. This is relevant information to consider when you're talking to this person.

"I'll take a vodka soda," she said. He cleared his throat and spent a few seconds longer than necessary unraveling and folding his scarf.

"I'm not sure it's a great idea for me to buy you alcohol," he said. "I think we're probably squeaking by right now because, this early in the afternoon, this place is sort of a restaurant, too. But it's basically a bar, and if they haven't noticed you in here yet, I don't think we should flag ourselves."

"All right," she said, "you're probably right. I shouldn't be here at all."

He went to the bar.

What's the harm in talking to him again? Amanda had said to her. *You haven't even looked at any of the papers. You haven't asked your dad about them specifically. For all you know, the key isn't still in the same place. You have literally no information yet, nothing he'd want to trade. So what could it possibly hurt?*

"I'm glad you called," he said when he returned. He lowered his neck to sip directly from his full glass, swiping at the foam that clung to his lip afterward with one finger. Then he pulled out a reporter's notebook, a pen, and his iPhone.

She had looked at his card so many times. She'd been keeping it in her wallet, next to her school ID and her Pinkberry punch card. She slipped it out sometimes in the middle of class, slowly, letting the sharp, thick corner poke up out of the wallet. First she'd thought she'd call him right after Christmas, and then it seemed that she'd left it too long. And now she was here.

"No," she said. "I'm not going to talk about anything with you today. I have some questions for you."

She marveled at the smoothness of her voice, the way she wasn't even having to pause at the beginnings and ends of her sentences to take a breath. With every sentence uttered this way, she felt better, more confident, felt the hard, glassy shell she wanted to feel all around her when she talked to this guy.

"Fire away," he said.

"I want you to tell me a little bit more about your site." She removed the two thin red straws from her glass and wrinkled her nose, dropping them onto the etched and re-etched wooden table.

"It would be financial news, from a human angle. It was an idea I'd been batting around for a while, with a friend, actually, but when Bear happened last spring, we figured it might be even more essential now than ever."

He didn't interrupt his speech to ask her if she knew what had happened with Bear.

"Basically, you know, what's happening now in very specific neighborhoods in Manhattan is going to affect everyone in the country. But so few people in this country even understand what's going on. And it's so easy to fall into a very simplistic view of what's happened—Wall Street is evil. That's what a lot of people think. And we just think that fleshing these banks out, making these men real people, reporting on *every* part of what's going on—we think that could be a real game changer."

It must be so sad, she thought, to use that term, game changer, to refer to yourself. Not to realize that it's only people who will never be game changers at all who see that as an impressive way to speak.

"So, financial gossip," she said. He jutted his chin out slightly.

"Not at all. That's one way to go, of course, but we'd consider that a failure. That wouldn't be true to our vision, really, at all. And there's plenty of that already. The market's pretty well glutted with it. My partner runs one of the smartest ones—Of Hedonists and Hedge Funds? I don't know if you've ever read it."

"No, but that's a dumb name," she said, crunching an ice cube between her molars.

"It's not the snappiest title. I'd be the first to admit that. But in any case, what he's been doing over there is much more in the vein of overheard in the elevator from a first-year analyst, stuff like that. Gossip, just as you said. And he's very critical of that world, all the more so because he's a part of it."

"What's his name?" Madison asked.

"That's the thing. He's anonymous, and I have to protect that. He's an investment banker, and if he were to be found out, he would be summarily fired. And he'd also lose his access to that world."

"So," Madison said, crunching another ice cube, "he makes fun of the people he works with, and he won't sign his name to any of it?"

Gabe lifted his beer and took a gulp.

"Like I said, he's looking to make a change. And I'm obviously looking for a little more flexibility than I had at DealBook."

"I looked you up," she said. "You haven't written for them since last year."

"I left to do this."

"And why do you care about someone who doesn't even work in finance anymore?"

He set his beer to the side and moved her drink, too, leaning forward over the table.

"Your father works in finance."

"You don't seem all that up to speed, for a future game changer."

"You think your father's going to get a different job? Like what? Cardiac surgeon? Electrical engineer?"

She felt it suddenly as a struggle, the effort to hold her jaw steady, to keep her gaze even.

"Thank you for your concern," she said, "but I'm pretty sure my father is qualified for all kinds of jobs."

"Madison," Gabe said. "He'll be working in finance forever, now. One way or another. You'll be a daughter of finance for the rest of your life. You get that, right? This is exactly what I want to talk about."

She didn't know what her own face did, but his slowly creased as he watched her. He looked down at his beer and passed a hand over his face before drawing it away and leaving two index fingers pointed at his temple. As he spoke, he kept them cocked there, like a rifle, and every so often waved them into the air just next to his head.

"I didn't mean for that to sound the way it did. Okay? But I told you. I truly believe the most incredible things anyone could learn about Bob D'Amico right now would be, what is he like as a man? A husband, a father? To humanize him. People want to demonize these guys, but they don't know anything about them. All we know about you guys is, some of the wealthiest people in the country fucked things up for everyone else."

He held up his hand when Madison started to speak.

"I wasn't saying that critically," he said. "Your father couldn't possibly have known what would happen to the world right after he bought that second uptown apartment, for example. But that's my point. All people have from him is what's on paper. And, if they're motivated to do research, his congressional testimony. But most of America, even most *Times* readers, have absolutely no motivation to explore anything that might broaden their outlook on anything. Not to mention, that testimony is pretty dry."

Madison swallowed the rest of her drink.

"I haven't watched it," she said.

"No," he said, his voice softer. "Of course. I wouldn't, either."

She regretted, then, having told him the truth.

"All I'm saying," he said after a moment, "is just . . . tell the world what your family's life has been like these past few months. That is the most radical thing anyone could do to rehabilitate your father's image. To help understand. And very, very few people are in any position to do that with any authority. And one of them is you."

"And the only way to do that is to talk to a reporter starting a blog?"

"It'll be a lot more than a blog," he said.

"Sure."

"Well, you must think it could be something," he said, sounding almost angry for the first time. "It got you to this bar. You're sitting across from me right now."

She waited, and said nothing.

"Madison, I've done my homework. I'm not flying blind here. I've got some really media-savvy people on board. This world is changing—just look at Facebook in the past two years. Just look at Twitter."

He pointed at her phone, which she'd taken out and placed on the table beside her.

"You're too young to understand this, but when that was new, if you'd told me that in a few years I'd have that option but also the option of an iPhone? It would have blown my mind."

"Great," she said.

"I'd be happy for you to just keep thinking about it," he said.

"I don't know anything about his bank," she said. "If you think I'm some expert on what happened at Weiss, you're wrong."

He hesitated before seeming to reach some decision within himself.

"Not what I'm interested in. Other people are doing plenty of other—there are big questions about the earnings report Weiss announced last summer, for starters. And about their overall accounting techniques. But I'm not interested in investigating fraud, and I'm bringing all of this up right now not to upset you, but to prove that to you. I could care less whether your father knew about what was going on at that place. I could care less what was or wasn't illegal. That's not what I want to write about."

She stared down at her phone.

"I'm interested in you," he said. "Not the bank, not him. What *you* think of him."

SHE LEFT THE BAR ALONE, assuming that Gabriel Scott Lazarus, with his three names, would settle their tab. It had grown dark during the brief time she'd been at that table with him, and it was still so cold, for late March. The golden light from the bar washed squares of the sidewalk in its warmth. And when she looked up, preparing herself to negotiate the various ways she could get home, where surely no one had even noticed her absence, Lily was standing right in the middle of one of those squares.

When Madison looked back over her shoulder, as if to disavow the bar behind her, the people in it, she couldn't believe how cozy it looked from out here.

She turned back to Lily.

"You followed me? From Connecticut?"

"Madison, what's going on?"

"I'm going to miss my train," Madison said, and began to busy herself with her scarf, her gloves, checking that she had everything still in her purse.

"Believe me," Lily began. "Believe me when I say that I'm telling you this because I love you, not because I'm looking to get you grounded, or anything like that."

"Please," Madison said.

"This is not a good idea," Lily said. "Not like this."

"How did you even know I was here? *Did* you follow me?"

"This is not a good idea," she repeated. "You're young, Madison, to understand this."

Madison laughed, taking pleasure in doing it right in Lily's face. As she pushed past, she heard Lily cursing under her breath, *shit, shit.* Madison put her arm up for a cab.

"Madison," and then Lily had one hand on Madison's arm, bringing it slowly back down toward their bodies. "I can drive you back. I won't tell her you were here. But I need you to—I need you to tell me why you wanted to talk to him."

Madison opened her mouth and gulped the cold air, air so fresh and brisk it seemed to have weight to it. She kept gasping it in, feeling more confident with each second that she wouldn't start to cry. She knew that if she just turned back to Lily, she would be hugged, brought in close, her hair stroked.

"I can probably help," Lily said. "You think you already know what I'm going to say. But you might not. I might agree with you, Madison. I might agree with you. Just try me."

FORTY

L et's try this one," Jake said. "This one looks nice."

Amanda and her father turned into the small boutique just off the Avenue. It was a "concept store," an idea she'd only heard of for the first time from Zoë Barker, of all people, at that hellish Halloween party.

They were, improbably, in search of a hostess gift for Suzanne Welsh, as they would be attending her museum benefit that night.

Amanda had no more interest than her parents did in that night's partygoing. But after seeing Madison the previous weekend, Amanda felt like maybe her presence could be important, a stabilizing force of some kind. Something was bound to happen, tonight, the first time Bob went back out into Greenwich. The water would be bloody within minutes. Bob would have to make something happen, just so he had some say in what that something would be.

That was the thought that kept coming to her, the certainty of some sort of drama, and she told herself that her desire to be there for Madison was just that, *for* Madison. It was nothing like the TV news, nothing like the *Observer* and its recent, renewed obsession with Bob's whereabouts. Nothing like her father's "professional" interest in what had happened at Weiss.

In town, they'd wandered aimlessly into and out of the storefronts that Amanda always thought of as their town mascots. Every store was set up to cater to the same airy, dreamed-of woman. They wanted you to see it each time you walked in: what you'd look like at a beach resort, walking from your cabana to the pool, or what you'd look like on your husband's colleague's British country estate, fox hounds nipping at your boot-clad heels. But no, Amanda reminded herself, most of Greenwich wouldn't have to imagine some aspirational woman. They'd already established themselves as that woman; these stores were only here to reassure them that they wouldn't lose their grip on her, whoever she actually was.

Amanda trailed her father through the store until he stopped at an antique wooden hutch cabinet littered with votive candles and other tiny, faux-vintage baubles. He looked over at her, helpless.

"A candle is probably fine," Amanda said. "We can have them wrap it so it looks more, whatever. Extravagant."

"I truly do not understand why we are going tonight," her father said. "This seems, to me, beyond foolish."

He peered at the box, trying to see if he could pop it open without breaking its gold-stickered seal.

"You're nervous," she said. "Because we haven't seen him all year."

"I don't think it's wise for us to be in the same place," her father said, doffing his glasses and chewing on an end.

"Dad, you could have run into him anytime. All winter. You live in the same town. I mean, why do any of this if you actually care what he thinks?"

"I do not," her father said. "I do not care what that man thinks. Not one bit."

"I don't believe you."

"Amanda, you—I mean, I know you were angry with me initially, that I did not consult you before that first column. But please tell me that all this time later, you understand. The tragedy here is not the loss of Bob's good name, Amanda. Please tell me you understand that."

"I'm not stupid," she said.

"Then act like someone who isn't," her father said. "Bob is not the victim. The victims are people who have never even heard his name, whatever its value. You know that."

She nodded, once.

"Tell me you aren't going to get into this with him tonight?"

"Of course not. If there's any unpleasantness, it'll be painful for you. That's why I'm worried about tonight. For you."

"Oh," she said. "Yes. We mustn't do anything to make this difficult *for me.*"

Her father held the box with the candle in both hands, letting his arms sag as if he was carrying something much heavier.

"I know it's been a rough year," he said. "You know how I know that? Because you have become absolutely vicious on this topic. The way you speak to me, about this, it's gotten quite ugly. I thought I was getting through to you, just now. I thought we were communicating. All year I've thought, if I can just make my daughter understand who's at fault here, then I've done my job as a parent. But I see that, in this respect, I've failed."

He began to turn away, then had one final thought.

"You wanted to go to this damn thing. So we're going. And I'm paying for the privilege. So I'd watch your tone."

He walked back to the cash register, offering the young salesgirl a tired, still-boyish smile. She laughed at something he said, reaching out to take his credit card between her index and middle fingers.

They should just do it, Amanda thought. That's what she would tell Madison, tonight. Just give the stuff to the "reporter," who didn't sound all that legitimate, honestly. Just give it to him, let it be his problem from now on. Nothing bad would actually happen. There was no way Madison had enough information, enough power, to cause any actual harm.

Either way, somebody—Madison's father or her own—would have to stand up in public and say those words: I was wrong. I made a mistake.

That's what's been missing so far this year, Amanda thought. That'll ease things up around here. That might make this the kind of place I can imagine staying in for another two years without putting my head in the oven.

She'd read that phrase recently, in English, studying Sylvia Plath as part of the spring poetry unit. She knew it wasn't literal; Sylvia had just shut herself in the kitchen and tucked towels between doors and floor. It wasn't in particularly good taste, either, to invoke suicide as linguistic flourish. They'd sat through countless school assemblies, all their lives, about how hurtful casual wordplay could be, how easy it was to rub your own cavalier attitudes like salt into the wounds of others.

But the phrase itself was just so tempting, so appealing on the tongue. And the image itself, the idea that someone could just kneel down and put her face into the heat. There was something undeniably memorable, romantic even, about that.

Her father came up behind her again.

"What are you thinking about?" he said. Amanda decided not to lie.

"Sylvia Plath."

"Jesus," he moaned, rolling his eyes.

"You know she put her head in the oven."

"Everyone knows that. That, trust me, is the only reason she's famous."

"Hardly," Amanda said.

FORTY-ONE

On the night of the Welsh party, Madison went into her mother's bathroom to watch her get ready. This was not something she'd ever done as a child; there was no echo of past routine, no remembered tenderness in the act itself to make the evening any easier. But still she did it, walked across the second floor and into her mother's part of the house.

Isabel leaned forward at the waist, her face thrust toward the mirrored cabinet above her sink. She was still wearing only her bra and a half-slip. Two cabinet doors had been left open, the mirrored sides facing each other. When Isabel tilted her head back and leaned forward, her neck and breasts floating toward the mirrors, her reflection repeated into infinity. Dozens and dozens of identical Isabel faces springing forward and receding into some illusory horizontal distance, in the unreachable depths of the green glass.

Madison sat down at the vanity.

"You'll wrinkle your dress," Isabel said without turning to look. The dress had been waiting on Madison's bed when she came in from school that afternoon. It was floor length, silk that poured over her hip bones and pooled at her feet like water, bile green in some lights, yellow gold in others. When she'd found it spread across her taut white bedspread, it reminded her of a half-healed bruise.

Madison stood up again, without comment.

"Oh, go ahead," Isabel said smoothly, drawing down her bottom lid to apply a thin line of eyeliner to its inner rim. "What do we care if we show up wrinkled for Suzanne Welsh."

They cared very much; this was the first night the entire family, all five of them, would be going out together, as a team, since the summer. But Madison knew what her mother was doing, knew that sometimes you just say things to fill the air, to shield each one of you from the other's scrutiny. She nodded.

"Is Dad ready?"

"I'm not sure, sweetheart."

Madison looked longingly at the chilled glass of white wine sitting on the sink, where a bar of soap should be.

"Is Lily going to come? To watch the boys?"

"They're going to eat with us, then she'll come pick them up as soon as dinner is over. I know they're excited, and I don't want to keep them from tonight, especially. It's important for them to see your dad, out, around other people."

It's important for me, too, Madison thought.

Madison strained to hear any signs of life from beyond the door that led to her father's antechamber. He couldn't possibly still be downstairs, could he? If he hadn't started to get dressed, then he wasn't coming.

He might be hiding out down there. There were suddenly a lot of people in the house tonight. Lena and her girls, bustling all around. Lily cooking something for three nights from now, in the kitchen. It was as if they were getting ready to host the party here, or something. Suddenly, every single one of them needed a reason to keep her hands busy.

When she heard nothing from next door, Madison turned to her mother's vanity, to the potted creams and glass-sheathed gels and the shiny black square cases that signaled their contents as Chanel eye makeup. She picked one up and held it in the center of her palm. It was so old that the interlocking white *C*'s had begun to wear out in places. Her mother was always telling her how important it was to throw out your makeup every six months, buy all fresh supplies.

"Why aren't you doing your makeup over here?" Madison asked, frowning at herself in the bottom-lit vanity mirror. "I thought the whole point was to sit at this thing, isn't that why it's called a vanity?"

Her mother stood back now from the cabinet mirror, as if she'd look appreciably different from two steps farther away. She cocked her head at her own reflection.

"It helps," she said. "To get it right, you almost have to be too close to actually see it. What's going on? Why are you in here?"

Gabe Lazarus hadn't so much as mentioned her mother, Madison realized. This hadn't seemed odd in the moment, in the bar, but now she thought of it. He'd talked about the jobs her father could get, the ways her father's image could be softened. *Cardiac surgeon? Electrical engineer?* His voice childish with scorn, then wavering with regret for having pushed her to reveal her own embarrassment.

"Sweetheart? Why are you lurking like a ghost," Isabel said. "What's going on?"

Madison sat on the edge of the bathtub. She could say it, if she wanted. She was dying to kneel down under the weight and let her mother shoulder some of it, finally.

"I want to ask you about something," she said. Her mother was bent over, swirling a thick black brush through face powder. She looked up at Madison now, her eyes such a clear blue in this light that they looked almost deadened, inanimate. Her mother must know. Shouldn't she? That Madison's father had confided in her, that Madison knew important things, or at least knew that there were important things unsaid. Which meant that they could discuss the business card Madison had tucked into her evening purse, as carefully as if it were parchment.

"Can it wait? Is it going to be a problem at the party, or can it wait until we've gotten through this?"

"It can wait," Madison said.

Her mother blinked at herself in the mirror, then met Madison's eye there, in the glass.

"Did your father say something to you?"

"Not really," Madison said, truthful.

"Well, then, good," Isabel said. "Remind me tomorrow. Let's just get through tonight. Smile like we mean it. Right?"

Madison nodded.

"Have you checked in on the boys?"

The twins were still insisting on sleeping in bed together. Madison tried to recall any time she'd sat with her brothers in recent weeks, actually comforted or reassured them. Done anything more than pull on their earlobes or crack a few jokes that even eight-year-olds must find lame. She blinked the question away, and looked up at her mother.

"Go check on them, Madison. And get your purse together. We need to be downstairs to meet the car in ten minutes."

FORTY-TWO

Mina stood in her strapless bra and her thigh-highs and her heels, proud of herself that after such a stressful winter she had no need for any sort of control-top anything. She looked down at the butter yellow dress laid across her divan and wondered if it was too late to choose something else, something more muted. Tom came into her closet and whistled. She pretended to ignore him, and he turned away.

"Are you ready?" she asked, following him back out into the bedroom. He flopped onto their bed, the clinking ice in the glass he held answering her question. "I'm serious, Tom. We need to be out of here by seven at the latest."

Tom pondered this, and instead of turning on the TV, as she'd expected, or even disappearing into his own closet, where he had another TV he could have watched unharried, he stared down at his drink. Clear, so vodka rocks. Which was usually only before the nights he dreaded the most.

"You don't think he'll really be there, do you?"

Mina left nothing on her face. She could already feel her lipstick caking at the corners of her mouth.

"I'm sure he will," she said. "Either he's there or none of them are."

He peered up at her, and she saw that this wasn't the first vodka.

"I don't want to see that fucking guy," he said.

She flung down the gown she'd been scrutinizing.

"Fine," she said. "You don't want to go?"

"Can we have an adult conversation about this?" he said. "Or do you feel the need to be a smart-ass with me? Can I just admit to you what I'm thinking?"

She went over to him and bopped her hip repeatedly against the side of his leg until he scooted over, clearing a sliver of the bed for her to colonize. She pressed her body against his.

"I'm sorry," she said. "Tell me what you're thinking."

"I'm thinking he's either smarter than anyone's given him credit for," Tom said, "or he's a total fucking idiot. They still haven't announced whether there will be any indictments. And who knows, they might hold off on that. It'll be another year even before the examiner releases the report on the bankruptcy. He should be doing what Jim McGinniss has done, go so far underground that no one's even sure he's still alive."

"It's just Greenwich," Mina said. "He's been to a million of these things. They both have."

"But he shouldn't be going anywhere," Tom said. "He should be holed up in that eyesore of theirs out in Sun Valley. He shouldn't be escorting his perfect wife, who's done absolutely nothing to deserve this, to Suzanne Welsh's backyard clambake like they're in the same boat as the rest of us. What is anyone even going to talk about with him? He's been the ghost of Christmas Past all winter. He's been letting her run interference for him."

Mina tried to hold on to her sympathy, her warmth. She tried to feel it within her, to sense its fragility the way she could feel her anniversary diamonds when she wore them, light beneath her fingertips but heavy, solid, across her sternum. ("Since odds are we won't make it to our seventy-fifth," Tom had said when he gave them to her, then insisted he'd been referring to heart disease, not divorce or infidelity, when she burst into tears.)

But she couldn't. She tried not to focus on the one small part where he'd complimented Isabel, the place where she'd felt his throat constrict beneath her. But she was out of practice, maybe, and coming unexpectedly as it did, this rage, it tingled her limbs until she had to move.

She stood up from the bed and walked away from her husband.

"Well, then we'd better get there early," she said.

"Why?"

"He'll need some friendly faces."

"And someone nominated me? You know I can't stand that guy."

They watched each other for a moment, and for the tenth, twentieth, hundredth time that year, she saw her husband make the decision not to ask her how she spent her afternoons, or when she'd last seen Isabel.

"Please get up and get dressed," she said. "It's not exactly a clambake."

FORTY-THREE

Lily had been waiting in the foyer with the boys for almost fifteen minutes. Madison was in the kitchen with a towel thrown around her shoulders like a cashmere wrap, cautiously eating a grapefruit. The adults hadn't yet shown themselves.

"Why does Madison get to have a snack?" Luke asked.

"Sweetie," Lily said. "We've been over this. You'd make a huge mess. Madison's older."

Luke sank to a low step, propping his elbows on his knees, his entire body deflated by the denial of his request. Lily looked nervously, for the third time in as many minutes, up toward the second floor. Isabel's instructions were to have the twins ready a half hour ago. Here they were, with their gel-tamed hair and their matching tuxedos, their mint green pocket squares, and she could see that all they wanted was for their mother to come coo over their handsomeness.

Matteo walked to the staircase, too, and sat down beside Luke.

And then Isabel was rushing down the stairs in a floor-length black dress, her hand coasting along the banister. She saw the boys and clapped her hands, then turned to Lily.

"Have you seen him?"

Lily shook her head.

"Madison?"

"Kitchen."

Isabel passed into the kitchen without another word, and moments later Madison came out again. She walked down the hallway to her father's study. Her face, despite Lily's efforts, was impossible to read. Since their conversation on the way home from the city, the conversation about Gabe, Madison had provided no clues at all.

The boys were standing now at the foot of the staircase, turning from Lily to their mother and waiting to be told the plan. They'd inched closer so that, even though they weren't holding hands, their shoulders and arms were pressed together. Lily wanted to cross to them, but she knew that her portion of the evening was fading out, that Isabel and Madison were in charge now. Her services were no longer needed. From now on, it was the D'Amico hour.

Moments later, as if he'd just been waiting for his daughter to fetch him, Bob was coming down the hallway, also clapping his hands, calling for the twins and dropping to one knee to let them tackle him.

"What, is Mom still getting dressed? We've gotta get this show on the road!" he yelled meaningfully, looking up at the staircase.

Isabel came out of the kitchen and looked first at him, then at her daughter. No one was looking at Lily anymore. Certainly not the twins, who were tugging at their father's tie with gusto.

"Boys, enough," Isabel said, crossing the room to her husband, the skirt of her dress purring as she moved. She held out one hand to her husband, then pulled at his tie with three sharp motions, tucking it back properly beneath the jacket.

Before they'd finished, Madison was at the front door. Lily took Luke's hand, put her fingers to the back of Matteo's neck, but Madison was already beckoning them forward to the car waiting outside. Her parents followed her lead.

FORTY-FOUR

Madison had been to parties like this one before. She'd been to *so* many parties like this one. Parties where her mother or father was a guest of honor, parties where they'd been in some integral way involved with the event's planning. She'd seen them speak on the stage at the main level of the *Intrepid* or in the lobby of MoMA, for actual charities, things that were a much bigger deal than this little party at Suzanne Welsh's house. And still, as the town car crested the top of Wyatt's front drive, circled the fountain, waited in the line of Range Rovers and Jags and the occasional black town car like theirs, Madison held one wrist with her other hand to keep it from twittering, anxious, in her lap.

The car glided into place. The attendant, a man her father's age, was suddenly looming at the window.

"We could have just driven ourselves this year," Isabel said.

"This is important," her father replied, and Madison saw that this was only the most recent in what must have been a series of barbed exchanges. She saw that these had been resolved not through some harmonious arrival at agreement; they'd just been dropped in attrition, merely abandoned. But wasn't her father still sleeping downstairs in his study? So when were these minor skirmishes taking place?

The man outside was pulling the door open. He peered into the car, his neck tilted like a jack-in-the-box, then reeled back to urge them forward, to the house.

And then Isabel was gone, already facing the rest of the night with her back to her husband and daughter. She adjusted her stole, then extended a hand for each of the boys. Madison didn't know why her mother had chosen that wrap to wear. It was too heavy for the breezy night, and her mother's arms jutted out from the fur at extreme angles, like the legs of a spider.

The twins walked alongside Isabel, flanking her. Only Madison was left behind. Her father clutched her arm, just above the elbow.

"What is the point in coming out here tonight if we're going to slink in like gate-crashers? Right, Mad?"

She could smell the Laphroaig on his breath and fought a brief spasm of irritation that he hadn't wanted to talk to her before the party, have a drink alone together.

She winked at her father, and he kissed the top of her head. They followed the rest of their family.

She glanced back once, just before they were swallowed up by the maw of the front door, the house, its second fountain. There was a small, familiar blond woman climbing out of a limousine, two cars behind theirs in the queue. Madison felt her father's hand stutter against her back, felt him recoil if only for a second, and that was how she knew that he had seen the woman, too. Even if later she would want so badly to tell herself that he'd had no warning.

MINA KEPT THINKING that the house was different. There was a new addition off the old living room, new landscaping. A waterfall, for God's sake. It all had to be new; surely she would have noticed it, last year. But then, it was so hard to say what this evening would have felt like a year ago.

"It's so good of you," some woman said to Suzanne. "So generous, really. I sort of almost feel like this is the first time I've really been out of the house in months. We all needed this. It's tradition!"

"Of course, this year more than ever," another woman said. Mina could not remember either woman's name. She couldn't remember coming over here. Tom had left her alone shortly after they arrived, promised to be back soon with a glass of wine. Mina felt a sense of paying dues, fussing over Suzanne now to avoid trouble later. But what trouble was that? The worst that would happen was probably that some small gesture of hers would offend Tom, that she'd find herself thrown back into the car a few hours early, driven home alongside a husband in a white fury.

"The timing just couldn't be better. Everyone's happy to finally be here," Suzanne said. "It's been a touchy winter, no? Don't get me wrong—I can understand some of it. I mean, I hardly even feel I belong in a house like this, sometimes. It's all Bill! But what can you do?"

"Well, you're hardly Brad and Alexandra," another woman agreed, stretching her lips as she spoke and raising her eyebrows in that nice-lady-pantomime of a whisper, of actual discretion. "I don't see a house for the Zamboni anywhere on *your* property."

"Oh!" Suzanne said, putting one hand to her chest and dipping her contorted smile toward her champagne glass. This chick must be a newcomer, Mina thought. Alexandra Barker might pop up at her shoulder any minute. And once she did, any casual observer might mistake *her* for the party's hostess rather than Suzanne. Disapproving talk of the Barkers was strictly verboten in groups this large.

Mina could feel her nausea up in her throat now, tightening her jaw. Every day of her life thus far had depended on keeping two distinct and self-sustaining places clear in her brain, two places to put the data and details of the world around her. But now it was all bleeding over, barriers had been breached, and she didn't feel safe showing her face in public when she no longer knew what she might be accidentally giving away. What she might be trading, without realizing she'd agreed to a trade.

Many of these other women were like Mina, had grown up in places that were nothing like this, but they'd forgotten it so fast.

They'd blinked, and then suddenly they were women who deserved this, who could talk to Isabel D'Amico and pretend they understood her. The only thing that remained of their old selves was the survival instinct, the willingness to claw another woman out of the way.

Where was her husband? Mina looked over her shoulder. For a moment she saw him, champagne flutes in his hands, talking to another man whose face she couldn't see. He definitely saw her; he met her eye and then shook his head once, with finality.

Suzanne was greeting a new arrival, a much younger woman and her surely sweaty-palmed husband, probably a new hire somewhere, maybe even Brad Barker's fund. The woman Mina didn't know had drifted away from their group, moving slowly and as if without intent toward the bar. She was talking now to some other blonde, very put together, more hard-edged and in a low-cut gown. Just a little too much weight carried through her haunches to really pull it off nicely. Maybe someone in from the city for the night, some Carnegie Hill second wife? But she looked familiar, actually. Mina wished for her glasses, but she hadn't worn them out in public since she was twenty-six.

The party was gathering steam, now. What had been a few clusters of tinkling small talk was now the rhythmic churning of festive noise. People were moving on to the third glass of wine; it was flowing in them, heating their blood, reminding them that there was no point in being here if they were only going to act like this was a funeral. Women were permitting themselves to laugh, regretting it when their voices grew too shrill but not regretting the impulse itself. It reminded Mina, with the dark blue trees at the party's edge, the lights strung through them, of one of the books she'd read as an undergraduate. When she'd moved to the city, everything had been too fraught with the potential for disaster to leave time for reading. And even once her life had taken a shape it wasn't likely to lose, she hadn't gone back to novels. She'd spent these last twenty years just trying to keep her balance. Her life wasn't busy, maybe, but it was demanding.

She sighed, feeling the pain of exhaustion even in her fingernails. And then she saw Isabel, standing with Bob and Madison at a table at the edge of the lawn. Isabel already had a glass in her hand; she was leaning, slightly, to catch something Bob whispered in her ear. She was laughing.

How had they done this? How, when everyone on this lawn was just waiting for them to arrive, had they managed to shuffle themselves into the crowd like cards lost in a deck?

Mina checked that Tom was still facing away from her, that he wouldn't catch a glimpse of Isabel, before she walked over to their table. Just before she was within shouting distance, Bob looked up and grinned. He put his arms in the air, probably for a hug, but he looked like a drunk wind-up toy. She stopped, almost wondered if she shouldn't approach them. But then that was absurd, he'd already seen her, he was flailing for her. She smiled back at him.

There was laughter behind her again. But this time it was unnatural, synchronized, as if the crowd had begun, as one creature, to roar.

MADISON WAS LOOKING FOR CHIP. She hadn't texted him since she'd left his house; it seemed like it would be desperate, maybe. But now, here she was, totally not desperate, but with no way to prepare herself if he should materialize next to her with a pilfered drink from an unattended tray. She wasn't even sure he was back from Florida yet.

As she stood with her parents at a bar table, she tried to imagine some options for what to say to Chip if he should appear before them. But she could only think of his hands on her shoulders that afternoon on the couch, the way he'd pushed down on the crown of her head.

If I had any nerve, she thought, I would have let that man kiss me, that poor guy at the bar in December. Poor, balding Hugh. I would have practiced on him, and then the Chip situation wouldn't have been such a complete disaster.

"Ground control to Major Tom," her father said. "Hello in there." He snapped his fingers in the air just in front of Madison's face. She tried not to blush; it wasn't like he could read her mind, not yet. She smiled and sipped from her water glass.

So far, things were incredibly normal, more normal than anyone would have dared even to hope. Her mother had gone to the bar while her father remained with Madison; that was the only appreciable difference from routine, other than the fact that her father was drinking wine. It seemed like things could continue to unfurl. They'd be seated with Mina and Tom. Her mother, through some method, would have seen to that. Suzanne wouldn't have refused that request.

Mina came over to them, and Madison's father waved. He was making double gestures, everything exaggerated, as if it were being done underwater and so needed twice as much force to achieve its objectives.

"Can we leave yet?" Mina said, pouting theatrically. "Tom abandoned me as soon as we got here. He's punishing me for making him attend."

"He'll be fine once we get some grub."

"Oh, Bob, how right you are there."

"Is Jaime home?" Madison said. Mina paused to take a sip of her wine.

"Too much work," she replied. "She's cooped up in her dorm room for their whole spring break, can you believe it? Oh, Madison, she would be so thrilled to get an e-mail from you. Or even just a text to say hi. She hasn't been home since the summer, can you imagine?"

"We haven't talked in a while," Madison said. "But I can—I'll send her an e-mail."

She was willing to bet that the only homesickness in this situation was the ache always resident within Mina. But then it meant that the promise cost Madison nothing, it could slip right off her tongue without consequence. If her mother had taught her only one thing, it was how to grant those sorts of promises.

"Have you said hello to Suzanne?" Mina asked Isabel. Bob leaned his head in toward theirs.

"We're girding our loins," he said, and Mina threw back her head, laughed. Madison saw her mother's spine briefly torque, as if stretching a shoulder sore from tennis, before she snapped back to her normal posture.

"Well, you'll probably get the sanitized greeting," Mina said. "You should have heard the earful I got. She's 'scaled down' this year because it 'felt more appropriate.' She made a speech about how people don't understand, when they talk downsizing, how many people it takes to keep her house in order and her pool clean. She said that if we scale back, that's what gets scaled. Those jobs."

"Well, she may be right, there," Bob said. "I'm sure she said it for all the wrong reasons, but people who talk about revolutionizing 'how we live today' don't usually understand the first thing about what it would mean."

Madison saw Amanda and her parents disappear into the crowd near one of the bars. "Mom," she began, but Isabel set down her wineglass with ostentatious precision, as if afraid she'd break it. She fumbled with the clasp of her clutch, then looked up again.

"What," Bob said, and turned to follow the path of his wife's eye.

"Oh," Mina said. "Oh, God, I should have said something. I saw her but she looks different, no? I couldn't remember why she looked familiar. She's put on weight. And her hair, it's so much longer."

"Who is that?" Madison said.

They were all looking at a blond woman in the middle of the crowd. She was talking to a short, heavyset man with gray hair, but his face was obscured, at first, by all the other bodies.

"Who is she?" Madison said again. No one replied. They acted as if she hadn't even spoken. And so, fine, she thought, fine. She left them there. She went to look for Chip, Amanda, anyone.

She had seen the blond woman before, even before she saw her out front. She couldn't remember where. The man with her was Jim McGinniss, her father's former right-hand man, which did not make any sense at all.

LILY SPENT THE EARLY EVENING in the kitchen with a celebrity gossip magazine. It could be worse, she thought, she could nanny for one of *those* poor bastard's families. She tried and failed not to think about how the party must be going, ignoring the temptation to open a bottle of wine. What would she say if they came home early? It should have been enough, getting caught back in December, Bob's clear disinterest in ever reminding her that they'd caught each other. His certainty that they'd keep each other's secrets.

But it wasn't enough, of course, and that was what the experience had taught her. Misbehavior, wrongdoing, becomes both the appetite and the food; it creates a space for itself and then demands more and more to keep its desires sated.

She'd been thinking this way ever since her conversation with Madison the week before. Whether Bob locked his study when he left for his mystery afternoon "jogs." Whether Madison had really seen him hide a key to a desk drawer, and whether that meant much of anything.

Her phone danced on the tabletop, jerking over the uneven knots in the wood. It was Jackson, again. She hadn't spoken to him in several days, but he'd called four times since this morning.

She grabbed her keys from the glass dish on the counter. She wasn't due to fetch the boys for another hour at least, but she couldn't sit here alone in the house anymore. Every surface in the house looked like the temptation to touch, open, read, remember. And that wasn't her choice to make; it was Madison's.

She went outside and got into the car.

"HOW HAS IT BEEN?" Amanda asked.

"I'm not sure," Madison said. They were moving through the crowd together, making looping, directionless arcs around the bar. At one point Madison saw Jake and Lori, standing alone at a cocktail table, fretful and conspicuous. She linked Amanda's pinkie with her own and steered her off into another current through the crowd. Whatever had changed, in the way she felt about Amanda and her abandonment last summer, it felt far too rickety and circumstantial to survive a conversation with Jake Levins. If he was too chicken to apologize to a fifteen-year-old girl, well then, that was fine. He didn't get a cheek kiss.

Madison briefly cased the bartenders, wondered which one would be likeliest to serve her. All around her, everything looked and sounded only almost like a party. There were peals of laughter that sounded more like shrieks. The lime glow of the pool beckoned, its underwater lights distorted by ripples, the perpetual harassing whisper of its waterfall. The lanterns in the trees and the greenish moon low in the sky, together, cast unnatural shadows on the faces.

Madison wandered, with Amanda, closer to the dinner tables grouped around the dance floor. The microphones up on the dais would later be used to thank everyone for doing the exact same things they'd done last year, and the year before that.

Amanda kept peering furtively at the faces in the crowd; Madison couldn't imagine why.

The centerpieces were so much simpler than usual that they felt showy. Some general green frippery surrounding what was ultimately just a large glass bowl, deep and round, filled with water and one single floating gardenia. Madison breathed in that smell, the gardenias, felt it settle within her. And so when she saw him it was almost as if she'd summoned him, called him to her with a secret whistle.

Zoë and Allie and Wyatt were moving across the grass, and Chip dawdled behind them, his hands in his pockets, extending his legs slowly with each step. She didn't think she had ever seen him in a tux before.

"You're not really supposed to be over here yet, D'Amico," Wyatt said amiably, in greeting. "They'll make an announcement for dinner."

Allie gave Madison a jerky hug, her elbows hitting the soft parts of Madison's torso.

"When did you get here?"

"Ages ago," Madison lied.

"Your whole family?" Zoë said this without moving any part of her face but her mouth.

"Yes," Madison said. Allie let her gaze flit from Zoë to Madison with tangible unease.

Wyatt turned his back on the party and showed Madison the inside pocket of his jacket. He had a flask tucked against the patterned fabric of the lining, which matched his vest.

"You want?"

Chip was studying the crowd with effort, clearly seeking an excuse to walk away.

"I'm good, thanks," she told Wyatt.

"You guys both look *so* pretty," Allie blurted out. "Amanda, I love your dress! I can't believe you're here, I thought your mom hated these things. My mom always says your mom is way too smart for the rest of us."

"Well, ladies," Wyatt said, and Madison was actually impressed by the smoothness of his intervention. "No one seems very excited about my flask! Levins, I remember you knocking 'em back like a champion at Halloween. Come on. Do a shot with me."

Amanda ignored him. Chip still hadn't looked at Madison. As she watched him, she caught sight of her again, the blond woman from outside.

Too late, she felt Zoë turn to follow her gaze.

"Oh, right. That's the woman your dad fired, isn't it?"

The words were still in the air, ready to be ignored by all six of them, when Zoë turned to Amanda.

"Do you think that's her?" she said. "Madison, she told you how she saw your dad in the city with some woman, right? She told us about it at Halloween. God, Amanda, you were so hammered, do you even remember any of this?"

Then, without the announcement Wyatt had promised, the adults had begun to move. The crowd came in a mass across the wide lawn, dozens of women picking their way across the grass in their stiletto heels, balanced unsteadily on their husbands, who always seemed to move a few beats faster. Madison looked for her parents and didn't see them.

"I have to go," she said, but Chip was already leaving. He didn't turn back, but Wyatt did. He slid his right arm around Madison's waist, his fingers fumbling at her hip.

"My parents bought a few," Zoë was whispering to Chip. "They auctioned off all of it, my mother had a field day. Her mother collected so much amazing stuff."

Madison wanted to follow them, to grab Zoë by the roots of her fake blond hair and force her to say that again, say it louder, hand her the deejay's microphone and have her say it up on the dais for everyone to hear as the party sat down to dinner. But Wyatt's hands were still at Madison's waist. Her dress was cut on the bias, and all she could think was that his fingers would leave the fabric crinkled, that it would be obvious someone had grabbed her dress with his sweaty hand.

"Don't mind Abbott," he said. "You know what he's like, you know he's always going to be looking for someone who's on his level. Who wants to do the things he wants to do."

She blinked at him for a moment, unseeing, reluctant to understand. Wyatt pulled back from her, his brow furrowed with malice or concern, or both.

"Look," he said, "it's none of my business. I just wanted you to know that I know he was a jerk, that's all. He can be a jerk, right? And you shouldn't feel like it's because of anything else, like you're too damaged for him right now or whatever. That wasn't it."

His hands were on her again.

"Excuse me?"

"I'm just saying," Wyatt said. "You got good reviews. If you ever want to, like, move on to the grown-up stuff, I'd be down."

He contorted his face, his mouth closed, his tongue pushing lewdly against the inside of one cheek. His hands were still on Madison's hips, and she reared back to put her own hands to his shoulders. She was ready to shove him, hard. She wanted to see him flat on his ass, on the ground below where she stood.

But Amanda moved in, put one hand over Wyatt's, squeezed his knuckles.

"Not a good idea," she said. "When you sober up tomorrow, I think you'll agree with me."

"Fuck off, Levins," Wyatt said, cheerful and unruffled. He turned and began to thread his way through the dinner tables, hands in his pockets.

"By the time he gets to his mother, what do you want to bet he's not 'totally wasted' anymore?" Amanda said.

"What?" Madison said, and Amanda's smirk faltered.

"Look," she said. "Obviously I never meant to say anything to Zoë about it, I mean that's obvious, right? I just didn't know if I should—I didn't even see anything. I just saw him in the street with that woman. That's it."

Most people had filtered toward the tent, for dinner, but there were stragglers enough still to keep the bars mobbed. The waiters with their silver trays of untouched food were filing back into the house, the party's staging area, to get ready for the next part of the job.

"It was that blond woman?" Madison said. "The one who's here? She used to work for him. You saw them together and you just . . . decided not to tell me?"

"Madison, come on," Amanda said again. "What do I know about any of it? It was probably nothing."

"Please don't talk to me," Madison said. "You should go find your dad. Find your own table."

MINA AND ISABEL WERE SEATED, waiting for the others. Mina tucked her evening bag into her lap, and Tom appeared at her elbow with a tumbler in his hand. Her champagne was nowhere in sight.

A uniformed staff member of some kind, a middle-aged Hispanic woman who avoided eye contact with anyone else at the table, brought the boys to their seats, presumably at Isabel's request. Madison came next, arriving in a flurry—playing with her hair, kissing the boys, making sure they were both situated in the grown-up chairs and could reach their forks and knives, their water glasses. She looked up at Mina, expressionless, and then looked down at her lap. Mina could see that she was taking that moment to draw herself in, to *keep* the face expressionless. When she looked up again, though, her eyes fixed on something over Mina's shoulder, back toward the house.

Whatever it was, it was gone by the time Mina craned her neck.

"Madison?" she said. "Everything all right?"

Tom settled himself heavily in his chair.

"Where is he," he muttered. He touched Mina's hand and then looked at her intently in a way she could not interpret.

"Isabel," he said, without looking away from Mina. "Jim is here, too."

Isabel held herself erect, waiting for him to say more.

"McGinniss?"

Tom nodded, sucking his ice.

"Where's Bob?"

"I don't keep track of your husband, Mrs. D'Amico," Tom said. Mina looked at the boys, who didn't appear to be listening to anyone but each other. Her husband couldn't seem to decide whether he was Isabel's protector or her primary detractor, and what had seemingly begun with solicitous concern had in the span of two seconds become something darker, nasty.

"All right," Mina said, trying to pitch it so her voice would be audible to Tom but still lose itself in the tinkling and rustling from neighboring tables. Isabel was looking back at the house, scanning its many heaped stories and their darkened windows. She bit her bottom lip.

"Do you want me to go with you?" Mina said. She could feel her husband radiating heat just beside her. Their bodies were touching at the elbow, at the thigh.

"I don't know where he is," Isabel said. "Where would we look?"

"He just ran down that staircase," Madison said. "There's a ballroom down on that level of the house, by the pool. He just went down there."

Isabel looked at her daughter, but Madison hadn't taken her eyes off the twins.

"We'll both go," Mina repeated uselessly.

"No," Isabel said. "Just watch the boys for a minute."

She stood and left the dance floor, darting back across the lawn. Mina glanced at the neighboring tables without turning her head, and she could see that everyone was rigorously focused on their own conversations. Which meant that most of them would have been paying close attention as Isabel D'Amico walked away from dinner.

Tom sucked his teeth, and Mina whirled on him.

"What?" she said. "I thought she'd done absolutely nothing to deserve this. Sweetheart."

Tom stared at her for so long that she worried she'd need to get the twins out of the way, to another table. Madison mattered less. If she was paying attention, she'd already seen everything from Tom that Mina would have liked to keep private.

But Tom set his jaw and turned unexpectedly to the boys. He cut Mina off with his entire body, inching his chair away from her. He peered at the twins, dubious.

"You're really going to eat this food?" he asked them. Matteo gave him a robust nod.

Madison stood up and pushed away from the table.

"Madison, I don't think—" Mina hissed, but what power did Mina have to keep this girl from following her mother? Madison lifted her dress with an elegant flick of the wrist and hurried across the lawn. From a few tables over, Jake Levins's daughter, too, jumped to her feet. She raced after Madison, moving with longer strides.

Isabel had already vanished somewhere beneath the house. Mina tried to think of something she could do, any single thing that wouldn't make the overall situation worse. She turned to the twins. They gazed back, impassive. They didn't ask her any questions. Later, that would seem most chilling. Their lack of surprise at having been brought here, propped up, and then abandoned. This is what they expect, she thought. This is all they know to expect from him, from her. What are they going to learn from this? Later, when they understand that they were a part of this, what will they think was the point?

"You know Jim's here with that girl," Tom said, mumbling now. "That Erica girl they fired."

Mina put her napkin on the table and began to stand up, but Tom locked his fingers around her wrist.

"No," he said.

She froze, hovering above her chair, neither seated nor walking away.

"It's not—it's not about her," Tom said. "I'm not unsympathetic, Min. I'm just, telling you. Trust me, for once. Don't follow them. He is not your problem."

"She's my friend," Mina tried, but her husband's grip tightened.

"You want to lie to me all year," he said through his teeth, "keep me in the dark, like I'm your idiot kid. That's fine. I can look the other way. But right now, that's not *your* husband. That's not *your* problem. You sit down and you eat dinner with these little boys."

He kept his hand around her wrist, and he put his other hand to her lap, her thigh. He knocked her purse to the ground.

"MADISON," AMANDA CALLED, as she tried to close the last few feet left between them. "Please let me explain. I wasn't trying to keep a secret from you."

They had already reached the staircase, which led down to the lower level of the house, to the rooms by the pool.

"I'm sorry," Amanda said. "You should have had all the information. I shouldn't have kept it from you. I know that, Madison, I know."

Someone had mentioned a ballroom down here, Amanda remembered now, at that excruciating party. She could hardly believe that she'd actually come here willingly that night. But I guess I did it again tonight, she thought. And then Madison opened a door tucked into the side of the house, and they were in a darkened room with polished maple floors and a mirror that ran the length of one wall.

The only light came from a single sconce at the far end, placed to illuminate the staircase that led back up into the house. A group of people stood in the middle of the room.

Amanda wanted to reach for Madison's hand, but that was no way to communicate anything. Holding hands achieved nothing. And besides, she knew now, with a certainty she'd avoided all year, that hers wasn't a hand Madison would ever seek out again.

Twenty minutes ago, standing with Madison and trying desperately to intuit what her friend needed most, Amanda had seen this woman in the crowd and thought, it's the yoga pants woman. She had needed no time to shuffle through recollections in her head, no time to think of faces she might have forgotten. She recognized the face as soon as she saw it. She knew it was the woman she'd seen in the city, with Bob.

Now that woman was facing them, standing with an older guy at her side. Amanda knew from her father's past wrath that this was the former COO, that he'd once been Bob's second in command. Two other people were facing them, their backs to Amanda. And then they became aware that someone had come into the room, and turned, and Bob and Isabel were staring at Madison.

There was a suspended quality to the silence in the room. Everyone's hands looked uncomfortable in the spaces around their bodies.

"Why are *you* down here," Madison said, hurling her voice at her father with something almost like a cough.

"Mad, get out," Bob rasped. He was watching Jim McGinniss and the other woman, as if they might try to use Madison as a diversion, and escape.

"Madison, go back to the table." Isabel was watching her husband.

"No," Madison said. "What's going on?"

Jim laughed, the sound echoing, eerie. He turned to Bob and raised his palms to face the ceiling.

"You wanna keep going with this?" he said. "In front of your kid?"

"This?" Bob said. "What is it we're doing here, Jimbo? Do we call this extortion, harassment, or just bad behavior?"

Hearing him somehow made Amanda feel more frantic; it wasn't enough to be controlling her own emotions if Bob D'Amico couldn't control his. He had the power to change everything about the room, right now, but she didn't think he understood that. He didn't look like he understood anything now; he looked like a snarling dog, held back by a choke chain. Even though Isabel wasn't so much as touching him.

Amanda tried to remember everything her father had written about this woman. Her name was Erica Leary. Geary? No, Leary. The one they fired along with Jim, trying to stanch the bleeding—her dad's words—last summer. Maybe the only person in the world Amanda's father had less regard for than either Jim or Bob.

It was suddenly inconceivable to Amanda that she'd never Googled this woman, that she hadn't put together the scrubbed, drawn face she saw on Lexington that day with the woman from Weiss.

Like every other reminder that year of her previous ignorance, her careless inattention to the things that dictated the course of her own life, it made Amanda want to look away. But of course it was too late now; she was in the room with the entire lineup. She couldn't look away. The D'Amicos might feel that they had that luxury, but Amanda knew better.

"Madison, go back upstairs," Isabel said. She kept her eyes on her husband.

Erica Leary hadn't spoken a word. She was moving, one mincing step at a time, backward. She was trying to get to the staircase so she could leave the room.

"No," Madison said again.

"Enough." Isabel finally touched her husband's arm. "Jim, this isn't the place. If you'd like to discuss something, I suggest you call our lawyers. I know you have all the relevant information. You can set up a meeting in the city. I don't want you in our home."

"Of course not," Jim said. "Of course you don't, Mrs. D."

"Enough," Isabel repeated. We're all repeating ourselves too much, Amanda thought.

"You fucking show up to ambush me like this," Bob repeated, spitting his consonants as if from behind his molars.

"Ambush," Erica said finally. "Ambush, Bob? Really?"

And then Isabel turned, and Amanda could see her face in the mirror. She gave the woman a look that split the room in two. Something very delicate had been resting on this, the woman's silence, Isabel's refusal to acknowledge her. Amanda shuddered.

"You knew they were going to be here," Isabel said to her husband. It wasn't a question. Her voice slashed the air like a sharpened knife through delicate fabric, left a gash when it was through. No one should respond to that voice, Amanda thought, no one should ever want to speak next.

And Bob knew that voice well enough that he didn't even make the attempt.

"I thought that if we got the principals together in one room,"

Erica said, but she'd used up all the nerve she had to spare, Amanda could see. Isabel had cut her down.

And then the door behind them made a sucking sound, and someone pulled it open.

"Amanda, what in God's name," Jake said.

MADISON DIDN'T TURN TO ACKNOWLEDGE Jake Levins. Her mother had turned away from the blond woman, back to Jim. Why was her father even down here? How could Jim possibly be worth his time?

"Girls, let's go," Jake was saying. Madison could not reconcile anything in this room to the world they'd left outside, up the stairs.

"Jake, this is none of your fucking business," her father said.

"Happy to leave. Amanda, now."

"Dad," Madison said. "What's going on."

She willed him to look at her, only at her. She tried to imagine him reaching for her, beckoning her to his chest. If she imagined it, then it could happen. It was like that first morning, watching the news. When she'd felt the certainty that she could call her father home to her. If she could just turn her thoughts to him strongly enough, he'd know what to do, he'd come home. We need you at home. We *want* to flinch here, Daddy.

"Bob," Isabel said. "This is outrageous. Let's go."

"You don't know why he hasn't left yet?"

Isabel drew herself up and turned to face Jim, gave him a bland smile. She held a hand out to Bob, but kept her gaze on Jim, her back straight. She looked at once wild and contained, a series of small explosions within a thin-necked glass bottle.

Jim waved his thumb in Erica's general direction.

"What does he tell you, he's helping her prep her testimony? Does he tell you it's business? They're fucking, Isabel. They were fucking last spring, they are fucking now. Past tense, present tense. Come on, Mrs. D. If I figured it out, so did you."

Madison could feel Amanda's twitching eye on her, but she still didn't want to look at anyone but her parents.

There was suddenly a lot of noise in the room, but the effort now required just to stand there, not to shake, meant that Madison couldn't quite focus on anyone else, on all the other bodies around hers.

Somewhere near where she stood, her father tried to lunge at Jim. Amanda's father intervened, just in time to keep them apart. Jake backed Bob up toward the wall and held him there. He whispered something in a low voice.

Jim tumbled away from them and bent over, his hands on his knees. He was wheezing, even though no one had actually touched him.

"Give it a rest," he hacked, his breath rushing and receding. "We all trusted you. Everybody trusted you, and look at us now." He waved a hand toward the mirrored wall, as if talking about their own astonished reflections rather than the actual people outside, the rest of the world.

"We thought you knew what you were—"

"We all did!" Bob screamed. "I did, too! We all did."

He was so loud, and Madison could see something inside him slipping off a ledge, a fragile statue you touched with a fingertip, touched again, pushed and pushed and pushed until it toppled.

"Dad," she said again, her voice softer even though she'd tried to keep it hard. "Look at me."

He looked up, obedient. Jake let go of him.

"You promised me," Madison said. Her father said nothing, and her mother was looking up to one corner of the ceiling. As if this were a scuffle between strangers, something that didn't involve her in the slightest.

"Madison." There was no warmth at all in her father's tone, only warning.

She knew she couldn't go any further, couldn't actually beg him to repeat the things he'd said to her, alone. She couldn't beseech him any more than this. I shouldn't have to do this at all, she thought. He shouldn't be making me beg him for anything. I asked him the exact question, and he told me: I've done nothing wrong.

"Would I lie to you?" Madison asked, mimicking his cadence from that first night in the kitchen.

Her father looked down, away from her. Like *she* was embarrassing *him*.

And then it was all kaleidoscoped, as if Zoë and Chip and Wyatt were there, too. Every snide comment Madison had ignored since September, every time she'd reassured herself that no one else knew as much about this as she did. The pity she'd felt for all those other, lesser people. Those rubberneckers who were interested only in the scandal, not in the truth. And Bob D'Amico always told his daughter the truth, didn't he? He wasn't really the man everyone said he was.

Madison ran at her father, but Amanda's father caught her by the crooks of her elbows. She managed it, though, before Jake lifted her entirely up, off the ground. Before her arms buckled and he brought her back down to earth with a harsh groan, her heels hitting the floor. She got it done, first. Madison spat at her father, at his feet.

"You're disgusting," she said. "You disgust me."

She wrenched free from Jake, who seemed to know that it was time to stop holding her. The spit—an impressive amount, considering how dry her mouth had been since she came into this room—gleamed on the floor, like something radioactive spilled in an unusually elegant lab.

In the corner, Erica bent over Jim, as if he really had been punched and now needed nursing. Madison stared at her, willed her to look up, but the woman did nothing. Either she refused to meet Madison's eye, or it didn't even occur to her that maybe she should.

"Madison," her father growled, leaning forward, suggesting that he might try to stop her. She didn't look back at him and so she never knew if he was begging her, finally, or just angry. All she saw, in the mirror, was a brief flash of Isabel in her black dress, cutting him off with one arm.

"Absolutely not," her mother told her father. "Leave her alone. Absolutely not."

They were all silent, even Isabel, as Madison left the room.

HAD YOU BEEN at the Bruce Museum's annual benefit that year, during the very first public season of the financial crisis, you would have missed most of the action. It would be hard to tell later, from the way the stories were constructed—it would be hard to see any image but the two men prone, pummeling each other on the dance floor as the entire gathered party stood and looked on in horror, beneath an April moon. But that wasn't what happened.

If you had been there, you would have been pushing a frisée salad around your plate, avoiding the warm nuggets of goat cheese, at about the moment Bob made his aborted lunge at Jim. But you would have been quite aware of the two most noted absences, the empty places at the D'Amico table. And so you would have seen—everyone saw—the moment they all came bursting up from the house. You would have seen, first, Jake Levins—and why was he there, you might have asked your neighbor, this wasn't really his scene, was it? You would have seen Isabel D'Amico, like a deathly angel in that dress, a bit severe for springtime, her movements slow and deliberate. She would not look toward the party. You would have seen Mina Dawes bolt from her table, rushing across the lawn, nearly tripping over her dress, to follow Isabel.

By now the murmurs were spreading, and all eyes were on the house. Bill Welsh, droning his welcome speech up on the dais, would falter. Everyone would pretend not to look toward the house and the unpleasant surprises it kept emitting, like smoke from an ailing car engine.

Finally, you would have seen another, unfamiliar blond woman, and the entire gathered group would, as one body, question and then recall her name, and why she might be there. She would emerge from the lower level and linger, uncertain as to which exit strategy was best—and how appropriate, one of the Goldman husbands would later crack, as he told his version of this story.

You probably would have missed the daughter. She would have left the party already, without anyone seeing her, or knowing where she'd gone.

LILY ARRIVED AT THE WELSH HOUSE EARLY, as expected, and negotiated with the parking attendant. He agreed to let her park over by the garage, so she wouldn't block any latecomers. Who was he kidding, she thought. None of these people would have dared to show up late.

She had just settled in to wait when Madison came around the side of the house, pulling the Abbott kid by the hand. Lily got out of the car.

"Mad," she said, "what happened? What's going on?"

"Oh," Madison said, stopping short. "You're here." She said it without surprise. The boy stopped with her, looking not at Lily but at Madison's shoulders, her chest, letting his eyes roam across her body as she spoke.

"Are you leaving?"

"Yes," Madison said, her voice rising as if she'd been energized by the word. "Exactly. We're leaving."

Chip Abbott slid his arm around her waist, a pretty brazen gesture given that an adult was standing right there. He smiled at Lily. She saw a cramp move through Madison's body, the split-second decision to fight an impulse to push him away. Lily stepped forward in alarm.

"Madison," she said. "You can come home with me. Come on, I'll drive you right now. I'll come back later for the twins."

They all stood there waiting, comically backlit by the floodlights that lit up the carport. Madison slouched so that her hips jutted forward, her shoulders sharpened and curled as if to protect her breasts.

"Don't worry, Lil," Madison said. "I won't do anything *they* wouldn't do."

Chip snorted in involuntary appreciation, then bowed his head politely when Lily glared.

"Just come home," Lily said. "Whatever it is, we can talk about it."

But Madison shook her head with a vague gesture, her eyes already wandering away from Lily's face, up to the trees and the dark driveway beyond the house.

"I'm fine," she said. She took Lily's hand and looked right at her again. "God, Lily, you look like you're going to cry."

Lily shook her head.

"I wish you'd come back with me," she said. "Now."

Madison reached out and began to rub Lily's thumb with hers in just the same way Lily did for the boys, when they couldn't sleep.

"I don't know," Madison said. "They *should* be worried. I don't want to sound spoiled, but they should be at least a little bit afraid of me. If they even notice I'm gone."

Then she turned back to Chip and he took her hand. They moved away together, almost trotting down the hill toward the front gate. Chip gave a quick salute to the guard standing at the top of the drive, and Lily saw with dread that he knew this house, knew its systems and knew that they would be ignored in favor of letting him do whatever he wanted.

"Lil," Madison called back once, before disappearing down the hill. "You should show them to my mom. The stuff we talked about. You should show it all to my mom. Let her figure it out."

Lily cursed under her breath, looking back and forth from the guard to the creepy man in the tuxedo at the front door. It had to be that something had happened with Bob; Madison had looked too scattered, too removed from her own limbs, for it to be something less than that.

She's allowed, Lily thought. She knew she was justifying her own failure, her own inability to keep Madison from leaving, but still she

thought: Madison is allowed. She's allowed to choose her own preferred source of pain, if she wants. They can't tell her not to do that.

She turned back just in time to see Mina emerge from the same
dark garden at the side of the house, squinting at a black town car
that had just driven up. She had Matteo at her side and Luke on her
hip, his shoes surely muddying that gown.

"Mina," Lily said, "what the hell—"

"Oh, God. You're here, you're here. Can you get them home right
now? Just drive them straight home?"

"What happened? Where's Isabel?"

"She's just tying up a few loose ends," Mina said, with the kind of
vague look Lily knew meant she had no fucking clue, exactly, where
Isabel was. "I think she went into the house. I can bring her back
later, I had my car come back."

"The kids will want her to come home with us," Lily said. "Did
she just leave them here alone?"

She lowered herself to the ground, briefly, to meet Matteo's bab-
bling, the noises he was making more like keening than conversation.
She ran her hands down his arms, smoothing the wrinkles in his
jacket.

"I'm going to call your security," Mina said, ignoring the question. "They'll be ready to meet you guys there. You need to make sure
he's aware that they need to be on call tonight in case anything—
anything else, happens. And he can start having his guys look for
Madison."

"What happened?"

"It was . . . unpleasant. Jim McGinniss was here."

"Bob?"

"Well—yes. I didn't see exactly what happened."

"But other people saw it."

"Well," Mina said, and she looked at Lily with an evasive gaze,
like a child with a chocolate-stained face who's just been asked to
account for herself. "No, not too much. But—Madison was there.

She heard it, and saw it, and everything. I'm not sure, I wasn't—I wasn't in the room. " She wasn't looking Lily in the eye.

Any fool could have looked at Bob and told you he wasn't ready to be back out in front of everyone yet. As soon as they saw that Jim had shown his face, they should have tossed Bob right back in the car. Lily could have told them that.

"We don't know where Madison went," Mina said, clearly struggling to manage her frenzy. "I've made calls. We've got it under control. But we aren't sure yet where she is."

"Tell them to search the house," Lily said. "I'm sure she's just holed up in some upstairs guest bathroom."

The lie had formed on her lips before she'd fully made the decision to tell it.

"I did that," Mina said. "I did, I did."

"Well, then, good," Lily said, no longer trying to be careful with her tone. "You've got everything under control, clearly."

She pointed the twins into the backseat.

"Jim says Bob's been sleeping with that woman," Mina said. "The woman they fired last summer."

Lily slammed the door and closed her eyes for a moment, wishing Mina had waited until the boys were safely out of earshot.

"He said that when?" she said. "In front of Madison?"

"Apparently." Mina nodded her head manically. "I could kill him."

It was, quite literally, the last thing Lily had expected her to say.

"And he couldn't even be bothered to come help us look for her. And Isabel is—her mind is elsewhere."

Then it was Lily's turn to snort. But when Mina turned to her, the genuine, strangled anguish on her face was shocking, her expression as forlorn as it was confused. Then she looked away, off toward the trees down the drive, the same place Madison's eyes had wandered toward. She clutched her elbows, hugging herself, and talked up at the trees.

"If I'd just gone inside with them. Then Madison would have had me there, too. He just let his daughter storm out, Lily. You don't let a child in pain walk away from you like that. You hug her, you keep her close to you. You don't let her leave. Whatever they do when they find her, I mean—it's too late, she already knows that they let her get away. She's already seen them."

"Okay," Lily said. "I need to leave. I need to get the boys home."

Mina nodded, and Lily bottled her resentment, just for a moment. Her resentment that no one was asking her what *she* thought Madison needed, that Mina was so confident of what her role should be in these decisions. Her resentment at the ways in which Jackson, the ever-present buzzing of her phone, was right. She did not want to push it too far, her feeling that she and Mina had come down on the same side of this thing. But just for a moment she bottled it all, leaned forward, and kissed Mina on the cheek.

AMANDA HAD LEFT THE BALLROOM right after Madison, had followed her across the lawn as they both angled their bodies away from the party, but they were almost at the side garden before she caught up to her.

"Madison," she tried, but Madison immediately spun back on her.

"You want to know what you can do to help? You can make sure your father doesn't write about this. That's the only way you can be useful to me at all."

Amanda tried to control the convulsive sighs and gulps, her attempts not to burst into tears. How many times had she said something to Madison, since that day in October, how many times had she made the decision to lie? She knew exactly which moments Madison would be thinking of: I'm here for you, what do you think, what do you need. Let me help you. The only reason she hadn't lied to Madison more often was that Madison had stopped speaking to her, had robbed her of that choice.

When they turned into the garden, Madison stopped short. Chip was standing there, smoking a cigarette.

Amanda could see her friend's face, could see the unshackled feeling as it spread across Madison's features. That same way she'd looked at him back in the fall, as if he were dangling something in front of her, something essential.

"You're not at your table," he observed.

Madison shook her head and took another step forward.

"I didn't know you smoked."

He shrugged. "Whatever. It's off-season, I'm allowed."

"Is your car here?"

"Yeah," he said, "but Suzanne made me park it down the hill so it wouldn't be in the way. I was over here earlier, I left it down the street."

He said nothing to Amanda.

"Can we go somewhere," Madison said.

"Look, D'Amico," he said. "I don't know what you're really looking for, but I just don't think you and me are—"

"Can you just help me leave this party," Madison interrupted him. "I don't care if you talk to me or not. Can you just do me a favor? I just want to be somewhere else for a few hours."

Chip blinked at her, then took another cigarette from his pack. She put out her hand.

"Just do me a favor?" she repeated.

He stepped close to her, so close that their arms were touching, and put the cigarette in her mouth. When he went to light it he hunched his shoulders over the cigarette. He obviously only did it to keep any winds from snuffing it out, but Amanda could see Madison curl into him, shelter herself beneath his shoulders. She could see that Madison wanted to believe he'd done it for her, that he wanted to protect her.

"Madison," Amanda said, almost comically out of place, standing a few feet away from them. They were practically making out, at this point, and still she couldn't move.

Madison stepped away from Chip, the cigarette in her hand.

"I told you how you can help me."

"You can't just leave," Amanda said. "That's a terrible idea."

"Why?"

She had no answer.

"You shouldn't call him, though."

"Who's him?" Chip said. He blew a smoke ring.

"I'm serious," Amanda said. "Don't even look at the business card. This isn't—this isn't what we were thinking when we talked about it. This is private family stuff."

Madison laughed, then dipped her head to Chip's chest and let her hair fall across her cheek.

"Can we leave?" she asked him.

"Do you need to tell someone?"

"Can we please leave," she repeated. Her voice was frantic, but when they walked away from Amanda, toward the front courtyard, Madison was the one leading the way.

Amanda stood in the garden, waiting for something that had already failed to occur, and then went back to the party to find her father.

FORTY-FIVE

Mina sighed and watched the dark roads outside their tinted windows. She'd closed the divider that separated them from the driver, but still the strains of his music filtered through. Otis Redding, it sounded like. She smiled. Not her father's music, to be sure, and not her husband's, either. *Why have I always surrounded myself*, she thought, *with men who don't listen to good music?*

It hadn't been ideal, having to wait out front in this car until Isabel appeared, but there had been no alternative. And really, it was too late to avoid how things looked. Their table was sitting empty in the middle of the whole fucking party. Tom was waiting at the house's main entrance, waiting for the second car she'd called for him as a quick fix. Who knew where Bob had gone, how Jim and Erica had made their escape. She wondered if they'd even bought a table.

"It's not Jim's fault," Isabel said, suddenly, from her side of the car. She had her hand to her face, her knuckles pressed to her white mouth. Mina scooted closer to her.

"Well, he shouldn't have been there to begin with."

"No, I just mean he's only saying what he thinks we should all hear. He's trying to purge. It's not his fault. He's being honest."

"Well, honest doesn't mean it's right to say it out loud. And the fact that he thinks he's being honest doesn't mean he's telling the truth."

Isabel shook her head in frustration. Mina tried again, played every remaining card she had.

"They took risks, Isabel, and they bet wrong. That's not a crime. No one did anything wrong. Mistakes like theirs happen all the time. It could have happened to anyone."

"And yet," Isabel said. "And yet, it didn't. It could have happened to anyone means exactly shit, Mina. It fixes none of it."

Mina didn't know what to say to this; there was no counterargument there. Her own husband had pointed this out many times: it happened to them. They had to have done *something* wrong, those guys.

"You don't—you don't understand how they operate, Mina. You can't. I know you try, but you can't. Jim's just sticking to his own team," Isabel said. "Everyone's going to stick with their team from now on. You'll see it."

Mina's skin felt suddenly cool. She felt sure that if she put her fingertips to her forehead, she'd find beads of sweat.

"There are no teams," she tried, but even she could hear that it sounded more like a question than anything else.

"Well, there should have been. We should have known better," Isabel said, and Mina knew without asking who she meant by "we."

"They didn't want us to. They never go into specifics, you know that."

"It doesn't matter. They're *our* kids. Our daughters. What are we actually teaching them? Every good thing they know is just the absence of actual wrongdoing. We don't improve any lives, not even theirs. We don't work off our debt."

Mina closed her eyes, felt in her stomach the shifts and turns of the vehicle beneath her. It seemed unfair, she felt. What had been asked of her this year seemed unfair. She was constantly being asked to present the most palatable version of reality to everyone around her, all these different, conflicting palates. And then, when she did, she was told she was naive, clueless, on the outside. Her husband slavered over her friend and then told her *she* was the disrespectful one. Her friend wallowed in her own performed grief, as if she hadn't signed up for exactly this sort of humiliation. As if it hadn't been pure luck that Isabel hadn't experienced this sooner. So he sleeps around, Mina thought. This isn't actual suffering. It might be, down the line, but this isn't actual suffering.

And she knew what they'd all say, if she tried to express any of this to any one of them. You're so off base, Mina. You don't understand how it works. You weren't there, you don't know, you haven't been through this. You don't know as well as you think you do. You're on the outside of this, even if you think you're here with us.

Well, fine, Mina thought. Fine Tom, fine Isabel, fine Lily and Bob and anyone else who wants to take a potshot. So then who's on the inside?

Who the fuck is on the inside, now? she thought.

FORTY-SIX

Lily sat at the kitchen table, waiting for whoever would make it home next. Her competing terrors worked in shifts. Every few minutes she'd feel somewhat pleased with herself, pleased that she'd gotten Madison out of harm's way for a while and kept the secret. Then she'd remember that she didn't actually know where Madison was. That there was a contradiction: Madison couldn't possibly be young enough to need to be sheltered, away from whatever was going on in this house tonight, but at the same time old enough to be wise about all the other places that were unsafe for her.

But as her mind wandered these same spirals, again and again, Lily hit up against one idea. That it was still better. Better than Madison being here, seeing her father like this, hearing her mother talk about what had happened at the party. Maybe she'll leave for good, Lily thought wistfully. She entertained fantastical images of Madison and this kid buying a car together, with cash of course, and hitting the road. Driving out to the other coast, parking on the sand. Leaving all of this behind them.

But none of them, not even Madison, were going anywhere yet. We're all stuck in this house, Lily thought. We have to play our hands through. If we weren't going to do that, then we should have folded sooner.

She sat at the kitchen table, the thick stack of paper arranged neatly in front of her. She'd heard him come home while she was putting the twins to bed, making all the usual noises: throwing his keys on the front table, lumbering down the hall to his study. She couldn't believe it, so she'd come down, on tiptoe, to check. Until the very last second, when she saw him snoring on his couch, she refused to believe that he really would have come back into this house without asking where his children were, if they were all here and accounted for.

So she was especially pleased with herself for having thought to go into his study as soon as she got home, before he got there.

Now, the boys were in bed, there was an empty bottle propped against the door to Bob's study so that she'd hear him if he tried to come out into the house—another brainstorm—and Lily was in the kitchen with these accordion folders.

She hadn't read through their contents yet, because she wasn't sure how involved she wanted to be in whatever was there. She knew what Madison thought; she knew what Jackson would say if he were here. But she didn't exactly want to take them on her own shoulders, not tonight. She just wanted to make sure they were no longer squarely on Madison's. She wanted Madison to know that at least one adult was involved and on her side.

She was reminding herself of that, of her role as the twins' protector and as Madison's advocate, when Isabel and Mina came into the kitchen.

"What's wrong," Mina said immediately. Lily looked to Isabel. They couldn't talk about this in front of Mina; surely, even if she didn't know what was on Lily's mind, Isabel would intuit this.

"Is he here?" Isabel asked.

"He's down the hall," Lily said. "I don't know how he got home, but he's in there sleeping it off."

"He went to sleep," Isabel echoed. Lily nodded, and Isabel laughed. She crossed to the sink and poured herself a glass of water. "Good for him."

Lily looked pointedly at Mina, who was awkwardly attempting to remove the pins from her updo. She'd already taken off her earrings, as if this were her bedside and the night were already over. She froze and looked from Lily to Isabel, again.

"I can stay," Mina said.

Isabel fixed her eyes on Lily for a moment and gave her a gesture almost too brief to count as a nod. She turned, then, back to Mina.

"No," Isabel said. "You should go home. Get some rest."

"I can sleep in the den," Mina insisted. "I can make up something to tell Tom."

"No," Isabel said. "Thank you. For everything, truly. I think we all need to sleep this off. Including you. Tell Tom I'm so sorry for all the hassle. I'll send him a bottle of scotch."

Mina gathered her earrings in one hand, holding the train of her dress with the other. She looked back only once before she left the kitchen. Lily could feel the woman's plea, her anxiety, but she refused to look up and make eye contact. The fact that we both hate Bob right now doesn't make you family, she thought. Your part of the evening is over.

"You should call the police," Mina said finally. "Or at least have Teddy call them. You should do something so that later it at least looks, to her, like you were all frantically looking for her."

Isabel crossed the kitchen and walked into the pantry. Mina scoffed, and looked to Lily, her eagerness to recapture their earlier frankness written naked across her face. But Lily said nothing, and Mina turned to go. Isabel did not emerge until the front door had slammed.

She looked, for a moment, at the space where Mina had stood. Then she turned back to the table.

"So," she said.

"These are some papers he locked in a drawer," Lily said. "Madison saw him hide the key. A while ago."

"And you knew where to look?"

"She told me about them," Lily said. "Not at first. But I saw her—she snuck into the city last week, again. To meet with a journalist. I don't know—"

She caught her voice before it faltered, reminded herself that some secrets were still secrets.

"I don't know how she initially made contact with him, and she said she didn't tell him anything. But she's been thinking about giving him this stuff, because she thinks it's the proof that he didn't do anything wrong. Bob. I think she thinks these will—clear his name, or something. Wrap it all up."

Isabel laughed.

"Do you think she really believes that?"

"I don't know," Lily said. "I don't know what he's been telling her. I think he's probably talked about some of it with her."

Isabel waited for a moment. She stood up, got a bottle of wine from the pantry, and brought it back to the table.

"Why are you showing them to me?" she said. Lily bit the inside of one cheek before answering.

"I heard," she said. "About tonight. Mina told me, when I picked up the boys."

"Superb," Isabel said.

"I guess I don't think it should be Madison's problem," Lily said. "I don't think Madison should have to be the one to decide what to do with them. That doesn't seem, I don't know. That seems unfair to me."

Isabel poured them each a glass of wine. They had done this only twice before, together. The first time had been after the towers, when for all they knew Bob was gone. They sat here, and split a bottle of wine, and waited to hear from him. Lily had been new to the family then, well-liked but not yet trusted.

"My daughter is no fool," Isabel said. "She must know that, if he could save his own skin, or prove that he was right, lord it over everyone, then he would have done it by now."

Lily said nothing. Isabel sighed.

"Do you know where she went?"

Lily shook her head.

"I spoke with Teddy already," Isabel told her. "He called both apartments in the city. She's not there, but we've got people watching both anyway. She left her phone at the party, I have it. So now, I guess, we wait for her."

They waited there for three hours. They drank the wine in silence, and after the first hour or so, Lily made coffee. She could see Isabel's fear, her exhaustion. The woman wasn't a robot; she was afraid for her daughter. But Lily could see, too, that they both felt the same way, that a part of each of them dreaded Madison's return. That this vigil was their penance for having failed to uphold some agreement, for having failed to render some service Madison should have been owed.

But never once did Lily think that she should tell Isabel she'd seen Madison.

"What makes you think she'll come home tonight?" she said, after untold minutes had passed. Isabel didn't reply for so long, Lily had allowed her thoughts to move on. But then Isabel spoke.

"I don't know if she wants to put herself in real danger," she said. "I don't know if she wants to actually go find out what other people, outside her little world, think of her. I think she just wants me to know that she could. I think she wants to see what I'll do."

"She wants you to protect her," Lily said.

Isabel smiled, but Lily didn't know if that meant they were in agreement or not.

"Maybe," Isabel said. "Maybe she wants to force my hand."

An hour after that, the phone rang, and Isabel answered it. She spoke to someone for a few seconds, then hung up.

"They're at the gate," she said.

FORTY-SEVEN

Isabel knew that if she was wrong, then yes, later, she'd look like a monster. But she was doing the best she could with the information she had. People assumed that because she did not smother her daughter, they were not close. But she knew her daughter pretty damn well. And she felt certain that Madison would come home that night.

The impossible thought, that she might not, burned like a flame in the back of her mind, kept Isabel's white fury stoked and searching. Because if Madison didn't come back, it was because of Bob. Proximate cause, ultimate cause. Every kind of cause there was. If anything went any more wrong tonight, it was her husband's fault, and Isabel couldn't look directly at whatever that meant. She couldn't look directly at what she'd do to him.

She'd seen Madison's face, in that ballroom. As she heard that woman, Jim's lewd insinuations. Madison's face had crumpled just the way it used to when she was an infant, her beautiful, untrammeled skin wrinkling in on itself like the stone of a peach. She'd been ugly, exposed, in that moment. She was still, in so many ways, exactly like her father.

It all happens so slowly, Isabel thought. Every individual step is so insignificant as it happens. All the times her husband had told her what their life would be like, and she'd taken a stand. Or she thought she had. Balanced what she thought were gracious concessions with what she knew were principled refusals. When he told her they weren't going to be like anyone else on the Street. That the men who worked for him would be held to different standards.

(She saw, now, that she had never asked, different how?)

The life your parents chose for themselves, babe, the life we used to talk about at the beginning, that won't always fit. Can't always be tailored to fit the life I have in mind for us now, Iz. The things your parents choose to display, the things they choose to keep close to their vests. That's fine for them, but things change, people change. Money has changed. It means something different now, can't you see that? Just trust me.

She'd let him tear down the old house; she'd let him buy that new apartment before they'd even put the old one on the market. "Let him," as if she had any say. All he wanted when he asked her permission to do something was the reassurance that it wouldn't be held against him. And all she'd asked in return, the one thing she'd ever asked from him, was that he not do anything in his own life, away from her, that would jeopardize their life here. This fucking backwater, this land of women with whom she had not a single thing in common.

Or so she'd always thought.

It had felt smart, to make sure that the other women out here knew they weren't really her friends. It had seemed wiser to know, from the start, that these people were not rooting for her. But she couldn't say, just now, what that wisdom was. What she'd gained from that distance, these past few months. She'd leveraged so much in her marriage against . . . what? The bet had been so big, when she married him, so big that it dwarfed caution, made it feel inconceivable that she'd ever be punished for taking that risk. She hadn't left so much of Isabel Berkeley behind that it seemed plausible the new Isabel, this new married person she'd decided to be, could ever end up on the wrong side of fortune. Not really on the wrong side, not in the final tally.

That was his real transgression. He'd taken all the steps that led her to a room tonight in which Jim McGinniss could stand up in front of Isabel's own child and call her husband a man who cheated on his wife. The fact that he'd allowed that meant that Bob had called her every tactic—every single thing she assumed he'd married her for—into question.

It was funny, she thought, but she'd never imagined the others would look anything like Erica Leary. She'd imagined many women in residence at the old apartment, women who were rounder, or louder. Darker hair, maybe, or more doting. Younger than her, without question. But never really a small, harsher version of herself.

She could feel Lily watching her from the other side of the kitchen. Isabel was sitting at the breakfast nook, running her hands over the table's surface. She fought the urge to lay her cheek down to that precious reclaimed wood, its knots and slants. She crossed her arms over her stomach instead, digging her elbows into her flesh. She held the pose until the pain passed. Lily looked away.

Madison had been so little, the first time. The weekend Isabel drove out to Shelter by herself, with her baby daughter. They'd taken his car out of the garage in the city; this was before the boys, just after they'd bought in Greenwich but before she moved out full-time. It was still early in the season, too early for the summer people to be out in full force, and besides, Shelter Island had been quieter in the nineties. Everyone who was there in April was someone like Isabel's mother, someone whose forebears had bought the house decades earlier.

She took the ferry and parked the car. She carried Madison into the house, surprising her mother, who was baking. Her mother was delighted; she held Isabel's hand for a moment to express her pleasure. There was the usual clucking over the baby. And then Isabel told her mother about the envelope that had come to the apartment.

It had been addressed to him, but something caught her eye, some aspect of the thick cream-colored paper, the feminine lettering, the Audrey Hepburn stamp. The photographs were tucked inside, so careless and unadorned in their intimacy. Explicit pictures, but goofy ones. Silly, for lack of a better word. The woman's handwriting on the sheet of paper so much more vicious and jagged than the loops and swirls on the envelope itself.

The letter had clearly been sent out of pure spite and rage, the howling anger of an animal with its leg caught in a trap. *But what trap is she caught in?* Isabel thought. *I'm the one trapped. She sent these and that's it, she can move on. I'm the one trapped.* It wasn't even two years at that point since their wedding, since Bob had insisted on a much bigger party than she'd wanted. Since he had suggested she buy a new dress rather than wear her mother's, that she permit a *Times* reporter to follow her around on the day of, asking niggling questions about every last aesthetic touch. Since he had told her he wanted her to be good and pregnant by the end of the honeymoon, when she'd already said many times that she wanted to wait until thirty for kids. She'd been pregnant four months after the wedding.

She would have wanted to get married on Shelter, right out behind the house. With the Petonic behind them. But they couldn't get the attention they deserved if they did it at her parents' place, he'd said.

Is this it, now? The attention we deserve? She almost said it out loud, to Lily, but she didn't want to have to explain herself.

She should have known, back then. That whatever he said, what he actually wanted was a wife like Kiki McGinniss or Suzanne Welsh. She should have known he wouldn't want the reminders of everything that had, at one time at least, mattered to him.

"But I can't just give up now," she'd said to her mother, who held Madison on her lap, the baby's feet pedaling away in the air.

"No," her mother agreed. "We aren't those kind of people."

"What would you do?" Isabel asked. And her mother looked up at her, quizzical, genuinely confused by the question.

"Isabel," her mother said. "As I would think you'd know, I would never have opened the envelope."

That was it. They strolled to town, avoided speaking of Buck, who was abroad that spring. They walked along the windy beach just below the house. Her mother held the baby, played with her endlessly, touched her cheeks and cupped her little chin.

But she heard what her mother really meant. She'd chosen to marry someone who was not their kind of person, and now she had to devise a way to work within the new system.

But I did, she thought that night, sitting in the kitchen with Lily. I did, I did. She had explained to him very clearly, that weekend of the photographs, after the drive back from Shelter Island. And he understood, or he told her that he did. He promised her it would never happen again.

He made her all these promises, but the truth was that he could break any promise he wanted, there had never been any sword hanging over his head. She'd been as helpless as her mother before her, as helpless as Madison was now.

Even as helpless as all these other women who told themselves they hardly needed to understand what their husbands did. That it couldn't matter less whether they knew the difference between a hedge fund and a bond shop, if they understood why insider trading was illegal. The difference between a margin call and a collateral call.

Isabel knew that most of these women would ride it out, the rest of this shimmering, soap bubble year, without ever fully understanding the underlying structure of a credit-default swap, what role the naked shorts had played, what mortgage-backed securities even were. They'd tell themselves that an idiot in Ohio, who should have known he couldn't afford to own a home, had no bearing on their husbands or their work, their families. They'd wait for the rest of the world to lose interest, which would happen. Bob would go down, like a ship sinking beneath black waves far from land, and the rest of them would wait for the whirlpool to consume itself, and resume swimming.

"I'm going to make some coffee," Lily said, breaking the reverie.

Isabel nodded. She wanted to tell Lily to go to sleep, but she knew Madison might come home and choose to speak only to one of them. And she had no reason to believe it would be her, and not Lily.

"Yes," she said, "please do."

She couldn't fault these other women, could she? They were just hewing to the deals they'd struck. If her husband had done the same, she wouldn't be here now. And besides, Isabel Berkeley had always prided herself on understanding his career. On knowing the lingo, dropping the terms. But what good had that done? Where's the solace in understanding every single phrase of what's being said when your husband is on a television screen, seated before Congress, looking like it's all he can do to keep from upturning the table itself and strangling the men looking down on him?

All these years I've told myself that he's fierce, that he doesn't just love the nickname because it makes him feel big. But tonight, he left his daughter standing there, alone. She had to spit at him to get him even to look her in the eye.

That was when the phone rang, and Teddy told her that he had a "squirrely looking" boy down at the gate, a boy who had driven her daughter home.

WHEN MADISON CAME IN through the mud room, she was a woman on fire. Her hair was wild, her makeup trailing away from the corners of her eyes in rivulets. She still had everything, Isabel noted: her shoes, her purse, every piece of clothing. But she looked, somehow, destroyed.

She stared at Isabel.

"You had the security guy *question* him?" she said.

"I didn't have anyone do anything," Isabel said. "You showed up with a stranger, of course they questioned him."

"Well, that's great," Madison said. "Fantastic. He already can barely even pretend he's interested in me for more than one reason, but this is great. This is just my final humiliation."

"Okay, let's—" Lily said, rising from the table, but Madison moved back suddenly, as if the two women in the kitchen were predators.

"Why are you both up," she said.

"Because we were worried," Isabel said.

Isabel knew that she was a bad mother in one way: she rarely hugged her daughter. For some reason, it always felt so much thornier than it did with the twins. The twins, she would kiss and cuddle and lovingly maul with abandon. Their embraces were so unquestioned, so simple. But with Madison, it always felt insincere. Like she was hugging her daughter to *prove* that she loved her, when so many other things she did every day were much more straightforward displays of her obvious love for Madison.

As far as Isabel could remember, Madison's grandmother had been much the same. They had not been a demonstrative pair when Isabel was growing up, and so it had been all the more surprising when her mother had taken to Madison, the first grandchild, with such gleeful, explosive affection. She'd still been herself. She hadn't become a more casual woman, not in the slightest. But it no longer seemed to stiffen her shoulders, the idea of embracing another person.

Isabel could remember one night out on Shelter, a visit shortly before her mother died, when Madison had been angry. They'd had some fight, not even a fight, surely it had been minor. Madison dropped a glass while clearing the table, or left the suede ballet flats she'd begged for all summer outside during an afternoon thunderstorm. Something like that. And Isabel had responded, she felt certain, with an appropriate level of censure. She'd yelled at her daughter, yes, but nothing out of line.

A few hours later she'd been upstairs, calling the city from the hall phone. She looked down and saw her mother out by the pool, walking to its far end. Madison was on the edge, her feet in the water. Her shoulders were shaking. And Isabel's mother walked right over, without pause, and slipped her feet out of their kitten heels. She sat down next to her granddaughter, put one hand to her back, and just left it there while Madison shook with sobs. She stayed there until Madison folded, until she allowed her grandmother to wrap her in both arms, kissing the very top of her head.

Presumably, at some point when the hysteria had died down, they'd spoken. Isabel didn't know. She had already walked away from the window by then. And it bothered her for days, the way this closeness had skipped a generation, until it occurred to her: the same thing that had revealed this painful truth had also suggested its salve. Someday, Madison would have a daughter, a girl Isabel might be able to draw close without question, without pause. It wasn't too late for Isabel, not entirely.

She'd thought about that often, this year. How easy it might be, to hug Madison's daughter one day.

But now, Madison was standing in the middle of the kitchen. She looked like an open wound. *We were worried*, Isabel had said.

She began to walk toward her daughter. Every part of Madison's body recoiled from her approach, but still Isabel walked toward her.

"Are you okay?"

Madison stood completely still, and looked at no one.

"Are you all right," Isabel repeated.

"What do you think?"

"I don't mean that. I'm talking about Chip, Madison. Did anything else happen?"

"Oh," Madison said. "Chip is great. Chip's life will keep going and he's not going to think about me ever again. I have had absolutely zero effect on anything Chip thinks about the world."

"Madison, what—"

"I can't believe him," her daughter cried. "I can't believe him."

Madison bent at the waist, just as she had when she was a thick-armed toddler with a sharp pain in her stomach. She dropped her purse to the floor, crossed her arms over her breasts. She allowed herself to be pulled, with one arm, into her mother's chest. She allowed herself to be held.

Lily looked at them, then looked back at the folders on the table.

"I'll take them with me," she murmured.

Isabel shook her head again. She bent her neck to speak directly into her daughter's ear.

"Do you want Lily to stay?"

Madison buried her head more deeply in Isabel's chest.

"I don't understand," she said. "You can't be proud like that, and act like you know better than every other idiot, and then also be a liar."

"I know, sweetheart. I know. We can discuss this later."

But her daughter barreled on.

"I thought I knew," Madison said. "I thought I knew more—I thought I had all the pieces. He made it sound like he was telling me everything."

"I know," Isabel said. "I know how it must have seemed."

"But it was going on the whole time?"

Isabel didn't answer, and Madison erupted with a fresh sob.

"I thought I had all this inside information that other people were too stupid to see," she said. "I thought people hated him because they were jealous. I don't understand. I don't understand."

It was the repetition, most of all, that made her seem so young, so lost, that seemed to shrink her before her mother's very eyes. It was the senseless repetition of a useless phrase that stirred Isabel's anger, like a cold object tossed into boiling water.

"I can take her upstairs," Lily said.

"No," Isabel said. "There's nothing more to do, Lily. You should go to bed yourself."

"But I can stay." Lily looked again at the folders on the table.

"But we don't need you to," Isabel said, letting the chill creep into her voice. She could indulge this for a few minutes more, Lily's desire to feel central to the solution, but after that she'd be issuing an order, not an invitation.

Lily was clearly angry, but she had no other choice, she knew that as well as Isabel did. She left through the mud room.

Isabel waited for Madison to gather herself, to wipe at her cheeks. She offered Madison her hand and they walked upstairs. Madison let herself be undressed, let her mother slide the white nightgown over her arms, sat still while Isabel wiped at her makeup with a moist washcloth. Isabel could see her capitulation, could see the relief flood her limbs, and felt a pang at having denied Madison something for which she clearly had such a hunger, such a need. Her daughter didn't care that she was being comforted by someone equally furious. She just wanted the comfort itself.

Isabel turned off the light and crawled into bed beside Madison.

"Did Lily show you that stuff?" Madison asked, only once. Isabel nodded, pressed her lips to her daughter's hair.

"Dad was lying to me, wasn't he?" Madison continued. "That stuff doesn't prove anything, does it? He lied to me. So many times, Mom, we talked about it. I asked him the exact question, and he lied to me so many times."

"Go to sleep."

"He kept acting like he didn't deserve what was happening," Madison said. "But nothing bad has even happened to him yet. He just wanted me to be on his side already, before anything happened. He just didn't want to feel guilty."

"Sleep, Madison," Isabel said. "Just sleep on it, for tonight."

Madison spoke only once more, her words wisps into the dark room, before she fell asleep.

"I thought I got to see this version of him no one else knew about," she said.

Isabel stayed there until daylight was beginning to stain the sky just at the edges of the trees out back. She'd forgotten how pretty it was, the view from this bedroom. That was how long it had been, she thought with pain, since she'd come in here to be with her daughter.

In the end, Madison had been the one who'd taken best to life in Connecticut, wedged somewhere between city and country, between wildness and the manicured. Her daughter loved it there; it was her home.

That's what we're robbing her of, and it will come entirely as a shock to her. None of this was ever a gamble, for her. This was her home.

Isabel went back down to the kitchen. She sat at the table, with the papers, for nearly two more hours. She did not read everything, but she read a great deal. She understood most of it, not all. She recognized some of the names, some of the e-mail addresses, and others were unknown to her. There was nothing there that could remain a secret for long; that seemed clear. If he thought he could bury any of it, he was dreaming. It was just a question of timing, and proof. It was only a question of who would get this information, and how quickly.

And he'd spent the first months afterward, this crucial period, twiddling his clumsy fucking thumbs. Stashing folders in locked drawers, and confiding in his child, and screwing a woman who'd failed even worse than he had.

Isabel thought about making some more coffee, waiting for the boys to come rioting down the stairs. But she was suddenly blurry with exhaustion; it began to leave smeared trails across her vision, her thoughts. Lifting her hand to her face was an effort. She thought of the pills from Mina. There were still some left. She'd put them aside, months ago, because after that one time she'd sensed something just beyond what she'd be able to control if she didn't. But this was surely an exception. This was an evening like no other, wasn't it?

She stacked the papers in one tidy pile and left them on the counter, near the sink. Before she left the room, she strained to see if she could hear her husband moving at all.

It's their future, she thought. And what he's given them, now, is a future with his fingerprints all the fuck over it. There's no life for her that won't be defined by him. She's too old to forget any of this. He can't survive that, unscathed. It wouldn't be fair.

He's so worried about his own personal lifeboat, fine. But then he doesn't get to assume he can stay on ours.

She told herself she would deal with the papers in the morning. She told herself Lily wouldn't do anything without asking first. Lily, who clearly thought she'd kept that wannabe muckraker boyfriend a secret all these years. Lily, who must have discovered how good it feels to brag about your own virtue inside your head, the only place where you can glorify it to your heart's desire.

Maybe Lily would leave the folders on the counter, right where they sat. Maybe she would wait to be told. Probably.

But now, tonight, Isabel needed to go upstairs. She'd had about all she could take, for now. She turned off the lights in her kitchen. Outside the house, she could hear the leaves rustling and the crickets, the sounds her daughter loved so much.

Isabel D'Amico would sleep on it. She would sleep on all of it.

Madison had always loved the trip out to Shelter. They would usually stop in Greenport for dinner, catching a late ferry. Her brothers would jockey for seats in the small vestibule and her parents would stand, her father's arms ringing her mother's waist, at the metal railing.

But when you came in by day, you could see the island begin to appear, a dark pile rising out of the slate water. As you got closer, it defined itself for you, yielded up the details of its coast. The disintegrating gray wood pilings, the granular strip of public beach, the thick trees mounded up on the hills like the looping borders of a child's cloud drawing. And when you were close enough, there it was: Gran's place, with the poplars at the edge of the property. There had been more of them, once, a whole line guarding the house, but now only two remained.

During Madison's sophomore year of college, Hurricane Sandy had eaten away at the private beach just below the lawn, and the house now seemed so much more perilous in its situation. The ocean was closer to the glassed-in porch than it used to be, and somehow Madison was always grateful that Gran was gone by the time that happened. The house looked like a monument to hubris, now. It looked like someone had just walked out to the tip of that particular finger of the island and, preposterously, decided to build a house there. When that couldn't be further from the truth, from the story of Madison's family on this island. But then, what did that matter? All that people had to go on, at this point, was the way it looked.

She remembered Antoinette calling her to tell her about the hurricane damage. She hadn't known that Antoinette even had her cell number and she'd almost ignored the call when she saw the New York state area code. But she answered, and then she'd been in a women's restroom on the third floor of the Humanities building, crying into the mirror.

It was the second time that year that she'd found herself crying in a bathroom on campus, the first having come when she ran into the freshman girl whose father was the district attorney for the Southern District of New York. Most people on campus, thankfully, weren't able to put the pieces together—Madison had changed her last name before enrolling—but this girl sure as hell knew who Madison was.

Once she'd gathered herself on the phone, Madison had asked Antoinette how she'd found her number. And Antoinette had paused, then said, "Oh, honey, Lily gave it to me a few years ago. She wanted me to have it, if I ever wanted to call you directly. Without, you know, having to go through your mom."

Do you know where she is now, Madison had almost said to Antoinette, do you know what she does now. But the truth was that Lily wasn't family anymore; that was painful enough in itself, even if it had always been true, at base. What good would it do to have an image of her, living another life as a person independent of the twins, of Madison?

Isabel had taken her time, after Gabriel Scott Lazarus published the e-mails. She'd kept Lily on for almost another year, and at the time Madison had thought that this was her mother's reluctance to punish Lily for something she'd all but *told* Lily to do. One thing Madison had never doubted: that if her mother didn't shred those folders that night, it was because she wanted Lily to do something with them. She outsourced it, Madison thought now, smiling in spite of herself.

Lily moved her things out one day while Madison was at school. There had been no warning before she came home. No announcement, no tear-stained letter, just the absence of Lily. Upstairs, on Madison's bed, Lily had left the silver claddagh ring she'd worn every single day Madison had known her, a ring that had always entranced Madison when she was small. Lily had explained, once, what it meant to turn the ring, that it mattered which way the heart faced.

It had been a gift from Lily's mother on the night she got into Columbia. It had been in her family. Looking back on it now, it seemed such a pedestrian, girlish thing for Madison to have coveted—so simple, neither special nor rare. But this one had been in Lily's family.

Madison kept it, but she'd never worn it.

She didn't know if she still believed that Lily had been left dangling for so long out of ambivalence on Isabel's part. She didn't know if the boyfriend had still been in the picture by then. All she knew was that, once Isabel made up her mind, Lily was gone.

When the ferry docked, Madison shouldered her bag—she'd brought only essentials, clean underwear and makeup and the bourbon she'd bought in Greenport, not certain how long she'd be staying—and walked up the hill toward the house. It was only the third house from the dock, always so easy to find. She let herself in through the garage, with the code from Antoinette's e-mail, and retrieved the key from the butter dish in the outside fridge. And then she was there, again, for the first time in so long.

IT WAS A FEW DAYS to Christmas and she knew, if she was honest, that she'd go home before Christmas Eve. The twins were high school seniors now, and it was only fair to them. Last year Madison had stayed in California until just after Christmas, arriving at the apartment in TriBeCa to find it shut up like some Dickensian haunted house: curtains drawn, fires banked, the boys hiding from each other and from Isabel, who rarely left her bedroom. Madison couldn't do that to them again.

She'd need a plan, for after the holiday. She hadn't told her mother she was taking a leave of absence from grad school, and she didn't want to have to discuss it just yet. She'd have to put something together, some story, eventually.

She poured herself a glass from the tap and walked to the big window to look out over the water. The furniture in the living room was still covered with sheets. This year's renters had been gone for two months, and the new people wouldn't arrive until the early spring. The draped chairs all looked somehow cowed, as if they were crouched and waiting for some further debasement.

If only we'd stayed here, Madison thought. It was a childish fantasy, but she couldn't help remembering that week out here, the five of them. Right before it all began. She knew that had been so late in the game, really. But it just seemed like if they could have stayed out here together. Spoken to one another, and only to one another. Locked themselves away and stored up food and boarded the windows. It really seemed like everyone would still be here, like they might be celebrating Christmas out here, as a family, if only they'd stayed inside Gran's house for a while longer.

But these honeyed false memories, *the way it might have been*, did her no good. She'd been better, in recent years, at telling the truth, to herself, in her own mind. At clinging to the facts, rather than to their ever-alluring shadows.

Such as: Everything that had happened with her father probably would have happened anyway. Her mother did not turn him over to the authorities in some fit of rebellion. She didn't take back control of anything. All she did was let the nanny embarrass him in the slyest possible way, and if she was in a fit of anything, it was jealousy and petty fury.

The e-mails would always have been discovered, sometime later that year, during the bankruptcy-court investigation. All that would have been spared were those first months of gossip, of lascivious media coverage. The whole situation was still so raw, that spring. Madoff was recent news, it still seemed entirely possible Bob D'Amico would go to jail. People ate it up, the e-mail proof that her father had been fully aware of the shady accounting tricks that kept the firm's insolvency under wraps for so long.

And then the speculation about his affair with Erica. If Isabel had wanted to, surely she could have gone into overdrive. She could have kept that out of the papers. It might have remained, then, a Greenwich-specific scandal. But she'd done nothing.

In the ensuing years, everyone seemed to have decided that there was nothing much actually going on between Bob and Erica, that their clandestine meetings that year had been more concerned with fraud and illegality. Everyone waited just long enough for the idea of the affair to cement its place in the collective memory of that year, then shrugged and said it was probably nothing. But Madison knew better. She could see how it would have appealed to her father, the mixture of contempt and gallantry. The woman had fucked up, yes, but now she was in worse trouble than he was, and he could be her protector. He could be the defendant, take the fall for her, and for all the others. For the bank, his truest family.

That had been the worst sting of all, reading the e-mail from one top executive that described the questionable accounting tactic of choice as "anothr drug we r on, guys." *These* guys, Madison remembered thinking. *These* were the guys my father chose to be loyal to, in the end? These guys and Erica?

Everyone said that the DA was foolish to pursue the case. That he'd never be able to prove conscious wrongdoing, not even with all the embarrassing swagger captured in those e-mails. And he hadn't. He'd apparently been quite haunted by that failure, by the fact that Madison's father protected his people, walked free, granted his wife full custody and then moved down to Florida with the new wife. Madison knew this, how the DA had been tortured by Bob

D'Amico's cavalier renaissance, because the man's daughter had told her all about it in a public restroom on campus.

She hadn't understood, that day, what that girl wanted from her. She understood the girl's anger, her disgust, but she didn't know what she could do about it. She couldn't very well say so, but the girl wasn't spitting anything at her that Madison didn't already feel on the nights she lay awake. Yes, exactly, she wanted to say. Agreed. Tell me how to fix it.

Believe me, I understand the banality of my own pain. I understand so much better than you could ever force me to understand. I am unhappy for the least interesting reasons in the world. I thought it was something unique, something of tragic proportions. Malevolent forces from the outside. But my unhappiness didn't come from outside at all. It was my parents, their willingness to gamble away the things they always told me were so important, so essential to our family's character. And you can't tell me any better than I already know it myself, that this is the least special unhappiness in the world.

She hadn't said any of this that day at school; she'd just let the girl shriek at her until it was over.

SHE SLID OPEN THE DOOR to the sunporch, her hand coming away gritty and dusty, and walked out onto the grass. There, across the water, was the big estate that had so vexed Gran; God only knew who lived over there now.

It took a long time, years after Suzanne's museum party, but Madison had eventually watched her father's congressional testimony. It was available on YouTube. A lot of people still watched it in those first few years; she always kept an eye on its page views. After the documentary about the bank came out, she finally reconciled herself to watching it. And all the footage was there waiting for her, several different versions of it. Plus on the *Times* website, plus in CSPAN's archives. If she wanted, she could have played three different streams of the video simultaneously. Her father jammed behind a small table, the congressmen seated above him so that he had to keep his head tilted up deferentially throughout. But the only part she played over and over again was a final interjection he made, toward the end of the first part of the hearing. "Until they put me in the ground," he said, "I will wonder why this happened to me." This wasn't the father she had known; there was a touch of the poet in this man, a Shakespearean tragedian who had apparently been living beneath her father's tough hide his entire life.

But he wasn't anything from Shakespeare; he was a criminal. She tried to remember this when she felt all the old outrage at some new catty interview from a former colleague, some smirking report of her father's latest attempts to get back in the game. So many people had suffered because of him. He was a criminal. It didn't make much difference, in the end, that society had declined to slap that title on him.

Everything but jail, she thought now, crossing her arms against the cold coming up from the water. Jail would have been cleaner, maybe. All these years, she'd been hoping and waiting for the final, scalpel-sharp cut. But it wasn't going to be like that. Not ever, she didn't think. It was always going to be chronic pain, suspended. The chairs keeping quiet beneath their draped sheets, the windows sealed against the remote, future possibility of a storm.

No one, it turned out, ever told the truth about this kind of pain. It wasn't a crucible; it didn't always make you new. She thought sometimes that perhaps she was a nicer person than she would otherwise have been, but that seemed like wishful thinking when all the adults who had been there at the time, controlling her access to the information, seemed to have learned nothing at all. They had come to the brink of something, that night, definitely. They had come right to the brink of some disaster, and her mother had given the little push it needed. But they'd also been at some other brink, on the edge of learning some lesson, and they hadn't done that, either.

Her father left the house the morning after Suzanne's party, and she hadn't seen him again for months. During the trial, her mother dressed them all in dark colors and made them sit directly behind the defense counsel's table, even the twins. She kept them there, like his loyal army, until the day he was acquitted, then filed for divorce. She sold the properties and moved them to an apartment in TriBeCa, where they could live as she'd always wanted to live. A quiet life funded by her own money. No danger, but no ostentation, either.

Madison had been homeschooled for her final three semesters of high school, and they'd lied on her applications. They said it was a health scare. The family physician signed the letter.

MADISON HAD RUN INTO JAIME DAWES on the street in New York that year, sometime in the spring. Jaime was going to Oxford, and Madison remembered that her first thought, as they stood on a thronged street corner in SoHo and exchanged pleasantries, had been for Mina. Poor Mina; boarding school hadn't been enough distance for Jaime.

"I never thought I'd see you again," Jaime said. "It seems like our mothers have lost touch."

"I'm sure that's not true," Madison said, but she knew that it was. Tom Dawes, of all those men, had gained great respect and renown in the years immediately following the Weiss failure. Had become something of a bigwig at Goldman, against all expectations. She didn't know if that was it, why Mina and Isabel rarely spoke.

"Not Mina's choice, believe me," Jaime said, as if in counterargument to Madison's silence. "I bet you don't miss Greenwich, though."

They'd gone, somewhat awkwardly, for a drink at a small, dark bar with a leafy backyard. Jaime pumped Madison for information. Her disgust and disinterest seemed at war with each other, and no truce had yet been declared. In the end, though, Jaime ended up saying much more about Mina than Madison said about anyone.

"You see, though, right?" Jaime said near the end, before she picked up the tab. "You see why I had to get out of there?"

Madison had just nodded. She'd put Jaime's number in her phone, deleting it on the walk back to the subway.

She hadn't told Jaime the things she did want to say, the things she had no one to tell. That her mother had proved herself, in the end, to be the one true mate for Bob D'Amico. That she'd followed his codes, even when she felt she was turning on him. That there had been a moment, maybe, when Madison and her mother might have teamed up, sealed the leak, kept the boat in safe waters. But they hadn't, and she could only assume this was because her mother hadn't wanted that.

None of this, Madison knew, looked like learning a lesson. The fact that her mother had become a recluse, that she seemed desperately to miss the Greenwich life she'd always treated with such disdain before that year, didn't mean she'd learned a lesson. Nothing so lofty. So it was hard to fault the wider world, wasn't it?

You don't really learn anything so deep from embarrassment or shame, you just learn not to make all the same mistakes again. What, then, should she have learned? Weiss was treated as a bad egg, careless and cavalier. The exception that endangered the rest of the system rather than that system's purest product. No one in the world her father had once dominated learned much of a lesson, she didn't think. So then, what steps was she supposed to take to avoid this pain in future? She'd only ever been a cog in the system, a party to the long con. Whatever racket her father had been running hadn't taught her anything at all when it crashed.

HE LIVED NOW, in a fortress down in Florida. His finances were something of a mystery. She assumed the new wife had money. He still showed up in New York every now and then for speeches. He still got to be the man they'd nicknamed Silverback, sometimes. Their once or twice yearly phone calls were always at his urging, never at Madison's. So maybe she had, in the end, chosen a side.

She sat down on a lawn chair and looked across the water to the other part of the island, even as it got dark, even as the winter chill moved in. She bundled herself up and stayed there. There was no food inside, she'd brought nothing for dinner. When she went back in, there would be only a long evening alone with Gran's ghosts, only bourbon and the fireplace.

She'd chosen her side, and she'd stayed there. She had allowed Lily, the woman who had done so much to raise her, to be effectively cut from her life. She had never spoken to Amanda again after that night at the Welsh party. She'd followed all her mother's cues. She'd punished her father with her own distance, because that had seemed like her only option. Because she'd probably always known who he was. She couldn't, looking back, see that first winter as anything other than the last, grasping attempt of a child to keep her eyes closed to the sickly green sunlight her parents' shadows had once blocked for her.

And now, here she was, alone in the only place on earth that still felt like a home to her.

We should have holed up here, she thought again. We should have come here, my mother and my father and Lily and the boys and me. We should have closed ourselves off from the world until it was over, like plucky refugees from some apocalypse, trapped in our own adventure story. The kind of story that ends with survival.

She went inside, finally, when it grew too cold. She drank the bourbon. She called her boyfriend, but he didn't pick up. She found some abandoned pasta in a high cabinet. The bourbon was working, and she imagined for herself that the pasta was a remnant. It was an uncherished artifact, the last proof: they really *had* locked themselves up in here, they really *had* kept one another alive through that first winter.

After she ate, she curled up on the couch and closed her eyes and tried to remember. What it had felt like when she had a tribe of her own, when she had taken for granted that if her parents had a flaw, it was that they cared too much about her future, her brothers' futures. That they held their children *too* close, devoted *too* much to building them a life.

When she could have told anyone, without hesitation, what the word *home* really meant to her.

It never would have worked, she knew that. They couldn't have hidden away here. The threat was never out there. There were no febrile hordes scratching at the roof, no one coming to fight them for their last resources.

We wouldn't have been safe in here because we were the toxin. We wouldn't have been safe in here because the epidemic would have been locked in with us. Sloughing off our skin, reddening our eyes. Turning us on one another, eventually, our little, yellowed teeth.

ACKNOWLEDGMENTS

Thank you, thank you, thank you.

Thank you to the grad crew—Christian Caminiti, Essie Chambers, Amy Feltman, Eli Hager, Cory Leadbeater, Rachel Schwerin, and Sam Graham-Felsen. Thank you for being, by turns: drinking buddies, therapists, sounding boards, and—most of all—readers.

Thank you to Bryan Burrough, William Cohan, Steve Fishman, Michael Lewis, Nina Munk, Vicky Ward, and Andrew Ross Sorkin for their phenomenal writing about the world of Wall Street, much of which I found very helpful at the preliminary stage.

Thank you to the Edward F. Albee Foundation; to Ruthie Salvatore and everyone at the Ucross Foundation; and to Mary and Patrick Geary in Princeton, for rooms with views and blissful solitude. Ucross in particular was a haven for me during the stressful final hours, and I'll be forever grateful.

Thank you to my teachers. Thank you to Eric Schrode and Kathleen Neumeyer, two of the first and quite possibly the toughest—you both set the standard, to this day. Thank you to John Crowley and to Traugott Lawler. Thank you to Erroll McDonald, to Deborah Eisenberg, to Donald Antrim. Thank you to Sam Lipsyte, for his devilish grin as he told me to write a better opening chapter. Thank you to Elissa Schappell, who taught me what to do with a first draft.

Thank you to Heidi Julavits, for being the sharpest and smartest cheerleader at the moment when I needed it the most.

Thank you to Darryl Pinckney, who took me to lunch when this book was a mess and asked all the right questions, for his keen insight and timely encouragement.

Thank you to Patrick Ryan, for his early support of my writing, and to John Freeman, for making me a better thinker (about this book and countless others).

Thank you to David Burr Gerrard for frequent reads and constant advice, and for enduring more than a few of my rants and raves.

Thank you to Andrew Kaufman for answering embarrassing finance questions early on, for indulging in no more than the usual amount of mockery when faced with my total ignorance, and for giving everything a close look near the end.

Thank you to Julianne Carlson, Camille Fenton, Elena Goldblatt, Mark Iscoe, Emma Ledbetter, Andrew Segal, Nikila Sri-Kumar, Lisa Sun, and Chenault Taylor—for believing I would finish, for keeping me laughing even in the darkest hours.

Thank you to the many others whose kindnesses have been essential, including: Marilyn Aitken, Deborah Antar, the Botwick boys, Caroline Bleeke, Julie Buntin, Charlie Clark, Jenny Crapser, Tamara Day, Neena Deb-Sen, the Dewhirst family, David Dunning, Peter Jackson, Abram Kaplan, Denny and Annie Kearney, the Miller family, Denise and Keith Mills (and the entire Davidson-Dennis-Parent bunch), Kate Philip, Streeter Phillips, Anna Pitoniak, Alexandra Schwartz, Michael Seidenberg, the Shabahang family, Danny Seifert, Moses Soyoola, Annie Spokes, Nathan Stevens, Timbo Shriver, and Arturo Zindel.

Thank you to Caryl Phillips, whose generosity is matched only by his brilliance and his rigor.

Thank you to everyone at Ecco and HarperCollins, especially Sonya Cheuse, Dan Halpern, Miriam Parker, and Emma Dries. But most of all, thank you to Megan Lynch, who had a vision for this book and who took the most exquisite care of it and of me. I feel unspeakably lucky that I found my way to her.

Thank you to Marya Spence, Marya of the infinite patience, unparalleled eye, and extraordinary cool. She found me and saw something where there was yet so little, and it would be impossible to overstate her role in forcing this book to exist. Every day of this process, I thanked and thanked the universe for sending me her smarts and her friendship. (And thank you to Rebecca Dinerstein, for introducing me to Marya.)

Thank you to Monsita Botwick, my godmother and role model. I'm hardly the only one in awe of her humor or her grace.

Thank you to my brother, my favorite person on the planet. If I am ever, in flashes, cool, smart, witty, or wise, it's because I am trying to become the girl he's believed me to be for the last twenty-six years.

Thank you to my parents, whose astonishing (and, let's face it, foolhardy) support was a lifeline for the four years I struggled to write this book, and for the twenty-four years before I'd even begun. To my mother: the most voracious reader I know, and the toughest audience, and the most bottomless well of belief, all of which made her an invaluable resource. Thank you for putting books into my hands from the beginning. And to my father, who never once doubted me and who gave the rowdiest whoop when I told him it was really going to be a book. Every writer should be so fortunate as to have these two in her corner.

This book, like most everything worthwhile that I do, would not exist without the faith, humor, wisdom, and all around dreaminess of Connor Mills. This book is for him.

ANGELICA BAKER was born and raised in Los Angeles. She received her BA in English and creative writing from Yale and her MFA in fiction from Columbia University. She now lives in Brooklyn.